3:17 a.m.
...The Waking Hour

by

EITEL-CASEY

Copyright © 2014 Shera Eitel-Casey

Library of Congress-in-Publication Data

All rights reserved.

ISBN: 1500895024
ISBN-13: 978-1500895020

DEDICATION

I want to dedicate this book to anyone who has set a goal and achieved it. You can't always listen to everyone's advice, if no one ever broke out of the box than there would never be anything new.

CONTENTS

ACKNOWLEDGMENTS vii

PROLOGUE 1

CHAPTER 1 8

CHAPTER 2 27

CHAPTER 3 38

CHAPTER 4 45

CHAPTER 5 55

CHAPTER 6 65

CHAPTER 7 77

CHAPTER 8 94

CHAPTER 9 101

CHAPTER 10 112

CHAPTER 11 124

CHAPTER 12 137

CHAPTER 13 145

CHAPTER 14 162

CHAPTER 15 172

CHAPTER 16 183

CHAPTER 17	194
CHAPTER 18	211
CHAPTER 19	222
CHAPTER 20	239
CHAPTER 21	246
CHAPTER 22	256
CHAPTER 23	269
CHAPTER 24	278
CHAPTER 25	293
CHAPTER 26	312
CHAPTER 27	318
CHAPTER 28	331
EPILOGUE	338
ABOUT THE AUTHOR	343

ACKNOWLEDGMENTS

I want to give a big thank you to everyone who took the time to read my book and give me feedback. I want to give out a special thank you to Tracey Stapleton, Makayla Stapleton, Christine Drover and Carol Raabe who took the time and helped edit and fix plot changes.

Karen Eitel really hung in there with me through the rest of all my edits and my dad, Bob Eitel, through the final. If wasn't for their support and help I would have never finished.

I can't tell everyone enough how much I appreciate everything they've done for me.

Shera Eitel-Casey

PROLOGUE

We were walking hand in hand in a field that was long and grassy, surrounded by a thick wall of trees that didn't make a perfect oval but surrounded the property making you feel like you were in your own little world. When I looked back up the small hill we had just come from you could see a beautiful River Birch with several trunks perched on top of it, its snow white bark flaking off elegantly, and the leaves shimmering in the wind, from here it loomed over us and looked like it could touch the sky.

He leaned down and kissed me on the forehead, then my temple, cheek and neck. He cupped his hands around my face. I embraced him back, and then let my hands fall to his hips.

My skirt was blowing ever so slightly in the wind. The sun was out and the skies were blue. It was a beautiful day. I said cheerfully "let's keep walking." I slipped my hand into his and our fingers intertwined. He gave me a peck on the cheek and we turned. Arms around each other, we started walking across the field. When we were adjacent to the tree line he stopped and pulled me close to him, I let my eyes flutter shut. When I re-opened them I saw him place his lips on hers and pressed hard, she jerked back and told him "Stop, be gentle." His hands began to shake and then his whole body. I looked down at my hands and all around me, I was alone. I looked across the field toward the tree line where I saw them, kissing.

She was wearing a white gauze top and skirt with a shiny silver bracelet that sparkled brightly in the sun. Her skirt was blowing in the wind along with her long curly blond hair. He was wearing tan pants and a white button down shirt with only a couple of buttons fastened. He had no shoes on and his light long hair was messy from the slight breeze cooling down the otherwise hot day.

His shirt blew open a little and she placed her hand on his stomach and reached upward. He trembled, looked up, and stretched his face toward the sky, it changed. Then he grabbed her shoulders making her totter with him. He looked down suddenly and backhanded her across the cheek. She turned to run but he nabbed her shoulder. As she tried to free herself, his nails dug into her shoulder. I could see the blood trickling down her white shirt onto his hand. He looked at the sky, howled and let her go to lick his hand. She turned again, but only got a few feet when he wrapped his arms around her and ripped her shirt from her. She kicked and screamed. She kept looking to her left, into the tree line yelling "Help me, help me." He threw her to the ground; she's still looking over to the tree line nearest her as she scooted backward.

I looked beyond her and saw a pair of eyes glowing in the shadows. I tried to help but all I could do was watch. I tried to get closer but I never reached them, I started running toward them but I'm still yards away. He howled again and put his face to her neck.

In a panic I sat straight up, gasping for air. It was pitch dark. My eyes were opened so wide I could feel them straining trying to see something, anything. But the dark just held. I rubbed my eyes to get a bearing on where I was – 'it was a dream, it was a dream, it was a dream.' I kept telling myself. I was in my room, another bad dream. I usually have dreams of not being able to scream, run fast enough or other weird things, but they are usually about me. I don't think this one was about me this time. It was me at first, but after they crossed the field it definitely wasn't me. I was actually watching another couple.

Unfortunately, it was only 3:17a.m. and I usually can't get back to sleep once I wake up. So I got my notebook and pen out of my nightstand and wrote down everything I could remember, leaving the light off so I wouldn't wake my sister. I was hoping it would be legible in the morning. I have had a couple of dreams before that I swear have come true but I'm never really sure because the memory of them can fade so fast. Although, some I have just never forgotten, no matter how much time goes by.

Just this summer, our family went on a two week vacation. My dad said it would probably be our last hoorah, as we kids were getting older and probably wouldn't want to go anymore. We usually only vacationed for a week at a time but this time it was for two. He named it "The 1981 Gellar Family Extravaganza" and had his itinerary labeled with it.

The week before we left, I had a dream of a man on a silver shiny pay phone, he was on the third phone of eight hanging on the wall, and on the other side of the hall was a big family room with a lot of older people watching TV, bizarre right? But it was one of the dreams that just stuck with me. Mind you, it's a very insignificant dream, I think, but the combination was very odd. Eight pay phones next to a living room... Maybe that's why it stayed with me. I can remember every last detail of it and I didn't even have to write it down.

* * * * * * *

We were driving to South Carolina not a far drive from my hometown Richfield, Ohio but far enough that my dad planned stops on the way. I got an eerie feeling at a hotel we stopped at in West Virginia. The outdoor pool was located right next to a huge mountain, you could see clouds and snow gathering at its peak. The water was ice cold even though it was eighty degrees out and none of us kids went in until my dad called us all wimps. So I jumped in! Didn't even feel the water with my toe or try to get in slowly – that's how you have to do it, just jump right in, like ripping a Band-Aid off – you have to do it quickly.

The water was worse than freezing but my dad and I continued to swim and jump off the diving board a few times. My sister asked me to do a double flip off the board which I had just mastered recently and I did, plus a couple other dives I liked to do. And that's when I got that eerie feeling I get once in a while, I noticed some guy at the end of the pool just staring my way. His hair was either greased straight back or wet; he had a trench coat on and sunglasses. I brushed it off and went to sit with Tori and Kit, my brother and sister. I'm only 21 months younger than my sister but four years older than my brother. I'm stuck in the middle. When I sat down, that's when the spooky guy got up slowly and left but not without staring us down first.

What I call my "eerie" feelings, I believe, are when I experience "déjàvu" and I believe those feelings are brought upon me because I have experienced the event before through my dreams. I also believe lately, that everyone has dreams that come true, but most people can't remember them an hour after they wake. So they are forgotten. Some people dream more than others and some people remember a lot more than others, like me. Maybe I'm just hoping it's true so I'm not the only freak around who has dreams that come true.

The following day we drove until we got to the bed and breakfast where we were staying. I stepped into the lobby and had that eerie "déjàvu" feeling again. I knew what was coming next and gasped "Oh my gosh!" I took a few steps forward and turned to my left to see very peculiar mirror-like pay phones and a man just turning to use the third phone! I looked down the hall and there were five more, all spotless and clean – shiny silver pay phones..... The man had on a trench coat, sunglasses and a blue baseball cap -- everything was just like my dream. He had longer hair than most, wavy and dark; I could only see him from behind though. In my dream his coat was white; here it was tan, but still....

My eyes were wide, I was standing in the same spot that I saw everything from in my dream. And I said "Oh my gosh!" out loud again. It was pure adrenaline and I was happy my dream had come true. I turned to the right and it was set up just like a living room with a bunch of older people staring at the TV!

My dad asked me "What? What's going on?" So I told him about my dream and then pointed to the man on the phone and then pivoted to my right still pointing explaining about the living room. I was very excited when I was explaining what I saw to him, that I saw all of this in my dream last week.

Then my dad said "Yeah right!" with a half chuckle and asked "Then what are they watching on TV?" From where we stood you couldn't see the TV, and of course we couldn't hear it because the volume was turned down. With all the confidence in the world I said "Golf." I paused, "Water and sand on the left and a green hill on the right." He walked over looked up, his mouth dropped open and he didn't close it. Then he came back and said "Addie you almost had me going..."

3:17 a.m. ...the waking hour

I walked over to see the TV and golf was on – there was no hill or water or sand. Then they showed two guys on the next tee and a guy hitting his ball over a green grassy hill on the right and water on the left, but I saw no sand...until the helicopter went over the green to view from the opposite side and there it was! Sand on the beach....believe it or not!

I was excited, I bet I had a goofy grin on my face too, so I looked at my dad and pointed to the TV and he just shook his head. I let my hand drop to my side, I had mixed emotions, happy because I was sure my dream really had come true and yet disappointed because my dad disregarded it so fast. I was hurt because I believe I'm an honorable person, very honest and trustworthy. Plus, I'm like a vault of secrets.

Why would he think I was lying? I had nothing to gain from lying about some people on a phone and watching TV. Then I started to doubt myself, maybe I was wrong, maybe I just had a similar dream and I've convinced myself it was real. It kept bothering me all day. So I snuck a call to Nicole and told her the whole story; Nicole Newland is my best friend and has been since fourth grade. I call her Nic most of the time though. She was a strawberry blonde and had hazel eyes. She's taller than I but only by a couple of inches. She's thin but not too skinny, and has nice legs. She is very outgoing and adventurous, no qualms about doing much and a good listener. She tells me I am too, but I'm not, at least not to the extent that she is. We were told we looked similar; truth is I don't think so, although my brother, sister and I look alike. I have brown wavy hair some of it curlier than the rest, blue eyes, and I'm medium height and plain looking and my legs are just okay, I wish they looked more like Nic's. I do have a birth mark that I think is pretty cool because it looks like a butterfly on my left shoulder.

She told me she remembered me telling her about the shiny phones but not much else. That day, was the day we decided I should start writing my dreams down. That way when I find myself in the midst of déjàvu, the prominent flash of memory that brings upon me that alienated and peculiar *"eerie"* feeling, I can call Nic and double check it by reference from my journals or notes. Maybe that's what déjàvu is, your memory trying to access information you have already received, but you just can't put your finger on it.

Nic also suggested that I date and sign them, and she would do the same in return after she read them. Plus, to make sure I use pen so nothing can be erased, this way we have an official record. I dated this dream July 16, 1981 and it's my first official recorded dream.

Our parents were strict with us, we had to do all our chores and we had to get good grades or we couldn't do stuff with our friends; well my sister and brother got good grades A's, B's and C's, I was a bit below average. Chores included cleaning the house top to bottom, weeding the yard, cutting the grass, washing dishes, setting and clearing the table at dinner time and doing homework.

However, during our summer break, our parents Sean and Lynn, have us in a lot of sports programs to keep us busy and out of trouble; so we rarely saw anyone from school anyway. My dad, due to his job in sales, belonged to the Country Club. To take full advantage of the Club our parents had all three of us siblings into, Golf (yes, golf it was a country club with a full golf course), tennis and swim team. My sister and I were also in synchronized swimming and I was also on the diving team.

We did a lot of things around the pool because we grew up swimming. Our mom was a swim teacher and life guard when we were younger. As long as I could remember, we would go to the pool every day in the summer. And when I say every day I mean "every day," rain, shine, horrible storms, whatever, we were at the pool every day. As soon as we were old enough, my mom quit her job and we switched over to the Club pool and then my mom would just drop us off there every day, and as I said we were at the pool EVERYDAY.

Our neighborhood was awesome as a kid, everyone had a minimum of one acre of land; playing football or flying kites was easy to do, you could pick anyone's yard, all of them were large enough. Our street was a big soft shaped "C" with two hills, great for riding bikes. We lived in the country so no curbs or sidewalks and only one street light at each end of the street.

None of the houses were fancy; we had a three bedroom ranch with a full walkout basement. Our house sat at the bottom of a small hill and the backyard had plenty of room and the side yard even larger. Our driveway went down the hill, and ended in a big circle that wrapped around to the garage. Our garage opened up from the back of the house, which my mom loved. The huge circle made for an excellent basketball court. We also had a two story deck.

The houses on our side of the street had a ravine and tons of land behind them that extended all the way down the block. To access the ravine you have to run down a steep hill or go down our "dirty slide."

Our dirty slide is a path my sister Tori started when we were smaller, some older kids were taking us for a hike and they ran down this steep hill located directly behind our house, but my sister and I just stared at it and said no way were we going to run down that hill. They were yelling at the bottom of the hill for us to follow so Tori got down on her butt and slid down and I followed. The older kids thought it was a hoot and ran back up to try it out. One of the neighbors said "How fun you guys just made a slide!" and Tori replied "a dirty slide," hence its name. Once you get into the ravine there is great hiking, a creek and discoveries to be made.

Tori was shorter than me and thin as a rail, but shapely. She has the bluest of eyes and freckles dancing across her nose and cheeks in the summer, like me, though our freckles would fade by Columbus Day. She had long blonde hair with bits of darker colors in it too; the kind people pay to have their hair look like. I on the other hand have dark wavy hair. She always dressed nice, hair styled and make-up on. She never over did it in the make-up department though. Tori is unlike me, I always wear jeans or shorts and tees, who cares what my hair looks like and make-up takes too long to put on, so I don't wear it. The only time you'll catch me in a dress or skirt is if we have to dress up.

CHAPTER 1

It's mid-summer and my siblings and I were golden brown with freckles running across our faces. All three of us were on swim team; however none of us played tennis this year. Although I love to play tennis, swim team, golf and diving were enough for me. I was having a very good season this year, faster in swim team and hitting the golf ball much straighter and farther than before. My diving coach's confidence in me had magnified and she asked to work an extra hour a day with me and me alone. Usually the whole team practices together. I'm getting leaner and faster and I've noticed the coaches keeping a closer eye on me.

As it was getting closer to school starting Nic, my best friend, wanted to have a last summer adventure; where we almost get into to trouble but not quite. She always walked the line, like my cousin Peyton; I assume that's why they got along so well. Of course, they both got along with me because I had no issues following along with their hair-brained ideas. This year Nic wanted to talk to the dead, it of course involved candles, herbs, a ritual, chanting, a dead person and in our case, a cemetery. My idea, flash lights and gym shoes.

Peyton wasn't allowed to drive to drive to the cemetery 'cause she may scare the spirits, so Nic made us walk. We started out walking to the Richfield Reading and Speech Center for batteries. We walked in loudly discussing our plans of raising or talking to the dead. The back room door was open, it was empty except for threads and scraps of material laying on the floor, Margie the owner walked out with two women following, and started apologizing to them about the mess as her tenant had just moved out. I guessed the pair was mother and daughter taking a tour of the place.

Margie spotted us and gave us a cheerful "well hello girls" and introduced us to the possible new tenants. They both had dark hair; the daughter was slim with dark make-up, petite but pretty in her own way. She had a long black cardigan, jeans and black boots on. The way she dressed reminded me of the burn-outs at our school. The mom was shorter dressed in jeans and a black sweater, she seemed nice, like a cheerful person.

We had gotten our batteries and I got a Snickers. It was only dusk but by the time we crossed the highway, through a field, and an industrial office area. It was dark when we reached the massive black wrought iron gates that protected the entrance of the cemetery; all three of us popped our flash lights on at the same time. When Nic explained what we were going to do a couple of days ago it sounded fun and not scary at all; but now in the dark cemetery it seemed a lot more ominous than I expected. I hoped I wouldn't get cold feet.

As we footslogged through and around the headstones we finally came upon one that was very large and fancy. The name on it read "Harriet Winchester" I said "Hey! We know her!"

Nic replied "That we do… she owns the house down the street from me, well her two grandsons own it now, but they are never there because they travel a lot. That's why they pay me to look after the place."

"If anyone is in tune to us trying to talk to the dead, it would be sweet Harriet." I replied. I remember Nic and me going to her house and cleaning it and her kitty litters, she had several cats and I even remember going grocery shopping for her and putting it away into her original medicine green metal cabinets in her tiny kitchen. She always tried giving Nic money and she would be very insistent sometimes, in that case Nic would take it and then put in her cookie jar, where she kept all her cash. She didn't use a bank. I could picture her with her white hair all pulled back in a bun, hunched shoulders, short, walking with a cane and always in a dress. Nicest lady ever. I bet, Nic was going to ask her where the treasure was! She always spoke of one, among other scary tales but we always assumed it was a story.

Nic dropped her backpack and started setting stuff up; three white candles in front of the tombstone and lit them, she poured some kind of black spice or crumbs from one side of the gravestone in a circle around to the other side. Then she dropped what looked like red flower petals in the middle of the circle in front of the candles and said something Greek.

We held hands across from the gravestone she told us to concentrate on wishing to talk to Harriet and we were supposed to say "Talk with us in the land of the living we bring you no harm" over and over. Of course Peyton and I just giggled. Nic got mad, stopped us and said "Really? Both of you concentrate."

As I was looking at Nic trying not to laugh, I saw movement over her shoulder, a dark figure wearing a long dark hooded cloak. It looked like the girl from earlier if I had to guess, tall, slim but it was so dark and why would she be out here. I turned back to the grave yanked on Peyton's and Nic's hands and said "Let's do this so we can get out of here."

"Close your eyes." I said very seriously shaking their hands. "Talk with us in the land of the living we bring you no harm." I said strongly and the girls repeated it with me. I put all my energy into it and raised our hands. "We seek out your missing treasure." I felt a surge of heat go thru my body, my hair stood on end, the circle set on fire and I heard something say "It's at the base of my favorite tree, eleven paces out due west the treasure is yours my dearest Nicole." One of us screamed so loud, I didn't hear anything else. I wanted to run but had a flash of consciousness, stamped out the fire, blew out the candles and grabbed the backpack. I looked back and saw the cloaked person, let out a yelp, and ran to find Nic and Peyton huffing and puffing at the wrought iron gates at the entrance to the cemetery.

The two of them were giggling. "Addie don't do that, you scared the crap out of us." Peyton complained.

"Do what? I didn't do anything? It was Nic's séance."

"Oh no, it's under my favorite tree ha ha ha." Nic bantered.

I held my throat, "I didn't say that" I spoke softly, "I didn't..." The girls turned, started walking back home chatting away like nothing happened. I heard it, I didn't say it....

* * * * * * *

As far back as I can remember, we typically had family night on Friday nights and we would go out to dinner every other week or so. The kids got to choose where too, my brother would sometimes choose Burger King but we loved it, he would always get the ham and cheese sandwiches. I don't know why they stopped making them, they were good.

My favorite place to go was Quaker Square for pizza, it's in downtown Akron. I love going in the winter, steam would come out of the sewer caps on the ride home making for a very cool effect in the dark, and I could imagine a creepy supernatural movie scene when I see it. When we would get to Quaker Square we would put our name on the waiting list and then go visit these old full sized retired trains that you could walk through and see the many model trains setup inside. My father loved trains and that would take up most of our wait time. Quaker Square used to be the old Quaker Oats Mill up until 1970 when they converted it into a shopping mall, hotel and restaurants. Totally cool too, all the hotel rooms were round; we got to stay in them once for a wedding. They gave us a totally cool tin filled with Quaker Oats cookies too.

Quaker Square has the best Pizza in town, my parents say "If you can't get Chicago pizza this is as close as you'll get." After dinner we would walk across the parking lot to the shopping mall. They have a glass elevator that goes all the way to the top floor – since they used to be oat silos there were many floors to shop on and explore. We usually shopped around a little after dinner always hitting the candy store before going home; it was one of those old fashioned candy stores, where you give them a dollar and it bought a whole bag of candy.

Since our parents were going out with their friends tonight we got to choose a restaurant last night. It was Tori's turn to choose and she picked Skyway's Drive In, a fast food restaurant we love, it has *the* best cheeseburgers, toasted cheese sandwiches and onion rings ever! It was a drive-in restaurant so you had to eat in your car, always fun as a kid. A great benefit of Skyway was the cute guys that came to your car to wait on you. Plus, it's the hot spot for kids our age to go. Number one on my list is the Ski-Hi burger, next is the California Fizz which is a drink - they're outstanding! If you try and duplicate either, the burgers or the drinks, ya just can't.

Anyway, we were on our way to our parent's friend's house, the Monaham's. My dad was always on time and my mom always ran late, but today she was on time and our moods were all on high.

My parents were very social, they go out just about every

Saturday. We used to have a sitter but not this summer. Now, when they go out with their good friends the Monaham's, who also have kids, they bring us to their house to fend for ourselves while the parents go have fun. Of course, the Monaham's kids were always doing something they weren't supposed to. When we go there, depending on the week, one kid was always singled out and picked on, hurt or traumatized in some way or other.

Just after we got to the Monaham's, before all the parents left, we got the usual rundown of rules: "No fighting, no playing in the living room or dining room, no friends over and do not answer the door no matter what! Call us at the restaurant or theater ONLY in an emergency. And if any of you get out of line there would be consequences!" My neighborhood friends thought my dad was scary but I think Mr. Monaham was way scarier and we took every word he said seriously. As far as discipline went, we were grounded or even may have been paddled when we were bad, but I always had a sense that their discipline was way more severe! I knew they had family secrets too and if they ever told us them I *am* sure they would have to kill us! Maybe they wouldn't kill us, but I'm sure they'd get the highest punishment available, which in that house couldn't be good.

The parents didn't take long to leave; they left at 6:45 on the nose. Right after they left, it seemed to be a more somber crowd, not the normal fighting and screaming that usually started the minute the parents left the driveway. It was strange because normally Kevin would yell something funny to us and the screaming, yelling and running around would begin. It wasn't that way tonight, at least not yet.

I guess we just had to wait for it. Of course it came, the reason they were on their best behavior…. The Monaham kids, Kevin and Lucy, said "We are going to invite our friends over and if any of you tell on us, Kevin will kick your asses." Kevin, by the way, had a black belt in karate. So we believed them when they told us that.

All the kids started to fight and we were trying to keep Kevin from using the phone but he locked himself in his parent's room and made a call and five minutes later his friend Logan arrived. We all went into the living room – the living room where we weren't allowed. It was okay though, we sat around talking. I sat on the floor, across from the couch and coffee table next to Kit. I wasn't going to get blamed for anything, easy exits from where I sat. Tori,

3:17 a.m. ...the waking hour

Kevin and Logan were on the couch. Lucy was still upstairs in her room.

The doorbell rang again, Lucy bolted for the door, it was her friend and they joined us in the living room. Everyone was bragging about what they had and what they did this summer, except my sister, brother and I. Obviously, we were in a rich kid's neighborhood. Although, the houses didn't look rich or massive, but you knew they came from money. Everything was pristine, kept up and perfect. The kids and parents always had all the newest gadgets.

The Monaham's had a nice two-story house and although nothing looked really expensive everything looked immaculate. The grass and bushes all perfectly manicured and the inside so clean I doubt you could find a spec of dirt. The grand picture window in the living room was lined with expensive drapes and opened perfectly leaving enough window open to let in daylight. The kitchen was spotless, with a dishwasher, double ovens and all the perks a kitchen could have. The dining room looked like it had never been touched. The basement was finished so nicely it didn't even look like a basement. Everything was up-to-date, new, but not too fancy either. And the kids had every kind of toy imaginable, new TV's, all the Atari video games and attachments, considering it's the very first home video game available to the public, it was a big deal.

As Logan kept ranting about his playthings, Lucy and her friend got flustered and mad because they were duped by him – he obviously had more stuff. They got up and went to Lucy's room. That left the rest of us. Logan kept on bragging along, now he was onto the sports he was in and how well he does in them. My sister got so mad she decided to tell him, "You look too fat to be good." He wasn't fat maybe husky but not fat – okay he's chunky – scratch that he's fat – I'm always trying to be nice to everyone. She started telling him how all three of us were on the swim team and anyone of us could beat him. He replied by saying "I would love to see you in a skin tight swim suit." I was sitting Indian style with my elbows on my knees and my chin resting on my hands, I looked up at him quickly. He was looking right at me, but I dismissed him thinking he was talking to Tori.

Everyone flirted with my sister so he must have been looking at my sister when he said it, all the boys liked her. She was beautiful.

My sister told him about my diving and Logan said "I betcha diving makes you sooo flexible, I wanna see you twisting and flipping in the air," real sleazy like. Kevin and Logan were the only two that laughed.

Who does this guy think he was John Travolta? Give me a break. I just gave him a dirty look and said "You're sick" and he responded "Sick in love with you". He just grossed me out more, this guy is crazy – "You mean you're in love with Tori", and he replied "No, I mean you!" I was actually repulsed by this guy, and now I thought I'm glad I'm not Tori because she has to put up with this crap from a lot of guys, I've seen it happen before.

Logan was obnoxious and nothing to be obnoxious about. He looked very average to me, nothing special. He doesn't even look like he's fit enough for sports; maybe there is a layer of muscle hiding underneath that husky body of his, or maybe not I laugh to myself. He had short dark hair that was dyed a brown orange color, ick, and no extraordinary features to him, except for the fact that his ears stuck out. And the mouth on him, has he ever listened to himself, maybe that's the problem, he won't shut up because he likes listening to himself – he's the only one too. When he ran out of things to say I think he just started making things up, actually I think most of the stuff he told us was all lies.

He started bragging again, this time about how he was on swim team and he's sure we had nothing on him. My sister got so mad she blurted out that I was a wrestling manager and I can kick anyone's ass.

In eighth grade, Nic and I were what they called wrestling managers. We weren't actual managers though. We would just keep score and video tape their matches at the meets which included tracking, setting up and breaking down the equipment. There was no actual wrestling or training involved. The only people I have ever fought with before were Tori and Kit and I'm sure that didn't count for much.

At this point I was still drawing pictures in the carpet with my finger, bored, half daydreaming not paying attention to what Tori was saying but to look like I was interested I agreed with her and said "Oh yeah sure" while still looking at the carpet and drawing something else. I didn't bother looking up or even removing my face from my hand and Kaboom! I was flat on my back! Logan had launched himself over the coffee table onto me laying me flat out, his head hit mine making the back of my head crash into the floor. He said "Give me a kiss baby!" and in the distance I heard Kevin saying "Let's give the love birds some privacy." " Kevin, Tori and Kit all left. I'm assuming they went all the way down to the basement because that's the only place we were allowed to go.

I tried to get out from under him, "Get off me!" He grabbed my wrists and pinned them to the ground, I shook my head back and forth so he couldn't plant his awful lips on me. I wiggled to the left when he leaned to my right and tried to plant one on my cheek. "You know you want it; you know you love it baby." He said in this creepy awful voice.

I thrust my butt up off the floor and kicked my legs out to the left and was able to free half my body wishing desperately I could make this stop. Logan grabbed me at the waist and pulled me back to him. I yelled "Help!" but my voice was drowned out by TV's and stereos blasting throughout the house. He entangled his leg around my right leg and I couldn't move. Everything felt as though it was in slow motion and time was standing still, I tried to get free, I felt my muscles begin to tire. He ripped my shirt part-way open, "Stop!" I said "Stop it! Let me go!"

He told me "You love it baby, you know you want it."

My body began to shake, tears began to fall. He was working with my right arm trying to pin it down. I fought and moved any part of my body I could trying to break free. I couldn't move under his weight, my one leg was still totally pinned.

"You're hurting me! Let me go!"

He grabbed hold of my right wrist but had no control. As I struggled to free myself I tried to think of a wrestling move that would get me out of this mess. I quickly thought; roll over so I wouldn't get pinned and then try and get up. I could do this, I could roll over. I tried and tried to roll but I couldn't budge.

"Addie I know you want it, give me a kiss" he said with effort.

"Leave me alone," was all I could muster up and not very loudly, it was a struggle to speak. I pulled myself up on my elbow and suddenly, he whacked my head with his and my head hit the floor with such force that it throbbed and rang. When we locked eyes, his looked like reflective mirrors with no color to them at all, they alarmed me with such a frenzy my heart stopped. He got my right arm between our bellies and laid on it with all his weight and I could barely move. My right leg still pegged started to tingle. Me being panicked and struggling to get away so bad, I know, was making him more excited.

He pinned my left arm to the ground, pressed his head on my cheek and pushed so I couldn't move, I couldn't even turn my head. "Stop! Please! Stop!" I felt tears rolling down my cheek and his hot breath on my neck and he licked it and then I felt a searing pain. "Get off!" I tried wriggling some more and broke my left wrist free. I inhaled and started hitting him with my fist as hard as I could, in the back, arm and face, anywhere. I felt like I started to break free but instead I felt his hand in my shirt and on my breast. I pulled at his hand, "Leave me alone!" I yelled again and I'm sure no one can hear me. All I can hear is noise.

I free his hand from my chest and he moves it to my waist, my jeans open and his hand is..."Aaaaahhhhhh" I let out a high pitch scream. I started crying so hard I couldn't breathe. And then, just like that, he was off of me. I immediately sat up and scooched myself backward until I hit the wall. Logan was standing holding his eye "You bitch!" I retreated further into the wall pulling my legs into my chest, pulling my shirt closed as tight as I could. I looked over to the entryway, my brother was standing there backing up slowly, shaking his head, he looked really scared. "You asshole, if you ever touch my sister again I'll split your other eye open!" Kit shouted.

Everyone else came flooding into the living room, Kevin in the lead; my hands were shaking trying to hold my blouse shut tightly across my chest. I noticed buttons on the floor in front of me, I collected them and re-clutched my shirt. My hands were trembling, my wrists bruised and red, my head pounding, my neck all wet and I hurt all over. I wanted to feel my neck to see if it was split open, but I don't dare touch it without looking at it first. Everyone was looking at me, they seem puzzled like they had no idea what was going on. But how couldn't they? They had to know exactly what was going on. Kevin yelled "Logan get off the carpet!" He looked at me and exclaimed "What did you do Addie!" Like it was my fault, Logan headed into the kitchen and I ran into the basement and hid in the corner.

No one came down after me, I was alone. My hands and legs were still shaking, I let myself slump into the corner. I realized my whole body was trembling and I couldn't stop shaking even after I sat. There was extreme chaos upstairs. "We have to call 9-1-

1?" someone shouted. "Who cares if he's bleeding send him home, get him out of here!" The tears started falling again, they felt like hot rivers of lava running down my face that burned and moved in slow motion. I could hear someone, I think Logan telling his side of the story but I couldn't make out his words.

I heard someone coming down the stairs, I inched myself tightly into my corner. Oh please don't let it be Logan, please don't let it be him.... Kit came around the corner and up to me and put his hand out. As he helped me up my blouse fell open and I noticed my jeans were unbuttoned. I pulled my shirt down hoping Kit didn't notice, and squeezed my blouse together, only two buttons were left on my blouse. My hands were still trembling so badly, I had a death grip on the other buttons in my other hand. I sat on the couch in the corner farthest from the stairs and grabbed my knees.

Kit grabbed a blanket and held it out to me; he must have thought I was cold because I was shivering. I didn't take the blanket I just held myself tightly in my corner and he covered me not saying a word. I slowly held out my hand balled in a fist and he slowly put his hand underneath mine and I wriggled the extra buttons into his hand. Kit crossed the room and sat, we just stared at each other. I gave my shirt another glance and noticed the pocket was torn a bit and it had a couple of blood stains on it. I squeezed myself into the utmost corner of the cool dark brown leather couch and pulled the blanket up to my chin. I wished I could disappear.

The last time I was this sore and trembled this hard was when my dad sprayed us in the driveway with the outside hose after losing Tori's boot in the *'not quicksand'* we found. I tried to stop but I couldn't, the more I tried to stop the more I shook uncontrollably, just like that day.

I remember it being a cool fall day, just last year. The sun was out, the leaves were falling, my favorite time of year, my sister and I went hiking. After taking the "dirty slide" down to the ravine and heading north and then west, after a bit my sister got her foot caught in some mud and she started calling out to me that she was stuck. I ignored her at first, thought she was joking and kept walking, but the next time she yelled at me I knew by the tone of her voice that she needed help. I turned to look and she had one leg on the ground and one, well one I could only see her thigh and she was trying to grab something. I ran over and pulled her arm, she moved a little but there was suction or something pulling her back in, sucking her leg in so bad I couldn't get her out. I grabbed her under her arms and pulled as hard as I could. Still she only budged inches. Tori grabbed a little tree branch behind me and I dug my heels in on the edge and then we pulled and pulled until we got her out. We were both laughing and fell to the ground when we noticed she was missing her boot. We tried digging it out by hand so we wouldn't get in trouble, but after many hours (at least it felt like hours) we gave up.

Our arms burning from digging, exhaustion started to set in. It seemed like we would never get home. It was the longest walk I had ever experienced. Especially because we knew we were in trouble unless we could get in the house undetected.

When we got home and to our detriment, our dad was outside and we were muddy head to toe, and Tori only had one boot, no hiding anything there. Our dad started yelling at us non-stop, we went to go in the house and he yelled "There is no way in hell you are tracking that mud into our house." He took the hose out, pointed to the middle of the driveway, we trenched over to it while he sprayed us with the hose until we were unbelievably soaking wet and shaking uncontrollably from the intensely arctic cold water that seemed to come from our hose and the beautifully cool air now felt bitter. We were shivering so bad we couldn't stop, the sun wasn't helping. Tori's lips were a shade of purple; the same color our lips used to turn after eating a bowl of wild blackberries.

Our mother appeared at the door in the garage. My dad yelled at us to strip and get in the shower, our mother said "They can't strip out here Sean! Girls come in the hallway and hand me your clothes. We stepped in on the carpet; my mom sent our dad upstairs to cool his temper. Tori and I were shaking so bad and our hands so cold it was hard to take off our sopping wet jeans; eventually we had to peel them off, it was worse than peeling an orange. After this long process, we high tailed it up the stairs in our undergarments and into the bathroom locking the door. We turned on the hot shower water like we normally do, but touching it felt like it sent needles into our hands, we turned it to lukewarm. To stop the shivering we each rinsed off first, then rotated not speaking; all you could hear were our teeth chattering.

That's how bad I was trembling but a warm shower wasn't

going to help. I remembered having told our parents the whole story, boy was our dad mad. He had started yelling at us again, his voice became hoarser with each word. Then he said "There's no such thing as quicksand!" He went on and on how there was no such thing in our area! We obviously had no other answer for him other than quicksand. Duh! It was sucking her leg in and we couldn't pull her out. What else could it be?

"Fine." he said, "Show me where." We followed him to the shed where he got a shovel and he hauled us back out to the woods where he would dig up the boot. We found the exact sinking mud pit. Seeing it the second time we noticed it was actually marked pretty well with the roots of an uprooted tree at the base and plants that grew all around the edge of it but nothing in the middle and you could see where we struggled. There was a huge oak tree near it and the rest were all small skinny trees surrounding 'the little sinking mud pit.' Not quicksand according to my dad. If someone were to get stuck in the middle, I doubt you could get out.

Thank goodness Tori had been near the edge because it was a pretty big area, and our dad couldn't dig anywhere but at the edges. He dug and dug but the mud kept caving right back where he was digging. When he started sliding in and nothing to grab a hold of except for tiny little trees, my sister and I lent a hand hoping he didn't pull us in. He was turning red and starting to sweat and then he started to swear. This time he started shoveling the mud and flinging it further away. Still the hole kept filling back in. My sister and I were silent the entire time and didn't move, unless we were lending him a hand to keep his balance or from falling in. We didn't move or dare say a word or do anything to make him any angrier than he already was.

Another ten minutes went by, my dad was red as could be, he stood up rested his hand on the shovel for a minute, then slung it over his shoulder turned and started walking home. Tori and I just followed. You know he never found that boot and we never spoke of the incident or the *"quicksand"* again. We didn't even get grounded! I'd rather be there than here though, I'd rather be trembling because my dad hosed us, than because of the insane and grotesque encounter with Logan, I remembered him licking my neck and his hot breath on me and it made me cringe all over again.

Kevin snapped me out of my reverie, when he came running

down the stairs and exclaimed "You aren't bleeding all over too are you?" he looked at me and spouted "Good!" and took off back upstairs.

I put my hand on my neck and felt it; it wasn't wet anymore. I looked at my hand, no blood. Kit said with a quivering voice "There's a mark, no blood." His voice sounded like a base instead of the alto he's always been. I moved my hand slowly up to my forehead where there was a huge knot, I looked at Kit and he just shook his head referring that there was no blood there either. The tears just started rolling down my face again and I still couldn't stop shaking, the blanket wasn't really helping because I wasn't cold, I was actually warm. My body felt hot, my head throbbing, I couldn't move, I was exhausted.

I didn't want to move, but "I want to go home" escaped from me. Kit, not saying a word, got up and before he ascended the stairs I said "By the way," my voice crackling and deeper than normal "Another one of their friends was in the front yard." Kit paused on the stair and looked at me, "What?" he asked.

"They must be planning a party. I saw someone in the front yard when… after…. I mean.. when you came upstairs for me." My voice didn't sound like me in my head. I could hear every one of his footsteps as he made his way to the first floor, they rang in my head and loneliness hit me like a ton of bricks. Maybe it was the sense of my security that just disappeared that made me feel feeble.

I was sitting on the couch alone, not sure I liked being alone, but I didn't want anyone's company either. What I wouldn't give to be at home. What I would give if I could wake up and this was all a dream.

Kevin came down the stairs again and spat out words like venom "You hurt Logan bad, he might need stitches!" He startled me so badly I thought my heart skipped a beat, I just stared at him and didn't speak. He stared back "You don't even care that you hurt him. What am I supposed to do now? I can't even believe Logan said he still likes you, you're a cold bitch!" His sister was behind him and started pleading with me not to tell their parents. Although, I didn't really hear what else they said, it all seemed garbled and their voices sounded like they were in a tunnel. The words *"He likes me"* were just ringing in my head. "I just want all of them to leave." I said half to myself. The two of them heard my whispered voice and Lucy cried out "Why should my friend leave she didn't do anything!" My head was too heavy to hold up so I put my face on my hands and knees.

"Leave me alone" was all I could utter.

My head spinning, my mouth was dry and I just wanted to go home. Kevin started yelling at Lucy, Tori came downstairs and couldn't help but get in the mix. I just wanted them all to go away; I slouched further into the couch and let my head fall back into my knees and put my hands over my ears.

Tori sat next to me and asked if I needed to call mom and dad? I shook my head no and said "I don't think so. " Kit came down and sat on the stairs.

"Should we go to the bathroom and check your head and your... well, everything and make sure you're okay? " Tori asked. "Oh, look your shirt is ripped, but not bad we can fix it. Can you stand?" She helped me off the couch, I slowly stood up, she was checking my jeans; they were unbuttoned. I thought I fastened them but my hands were trembling so badly I must not have gotten it latched. She looked up at me slowly and held my gaze for a while. She started looking me over again. As we entered the basement bathroom Tori stated, "You have some blood stains on your shirt and jeans but just small dots, I think it's from Logan though. I don't think you're bleeding. Are you?" I shook my head. "Sit." She said pointing to the toilet, closing and locking the door behind her. I let go of my shirt finally. "You're missing buttons too!" Tori said more excitedly. "I had no idea, I thought Logan was just joking around, I mean I didn't know, but I should've checked on you or not left." She said shaking her head. "I'm sorry. Are you okay? She asked slowly as if I may not have caught everything.

She found a clean washcloth and rinsed it with warm water; she wiped off my face and then my neck, arms and hands. She rolled my sleeves down so my bruised wrists weren't visible. "Are you sure you're okay?" she asked again turning my wrists to evaluate the marks on them before buttoning my sleeves. I had on my heather red shirt; it wasn't red though it looked pink because of the "heathering." It used to be one of my favorite shirts but now I couldn't wait to take it off. I replied with "I think so" my voice still raspy and unfamiliar.

"Let's get you some ice packs and aspirin."

"... and water please." My voice pricked, from my throat being so parched.

They were all silent when we came out of the bathroom, so silent you could hear a pin drop. Lucy's friend and Logan were present. Logan was holding an ice pack and towel over his right eye. I stopped. When I looked into his eyes they looked normal, dark but normal.

Tori said "What the hell are they still doing here?" I was frozen in the doorway still holding my shirt shut. She looked at them and barked "Go home or I'm calling the police! And if your other friend is still lingering outside get him outta here too!"

Kevin started in "Logan might need stitches! The bleeding won't stop and I can't just send him home!"

"Sure you can!" Tori retorted "Get all your friends out of here including the guy in your front yard! Now!"

"What guy in the front yard? You're delusional! Your sister started a fight with my friend and now you're lying about us inviting other people over, next you'll say we're having a party!" Kevin yelled. Then Lucy chimed in and then Kit. Everyone was talking or yelling all at once, I couldn't hear anyone and I just started to cry again.

"STOP IT!" Stop yelling at each other!" Tori shouted "The only way we're going to clean up this mess is to have all guests leave the house." She eyeballed Logan and Lucy's friend and pointed toward the stairs. "We need to make sure the house is in good shape, no blood, nothing broken and we'll re-vacuum the carpet so they cannot tell anyone's been in the living room. Everyone will leave Addie alone, if she chooses to tell, that is up to her!" She put her hand up before Kevin and Lucy even got another word out. "Kit go get Addie some water, Lucy find a needle and thread. Kevin get her an ice pack and a couple aspirin."

They didn't move. They all just stood there with their mouths opened, come to think of it so was mine. Tori never took charge like that over here; sure she was really bossy at home but never anywhere else. "What are you looking at? Move! Or I'll tell our parents!" she yelled. It made me jump but they all hopped to it. Tori turned to me with such empathy in her eyes and said "I am so sorry Addie, I am sorry; no one will touch you now I promise." She intertwined her fingers in mine. The two of us need to stick together, two are better than one" and she gave me a wink. In that short moment I thought I saw a flash of my grandmother in her and I stopped shaking.

3:17 a.m. ...the waking hour

"So we aren't going to tell anyone what happened?" I asked Tori. She put her arm around me. "That's entirely up to you or if you want me too..." Kevin had come down with a towel and a baggie filled with ice. He moved his hand toward us and shook it impatiently. "So are you gonna keep your mouth shut? You know you started the whole thing. If you wouldn't have teased Logan none of this would have happened." Kevin said defensively.

Tori stepped right in front of him and said "Your friend is an asshole and if you or your friend come near my sister again, or any of us for that matter, I'll sic my boyfriend and his friends on the two of you! Now back off Kevin or I'll be the one to tell our parents!"

Tori was great, she turned to me and said "This isn't your fault" Tori repeated it a couple of times. As I tried to speak my voice kept cracking. "I just want to go home and I never want to come back." Tori agreed, but turned to Kevin and said "You forgot the aspirin."

As the Monaham's and Kit appeared back in the basement each retrieving what Tori had asked for, everyone was silent. I know they wanted to know if I was going to tell. I just wanted to go home. No more talking, I wanted to be left alone. No one spoke another word the rest of the night. Tori sewed my buttons back on and fixed my shirt up pretty good considering. I started to shiver again even with the blanket, I thought it was from the exhaustion starting to set in. Even so Kit got my jacket, it helped cover up my shirt. Tori fixed my bangs to cover the bump on my head. Everything looked fine on the outside.

A week passed and I never spoke of the incident to anyone, not Tori, Kit, my parents and not even a word to Nic. My brother and sister never brought it up, and I'm sure the Monaham's didn't either. If Logan needed stitches, I'm sure he lied about why he needed them, because if anyone ever found out what really happened I'm sure Logan and the Monaham's would be in monumental trouble.

That was until the Friday after my incident, my mom called me into the basement. She was putting clothes into the wash. I saw the shirt I wore that night and I felt a wave of heat flush through my body. She was holding my shirt above the washer. She started saying something that I couldn't hear. Then she dropped it in, next was my bra. I could see that the lace was still torn and hanging off of one side, I forgot to fix it. My body got warmer and warmer, I felt sick and light-headed. My mom knew something happened, she was going to ask me about it. What do I say? Then, I felt a faint pang of relief and my eyes welled up. I could finally tell my mom.

"Addie," my mom said loudly. "Addie are you feeling okay? You're very pale and why are you crying." She dropped my bra in the wash and I felt myself exhale. She stepped toward me and I flinched. She said "I am just going to feel your head Addie, are you getting sick?"

"I'm a little tired mom and my eyes are burning." Burning eyes in our house was a tell-tale sign for too much chlorine from swimming but my voice had cracked too. "What did you call me for?"

"Never mind sweetie, you go lie down."

I went to bed and cried myself to sleep.

That night I had a dream; it was about me and a wolf running peacefully in the ravine behind us. When I ran up the dirty slide and turned to wait for the wolf he was gone. It wasn't unpleasant but unusual, plus, my dream didn't wake me.

That week we had a swim meet. I was glad for the distraction for something to do. It was quite comforting knowing I could swim and be able to go to swim parties and other such water events and not worry. I'm always very comfortable in the water. It's like walking or breathing air to me. When my parents saw how bruised up I was I had to lie and tell them it was from the roller rink. At times at the roller rink we would all hold hands, skate around rink as fast as we could and then let go of the person on then end. I have gotten bruised up from it before. However, when eighth grade ended so did our trips to the roller rink, not that my parents knew that though.

Today was my first swim meet of the year, I have never been a great swimmer, just average, but I enjoyed it. We missed our first three swim meets because of our '1981 Gellar Family Extravaganza'; you know the one with the shiny pay phones. After the third swim meet, everyone gets placed in the lanes by how they've won in the previous meets. Megan was a nice girl on the team, usually an average swimmer just like me. Today, however, she got the middle lane; everyone was bragging how well she did at the first three meets and that she took first place in breast stroke all three times. The best swimmers are always in the middle, there are six lanes and every other lane is someone from the opposing team. She was the one to beat.

For the fifty meter breast stroke race I was in the outer lane right next to the wall, the norm for me. I was very determined to win, or to do well, when I finished I tagged the side of the pool and looked to my right and saw no one. I had a memory flash back of the first race I was in when I was four. Some memories fade after time, but some stick with you like they were yesterday no matter how much time goes by. I started swim team after that, it's an amusing story how my first swim race went.

On a normal day we would usually leave the pool around three or four in the afternoon but this time we had stayed to watch the swim meet. Just one random summer night my mom had decided to stay late. She was still a lifeguard and swim teacher at the time. In the six and under group they only had three swimmers and six lanes, one swimmer was on our team and the other two were from the opposing team. So they needed another person and because I *could* swim all the strokes my mom volunteered me.

Of course, every kid always says "yes" when asked if they want to swim, I was no dummy, I said yes too. They asked me if I knew how to dive, "oh yes" I said "I can". So they told me when the gun goes off dive into the water, swim as fast as you can "freestyle" to the other end of the pool and stay in your lane. The lanes were lined with floating guides, it looked easy enough. I was still small and someone had to help me up on the starting block but up I went. There wasn't enough time to be nervous. I was watching one minute and then the next I was on the starter block.

The referee said "Take your marks", I didn't move, "Get set", *"POP"* went the cap gun. I shook at startling noise but then I jumped into the water doing the most horrid looking dive, I guess you couldn't even call it that. It was more of a jump smack dive combo I was told. I came up and took a deep breath and I started swimming as fast as I could. I didn't look around, just like they told me, I just swam and swam and swam. I swam my heart out! I got to the other end of the pool! I looked up and saw no other swimmers I must have beat everyone! Leaning on the edge of the pool I said "I won, I won!" I couldn't make out what everyone was doing outside the pool, they were holding their stomachs and their faces were red, some were jumping up and down, they were laughing and cheering. Coach pulled me out of the water and wrapped a towel around me and gave me a big hug. He held me up under my legs cheering with his other arm.

So of course I asked "Did I win?" and another roar of laughter washed through the crowd. I never saw my mom laugh so hard before, she wiped her eyes and said "Oh, no honey." I heard chuckle, chuckle. "You came in dead last! You came in about two minutes behind everyone else!" Another roar of laughter came about. I remember it very clearly; some memories just really stick with you. That was the day my sister and I were signed up for swim team. My mom, of course, was harassed for the way I swam, I guess I swam like a wiggle worm; my butt was going side to side. Even her boss gave her a hard time about it because she was one of the pools swim teachers. However, it didn't take her long to straighten me out.

As soon as I tuned back into reality, I heard the clapping and turned around again to see the rest of the swimmers starting to come in. I had finally won and by a lot!

My next swim meet was the same, but I won in freestyle and breast stroke. It kept happening all summer. From then on out I swam in all the relays and all the swim strokes, breast stroke, freestyle, backstroke and eventually butterfly. It's funny how everyone wants to be your friend when you're winning. That was okay though, I already knew who my real friends were.

I guess I didn't have to write this dream down anymore because for the past couple of weeks, I kept having the same dream of the girl and guy in the field. Better than the nightmares I was having of Logan and his eyes that were very unnerving, why couldn't I have dreamt about that before it happened? In any case, both dreams are haunting me. I wake up at exactly 3:17a.m. every time I have a dream about the guy and girl in the field. Instead of writing down the whole dream, I only jot down the new details I remember. Like one new detail I noticed, the girl had a silver bracelet that glistened in the sun before the attack but not after. Normally, or at least what I thought was normal, once I recorded my dream I wouldn't have it again, but not this one. Normal, what's normal, normal is probably having dreams that don't come true. I guess I don't know what normal is for me, I hope this one doesn't come true.

CHAPTER 2

My sister and I were freshman and slated to graduate 1985. I was the youngest one in our class; I'll be the last one to turn fifteen in November. When I arrived at school on the first day, I was feeling very young and confused. As I walked to my locker which was near the front entrance and Nic's locker I noticed a ton of students piling out the front door. Why was everyone leaving school? Did I come on the wrong day? Did the fire alarm go off? Am I awake? No, couldn't be the wrong day, buses picked us up and everyone else is here; maybe it's another practice day. I paused in the hall to notice they were all crossing the street to a church across the road. Another freshman stopped by my side and asked me "What's up?" I replied "I have no idea." I looked around me and needless to say it looked like all us freshman were pretty much clueless to what was going on. It seemed like all the older kids were going to church. Do all the juniors and seniors go to mass the first day of school, or before school, do they have religion classes over there? I had no clue what was going on.

I felt Nic come up beside me, she asked me what was going on and I of course gave her my 'I don't know' explanation, but rambled off all the possibilities including the fact that maybe we were still sleeping. So, of course, and I should have expected it, she pinched me. I let out a loud "Ow!"

"Nope." she said "You're awake."

Storm breezed by us and grabbed one of each of our hands and said lets go. "Wait" I said as Nic and I tossed our books in my locker and slammed it shut. He gave us a tug and led us into the mass of people that went out the doors and across the street into the very crowded church. The people were so thick it felt like we were being herded like cattle. I squeezed Storm's hand so he wouldn't let go and he squeezed my hand back.

We entered the church through very large wooden double doors that were propped open. It was a very basic one room church but very pretty. They used huge wood rafters and supports all along the ceiling and behind the altar were large stained glass windows. It was a beautiful church; all the pews were classic wood and all the side windows were stained glass as well. Storm found us this niche near the back of the church, he sort of led the two of us so we were in front and he was behind us. Nic tilted her head sideways to look at us and asked "What's going on? Are we supposed to be here?"

"Just wait" he said.

Students were still coming in the doors; I caught a glimpse of a coffin in front of the church and I instantly got nervous. Excitedly I blathered softly "Why are we at a funeral and whose is it? Do you know that person? I am so sorry Storm, are you okay?" I could hear Nic mumbling a couple of questions too.

He half laughed and smiled at us "Could you two be a little patient, let's just wait until everything settles down a bit." There were rows upon rows of pews that spanned the length of the church. Right then he took our hands and swooped us in the last row of seats and sat between us. Students got settled in and almost simultaneously everyone sat. You could see the minister at the lectern trying to get the microphone to work, everyone got really quiet, the sounds were down to a murmur. Storm brought us in closer to him, so close I felt like I was sitting on top of him and sure enough more students scooted in our pew. There was standing room only. I couldn't help notice some of the students were crying and the mood was very somber.

I felt the warmth and the aura of the room envelop me immediately and then a slight breeze from the doors propped open behind us. It smelled of wood and candles; none of the beautiful stained glass windows looked like they opened. I noticed sunlight shining in the front behind the Reverend and casket, coming from

3:17 a.m. ...the waking hour

what looked like another door around the corner. I could only hope the breeze would continue. Storm began to tell us the girls name in the coffin was Jewel. She was supposed to be a senior this year and that both his brothers knew her. "The investigation isn't over but there was definitely foul play and they're saying she was murdered. They aren't letting out any details on what happened, but my brothers said she was dating some guy but nobody knew who. After dating him for a couple of months she was looking very ashen and had circles under her eyes like she was starving herself. Her parents were really worried about her and rightly so. The boyfriend can't be found, it looks like he took off, they think out of state."

As soon as I heard the word murder everything Storm said started to sound further and further away, like I was in a tunnel, I felt my face get even hotter and I flashed on *"his"* face, my heart began to race and I pictured myself in the coffin. I told myself, think of something else something positive – I looked right into Storm's eyes and he looked at me quizzically scrunching his eyebrows together. Why was he looking at me that way? Probably because my face was red and hot, my eyes were welling up, but it was hot in here and it was a wake. But realized I had a death grip on his hand. I tried to relax and tried getting Logan out of my head.

He leaned over, although he didn't have very far to lean because we were sitting so close. I tried to focus everything I had on Storm, but that *"guy"* that *"leach"* was there on top of me again. Storm whispered "Breathe" and I took a deep breath. Storm was looking straight ahead and I just stared at him, I thought of our long conversations on the phone the year before when we had sort of dated briefly, well we had one sort of date. I didn't appreciate him then, but I was appreciating him now. I was remembering how he kept checking up on me at the roller rink, which at the time I found annoying, I thought he was being intrusive but now I could see it was just because he cared for me. The last day of school last year was the last time I talked to him and told him "I guess the next time we'll see each other we'll be freshman." He just agreed with me and we went on our separate ways. I was right, our paths never crossed and he never called, I didn't call him either.

Storm was on the wrestling team back then and Nic and I were wrestling managers. He was very skinny and gawky looking then but he didn't look that way anymore.

I was breathing more normally and I was having visions of Storm holding me instead of that dreadful moment in my life that was defining me. I leaned right back into Storm's ear and whispered "Sorry." He looked back at me and asked "What for?" I replied "For being difficult and acting all weird. I'm nervous; I've only been to one other wake." He turned his head looking at me scrunching his brow. Then relaxed them and said "No problem" like he hadn't even thought about it twice.

I hadn't a clue on how to act, what to say or ask; Nic looked at me, shrugged her shoulders and pushed the corner of her lips downward, I did the same. Storm began "On another note, she isn't the first one to die in this school of something suspicious." We both looked at him, questioningly. He responded "My Uncle's a cop." Nic and I looked at each other and shrugged our shoulders again. That explained a lot.

Storm was holding our hands and I wasn't about to let go, it was nice; it made me feel like all three of us had a connection. Plus, I'm glad Nic and I were with Storm, he needed a friend. As the minister finished his sermon, I heard him mumble something about last respects when passing by the casket..... That's all I heard. The students in the first three rows stood up and made a single file line that went to the casket and ended at the pew, just like when you went to take communion, except they emptied the pew to the right instead of the middle aisle and made a line. As students passed by the casket to pay their respects you could hear some crying and sniffling going on. We were in the last row on the right side. I was hoping we would high tail it out since we were so close to the doors, none of us knew her personally so I was thinking we didn't need to pay last respects especially to someone we didn't know.

I nudged Storm and nodded my head toward the door and he shook his head with his eyebrows rumpled. That's when I noticed a guy sneaking out the back door. Storm must have been worried about me because he took my hand and put his arm under my elbow and then re-gripped my hand and whispered "Are you okay?" I nodded. It wasn't my first wake it was my second but when I passed by my first dead body, my Grandmother's, it was different. I knew her and when I saw her I actually saw her peaceful and asleep. Before she died she was miserable and in pain. Then I saw her in peace, it was different.

That's where I got my name, from my Grandmother, her name was Adele too. We both hated it, but after she passed the name grew on me because I was reminded of her simply by saying my name. My grandmother used to smoke and sew and even though she was stubborn and bossy, I loved her. Yes, she had lung cancer. My mother and she quit smoking cold turkey the day they found out she had it. I thought I hated shopping with her on Saturdays and helping her cut patterns out all day, but after a while it was actually okay with me, and now, I missed it, I missed her. She used to take us to a candy store and they only sold it by the box, making it super cool, that was before the big bulk stores existed.

Plus, we used to go to this Lithuanian Deli; they had great lunch meat, fresh polish sausage and the best bacon buns on earth. That's where Tori and I got the saying "Two are better than one." My Grandma used to tell us that when we fought, and we used to fight all the time, that we needed to stick together. She had us go outside once and collect three sticks. She told us to try breaking one, pretty easy right. Next she had us try and break two sticks, not as easy right...she told us. "Two are better than one." So Tori and I were always trying to use that saying around my grandmother. She found it humorous.

I'm glad I can get my mind to focus on other topics easily. Since we were in the last row we would be the last students to view the casket and last ones back to class. I'm sure that's why Storm picked these seats. When we stood up I was first out of the pew and Storm leaned into me and I could feel him smell my hair "You smell good." I turned to him and gave him a look. "Are you flirting with me?" I saw him give me a half smile out of the corner of my eye but he didn't say anything. I whispered "We're at a wake!"

Storm had sandy brown wavy hair, a prominent jaw line and the most piercing green eyes I've ever seen, and now that I was paying attention, a very sexy smile. When Storm looked at you it was like he was looking into your soul, but knowing him he wasn't. When we first dated he was skinny, had braces and was the same height as me. Now he was taller and filled out a little more with bright straight pearly whites. My mom used to tell us we were too young go steady and have serious feelings about anyone back then. She also said we were too dramatic and I think she was right. Sally liked Tom, but Tom liked Megan, and so on.

Although, Storm and I kissed a couple of times, it was first time kissing for the two of us so they were only soft tender kisses, nothing more; just innocent and sweet. We used to call each other on the phone and stay on it for what seemed like forever while never saying all that much. And that was it to our relationship, it ended because school ended and I guess I never called him because I wanted someone who knew how to really kiss, seeing I was a novice myself.

I remember my neighbor Gus asking me why I broke it off with Storm last year and I told him that I didn't, school just ended. "Why else did you end it?" he asked. I thought he was asking because he was curious and maybe for future reference, so I told him about the kissing thing. You know he told me I should have told Storm what I thought about the kissing thing. I was appalled! I thought it was ludicrous to have to talk to him about it. Then Gus asked me if I wanted to practice, and I was flabbergasted by the things coming out of his mouth, but then we did a couple of times later that summer – he was a good kisser. Maybe he was right, maybe I should have said something.

I started walking slowly and followed the line of students. I gripped Storm's hand a little firmer pulling him into me and I felt Nic bump into Storm, a little chain reaction. My hands were becoming clammy. Since I've only been to the one wake before I was hoping I wouldn't cry. I wondered how Nic was doing. I wish she was in front of me. The line moved slowly and we were all very close together, mostly because of me. As we kept inching closer I was getting more and more nervous and kept pulling Storm closer to me with Nic in tow.

"Relax." Storm spoke softly to me, "Just do what the person in front of you does and I'll be right beside you when we get to the casket." I got a chill feeling his hot breath on my neck "And don't cry" he added.

Don't cry! I'm about to see a dead person and I'm not allowed to cry, how am I going to manage that? Especially, because when I pictured the casket I kept seeing me. I wished I wouldn't waste any more time or tears over *"Logan."*

There were only two people left in front of me. I turned sideways pulling Storm even closer, he nudged me. He said nothing, then tucked his arm up underneath mine again and re-gripped my hand. He had nice hands not too big and not too small, and if hands can be muscular they were and warm, he gave me comfort.

"You're fine, don't look down if you don't want to and you don't have to touch her either. Just keep breathing" Storm whispered trying to re-assure me.

I looked at Nic she mouthed to me "Are you okay?" I said nothing, Nic looked perfectly fine then she said "don't look down." I looked down, as soon as they told me not too, that's what I did, I looked down. There she lay perfectly still, she looked so peaceful, I took a deep breath. She had a nice royal blue shirt on buttoned all the way up and khaki pants. I would never wear my shirt all the way buttoned up. I wonder if her eyes were blue too. She had a couple of scratch marks on her right hand, and one just under her collar. Other than those marks it looked like she hadn't a thing wrong with her. No reason to die at all.

Keep moving, keep moving, I told myself side stepping slowly. I looked at her face she was beautiful, young. There was a poster size picture of her at the head of the casket and her full name labeled it "Jewel Ann Richardson Class of 82." It sent a chill down my spine and I felt my eyes well up and my cheeks got hotter. The girl in front of me did the sign of the cross when she was at Jewel's head and mumbled "She looks so weird in pants, why couldn't they put her in a dress, something normal." Her girlfriend, whom was holding her hand, agreed.

I wonder what normal was, jeans and a tee are normal for me. When I got to the end of the casket by her head, I mimicked the girl in front of me, by using the sign of the cross. I can do this, keep breathing, we are almost done – I felt myself trembling a bit inside but couldn't help it. Storm gave my hand an extra squeeze. Could this have been me this summer if my brother hadn't stepped in? No, no, no don't think like that, shake it off. I was in a house with others around and Kit did intervene.

I was at her head and looked at her face and down to her wrist where I caught a glimpse of the scratches on her hand again. I got that eerie sense of déjàvu. I thought I was going to see me when I looked down but instead I saw the girl from my dreams and it jolted me. I shook my head, what the heck had Storm gotten me into, I'd rather be in class. I felt my eyes well some more and finally a tear escaped. Breathe I told myself, I turned my head away from the other two and wiped my tear quickly and took a deep breath.

We finished, thank goodness, as we rounded the corner Storm

put his arms around our shoulders and gave us a quick squeeze, I felt relief. Storm thanked us for coming with him, and that he came for his brothers, and I guess in turn Nic and I came for Storm. Although, I think it had to do more with cutting class for Storm. My body still felt shaky, I imagined it felt something like the aftershock of an earthquake, and I couldn't shake the eerie feeling I had, like I knew that girl. I took a deep breath in through my nose and out my mouth, trying to relax.

Storm asked me if I felt okay and I squeezed his arm around me. "Are you cold you're shivering?" I turned into him to give him a hug and kiss on the cheek. He turned his head at the last minute, classic move I might add, and his lips touched mine then he pressed firmly and our lips parted. After a second, I pushed back lightly and looked at him quizzically. He had a devilish look in his eyes.

Nic said "Break it up you two," but I kept on looking at him, his eyes were mesmerizing. We were in a people traffic jam trying to get back into the school. He kept his arm around me as we moved through the crowd and I realized I wasn't trembling any longer. I choked back a swallow and realized that it was fear I was feeling.

I touched my lips with my hand and thought that kiss; his kiss wasn't familiar like I thought it would have been. I couldn't help wonder if he may have had practice this summer too, and smiled.

We got to the front school doors and teachers were handing out new schedules, we still had to go to all our classes but all of them were cut shorter. Half the high school student body made it to the wake or blew off class. I noticed Storm was still holding my hand and not out of necessity anymore. I opened my hand to release and had to jiggle my hand free. I looked at him and headed straight so Nic and I could get to Art class. We walked ahead of him; I gave him one last glance behind us. He was gazing at me with those gorgeous eyes and it was like getting lost in a sea of green. I smiled softly back at him.

While Nic and I were walking to class I said "I can't believe he kissed me."

"I can't either!" She replied snottily.

"Why would you say it like that?"

"Because Addie, he has a girlfriend!" She said with another snarky bite. "At least that's what I heard."

3:17 a.m. ...the waking hour

"You've got to be kidding me!"

By the end of the week Nic caught a rumor to verify Storm was dating a girl named Shelby. I wasn't speaking to him; of course, I was giving him 'the cold shoulder' in history class all week. He had to know why and if he didn't, I didn't really care. He was making no effort to find out why either; except for consistently poking me with his pen which just irritated me more. Whatever, I thought, let him stay dumbfounded.

Nic told me she found out all the details on Storm from Declan, who said he'd been dating since this summer. I would've asked Declan myself but he hadn't been on the bus yet.

Declan was a friend of mine. We've been riding the bus together since seventh grade so this will be our third year together. He's a nice guy and we have no interest in each other except for being friends, we can talk about anything. He was my height, had brown curly hair, slim, a good build, muscular, not overly either like a steroid junky or anything... He always knew all the gossip on everyone, the unfortunate thing was I didn't know half the people he was talking about before, but this year would be different since we're in the same school now.

Friday, on the way to class I decided I loved my Art class because I loved listening to the radio and drawing, it's a great class to start the day. Another reason to love Art, are the two hot guys sitting in front of our class, seniors Topher and Cale – a very nice view.

While we were in class today a news report came on the radio, Topher the hot guy who sat up front turned it up so everyone could hear. Our class is the first to hear news updates, another plus.

The newscaster stated: *"Jewel Ann Richardson of Summit County died two weeks ago, August 18th. Which at the time, the Police thought was an accident. They are now stating that they believe foul play is at hand. They believe she was killed in another location and that her body was dumped at Township Park. If anyone saw her on the day in question please contact the Richfield Police Department at 555-1266 ext. 47 or ask for Detective Grey the lead investigator."*

I flinched and my throat tightened, panic set in. I flashed back to the girl in the white dress I had been seeing in my dreams, then to the girl in the casket. I squeezed my eyes shut and recalled being trapped under his body with all his weight on me, his tongue on my face, ugh, I couldn't breathe. I felt Nic tugging on my shirt saying something. I focused and I heard "Breathe Addie, breathe, are you all right, do you need to go to the nurse?" I held my eyes with hers and handed her my note from the front pocket of my jeans, my hand was trembling as she reached for the folded up piece of paper. She looked down at it flip flopped it in her hand and then looked back up at me. "Did you have the same dream again? Do I have to read it?" I tried hard to swallow and speak but instead I just nodded.

When Nic was done reading it she asked, "When was the first time you had this dream?"

I inhaled deeply, trying to relax. "This summer?"

"How many times have you had this dream?"

I shrugged my shoulders, "A lot"

"Should we call the police?"

I shrugged my shoulders again, "And say what, that I have these dreams and I write them down and you sign and date them so we know they're real? And I know where Jewel was killed, sort of, because I saw it in my dream..." I cleared my throat as my voice wasn't steady.

"Oh yeah, that does sound kind of weird, huh. What if we tell them we were friends of hers and see if they found her bracelet because she always had it on?"

"Don't you think they would find out we were never friends with her?"

"What if we, I mean you, drew a picture of where she was killed and wrote a few notes down and mailed it to them anonymously?"

"I don't know" I said sounding defeated because I felt it, "I'll think about it."

I don't know who made up the saying, but by the end of the day our class had a new motto "85 Stay Alive." Not that I think a lot of murders were happening but each class had more than a few students die each year and we were going to be the smart class, the one where no one dies before graduation. It's not like we had that many students in our high school, we were in the country more than less. Richfield only had about 2,000 residents, so when you lose a couple of classmates you could feel the emptiness from their absence.

We have lots of hills everywhere, no sidewalks or curbs and not many street lights either. So when students were screwing around when driving, especially at night, accidents happened. I heard car accidents were the leading 'cause of death in teenagers, then comes homicides and these two seem to be very high in our school. Plus, there are the normal run of the mill deaths, suicides, cancer, heart disease and silly accidents. However, I'd like to find out how many we lose by foul play.

CHAPTER 3

Nic and I went to see Journey in concert, it was really good but I just couldn't seem to get into it and I think Nic sensed it. Afterward we went to her house, I was spending the weekend. Her mom was very cool about dropping us off and picking us up places. Plus, we could get away with more stuff around her mom, if she knew what we were up too, she didn't let us know.

When we got back to Nic's house she looked anxious, and as soon as her mom announced she was going to bed Nic smiled and waved me on to follow her, intrigued by the cloak-and-dagger I followed. She turned off all the lights until we came to her back sliding door. For a minute, I couldn't see a thing, then Nic flipped on the outside light, she had a menacing smile on her face. Her dog was just as intrigued and stood right next to us; Rusty was a good dog never barked, well trained and always stayed near the house. She grabbed my hand and yanked me out the door called for her dog but Rusty didn't come. We were running, the light faded fast as we ran away from it, the darkness enveloped around us quickly, I had a hard time seeing Nic in front of me. We ran through her properties first tree line as far as I could tell. Her feet found every step with familiarity and ease, where I fumbled behind her slowing us down.

We began to giggle and finally slowed to a brisk walk, through another tree line and there it was, her pond surrounded by nothing but trees and fields. She brought us around by a dock and we stepped onto it.

She turned and said "I've always wanted to skinny dip so we're going to tonight and you're doing it with me." She started taking off her shoes and then her jeans.

"Since when do you have a dock and a beach?" I asked.

"My dad and I finished it last week!" Nic said excitedly.

"We put sand in the water too." She pointed to the area where the beach should be, I think I could see it, I felt it under my feet. I would definitely have to check it out during the day.

Before Nic pushed her jeans down she started talking slowly and cautiously "Addie, I know there is something very wrong with you... I know because I can feel it and because of the way you've been acting lately. Plus, you were trying to hide the bruises and scratch marks on your arms and legs." She took a deep breath, I said nothing. "You are my very best friend and I thought we told each other everything." She paused; I could tell she was choosing her words carefully. "I'm not going to make you tell me but, if something bad is happening at home I can help. You can stay here until we figure it out. Or if it's something else, if you need any help at all tell me, your parents, or if you can't tell us you should go to a counselor or the police."

I started crying, of course, me who usually never cries was crying again; I wasn't sure what to tell her. I just wanted *it* to go away and never think or talk about it again, but obviously ignoring it doesn't mean it's not so. "You are my best friend" I blabbered out. "I'm just too ashamed to talk about it."

Nic threw her arms around me; giving me a huge hug "You don't have to tell me," she said rubbing my back.

Well that did it, I felt compelled to continue. I cried like a baby sobbing the whole time but I told her about my attack from Logan. Thank goodness I didn't have to beg her not to tell her mom or anyone else for that matter. She's the most trustworthy person I know, so if she tells me she won't tell anyone I know she won't.

After I settled down a bit Nic said "I am not doing this alone, strip Addie, we're going in!"

I'd never been skinny dipping before, didn't really want to either but found myself wiping my face and taking my shoes off and then I heard a splash! Nic was in. Nic's family owned 150 acres so I couldn't imagine running into anyone else here, so I thought why not.

You could see a little bit, the moon reflecting off of the pond gave us some light, but everywhere else it was an abyss of blackness.

"The water is warm hurry up!" Nic yelled. I continued and took off my jeans and then everything else. I ran and jumped in the water, it was warm, I had jumped right in like always, no reason to test the water I was going for a swim regardless.

"This will at least wash away the smoky smell from our hair" I said. It felt like more than a cleanse of my hair, it was also cleansing my soul, I felt better and was glad I shared my story with Nic.

We swam for a while, it was very relaxing but the fun had to end... Boy did we miss-calculate, it was freezing cold when we got out, plus no towels! We got out and started shivering immediately, as we headed for our clothes at the other end of the dock, my teeth were chattering so loud it was earsplitting. I turned around and ran off the end of the dock, making a big splash, Nic followed. "Crap" she said between chatters. "I didn't think it was going to be that cold when we got out, I thought it felt warm outside."

"Yeah" was all I could blurt out.

"I'll go back to the house and get towels" Nic suggested.

"And what, leave me out here alone, in the perfect setting to meet "a spooky killer" where I can't run fast enough, and I trip and fall and.... I don't think so!"

"Okay, well then we'll just have to freeze. We'll get out, put our clothes on real speedy run back to the house and take hot showers."

"Sounds good" I retorted "You first."

We got out, getting your undies on wet was harder than you'd think, I gave up on them and threw them to the ground and pulled on my jeans, not easily though. Nic was mumbling.

"Forget the bra and undies; just pull your pants and shirt on." She looked at me I was already dressed holding my undies, socks and bra in hand. I waved them in the air. She smiled and did the same. We ran back to the house hair dripping wet, it felt colder than cold, it was darn right frigid.

As we approached her house we could see a silhouette standing in the doorway. Nic's mom, waiting for us, she was holding towels. "What are you two insane going out there without towels? Your lips are blue, go take warm showers. Addie where is your bag I'll get it for you." I pointed to the other room. As she left I nudged Nic "Your mom didn't yell." She looked as shocked as I did.

"No, but maybe she thinks we wore swim suits? Hurry into the shower, maybe she won't ask or notice." We made a mad dash to turn the water on and close the door behind us. Nic's mom knocked a couple seconds later and handed me sweats and a t-shirt for Nic and my bag. We each took nice long showers, and wrapped towels around our heads and went straight to Nic's room. She hadn't said much since our swim. Little tid bits here and there, however, when we were lying in our beds saying nothing, I could sense she wanted to talk to me some more. I told her "I can feel it – go ahead."

"Are you *sure* you're okay Addie?"

"Yes, I'll be fine. I'm just hoping no one else finds out or that Logan doesn't blab it to his friends."

"I don't think he ever would, he has to know what he did was wrong and if he told anyone, the truth would come out." Nic explained.

I got all choked up, but after I got control of my emotions I said, "Maybe this is from the consequences of my actions, you know what comes around goes around."

I could see the outline of Nic as she sat up in bed "Are you kidding me, you didn't deserve this and it wasn't your fault. You were unfortunately in the wrong place at the wrong time." I sucked in a deep breath and attempted a little humor. "Well, I am a hussy! After all, I go around kissing other people's boyfriends; just give me a "Red Letter" on my chest."

Nic started laughing "It's a scarlet letter."

"Whatever, I *am* damaged."

The next night her mom dropped us off at McDonald's. It was right across the street from Montrose Swim Club which had a miniature golf course. We were kids always looking for something to do. We got to McDonald's, ate and hung out for a bit, saw some kids we knew, chatted and then walked across the street to go golfing. The guy in charge wouldn't give us a discount, we were supposed to get a discount when my mom worked there but he never gave it to us before and he certainly didn't give it to us this night either, even though, we were very charming.

I thought I was bad at putting but Nic was worse. We had fun though, we always do. As we finished up, we decided not to let our balls go into oblivion on the 18th hole. We pocketed them instead. As we were walking back to drop off our putters, we ran into Declan and his girlfriend. So we gave our putters and golf balls to them – that'll teach the guy for not giving us a discount!

As we crossed the street back to McDonald's we were trying to decide if there was anything else we could do before calling Nic's mom, when a pickup truck pulled into the Mickey D's parking lot. It was Ben and a couple of his friends. I knew Ben vaguely but Nic knew him pretty well from the camp she volunteered at last summer. They yelled for us to come over, told us they were having a party, they were just here to pick up dinner. We jumped into the back of their truck without saying a word to each other.

They were kind of gawky, but respectable. "Before we take off" Nic announced, "You've got to promise to drop us back off here by 11." Ben promised. However, when we got to Ben's the only people there were Ben's older sister and her boyfriend. Another thirty minutes went by and still no one else came, so I guessed they weren't really having a party. It was just us and them.

It was all right though, kinda fun, us kids were in the basement while his sister and boyfriend kept to the kitchen upstairs. The boys were pushing drinks on us the whole time, Nic and I kept saying no, although we kept thinking about it. Like we wanted to get drunk at this sort of *"not"* party. We broke down and had one drink which we called a social drink. The boys started doing whip-its, Nic and I had never even heard of them. The gases to make whip cream supposedly gave you a quick buzz that went away rather quickly, hopefully, undetectable by parents, as the effects didn't last. It took some coaxing but Nic tried one and then so did I. Right after though, Nic attempted to do the stairs and didn't quite make it. Then we both finally agreed to another beer.

One of Ben's friends came to sit next to me on the couch. We made small talk, and then he scooted closer and put his arm around me and planted a kiss right on my cheek. I pushed him away and told him to get lost. He placed himself in front of me and tried kissing me on the lips. That was all it took, I freaked out and I don't remember anything else besides crying, his sister trying to calm me down and then Nic. No one could touch me or I would start freaking out all over again. One minute I was on the couch all relaxed and the next I was a crazy person!

3:17 a.m. ...the waking hour

I couldn't stop crying hysterically. After several attempts by his sister to calm me, Nic came over to me and in one fell swoop said, "I'm so sorry Addie, I am sorry, no one will touch you I promise. We'll get over this together, this was too soon. The two of us together, two are stronger than one, right?" She squeezed my hand and winked at me. And in that exact moment I stopped crying. I wiped my face with my sleeve "My grandma used to say that."

"I know." Nic replied.

I could hear his sister saying *"Get her the hell out of here! Take her back where you found her, she's crazy and has huge issues, take her home!"*

They had me in the truck quicker than we could blink. On the way back to McDonald's, Nic asked everyone to never mention this to anyone, they all agreed pretty quickly. Nic hopped out of the back, I had both hands on the side of the truck ready to get out when the boy who had his arm around me earlier, that started me tumbling into my horribly embarrassing frenzy of delirium said "I wanna know if you wanna go on a date....."

His friend chimed in and said "He's in love with you!" I finally got mad, I wanted to reach across the cab and smack'em, when I felt Nic put her hand on mine and said "Addie my mom's here." I climbed out using the tire to step down and could feel my inner body still boiling from anger, like a pot about to boil over. I turned and apologized to everyone quickly for my actions and walked away and didn't look back.

We got in the car and her mom was totally silent the first couple of minutes. Then chimed in, "Have you been drinking? And smoking? You two reek of alcohol and cigarettes!" She was mad and even though we weren't smoking others had been.

Nic replied "Mom, Addie and I had one beer each and we won't ever again, it was gross, we went to a party at my friends Ben's house. It was horrible they were all drinking and smoking so we asked them to bring us back."

She nudged me "Oh, yeah it was horrible." I replied. She looked over at me and gave me a small smile.

"As long as you don't do it again and you tell me the truth, you aren't in trouble, but this is a warning. Another incident like this and I'll have to tell your parents Addie, and Nicole you'll be grounded."

"I promise." Nic said. "Me too," I mumbled.

The rest of the ride back to Nic's house, was quiet, she kept looking at me nervously like I'd lose it any second. I felt weird. She turned to me in the car and whispered "What was he thinking?" she shook her head in disgust. I wasn't quite sure if she was talking about Logan or the boy from McDonald's and I didn't care. I didn't say a word.

When we got to Nic's room she closed and locked her door. Looking at the floor ashamed of my behavior, I told her "I don't even remember anything. I don't know what happened. I remember crying upstairs, but I don't even remember going upstairs. I'm sorry."

Nic's voice cracked, "Don't apologize, you were due, you needed to cry it out.... It was a delayed reaction." She paused, "you ran up the stairs screaming. You went on and on about how you didn't provoke him, it wasn't your fault. You asked if we thought it was your fault, I think it had to do with that night that you told me about." A long time passed before she started again "You also asked if you should tell someone. Thank goodness you told me what was going on so I at least had a clue, not sure I helped but at least I had an idea." She cleared her throat "You kept repeating, 'I didn't ask for it, he started it, I didn't start it and it wasn't my fault.' And you're right Addie..... It wasn't your fault and you didn't start it, nor did you deserve it. If you need to tell your parents I'll go with you."

I laid down and starred at the ceiling in silence. We never spoke of that moment or the incident again, either of them.

So with all that, why did I wake up at 3:17a.m. again? I had a dream of receiving several red roses. Why? I could see it if I dreamt about getting a red "A" sewn on my sweater. But roses?

CHAPTER 4

When I woke Sunday, I tried to think of other things, to think of other subjects, normal things. I wanted to smother those *other* memories and make 'em go away. I tried thinking of something that made me happy and my mind started to wander a bit when my thoughts turned to Storm, him holding my hand at the wake and kissing me. I day dreamed of him saving me from Logan, as soon as Logan knocked me to the floor Storm was there saving me from that dreadful night. And when that guy tried kissing me on the couch Storm was there too. I had a lot of time to think of Storm and I was coming around to actually liking him, of course it was me making him into my knight in shining armor. The reality of it was he had a girlfriend and he kissed me while he had a girlfriend, so I need to smother him too, the thoughts of Storm and thinking he's boyfriend material.

That week at school, I noticed he had a great smile and beautiful eyes, and even though someone can become more attractive the more you know them, he really was attractive. In history class, Storm drew a picture of Jesus on the cross and gave it to me. We happened to be talking about religion that week in class. I thought it was a really good picture too. Because of his drawing, I thought we had a lot more in common and he was growing on me. By the following weekend I was very happy about the aspect of knowing Storm. I thought about the time we dated in eighth grade and then about the kiss after the wake, it was weird, not the kiss itself, but weird because he did it.

Maybe he would never go out with me again, anyway. Still, maybe he just kissed me to show me what I'm missing and now he thinks he has the upper hand. Quit wasting my time thinking about him, he has a girlfriend; maybe I'm over analyzing the whole situation. Maybe I just wanted any old boyfriend, a protector, someone I could trust and rely on. I spent way too much time this week thinking about him and it took me twice as long to get my homework done. I decided I would focus on getting a boyfriend, not that it will happen but I'll give it a whirl.

That night I watched a Bruce Lee movie and dreamt I knew Karate. Maybe it was time I learned some self-defense, maybe if I had, Logan wouldn't have gotten me pinned down. When I think of the incident I picture every scenario of what I should have done to have avoided the whole mess.

In my dream, Bruce Lee was my teacher and we were training in the field across the ravine. After, we started running that same wolf from my dream before began following us. I ran up the dirty slide and the wolf stopped mid-way, his eyes were glowing.

When I got to school on Monday, to my surprise I saw Storm in the hallway before first period and he came up and chatted with me and gave me a peck on the cheek and said "Catch ya later". I thought holy crap, pining over him all weekend may not have been a waste of time. If he gave me a kiss like that he can't be all that serious about his girlfriend. I was going to have to find out more about this Shelby girl and see if maybe they broke up. ...or find out if he's just messing with me.

I had decided to wear my white jeans today because there weren't many more days I could wear them, probably none. And I wore my favorite striped colored tee that looked really good with them. Lo and behold when I got to Algebra, my third period class I sat down in the middle row, middle seat, like I usually did and a girl to the left of me one seat back tapped my arm to get my attention. Class hadn't started yet and it was noisy. She scooted her chair really close to me and said "I think you sat on something." She paused "Your jeans are dirty in the back....." she had a longer pause. "I think its blood, I think you got your period."

My face had to turn all sorts of shades of red. Could it be that I finally got it, I thought you were supposed to get a warning of cramps or spotting or something, but no, not me of course. It happened today because I decided to wear my white jeans after Labor Day. I looked back at her and said "Really, crap I had no idea."

She said "Stay there," like I was going to go anywhere at this point.

She got up; she had long black straight shiny hair and was very slim, her jeans so tight I'm not sure how she got them on. She whispered something to the teacher and came back to my desk and said "Grab your books, come with me." She handed me her jacket "Tie this around your waist." I quickly tied the long sleeved rain jacket around my waist and got up hoping nothing was showing. She made me go first, I stopped outside the class and she pointed right, so I turned right went up the stairs, we were headed toward the nurses office.

She introduced herself as we were walking and….she said "Hi I'm Shelby, the jacket is covering everything perfectly, don't worry I know just what to do. This happened to me the first week of school, just tell the nurse you are very upset and embarrassed and she'll let you go home." She said quickly and with a great big grin. "Really?" I replied. I was mortified and embarrassed and to top it off my mind was going two-forty. This was Storm's girlfriend…. does she know who I am? Has Storm ever told her about me? Does she know he kissed me? Couldn't I have worn blue jeans today or black for that matter? White pants were definitely out of the question for me for a while…. Dude this was Shelby the girl I was supposed to find out more about!

"Thank you so much." I said as calmly as possible. "I'm Addie, Addie Gellar. I wondered how long I had been walking around like this." And I put my hand out to shake hers. It couldn't have been too long because I went to the bathroom just after first period and no signs then, I calculated in my head. The nurse was on the phone when we got to her door, we waited a minute outside. Shelby was a fast talker, and she talked a lot, she was telling me about her classes. I read the name plate outside the door, Nurse Melinda.

When the nurse was off the phone she waved Shelby in and asked "What can I do for you today Shelby?" with a great big smile. The nurse was older, I am not good with ages but she had to be in her fifties, she was a little chubby but still had a nice shape with salt and pepper hair. I walked in behind Shelby and she replied "My new girlfriend Addie is sick just like I was the last time I was here," and she gave the nurse a wink.

The nurse stayed in her chair and winked back "I'm so sorry to hear about that Addie, would you like me to call your parents to come pick you up?" Wow was that easy, I didn't even have to grovel or anything. I just shook my head yes and smiled.

Nurse Melinda asked Shelby if she needed a note to get back into class. Shelby replied, "Yes, please." As she was writing up a note, I turned to Shelby and said on the down low "Thank you so much for helping me out – I wonder how many others noticed and didn't say a thing to me – I wish I knew so I could spite them later." We both giggled.

The nurse handed Shelby a note and off she went, "See ya tomorrow" she said as she walked out the door. The Nurse pointed to her chair and I said "I don't really want to sit because I have actually leaked through my pants." She said "Go ahead and sit I will take care of everything." So I sat on my knees. "Now Addie what is your last name?" I told her "Gellar G - E - L - L - A – R"

"What is your home phone number or a number I can reach an adult that can help you out like a mom, aunt, guardian or grandmother, I am asking for a female due to the nature of the illness. She gave me a wink, "it may be more comfortable for you this way."

I smiled back, I was definitely more comfortable calling a female, like a man would understand, but the only person I could call was my mom anyway. I gave her my home phone number. She continued "This happens to lots of girls every year. I don't want you to feel bad or be embarrassed. It happened to me a few times myself when I was in high school." She put her hand on top of mine which was resting on the desk and gave it a little rub. She handed me the phone "Why don't you talk to your mom."

That night I had a weird dream that woke me up, I felt panicked and wonky, like it actually happened to me, it seemed so real. It was 3:17a.m., this was becoming a habit. It took me a minute to get my bearings; I had another dream "not" about me. Again, this one started out being me but then I was watching the event unravel. I have noticed the last two dreams I had that came true had something white in them. The white object was usually the main object of the dream. The girl in the field had on a white outfit, the man on the pay phone had on a white trench coat and tonight there was a white pickup truck, not that this one has come true yet but if it does then my point will be proven. I made a mental note; these items are not likely to be white in the reality version but are labeled white as the significant part of the story. The fact that I have been waking up at 3:17a.m. may be a factor as well.

In this dream, I was driving a white pick-up truck, it was unusually cold, the heater was on and it was raining. I put my wipers on, I could hardly see, visibility was rough. We were speeding up Route 77, north, toward Cleveland. We were on a bridge near an exit before the turnpike and we were in the left lane stuck behind a smaller black car that was moving slowly and wouldn't move over, so we started to pass on the right. As we were passing, the truck's rear end slipped right then left, we swerved to miss hitting the small black car and the truck did a 180! I wasn't driving anymore I was now watching. I watched as the truck spun out, and I saw two silhouettes in the cab. I couldn't see their faces as it was all a blur, but I got the feeling I knew them, they felt familiar. They spun to the edge of the highway, hit gravel and debris, and the truck started rolling down the man-made hill. I saw hands pressed on the window. The truck rolled onto its side and then over and over again.

The small black car took its time changing lanes and then finally pulled off to the side of the road. He backed up a bit and I saw him open his door and jogged back toward the truck. The truck laid upside down, its wheels still spinning and that's when I woke up. I wrote it all down just like Nic and I planned, dated it too.

The next day I didn't want to go to school afraid everyone would tease me about my incident, I was sure the rumor was all over school by now. I walked in expecting the heckling to begin immediately. Someone smiled and said the usual "Hi" in passing, no weird looks from anyone, or name calling either. I realized Declan didn't say a word to me about it on the bus either.

Declan hadn't mentioned a thing to me this morning on the bus; not even that he thought it may have been someone else. So maybe no one knew, then again, maybe only half the school knew by now. Grin and bear it, I told myself. I'm sure I'd hear something in first period, no pun intended. I got to class and sat down quickly vowing never to wear white jeans again.

Class started and class ended and not one word about yesterday's incident. Algebra came, I saw Shelby and she didn't even bring it up, she acted as though we were new friends and that nothing ever happened. Shelby must not have told a soul! I guess she is a new friend, except for the fact that she is dating Storm. From here on out I will put Storm and Shelby in my head as a 'couple' and as friends.

I have clean clothes, a clean start and a new friend. It's all good, I'm just a freshman in high school and no one knew anything had happened to me. While I'm on a new kick, I vow to stay out of trouble, I will never drink again or do whip its. I am a clean, honest person that's going to stay out of trouble.

We were going to have our first football rally today; I guess they have them on Fridays before home games. Before the rally all the freshman girls met in the gym first, we were wrangled there fifteen minutes prior to the real assembly. The teachers warned us to stay away from the senior boys, that they would all be interested in the freshman girls to try and "*score.*" They didn't use the word score but that's what they meant. They told us not to feel pressured to have sex with a boy and if you did there were safe sex measures to take. If you were thinking about having sex you should talk to your parents – ew! All of us had to take a "Health" class this year too. Of course, they warned us not to buy an elevator pass, because there's no such thing and a few other such rules. It was a little embarrassing but not so bad in a group.

Afterward, everyone scattered and the rest of the school started to come in. Nic and I moved to the top of the bleachers thinking this was going to be lame. Declan found us, Tori sat a few rows in front of us, she was hand in hand with Alec. Storm and Shelby found us and sat in front of us.

The principal came in and made a few announcements and then said "Here are your cheerleaders!" And the crowd cheered, the principal came back with "Did you say something?" Cupping his hand around his ear, "I said, here are your cheerleaders!" he shouted. The cheerleaders came tumbling into the gym and the crowd roared loudly, shouting for the cheerleaders. Very loud music was played and they did a dance, an awesome dance, actually. The football coach was up next and announced he thought they were going to have a great year; the crowd cheered, introduced a few star players and then the whole team. We all roared some more. The team leaders made an announcement and then four other football players came out dressed as cheerleaders and did a short dance to some music, hysterical! Then the team captain said "Thank goodness we have professional cheerleaders, let's give them a round of applause!" and we did.

The cheerleaders did a cheer and everyone cheered back! And then they did another dance and everyone roared again. All the players came back in, students and teachers were riled up and screaming from the stands. Afterward, everyone was in a great mood, including me. Everyone met on the gym floor and it was over. Now all I needed was something positive to happen for me; so far my High School luck stunk. I definitely needed something positive to happen. And I may need to make it happen.

My mom and I, along with Tori and her friend picked up Nic to go to our first home football game of the year. We were stoked. We got there early which was fine with me. It only took a few minutes after we got there for the parking lot to get all jammed up with traffic. Parents and students started coming in the gates. Nic and I walked around the entire football field just checking everything out, and then started to tour our side of the bleachers. Nic knew a lot more adults than I did but we chatted with all of them a couple of minutes regardless. We even went over to Tori and said "Hey" but, that was short lived.

We leaned against the fence that encircled the field to watch the first kick off. Everyone was cheering and the cheerleaders were actually really good, they kept the crowd cheering. Declan walked up to us while we were leaning on the fence. We chatted for a bit and just as Declan left three other boys came up to us. The one in the middle was Frank; he was in my history class and a freshman like us. I hadn't realized he knew I even existed seeing he was the most popular boy in our class. He was very good looking with smooth light skin and brown hair with natural blonde highlights most likely from this summer. He said "You're Addie Gellar right?" And of course I agreed with him. I thought finally my luck is going to turn-around. We had the most popular boy in our class talking to us!

He continued "Your boyfriend is Logan Harper right? He told me that he's madly in love with you and he needs your phone number." I just looked at him with my smile frozen in place, Nic said "Logan who?" He started to laugh, "You don't know who

Logan is? Well he went on and on about you. Said he met you this summer and that you are awesome and he can't wait to see you again."

Frank was looking at me waiting for a response. I didn't move or say anything, my mind was blank. "You supposedly met him at Kevin's house. Ring any bells?" He said a little sarcastically. My smile dropped and I went still. I lost all expressions and felt all the blood leave my face, my body felt limp as if I had no control. Still nothing came from my mouth, I couldn't speak.

There was what I thought the longest intermission in a conversation ever, until Nic chimed in "Logan is an ass and Addie has no interest in him at all." He just looked me up and down and said "Cat got your tongue or what." I cleared my throat "No I'm just trying to figure out what he looks like, I barely remember him." I said shakily and without confidence. I hadn't even thought for a moment that Logan, Kevin or Lucy would say a word to anyone about anything. I just assumed everyone was keeping it quiet like Kit, Tori and I. I certainly didn't think anyone here at my school would find out about it.

I turned around and leaned on the fence, reminding myself to breath, hoping they would leave. I pretended to be interested in the game, so much for my lucky day.

From behind me he said, "What do you want me to tell him?" Nic replied "That she thinks he's an ass and to bug off." I turned around, and gave him a half smile in agreement with Nic. She grabbed my arm and we walked a little ways down the fence.

Was Logan insane? Doesn't he know that what he did to me was wrong? I barely had a conversation with him and he attacked me as if that was normal for him. Nic turned to me put her arm around me and said "You okay?"

"Yeah, I am fine....is that weird or what? Is Logan insane or what? I didn't flirt with him I swear I never even talked to him alone!"

"He *is* obviously crazy" she said.

Nic's my best friend and I knew she would support me no matter what but I wanted her genuine opinion about what she believed. I hadn't said a word to her; it was like she knew what I was thinking. That's what I like about Nic you don't have to spell everything out to her.

She just started talking "Look Addie I believe every word you told me. You don't have to convince me it's not your fault, or that it happened exactly like you said it did. Since Tori already knew, I verified it with her, and you made it sound less dramatic than it was too. She's worried about you but she's glad you told me." She took a breath and she held up a finger and pressed on it with her other, "My thoughts are, number one - why would you lie about something like that? It doesn't make sense. Plus, we always tell each other everything no matter what, whether we're at fault or not. Number two," she held up a second finger "if a guy likes you or you flirted with him, him attacking you or even laying one finger on you without your permission is wrong. Number three - I don't care what any girl has done or said she doesn't deserve to be sexually assaulted. Number four and last but not the least - if he violated you like I know he did, because I saw the bruises, then he is a mean, vicious, crazy son-of-a-bitch who probably has a screw loose or two. So of course, he thinks he's in love with you, he is demented! He sexually assaulted you because you're gorgeous and he knew you were out of his league. Plus, he's probably never had a girlfriend before."

I let out a little laugh. "Thanks." I said and wiped a tear from my eye. We waited there until I was able to push them all back. I concentrated on the game and Nic stayed close by.

After I pulled myself together, Nic and I walked all the way around the field. She took a plastic bottle out of her pocket filled with a clear liquid and she pushed it into my chest, "Here." It was in a rubbing alcohol container.

"What's this?" I asked.

"It'll calm your nerves." She said. So I took a sip, it tasted awful, I handed it back to her saying "Ewww." She took a sip and said "Ewww" too.

"I told you it was gross."

She handed it back to me. "I don't want any more of that." I replied. "It's awful."

"Come on, one more sip you'll feel better, it'll calm your nerves." Nic said. So I took another swig and so did she. "It is awful" she retorted. "Next time I'll add juice."

We ran into people stopping to chat and before I knew it the game was over. To my amazement we did not sit down the entire game, and I did feel better, more relaxed. I hit Nic in the arm "Hand it over – I need one more."

We headed out to the bonfire and not five minutes into it Frank came up to me, this time he was alone. I'm standing at the edge of the huge roaring fire and he stood next to me, casually, like he knew me and nudged my arm. "I'm glad you aren't seeing Logan, that guy is bad news and I can tell you're a nice girl."
"Thanks." I said. "You know if he actually was my boyfriend I would have given him my number."
He laughed and said "Yeah good point."

CHAPTER 5

After the first four weeks of school I hadn't been approached by any boys, no dates for me. Of course, I guess I wasn't expecting it either. My sister, on the other hand, had been asked out several times over even though she had a boyfriend.

My sister Tori was short, petite and pretty and all the boys liked her. She had the same bra size as me but since she was short she was what the boys like to call '*stacked*'. Because I'm taller I don't look as '*stacked*'. I thought that was unfair. All the boys were always fawning all over her and when she would turn them down, she turned them down flat! After they'd come crawling to me for help. I never had any help for them but I would get to know them and sometimes I would be second on their list, never accepting any dates, thinking they had no real interest. Most of the time I just made another friend and friends are good.

All in all she was much prettier than I. She told me it was only because she took the time to do her hair and make-up making her appearance better. We do have similarities. However, I get to sleep an extra 45 minutes a day! She gets up earlier to shower, style her hair and put on make-up, and dress nice. I don't care so much, I get up wash my face, brush my teeth, throw on a t-shirt and jeans and I'm good to go. Sometimes, I put a brush through my hair, but sometimes I don't, with my hair being curly-ish leaving it alone looks better. Tori got all the attention and I didn't really care, we usually didn't like the same type of guys anyway.

Since my sister and I were in the same grade, I was hoping *not* to have any classes with her in High School, but of course, we had first period together which neither one of us liked. The class itself I loved, it was Art class and since it was the first class of the day maybe she'll be too tired to fight with me.

We used to fight all the time like any siblings would, but, we did get along when we needed to. My sister was held back in first grade because my family was transferred that year, plus to boot, she got pneumonia which put her behind even further, so they held her back. And my mom started me early, which she liked because we always had the same school schedule that way. So there you have it our small story of how we got to be in the same grade. Since we looked similar, we always just told everyone we were twins. It was easier and shorter to tell. Everyone believed it.

Four weeks into the school year and my sister and I hadn't even spoken in class. Thank goodness it was the only time I saw her during the day. We had no other classes together not even lunch. I was happy about it and I think she feels the same. I was really hoping she wouldn't speak to me at all in class or embarrass me in front of my friends or potential cute boyfriends either, because I wouldn't stand for that.

It was Wednesday morning, our Art teacher gave us our assignment and as usual the radio went on and we could talk. The two really cute guys that sat at the front of the class controlled the radio. No one else cared or ever said anything to them because they were the super cool guys of the school. They made sure the music was good, I had no complaints. It was a ritual, teacher gave assignment, radio's turned on, the two cute guys sat at the front of the room where the teacher normally would and they could screw around and leave class. Sometimes they didn't even show up, however, no one else could get away with any of that.

This particular day a report came on *"A girl was found dead off of Route 77 and even though she wasn't in or near a vehicle when they found her, her injuries were consistent with that of a vehicle that had rolled several times. An abandoned car was also found near the scene of the crime, the vehicle was left with the keys in it and the owner nowhere to be found. Investigators believe the owner of the car stopped to help and was a witness to the accident. The police are still investigating whether the disappearance and the death are connected."*

3:17 a.m. ...the waking hour

Nic said loudly "Oh my Gosh, that's what you saw!" Several people in the class heard her and looked right at us. I shrugged my shoulders, made a goofy face like I had no clue what she was talking about and everyone went about their business. I looked at Nic dumbfounded "What? ...shhhh..."

"The last dream you wrote down! I read, signed and dated it on Monday!" I put my backpack on my chair and shuffled through my papers until I found my journals, I found the newest one and reviewed the details. I actually didn't have to read it, I remembered, but I wanted to see if what I wrote down was the same as I had remembered.

"We'll have to investigate all these facts and see how accurate your dream was!" Nic sounded excited. "Come over after school so we can start right away!" Nic started writing down a list of all the things we should check, number one on her list *'Drive down 77 to see where the accident occurred.'*

We had Peyton drive us down 77 that afternoon; it was nice because she never asked a lot of questions so we just told her we wanted to investigate. It was hard to tell from the road where anything happened, but I knew the spot so I pointed where to pull over. We got out of the car and looked over the area. Nic pointed "You can totally tell something rolled into the grass, right there." She had a smile on her face, both of us were flabbergasted.

"Now what?" I asked.

"I don't know — do you remember what the driver of the truck looked like?"

"No"

"Do you remember if it was a boy or girl?"

"It was a guy driving and a girl passenger, a girl with long brown hair."

"Well that's a clue." She wrote it down. "I'll write down all our findings, anything you remember or anything we find. Do you remember what kind of truck it was?"

"You mean besides a pickup truck? No, it was plain and dark in color."

"I thought you said it was white."

"It was white in my dream because it was the main subject and when I was driving it but when it rolled it was dark, like navy blue, keep in mind it was a dream.... now what?"

She kept writing down more notes, probably something like

'Addie's lost it, she's Looney Tunes.' I started walking around the matted down grass to see if there was anything left behind but there wasn't.

That following Monday in Art was quiet; everyone was working on their projects listening to the radio as usual. I looked up to glance around and caught notice of the twins. We had actual identical twins in our class and they sat together and they did look exactly alike. Both had this perfect red curly hair and freckles, very cute. My sister and I never sat together. Why chance it? She and her best friend sat next to the twins. I looked down at my paper and started drawing again, and BANG! I almost jumped out of my skin. A stool was pushed over by one of the twins.

The next thing we knew a cat fight broke out. The twins were hissing and screaming at each other right in front of everyone! The entire class went silent; I was in awe that they were actually fighting like that in public. They were both standing, one of them started swinging. That's when the teacher got involved, a couple of slaps and it got very loud - - the teacher had to yell to get them to stop - - and he told them one more outbreak like that and they'll get detention! They were lucky Mr. Walker was a very laid back guy who didn't like confrontations…

My sister and I exchanged glances from across the room and we both shook our heads. We both knew it meant we would never fight like that again. When the fight was over and everyone had settled back down Tori came over to me and said, "They looked bad didn't they?" I shook my head. "Do we look like that?" Tori asked.

"I don't know and I don't want to know, let's just never fight like that again." We both agreed. I felt like we became instant best friends at that moment. Between this and my other incident we just kept getting closer, nothing like pure chaos to form a bond.

She sat back down and in that same moment we made eye contact and a new pact for life had been made between us. My sister's smile turned into a surprised look and she pointed her finger toward my right. I turned to see one of the gorgeous guys walking toward me.

He started talking to me "Can you believe those two fighting like that?"

"Of course not," I said, giving my sister a glance and a smile. I

3:17 a.m. ...the waking hour

looked back at Cale, he was looking right back at me. "How embarrassing..." I commented.

"Isn't that your sister over there?" Cale asked thumbing over his shoulder pointing in her direction.

I lost my smile and took a deep breath and exhaled "Yes it is. Do you want me to introduce you?" He interrupted before I got my last words out "No, no, no, I came over to talk to you. You two are nothing but nice to each other, it's very nice to see. Are you twins?"

I could have choked, I said "Yes" – because my sister and I are now buds. I looked at her and winked, she just smiled and raised her eyebrows at me a couple of times.

I can't believe this boy was talking to me, well a boy wasn't a good description for him, he was more like a God. He was gorgeous, beautiful, mature and cool! His hair was light brown, shoulder length and a little wavy, fine but lots of it. His hair was so nice and looked so soft I just wanted to run my hand through it. He was tall, I think six foot, plus, he wore Frye boots. I love a guy in boots, almost any kind; cowboy, Frye, construction or other leather boots. They are very masculine and sexy at the same time. He had soft grey eyes with bits of gold that were easy to look at and a narrow face (he also had a cute butt).

I introduced myself "My name is Addie, what's yours?" Yes, I knew his name but why should he think I ever really noticed him or knew his name. He chuckled and said "You don't know my name?"

As my sarcasm escaped me again "No, should I? I'm sorry" but then turned it into sincerity.

"I guess not, my name is Cale Winters" he said with a big smile that could just make you melt. His teeth nearly perfect, making him totally adorable. I like a guy with a nice smile and teeth.

"Nice to meet you" I replied and put my hand out to shake hands. "What can I do for you Cale Winters?"

"Nothing" he retorted and asked me what classes I had, what hobbies I liked, what sports I was into. Afraid to tell him what sports I was into like golf and swim team, I told him I wasn't in any. Nic shot me a weird look.

He told me he was in a band and that he managed a couple other bands too. He also mentioned that he was a senior and played basketball, and he told me all sorts of other stuff he liked to do. My hands were starting to sweat not knowing what the heck he wanted.

When our conversation started to get a little thin I repeated, "So what can I do for you today Cale Winters?"

"Wow you like calling me by my first and last name, am I bothering you?" he asked and laughed.

I laughed too, "Of course not, but it just kinda seemed like you were on a mission and I thought I'd help you get there quicker."

"Well then let's get down to business." I was leaning on my desk but straightened up when he put both his hands on my desk and leaned in a little. "I have been taking notice of you since the first day of school and wanted to know if you were dating anyone. If not, maybe we could go out sometime."

I let a long pause linger, I was a little shocked. I felt my face scrunched in a questionable *'really'* kind of look. My hands were clammy now – I came up with a reply. "Well, if you can change the radio station to 101.9 I'll think about it..."

He turned to look at the radio and then looked back at me. I just never know when to shut up do I, and Nic elbowed me like I just ruined everything. She laughed and said "Yeah 1-0-1-9 is a great station." In reality the more nervous I get the more sarcastic I get and if he doesn't like it why bother dating me. He may as well know how I am up front.

Cale looked at me funny, spun around on his heal hopped over the table one armed and then stood at the art table near the radio and started chatting with Topher and they both looked over then laughed a little to themselves, but he didn't change it.

Nic and I started giggling softly as soon as he sat down. I hope he didn't see. "Nic, did you see that? He came up to me, I mean right in front of me and it was unmistakable that he came up to me! Did I say he came up to me.......to talk to me?" I said in a whisper, she nudged me with her elbow giving me a nod and we both giggled again. We decided that he had a bet with Topher, to see who could collect the most phone numbers in a week, or something ridiculous.

They always seemed bored and not really into the class, I never saw any art projects that they did either. Who cares though, it was nice having them in class. From what Nic and I have heard, Topher is the most popular guy in school. I could see why, his friend Topher was also popular; he had blond wavy hair not quite down to his shoulders. A great smile and the bluest eyes you have ever seen, bluer than Tori's, not as tall as Cale though. Possibly too pretty for me though.

When the song was over Cale looked over at me did a half nod upward and changed the station. I was a little surprised as he motioned for me to come by him with his finger, his eyes just staring at me like he'd won something. He wanted me to go in front of the class and talk to him, my legs just became a little jello-like, I wish I could send Nic or Tori for me. Tori was good with all boys, knows how to talk to them, I should send her. I looked at Nic and she nodded for me to go. I slid off my stool and walked slowly toward him trying not to lose my balance or trip over my own two feet in the process, attempting to look cool at the same time; it's not as easy as you'd think. Nic said "Don't forget to breathe." I shook my head and thought good advice.

I looked up and he was still looking right at me, I of course kept his gaze, I like to look people in the eye. Trustworthy people always look you right in the eye, my dad says. I made it to the table and hoped my make-up and hair were okay, oops I don't wear make-up – note to self - rethink wearing some make-up. I wasn't a slob or anything but never really cared about that stuff before, I was a little worried now.

Cale immediately told me "I changed the radio station. I think you owe me something..." and he smiled a sexy crooked little smile at me, even better than the one before. "Well as long as the radio station stays on this channel for the rest of the class I think we have a deal." Topher started laughing and said "Boy you are tough."

I replied "A girl's gotta try."

I turned to go back to my chair and Cale caught me by my arm gently turning me toward him and said "You're not going anywhere, don't you trust me? Where's the faith?" He stared right into my eyes; most boys don't give you a steady stare right in the eyes. I stared back, he was so nice to look at. "I'll keep the radio station on the rest of the class, you need to trust me." He said with more emphasis but then lightened up "A deal is a deal, now you owe me your number."

Oh, I wanted to cave, a gorgeous guy was asking me out *"hello"*, and a deal was a deal....I looked at Nic she kinda gave me a look to do it, to give him my number. So I did, I quickly wrote my name and number on his blank drawing pad, and went back to my desk. I could feel my face flame, I'm sure it was a crimson red. I hope he isn't looking at me now, I'm overheating.

As soon as I sat down he was right at my desk, he startled me, I didn't even have time to breath, he leaned on my desk and said "Can I ask you something? Why did you write your name down?"

"I didn't want you to confuse my number with all your other girlfriends." I pointed to the paper and said "That's A-D-D-I-E, I wrote pretty neatly, you shouldn't have a problem reading it." I smiled.

I could hear Topher chuckle in the background. Nic's and my desks were up front near Cale and Topher's desks, well the teacher's desk, as soon as you walked in the door and straight back. The desks were formed in a "U" shape with a grouping in the middle. We were at the end of the "U" furthest from the door so no doubt Topher heard me.

I at least got a flash of his crooked smile again. His hair looked so smooth, he was close enough I could touch it. It fell around his face when he bowed his head. He looked up at me and put his hand through his hair, still smiling and said "Let's start over.... Addie I would like to know if you'd like to go out with me sometime, soon."

That's all I remember really, the next thing I know and to my surprise I was giving him my number, again. I don't remember talking to him or what he may have said after that, but before the bell rang I had given him my number sincerely.

I slid off my stool and started collecting my things. "Holy Crap! I was asked out!" I whispered to Nic. "I think, and by a gorgeous guy!" He was the first boy to ask for my number in High School and he was hot and popular - I have not been asked out all that much before. I hoped I did okay – I looked at Nic as I was packing up my stuff, "What just happened."

She looked at me and laughed and said "You've gotta date!"

I laughed, "Really when?" My face must have been flush because I felt very warm.

"What did I say to him?"

"You were your usual cute self."

"So I didn't drool or anything."

"No spit hanging out of your mouth at the time."

"Good, did he really ask me out? Did I give him my correct

3:17 a.m. ...the waking hour

phone number? Holy crap - I wonder if he'll actually call." I said in a hurried whisper.

"I'll see you in Home Ec" Nic chuckled as she walked out the door and down the stairs and I went the other way. The bell rang.

As I headed down the hall to my next class, someone put their hand on my right shoulder so I grabbed it and pulled it down by my side, pulling them next to me. "So you do like me" Cale said.

"Crap" I said throwing his hand out of mine. "You scared me, don't sneak up on me like that!" My heart was racing.

"You grabbed my hand." he said sweetly.

"Well I thought you were someone else."

"Who else were you going to hold hands with?" he asked as I picked up the pace.

"No one, look I'm going to be late." My heart was still pounding. I started to turn into my class then stopped and turned to face him. "What can I do for you?" I asked as nicely as I could. He backed me up against the wall put one hand on it, boy is he tall. He's definitely at least six foot tall or taller. He leaned in closer placed his mouth down by my ear and whispered, holding out the peace of paper I gave him in between us. "Is this your real number?" As he whispered in my ear, I felt chills go all the way down my spine, I tried ignoring it. I closed my eyes and breathed him in. He smelled clean, like fresh air with a bit of evergreen. I tried to bring myself back to reality, he sounded serious, he thinks I lied to him.

I opened my eyes, straightened up a bit, looked him in the eyes, took the piece of paper from his hand with my left and put my right on his chest backing him up a little. I looked at it and said "Yes, of course this is my real number." I gave him a crooked smile back. "I actually hadn't even thought about giving out a fake number to you or anyone else for that matter. Good idea though. I'll have to keep that in mind for the next guy."

"I hope you don't give your phone number out to anyone else, at least until you give us a chance," he replied.

Pretending to ignore his response I said "I also labeled my number with my correct name so you don't confuse it with the other numbers you've collected."

He laughed. "Why are you giving me such a hard time?"

"Well, I am sarcastic and besides, I'm sure no one else does, gives you a hard time that is."

I hope we are done here, I didn't say it, I wanted to but I didn't want to mess it up any more than I already may have. He breathed in, and exhaled, he put his hand on my flaming cheek and said "All right, but know this, I *will* call you Addie Gellar." My face was so hot and his hand felt ice cold but I bet it was normal, in any case I felt every one of his fingers pressed lightly on my cheek. I got to watch him walk away.

I sat down next to Storm like I did every day because we had assigned seating, he gave me a dirty look and we didn't speak the whole class nor did he look at me again. I wonder why he's mad at me this time... What do I care if he ignores me, he's dating what's-her-face and now I may have a date!

I was excited up 'til third period, but realized Cale might not call and if he did maybe he just wanted to see if he could get 'lucky' as the saying goes. I decided to be in a good mood regardless. Until, I thought about being alone with him and only him and then about *that* night and had a flashback. I started feeling very uneasy my chest tightened up and I could feel my eyes start to tear. Shelby looked at me and mouthed, *"Are you okay?"* I nodded my head; think of something positive, diving, swimming, golfing. I thought of my cousin Peyton and some of our escapades, I started to feel a little better and decided I wouldn't go out with him. I can't, I'm a mess. I thought I had nerves of steel, but I guess not.

In Home Ec, Nic declared that if he wanted to date me I should take the chance and see what happens. I just told her "We'll see."

CHAPTER 6

The next day in Algebra, Shelby caught my attention. She was sitting in the same seat as the day before. In my confusion and out of nowhere I asked her straight out "Are you dating Storm?" Shelby confessed she was and sleeping with him, that she couldn't get enough of him. She said she couldn't help herself that's all she wanted was sex, sex, sex, and then she laughed. She talked a lot and fast, but seemed very nice. Storm was dating a nympho, great. I wonder why he has been so hot and cold with me all the time. "Storm's not talking to me again, is he in a bad mood or what?" I asked point blank.

"He was fine when I saw him before first period. I'll ask him at lunch." Shelby said. I realized I really didn't care, I went from extremely happy yesterday to nervous and confused, her conversation was a great distraction and I didn't need to say much to get her to talk.

After English I had gym, as I was walking there I saw Cale, I almost froze, but then kept on walking. Should I stop and say "Hi", should I wave, hell no. I'll put my head down, walk fast and pretend I don't see him, maybe he won't notice me. I'll just walk quickly and see if I can fly right by him. I averted my eyes and kept walking... I passed him and was almost ready to turn the corner when I heard someone shout "Addie!" I jerked when I heard my name and slowed but kept walking, please don't be Cale.

I heard "Addie!" again. I stopped and turned, it was six foot, sandy brown haired, sexy crooked smiling Cale. I smiled back, "Hey! Wow, nice to see you, am I lucky."

He flashed his bright whites. "Topher and I are thinking about going to a movie Friday night, talk to Nic and see if she wants to go, we can make it a double date." He started walking backward and said "I'll call you later." Storm checked him with his shoulder as he walked past, glared at me and mumbled something to me about blocking the way and hit the gym door open.

I walked into the girl's locker room and grabbed a locker in the first row, we hadn't been assigned permanent lockers yet, and who popped up beside me but Shelby. She was wearing super skinny jeans that were skin tight; when she took them off they left an impression of the inseam all the way down her leg. She started talking, she said still talking a mile a minute "Storm's in a good mood and he said he didn't know what I you were talking about. He can be moody." As we were walking into the gym she told me that Storm transferred into our gym class so that they could have a class together. I rolled my eyes, she didn't see, great I get his moody ass in two of my classes.

She confessed she knew that Storm and I dated and that he had talked about me before and was glad to finally meet me. That she knew he still had feelings for me before they started dating. I was shocked; I assured her that we only dated in eighth grade and that we weren't serious at all. "Plus, I have a date with Cale Winters." I told her.

"Cale Winters!" she screamed in the hallway grabbing my arm, it echoed and since we were by the entrance of the gym I could see all the boys look up, they heard. Great.

Shelby and I were becoming friends. She was different, eccentric but nice. We got paired into four groups, Storm ended up in mine and Shelby in another. He came right up to me and said "Nice to see you've become such a slut!"

I was startled, where did this come from? I turned to him "Where do you get off calling me names, you don't know me, we don't even talk! What do you know about me? Nothing! We dated in eighth grade for what two days, you know nothing!" I said under my breath with my teeth gritted "You're dating Shelby and she's a...." I didn't finish that sentence. "I haven't dated anyone since you and you're calling me a slut! Don't you think you should wait

3:17 a.m. ...the waking hour

until I've had sex with someone before you go around calling me... that?" I had started in a lower tone but my volume grew. I put my finger down took a deep breath hoping no one else was listening and said "You know what, we're not friends, don't speak to me again."

I walked over to Shelby's group as the gym teacher was yelling at me to go back to my group. I told Shelby "Storm wants us to switch."

I'll be glad when this day is over.

That night after dinner, I was washing the dishes when the phone rang and my mom answered, she talked for a while I heard her giggle and then she called me to the phone. She put her hand over the receiver, but you know that never works – whoever is on the other end can still hear. "Cale is on the phone he would like to take you out this Friday, I told him you were available!" She said way too enthusiastically, like she had doubts I would ever find a boyfriend, and handed me the phone. Of course I was mortified. "I go to the football games on Friday's mom." I told her smartly.

I got on the phone and said "Hi!" With a little bit of attitude but ended up having a very pleasant conversation. I told him how Nic and I usually go to the Friday night football games but he said he and Topher already picked the show, however, if I really wanted to go to the game we could. He asked if I talked to Nic about going on Friday and I told him I hadn't. He seemed a little shocked.

"I'll ask her in Art class tomorrow."

"You aren't going to call her now, talk to her and then call me back tonight? I thought you'd be a little more excited."

"Too many phone calls for me." I said "I didn't have a very good day today. I'm going to do my homework and go to bed."

Cale interrupted "...and finish doing the dishes?"

"How did you know I was doing the dishes?" There was a slight pause some rustling and he replied "I can hear you through the phone." I dismissed it.

"Can we talk tomorrow or would you rather not be seen talking to me in public." I felt his hesitation to answer because I was being spiteful and for no reason, at least not to him.

"I guess you did have a bad day, the morning will be fine. I'll talk to you tomorrow." Click. I hope I didn't make him mad. I am exhausted and can't even think about it right now. As I got off the phone my mom came in the kitchen to tell me how polite Cale was and that she really liked him and looked forward to meeting him. And then she announced she and my brother were going to the store for milk and that my dad and sister should be home any minute.

I really did just want to finish the dishes, do my homework and go to bed. I was tired of talking, tired of thinking and just a little irritated.

As the sink was emptying, I heard a noise just outside the kitchen window. I became absolutely still, my mind and heart began to race, waiting to hear the noise again. My heart was pounding so hard I wasn't sure I could hear anything else over it. I saw something go by my window out of the corner of my eye! Did my mom close the garage door, was the patio door locked?

There should only be so much horror a person should have to experience in a lifetime, or in my case, a year. I felt a little light-headed. I – will - not - be – afraid - I - am - not - afraid. If someone comes close I'll hit him with this...I looked around.... grabbed a frying pan from the sink, I'll hit him with this pan and then I'll run out the front door I told myself. Since my incident this summer, I'm always thinking on the morbid side of things. I imagine someone jumping out and attacking me and then I find myself pre-planning what to do in every scenario, when I get a little startled, feel anxious about a situation, or hear a noise I shouldn't have, a little like now.

My heart still racing I checked all the windows to make sure they were locked and then walked slowly over to the sliding door, opening my basement door on the way, another possible escape route. We had a ranch house with a full walk-out basement that had full windows and doors on the backside of the house. In the front middle was a living and dining room, behind them lie the kitchen and eating area connected by a short hallway and a door to the basement. Off the eating area, where I am now, is a sliding door connecting a two story deck. Below the deck is a storage shed. The kids had rooms on the right side of the house and our parents the left.

I felt my eyes pool up, stop it don't cry no one was here to attack me. I am just hearing things. I gathered up a bit of courage

3:17 a.m. ...the waking hour

and realized the chances of another attack actually happening to me must be slim to none. I have never heard of a girl getting sexually assaulted or attacked 2-3 times a year.

Once I got myself to imagine that I just heard a stray cat, or Rocky the Raccoon I felt better. We have a raccoon that comes up to our back door once in a while and we feed it by hand. We obviously named him "Rocky the Raccoon" but once it started knocking over our outside garbage cans digging for food and bringing friends, making a huge mess we stopped feeding him and eventually they stopped coming around. I inched toward the sliding door to peek out. I heard something again. I flipped the outside light on and peeked out the sliding door and saw a raccoon flinching on the porch on its side, not quite dead yet.

I heard another noise, screamed and held the pan over my head, my heart leapt so hard it hurt. I saw a shadow of headlights flash threw the house. My dad must be home. I ran to the front window and saw him pulling down the driveway and then went and looked out the kitchen window. I didn't see anyone.

I ran down the stairs and told my dad about the noises and the raccoon. He told Tori and I not to move and went out the garage door. I saw him grab a bat and sneak out of the garage. We were standing in the hall not making a peep or moving an inch, I was still holding the pan when my mom pulled in the garage. She came in the door holding two bags said "I got ice cream!" Kit and Tori ran upstairs and she followed. My dad came in "Yep a dead raccoon, nothing to worry about." he said and rubbed my head. And that was it, no one else thought another thing about it.

I went in my room to do my homework and started thinking about my date with Cale, I got really worried about our first date – I imagined going out to dinner, after he tried kissing me and I tell him no, WHAM! He's on top of me and I'm struggling to get away and then I'm the crazy girl crying again. Same vision I always have where I cannot get out from under him and I can't scream. My sister startled me and asked if I was okay, "Yeah, I'm fine" I said sarcastically. "Just asking!" she replied in the same tone, total sister *'I don't care'* jargon.

I have to stop worrying about it, I thought of Cale and then I thought if mom likes him he's probably a geek. On the other hand if he is one of the most popular boys in school, maybe he just knows how to talk to adults. I think I'll cancel; I can't do this and went to bed. I had bad dreams again, this time I was at the football game and Cale came up to me and started shaking me, but when I woke up my mom was waking me for school.

As I got ready for school, I was still preoccupied with the notion of whether I would even go out with Cale or not. When I got to the kitchen, my mom and dad were talking, my dad turned to me and grabbed me by the shoulders, my mom hovering over "I guess you may have seen someone in our yard last night, the White's house got broken into last night."

I was too tired to make any sense of this or anything right now. The Whites were our neighbors and although we had large yards, the sides of our two houses were kind of close together.

"I told the police you saw something but didn't see any details. Is that right?" My dad asked me.

"No" I said slowly "I mean no, I didn't see any details on who or what it was, I just heard stuff and found the raccoon."

"Yeah about that, it wasn't there this morning."

"What?" I asked still in a fog, time for some coffee.

"The raccoon, from the porch is gone, another animal probably snatched it up for dinner."

"Ewww" was the response he got from me and my mother. Tori walked in "What'd I miss." No one answered her. I went about the business of getting my breakfast together. We've never had any problems in our neighborhood before, Tori and I talked about it on the way to the bus stop. I think it was the first time Tori and I actually socialized at the bus stop, it was kinda nice.

I was too preoccupied by the break-in, it was consuming my head but not for too long before I remembered the fact that I had to make a decision about dating Cale came back to me. I wondered if Nic even liked Topher or would consider a double date. Who was I kidding of course she would, Topher is gorgeous. Maybe if they went with us it would be much easier and less pressure for me. I guess I'd be finding out soon enough.

I met Nic at her locker. I was in a better mood, but still a little weirded out about our neighbor's house getting broken into. I told her the deal about Friday night and she said "You should have said yes, you know I don't have plans and if I did I would have canceled. Why didn't you call me last night?"

"I'm asking you now. Would your answer have been any different last night versus today?"

3:17 a.m. ...the waking hour

"You know you are always a smart ass. Yes, I will go." Nic said excitedly.

"Sorry, I just don't have a very good filter. Plus, I don't know if I want to go, I'm not sure I'm ready to go. I get all wigged out when I think about it." I looked at Nic and I knew she understood what I was talking about.

"Addie, if we go on a double date we'll stick together, I'm sure there will be nothing to worry about. Girls always go to the bathroom in pairs so we'll just make sure we stay together. It'll be fine."

I looked at her with a hard face and said "You better, promise me."

"I promise, besides us girls have to stick together. Two are better than one!" As we walked to class I could tell Nic was super happy, she couldn't stop smiling. I briefed her on my dream and my neighbor's house.

I waited for class to start, the lecture and assignment were given and the radio turned on. Cale came up to me right after the teacher was done talking. "Addie why didn't you call me back last night?"

"Hmmm, there are only so many phone calls I can make in a night, besides I told you I would see you today and the fact that I didn't write down your number made it a problem." I continued "Just so you know I am not a typical girly girl."

Nic chimed in "She's not." Shaking her head in agreement with her lips pursed.

"I don't like to talk on the phone a bunch. You know girly stuff really isn't me, like putting make-up on is okay, but I don't want to spend hours doing it, and I am not one to spend hours in bathrooms like most girls either. However, I did put a brush through my hair today just for you." I said pushing my hair up at the ends, then held a slight pause and smile. Cale just looked at me with his crooked smile and puts his head down.

"You really are somethin'," he said.

"Nic and I are fine for Friday. Shall we make it a date?"

"Yes, good" he said letting out an exasperated breath. He looked up at me, looking me in the eyes so I couldn't look away "You should wear your hair up tomorrow." He said, and it sounded more of like a command than a suggestion. So my smart mouth replied, "Yeah, okay just because you asked my dear." and I laughed. Nic nudged my side. "Oww!"

"Next time call me back would ya, I was going to skip first and second period today, but came in just so I could talk to you."

"Ohhhh, sorry." I said.

"You are being sarcastic aren't you? It works for you though." He squinted his eyes at me and gave me a half smile.

"Addie is a bit cranky today, she had a bad day and night yesterday. Her neighbor's house got broken into," Nic said. I think she's trying to cover for me, I guess I need to chill.

"I didn't mean to be sarcastic that time, I would never interfere with cutting classes, really," and although I meant it to be serious, it wasn't coming out that way. I am surprised he didn't cancel with me on the spot.

Cale looked down at his feet and then over at Topher and nodded his head toward us and he came over to talk with the three of us. They were leaning on our desks just chatting; Topher is very funny, we all laughed with him. Nic said under her breathe "Check that out."

"What? Check what out?" Topher responded.

"All the girls, look at all the girls in the class, they're all staring at us." The boys turned their heads slightly to check out the scene and gave a half quiet laugh.

I said "They aren't staring at us they are gazing at the good view they have."

Cale stood right up knowing I meant that the girls were staring at their butts. Cale admitted under his breath "They aren't staring at our butts." He actually turned a little blush. Topher changed his stance; he leaned on the desk sideways so his rear faced the front of the class where no one else sat.

"Trust me if I was sitting over there that's what I would be looking at – do you think they are looking at me because I look so good today???" I batted my eyes. They both pursed their lips together which led me to believe they agreed with me.

"And look you're both blushing too!" I continued.

"Cale, she is sarcastic but funny and… on that note I'm going back to my desk and... I am going to walk backwards." as Topher began to walk backwards and try to navigate himself around a bar stool he fumbled a little. It was funny, we all laughed. Nic said "Really no viewing for us?" he bumped into the cutting board table still blushing and turned around to look where he was and then turned around again to get back to his desk. We both caught a glimpse, "It is a nice view." Nic said and I agreed with an "mm-hmmm" we exhaled and giggled under our breath.

"Addie and Nic, I can't believe you two. " Cale said still blushing.

"Me either, we are in rare form today." I replied. Cale had changed his stance and actually seemed uncomfortable looking right at me with his crooked smile and a twinkle in his eye. "You are worse than guys."

"What's wrong Cale?" Nic asked sweetly. He took my notebook wrote his number on it leaned back on my desk on his elbows pushing himself a little closer to me and said softly so no one else could hear "Paybacks!" When he said it he gave me a chill down my spine and he walked away.

But a fine walk that was – Nic and I looked at each other - what did we get ourselves into, we sure hope they don't pay us back. Because now that I think of it, *if* I knew the whole class was looking at my butt, I would most definitely be a little uncomfortable myself, *maybe*.

As soon as they were out of ear shot I turned to Nic – she was smiling ear to ear "Holy crap Nic I cannot believe that you and I have a date with some of the hottest guys in school and Topher is totally funny too! And you're right the two of us will be fine together on a date and I think it'll be fun!" Nic started saying how nice they were and how excited she was about the date when my sister walked up.

I froze and looked at her, she said with a big sincere smile "Hey! Why were Cale and Topher over here? "I decided to be nice about it, and I told her straight out, "Nic and I have a double date with Cale and Topher on Friday." I expected some flak from her but instead she was cool and asked us the details. I ticked another one off for our new found relationship.

Nic and I had a plan. I decided to wait until about 5 minutes before the class was over before I went up to Cale and Topher, so I didn't have to talk too long. At five 'til I went over and said "Hey sorry about my comments earlier I really didn't mean to embarrass you, I sometimes have no filter, I just say what comes to mind – no thought process involved obviously…"

Topher interrupted "Don't apologize – I thought you were cooler before. Besides we have already plotted our revenge."

Cale asked me what I was holding and I replied "Nothing, it's a drawing but it's not done, I'll show you later." I felt both their eyes on me while I returned back to my seat, it could have been the sign I was holding over my butt as I walked, it read "Bring it on!" with a simple curved shape "W" under it. I heard them both laugh as I walked away. I barely made out Topher's words.. "I like these girls!"

The bell rang and we piled out of class. Cale was waiting outside the door and grabbed my hand. His hand was cool and soft.

"Where are you headed?" he asked.

"Class."

"Which class"?

"History."

"I remember, I'll walk you," we walked a few steps and Cale said "So now you're blushing, so it's not going to be that hard to get you back then. Or is me holding your hand embarrassing?"

My face felt warm, I was completely flushed, I felt uncomfortable, edgy, I wanted him to let go, though I wasn't sure why. All I could say was "No, of course not, you just caught me off guard." We walked in sort of an uncomfortable silence.

We reached my class quickly, which I was happy about. I let go of his hand and said "Here we are. Soooo the four of us are going out Friday. We should have fun." I was leaning against the wall and Cale across from me when Mr. Emotional comes up and just stands right next to us.

"Can I help you?" Cale retorted.

"Ah no, but Addie I have a message and love letter for you from Logan." He held up a folded piece of paper. I froze and said "What?" shakily.

"He said he loves you and to call him." Storm said it with such a bite I wanted to smack him.

He waved the note "It says it in the note too."

Cale just chuckled and didn't seem concerned at all. Storm walked into class still holding the letter in the air. "Jerk" I looked back at Cale thinking he was going to have questions for me but instead he bent over and whispered "He likes you." He kissed me on the cheek and said "I'll catch you later," and left.

I sat at my desk and the folded note was sitting on my desk. I sat down and picked it up like it was a diseased piece of paper and put it on Storm's desk. He didn't touch it he left it there the entire class, and he gave me the cold shoulder so badly I could feel a chill in the air. What's his deal? I tell you Storm has more moods than Jekyll and Hyde, but his main mood is grouchy.

He got up in a hurry after class and bolted for the door, leaving the note on his desk. I of course couldn't leave it there so I grabbed it and threw it in my bag.

Later that afternoon, Nic and I met for a bathroom break. We never actually went to the bathroom, we would just pick a time and place and meet up and chat some. Today I brought both my notes, I gave her the note about my dream, we both leaned up against the wall just around the corner from the elevators. "That truck keeps on coming up everywhere." I told pointed to the place in my letter where it mentioned it. "Yeah, I see that..." she said, we were deeply engrossed in my note when we heard a noise.

I stopped holding up the wall and looked around the corner but saw no one. We finished up that note and I handed her the one from Logan.

"I wonder if they ever found Jewel's bracelet and if she was really attacked like I saw?" I was rambling "I can't take it that Logan's trying to contact me, and what if he's telling everyone what happened and better yet what if he is embellishing the story, telling everyone a bunch of lies."

I think Nic was listening to me, at least as much as she could while reading at the same time. "This guy's unbelievable, and I don't think he's going to leave you alone unless you say something to him or send your own message back to him." Nic said. She looked up at me with sympathetic eyes. But then they got really big. "Hey Cale!" she said and handed me my notes back "see ya."

I folded the notes up as fast as I could and jammed them into my pocket and turned around slowly, not sure of what to say, I just smiled.

"You're lucky I'm not the hall monitor" Cale said with a no teeth smile. "She's on the second floor right now."

I replied "I know, funny seeing you here."

"I should say the same. What are you and Nic up to?"

"Swapping notes."

"Hmmm," was his response. He took my hand and kissed it, "I gotta go, I'll catch ya later" he said pulling my hand gently with him letting it go slowly and giving me a wink. I shook my head, who is this guy Romeo or what? I wonder why he didn't ask me about that darned note again, here he sees it twice and could care a less about it. I wonder if he heard us talking. I hope not.

I flashed back to my dream about my wolf, its grey eyes against his sandy brown coat and white under belly.

CHAPTER 7

Nic and I were sitting in Home Ec and I was daydreaming when the class got interrupted, in walked Topher, he whispered to the teacher and then toward us and announced to the class "This rose is from an admirer *butt!*" he said putting the emphasis on the word 'butt'.

"...he doesn't want to disclose his name!" He cleared his throat and started again. "...'*butt*' *h*e really wanted to send... this message to you my dear Addie...

I like you very much *butt*
We owe you big because you started it
You need to challenge me *butt*
Not run and flee
Although you may want to
Cause paybacks are coming to you, *butt*
Just so you know they'll be fun and gentle
Cause our meeting was not accidental
Will you go out with me?
…..this is a special gift for you."

He handed me a single red rose. The class "Ahhh's" but he wasn't done "*Butt* in return my dear he would like permission for a date this Friday."

My face flushed. And he waited, I nodded. Topher started again "*Butt* there is another message - Mizz Nicole Newland you got off easy this time." He mouthed you're next, took a bow and the class clapped and he ran over to Nic gave her a peck on the cheek, and said "We really tried using butt more butt it just didn't work for us we're not really good poets as you can tell." And he high tailed it out of the class. Nic's face was smoldering red and I was having a hot flash of embarrassment myself! I covered my face.

Nic received the same treatment from Cale in her sixth period class.

Cale showed up early Friday night for our double date. We were going out to dinner, and then the football game to follow. He brought me one red rose. I glared at him when he gave it to me "How thoughtful." My Mother said. I couldn't help but smile, I placed it in the vase with the other one.

He flashed his eyebrows "So you kept the other rose I sent you."

"Yes, I did." I said with a smile. He was dressed in tan corduroy pants, a jacket and a button down shirt. He looked like my dad would dress when they'd go out for a casual dinner with their friends. It was a little disappointing for me. He looked much hotter at school. Maybe he dressed that way for my parents.

He was very mature and polite when he met my parents; he had a long conversation with my mom. They sounded like two old friends that hadn't seen each other in a while, him getting along with my parents so well, worried me. And my parents letting me go with him, in his van, with no windows – and didn't even give me a warning and they didn't announce my curfew in front of him, well that worried me too. Since my mom didn't mention it, I think Cale felt obligated to volunteer information. I tried to stop him "Don't worry about the van Mrs. Gellar, it's a work van filled with equipment, there's only room for two." Cale said looking her in the eye steadily and not breaking that bond. Until my mom laughed and said "That's fine Cale, I trust you." Red alerts were going off in my head.

I had told my mom earlier that we were going to the game, so when she asked Cale what we were doing, and he replied going to dinner and a movie, I freaked out and retorted "I thought we were going to the game!"

"Oh, that's fine Addie we can go to the game, we hadn't talked about what we were doing after dinner, but there are a couple of movies showing at Summit Mall, or we can go to the game." He pulled two football tickets from his pocket. "My mom makes me buy tickets whether we go to the game or not she likes to support the school." Cale said with an arch in his eyebrow looking at me calmly. I sat and smiled at Cale for just a moment as relief set through my body. I think I'm a little more tense than I realized.

We got in his van and I gave a quick look in the back, it was empty! "What would you have done if my mom checked your van? I can't believe you lied like that!" I said a little excited. It only took me a minute to calm down and get extremely overwrought again in his huge empty van. I felt a lump in my throat, my head was spinning. What was he expecting, I wanted to know his game plan but because I had no experience in this area, and I could feel my ignorance and inexperience creeping up on me, I just had nothing to say.

As soon as he pulled out of my driveway I started chattering, talking way too fast. "Who are we picking up first? Are we really double dating because Nic thinks we are and she's waiting on us? I thought we were going to the game obviously you have other plans. How come I wasn't aware of all these plans? Is Topher really coming and why is your van empty what do you expect and furthermore don't you own a car? And if we aren't going to the game why do you have tickets?"

Cale put his hand on my knee, I flinched. "Relax," he said, "it'll be fine, Topher and I wanted to see the movie at the drive-in. When we pick the other two up we'll see what everyone wants to do. And obviously, under the circumstances," he gave me look like he knew I was nervous or maybe it was a look that he knew I've never dated before, "we'll pick up Nic first. "

I let out a breath of air. Cale continued "I didn't ask you about the movie ahead of time because I didn't want you to have to lie to your parents about the van, the drive-in, etc."

"....Oh....." is all I could say. I was silent except for a few instructions on how to get to Nic's. Somehow that didn't make me feel any better, he started sounding like a player to me and why did they want to go to a drive-in, in this big empty van? Maybe I should cancel, say I'm not feeling well and have him drop me off at Nic's and we'll call it a day.

I knocked on Nic's door, she answered with her coat on and a big bag of popcorn in hand. I told her on the down low that the van was empty!

She said "I know isn't it cool! Topher is going to put bean bags in the back!" She sounded excited.

I didn't think she heard me over the dog barking, she told Rusty to shut up and get in the house but he just kept on, very unusual for him. Cale stayed in the car I didn't blame him, Rusty was going to get him if he got out. "How come I wasn't told about any of this?" she shrugged her shoulders.

"We didn't want you to worry."

"What did you tell them?" I was completely panicked.

"Nothing!" she said back "Nothing! I swear it! I just told them it would be better if you didn't have to lie to your mom. I knew you'd panic if you knew all this stuff but it will be fine, I promise, two are stronger than one." she said, putting her hand on my shoulder.

"Let's not push it Nic." I told her giving her a stern look. We walked to the van together.

Nic said to Cale "Sorry about my dog he usually never barks unless he feels threatened. I just talked to Topher he's ready, he said he wants pizza, and the movie starts at 8pm" I turned to look at her with a confused and exasperated look on my face.

"So we *are* seeing a movie? What movie?" My head was spinning, how did Nic know all this and I didn't, it was supposed to be my date.

Didn't Nic feel trapped that they had a plan; of course not she was part of the plan. What was she thinking, I wish I could talk to her alone, give her a piece of my mind. She hopped in the back and sat on the floor then announced she had to be home by one, I had to be home at midnight, she always seems to be one up on me.

Cale helped Topher load four bean bags into the van. As soon as they both got in the car Cale and Topher argued over where they wanted to eat, Cale complained Topher always wanted cheap food. Topher argued Cale acted like a Grandpa and wanted to have meat and potatoes all the time. I laughed when I heard the Grandpa remark, thinking he dressed like one too. Cale finished the argument by asking Nic and me what we wanted to eat, "Whitey's of course," we said at the same time.

Cale came over to open my door which I thought was geeky, he also put his hand on the back of my neck as we walked into the restaurant, just like my dad does. When we got inside Topher

3:17 a.m. ...the waking hour

and Nic were getting along just fine, but Cale was acting like my dad, he ordered a salad for me, asked me if I had to use the washroom and other oddities. What happened to the cool guy at school – maybe at school it was all an act and he really was a geek.

The rest of the night was just weird, Cale and I sat in the front seats the whole time while Topher and Nic were talking and seemed like they were having a lot of fun in the back. They were cracking jokes and laughing the whole time. I just felt uncomfortable.

The highlight of my night was when we all had dessert in the back of the van on the bean bags – they even set up a couple small tables. We had chocolate and popcorn the best combo, something sweet and something salty.

Cale was super polite all night, almost a little too much. He didn't try to kiss me but we did hold hands for a bit. He didn't make a pass at me or anything, which I thought was odd, not that I wanted him to. I hate to say it, but I felt like I was on a date with my grandpa.

He started the van before the second movie was over and turned the radio to the high school football game, I didn't even know they had a radio station for it. We left and didn't see the end of the movie which was fine because Nic and I saw it the week before. To my surprise we pulled into the school parking lot, he parked right by the gate and we all stepped outside the van and just hung out. The football game only had a few minutes to go. Cale leaned on his van, pulled me close, told me he didn't want me to get into trouble with my parents, then tucked my hair behind my ear. I didn't put my hair up, I couldn't, not after he asked. And he put his arm around me and gave me a squeeze.

I think I paid attention to more details of tonight's game than I had any other game. As people started parting the gates, Cale told all of us to tell anyone we talked to that we sat on the visitor's side. We had the radio on while leaning on the back of his van with the doors open, and who did we run into but my own sister Tori. He couldn't have planned it better.

I, of course, got home a few minutes early, Cale kissed me on the cheek, and said good night. Topher made fun of him said he should give me a proper kiss and Cale told him to grow up. I thought it was weird too, I felt uncomfortable, especially with Topher and Nic watching our every move. I'm glad this night was over.

Even though the date was odd it went fine; the oddness could have been my fault. I liked him even though his hair was nicer than mine, at least better groomed, it was always washed and styled, none of the dirty grunge look. He dressed cool, at school anyway. He was tall and slim very nice to look at and always wore boots.

I had dated some boys in seventh and eighth grade but Junior high dating was never serious, everyone usually went out in large groups and we were all dropped off by parents. None of the gatherings or so called dates were as well planned out as tonight. I actually think I could consider tonight my first real date.

I was dreaming about my wolf, we were running in the ravine behind my house. When I got to the top of the dirty slide Cale was standing there, I turned and the wolf was gone. Then Cale and I were by my garage door and he was being mean to me, shaking me. I said to him "Cale stop, it's me. What are you doing?"

"Cut" someone said. And just like that we were interrupted; we were on a movie set, people and cameras everywhere. Cale let go and said "I don't know, sorry." The look on his face changed, he felt his chest and arms, checking to see if he was really there or was he dreaming. We looked at each other and then around us and everyone from the set was gone. It felt like Cale had really stepped into my dream. I woke up with a pounding headache, it was 3:17a.m.

We went to a movie on our second date and he brought me another rose. We went out on a Tuesday because he said he had a gig that weekend. My mom actually let me go out on a date during the week. Maybe she was letting me because she liked Cale or maybe it was because we were in High School now. The date was just all right, I was less nervous this time, I think. He wore thick striped corduroy pants and a button down shirt and he styled his hair different, and not a good different either I thought he looked a little geeky. I told him he looked too old to be in high school and I ran my hand across his unshaven face, he could grow a full beard. He grabbed my hand, looked at me, I swear he was going to tell me I was right but replied, "Yeah I graduated a long time ago but decided to re-enroll in high school for the fun of it" and laughed.

Before we said good night he asked "After our date the other night did you sleep...I mean did you have a dream... I mean a good dream... did you have fun?" What was he really asking me? Was he asking me if I had the same weird dream as he did? Noooo, it couldn't be. I just stared at him and realized my mouth was open and replied "I had a lot of fun but I don't remember my dreams..." I lied. He kissed me goodnight on the cheek.

The third date we went on was the following Thursday and he gave me another rose. We met the guitarist from one of the bands he managed for dinner and they talked business, it was fine I guess, boring for me. He was dressed nerdy again, he never dressed or acted like he did in school on our dates, in other words not cool and not hot looking. Maybe Storm wasn't the only Jekyll and Hyde, maybe Cale was too, hot guy by day, nerd boy by night.

Every date from then on, he would come a little early, give me a single red rose and chat with my mom and or dad. I started to notice that, at least it seemed as if, he liked my parents more. It was like waiting for my parents to get done talking to their friends so we could get going. He was much more interesting and sexy in than outside of school.

Every conversation we had was all about him. Anytime I brought up something I had done, he had done it and of course, he did it better. Like once, I told him about Nic's and my ski trip and that Nic had all sorts of bruises all over her because we were knocking each other over. He did it and did it better, he and his buddy broke arms and legs when they went skiing. I talked about swimming and he of course he did that too and his experience was superior to mine. Plus, he had done a million more things than I had, I'm not sure how someone so young has accomplished so much already. Maybe I was just jealous, however, I found him to be very boring and I wasn't interested. After my seventh rose I couldn't take it any longer, we had never *really* kissed. He always just kissed me on the cheek or forehead. Weird, especially after seven dates. He didn't seem interested in me that way.

The final straw that broke the camel's back, as the saying goes, was when we were on a date that I don't remember much of. He had coaxed me into having a glass of wine at dinner, a dinner he made for me at his apartment. His parents weren't home either. I remember it being so clean it didn't even look like anyone lived there. I was very nervous about it so I drank the wine, it didn't even taste that good. After dinner we cleaned up and I remember putting my coat on, when I woke up we were parked in a driveway of a house I'd never been to. The house we were at was a white ranch with green shutters in need of a fresh coat of paint. A couple trees in the front and one that peeked over the top of the roof from the back. I saw Cale come out of the side door and shut my eyes quickly before he got back in the van so he wouldn't know I was awake.

I'm not sure why I faked it for a couple of blocks but I did. I wanted to know where we were coming from so I pretended to wake up. I think I took him by surprise by the look on his face but he put his hand on my shoulder and said "Hey, sleepy head." He smiled at me and I forced a smile back.

"I'm sorry. Did I fall asleep long?"

"No, not long at all," he glanced at me as a cars headlights passed us by and his eyes glowed just like Logan's did that night, the same mirror-like reflective looking eyes that showed no color at all. I froze not able to breathe or move, but made myself look out my window so he couldn't see my reaction until I forced myself to breath and swallowed back the bile that began to rise in my throat. Something definitely wasn't right.

I didn't notice the names of the streets we turned on, it was too dark and my vision hadn't returned its focus yet, but I bet I could find it again. We were in Brecksville and weren't far from the highway. I didn't say much on the ride back home and neither did he thank goodness, I didn't want to have to force another smile on my face.

That night when I got home I noticed I had a bruise and a couple of marks in the crook of my arm. I didn't feel like anything else was out of place, I don't think he *did* anything to me but, whatever happened wasn't right. It felt creepy and sinister, maybe even vindictive. That was it for me, way too outlandish for me. I was going to have to end it, but before that I should see if I could find out why his eyes looked the same as Logan's did, it seemed a little too coincidental.

I went up to him in Art class and was going ask him straight out if he knew Logan and then tell him flat out 'we should just be friends' but when I got to his desk he started talking about this and that and how awesome he was. I think he liked to hear himself talk. Then he announced he was going out of town for a long weekend and wouldn't be back until next week. He started talking about his trip and what he was going to do. It was business mixed with

3:17 a.m. ...the waking hour

pleasure and by the end of it I had no idea what he said. Nor did I say a word to him, I just walked back to my desk.

Nic asked "How did it go? What did he say?" I looked up at her in confusion and shrugged my shoulders.

"Huh, you didn't do it? Addie, you've just got to do it."

"Maybe later today."

"Yeah, later today" she agreed. "I have to tell you something..."

"Ok"

"The notes of your dreams you gave me, they're gone."

"What?"

"Yeah all of them – gone into thin air – I asked my mom if she'd been in my room and she said no and I believed her. Everything in my room was out of place like someone was looking for letters or something. It had to be the other night 'cause mom said Rusty was barking his head off at something even though we always said if someone robbed the house he wouldn't bark." She just looked at me. "Aren't you mad or worried? ALL your notes are gone."

I replied nonchalantly "Not all of them I still have mine."

"What do you mean you have yours?"

"Well I held on to some 'cause they just seemed silly or odd or were repetitive, so I didn't give them to you."

"I'm not sure if I should be mad or not."

"Well don't be you can see them, they're silly."

I sat down and started to work on my project. I was concentrating on how I would break up with Cale when I remembered he told me he was going out of town for a long weekend. In fact, he made it sound like he'd be gone for at least five days. That's five days I don't have to talk to or see him that perked me right up.

Even though I wasn't bold with Cale, when I got to history I decided to be bold more of the time with everyone and I was going to start now. I looked Storm square in the eye and asked him "What did I do to you to make you hate me so much?" He looked stupefied like he had no idea what I was talking about.

I continued "I like being your friend and if you don't want me hanging out with your girlfriend, I don't have to. If I did something stupid, because I do stupid things tell me what I did and I'll try and fix it. But you acting all huffy and cold around me is awful and I'm done with it."

He looked at me with his piercing green eyes and said "I don't hate you, what made you think that?"

"The fact that you treat me like crap, say rude uncalled for things to me and completely ignore me other times. You're just down right mean to me sometimes."

Of course he didn't deny it but said "Sorry I... I'm not sure why.... actually I do know." He paused and I gave him a look to go on.

He continued "It's just that Cale is the biggest playboy in school and he's just dating you to screw you, then dump you and now all the other guys will think you're a slut. Plus, I don't like the guy."

"Why do you talk to me like that? It's rude – don't do that. And why do you care what everyone else thinks?"

He shrugged his shoulders "Well it's true, he always dates younger girls and he does it so he can...... get lucky with a..... a non-experienced girl." He stammered on "Did I state that lady like enough for you?" with a disgusted look on his face.

"Well for your information we have been out with him seven times and he hasn't tried *a thing*. "I said making quote marks in the air with my fingers, and then thought at least not that I remember.

"He will..." Storm warned "...and then he's going to dump you."

I interrupted him waving my hand and smiled, I leaned closer to him and said "Me first." Storm looked at me confused "I tried breaking up with him this morning but I didn't.... he talks a lot." I paused, shrugged my shoulders and then leaned back toward him. "He doesn't know it yet, so please don't tell anyone."

Storm winked at me as if he knew how to keep it a secret, he leaned back in his chair with a self-satisfied smile, or was it more of a smug look. A few minutes passed he reached over and put his hand on the back of my chair, "Do you want to sit with me at lunch today?"

"Come again?" I replied.

"Sit with me at lunch and you can tell me all about it." I smiled at him. That wasn't so bad; it felt really good to get my friend back. Plus, admitting I was going to break up with Cale out loud, made me feel like a cloud had been lifted and made it seem more real. I was going to break up with Cale.

Nic was going to be late to lunch today so when I got to the

3:17 a.m. ...the waking hour

cafeteria, I spotted Storm, grabbed some lunch and went to sit with him. He looked like a cat that just ate a canary.

"What's up? You look really happy or like you just did something mischievous?"

"Nothings up, just in a good mood, so spill, why are you breaking up with Stud Muffin?" Storm asked with a tinge of sarcasm.

"Well... he's actually boring, he talks about himself all the time and I just don't think he's my type.... Why are you smiling so much?"

"I just don't like the guy. I never thought he was right for you."

"I never knew you had any thoughts on who was right for me."

"I've thought about it, so you're breaking up with him because he's boring?"

"That plus we didn't really kiss, kiss. What's that about? I think he would since you say he has such a reputation."

"Addie, you have kissing issues."

"What do you mean by that?" I shook my head "I do not! I just think that after several dates..." I leaned in toward him for a more private conversation "maybe he should have *like really* kissed me not just a peck on the cheek.... What do you mean I have kissing issues?" I said softly and my face blushed.

"If you wanted to be kissed why didn't you kiss him, ugh, never mind."

I leaned in close to him "I thought guys were supposed to lead with that stuff. You did and I thought you were a good kisser...... Huh!" I covered my mouth. "Oh my gosh, I'm a horrible kisser."

"You're a good kisser...just so you know..." He looked a little uncomfortable; he was looking at his lunch tray. "I don't know, maybe I don't know what I'm talking about." He squinted his eyes looking right at me when he said it. He cleared his throat and continued "So you're telling me Cale never *really k*issed you, and never tried anything else?"

"No!" I said "Weird right, not that I want this conversation to go anywhere else, but no." Storm just looked at me wide eyed, and said he didn't believe it, and laughed.

I felt some tension leave us "I know!" I said half laughing with him. "It's like I was dating my grandpa or something, he was always kissing me on the cheek or forehead and dressed geeky when we went out."

"And that's it?" Storm asked looking at me trying to detect deception.

"Nothing else at all I swear," I shook my head no.

"Break up with him" was all he said.

"I don't know what to say to him, I've never broken up with anyone before." Storm laughed sarcastically and turned his head.

"What is that supposed to mean."

"You broke up with me."

"I so did not! We weren't even dating exclusively and since school ended I never heard from you, when I said goodbye to you, you didn't say anything like *we should get together this summer*.' I believe I...you know what, it's a moot point. I didn't break up with you because we never went steady, we went out a couple times, but we weren't exclusive, and besides, what does it matter now you're dating a nympho."

He looked shocked. "You're calling your friend a nympho, that's not very nice."

"I take it back, I like Shelby but you know she tells me everything." I gave him a look back squeezing my eyes together, studying him back... "Who's the slut now," I mumbled.

"So you thought we weren't even dating".

"No, I didn't say that, I said I didn't think we were going steady, there is a difference. You know that has to be mentioned in some conversation and I never remembered any conversation like that between us."

Shelby and Nic had found each other and came to sit by us, I was thankful. I didn't want Storm and I to get back to the "cold shoulder" phase again although it may already be too late for that. Storm and I didn't talk much after that, didn't have to not with Shelby there. But I was dumbfounded, was he treating me like crap the whole time because he thought I broke up with him last year?

I couldn't hold it in any longer, I fired out "So that's why you've been mad at me all this time, from eighth grade!" Storms head snapped up in surprise. "Well that's just great, there's nothing I can do about it now Storm, it's done it's over, get over it! I'm sorry Storm but let's not blame it all on me – you did nothing about it either!"

I'm not sure why I was so mad, but I got up without a further word and just started walking. I found myself in front of my locker.

Nic caught up with me a couple minutes later, "What was that all about?"

"Storm is mad at me and has been treating me like crap because he thinks I broke up with him last year."

"But you guys weren't exclusive, right? I mean you dated a couple of times but nothing serious."

"Well that's what I thought but he thought otherwise, and it's irrelevant now. I mean why bring it up? You'd think after he had a girlfriend that our so called break-up would have been a faded memory by now."

"Maybe he still likes you."

"Maybe he doesn't. If he did why is he dating Shelby? That doesn't make any sense to me. In any case, I don't like him that way... I guess I have other things on my mind."

"Well we know guys are unstable."

"And Storm is majorly the king of unstable." We both had a good laugh over that.

I decided my blow up may not have been about Storm that maybe this Cale thing was weighing on my mind more than I anticipated. I decided to try and break up with him before school was out, but he was nowhere to be found. He must have left school early.

Nic and I decided to hang out all weekend, have some girl time. Since Cale was going to be out of town, we concocted a scheme to try and find the house he took me to, see if we could find any clues. Even though we were going to spy on him, I felt more relaxed, like my life was back to normal. I felt more at ease than I had in a long while. Although, in the back of my mind I was still thinking about breaking up with him, the crazy guy who drugs girls and does who knows what with them – I wanted to think he was crazy, but I just didn't.

Nic got to my house around 3:00 and so far our *'spy'* plans have been foiled since we have no one to drive our getaway car. We hung out at my house Saturday night, my sister hung with us too. I was very surprised, she usually always has plans.

We were all bored stiff so we decided to go down to the neighbors to see if any one was home. To our amazement Gus was and he had a friend over. They came out to hang for a bit, they must have been bored too. We talked on the porch until dusk, when I noticed an unfamiliar car in the driveway. I nudged Nic and pointed to it.

Nic said excitedly "Oh my Gosh! You guys are bored and you can drive and have a car!" She said pointing to Gus's friend. We started laughing. "Can you take us somewhere?"

"I'm not allowed out past eleven with the car."

"We only need it for about an hour...door to door." Nic said getting all excited. "We need to get something from Addie's house first. Pick us up in five minutes!" She yelled as all three of us girls ran back to my house. We got inside huffing and puffing, we each grabbed a pair of rubber gloves that my mom used when cleaning her paint brushes. Tori had no idea what we were doing but looked excited so she just grabbed all the same supplies that Nic and I did. We ran upstairs and I gave everyone sandwich baggies, in case we found something. My mom came in the kitchen and we all froze.

"What are you girls up to?" she asked.

Tori, quick on her feet said, "We're going to pick up one of Gus' friends and then we're going to play football." And asked, "Where are the flash lights?"

"There are a few down in your dad's work room." she said as she reached for one above the fridge and handed it to Nic not knowing she was aiding and abetting future convicts.

"Thanks Mrs. Gellar.

"You're welcome my dear. You three stay out of trouble ya hear?"

"Really, she says that now?" I said in a whisper taking two stairs at a time into the basement.

"We will!" Tori yelled back as she scrambled to follow Nic and me. We found three other flash lights and then booked to the top of my driveway where Gus and his friend were waiting. All the girls jumped in the back.

Gus turned around to face us and asked, "Where to?"

"I know the approximate location." and I rattled off the first few directions.

"We aren't going on a wild goose chase are we?"

"It's possible" Nic said, but added "If we don't find it in fifteen minutes than we'll come right back.

He didn't look very satisfied with that answer. "What else do you have to do tonight?" Tori asked.

"Good point, but we get to do what we want when we get back." Gus replied.

"Fine." she said. I just rolled my eyes hoping she wasn't getting us into trouble.

Thinking about trouble, I started concentrating on our route. "Turn here." I pointed. It wasn't the street, we had to turn around and go down the second street, and then a third. As Gus's friend turned down the street slowly I got an eerie feeling, the same one I get when I've had a dream that comes true, this time it sent a chill down my spine. The houses were not close together at all, Gus' friend (I wish I could remember his name) was driving slowly making the moment seem more suspicious than it was, or maybe not.

I grabbed Nic's arm and pointed, "That's it." I whispered loudly enough for everyone to hear. He drove slowly past it and down one more house, turned around, parked and turned off his headlights. Both the guys flung their arms over the front seat to look back at us. We gave the boys the details on why we were here, but we didn't have to, they knew something was up.

"Now what?" They whispered, they were intrigued.

"Should someone stay here to keep the car running in case we get into trouble?" The guys looked at each other and said "Naaaa."

"What are we doing?" They asked.

"We're looking for clues." I said.

"What kinds of clues?" Tori asked.

Nic and I looked at each other, she shrugged, and responded "We need to know who lives here, what kind of people they are and look for other clues like drugs or weapons, anything out of place."

Gus replied "That's easy, check the mailbox."

"Glad we brought you, I wouldn't have thought of that." I said.

Tori the organizer, pointed to Gus' friend and Nic and I, "You three are in one group. Gus and I will be in another. You guys go to the left of the house and we'll take the right."

I nudged Nic "I'm just guessing but maybe the bracelet's here."

"Noooo." Nic said exaggeratedly. I replied "It's a big maybe."

We all snuck out of the car and closed the doors quietly, I wonder if anyone else was as nervous as I was. Nic and I went right and Tori followed and then the two boys followed, so much for the plan. Until the boys stopped at the mailbox, filtered through all the pieces, and then flanked the house left.

There were no lights on in the house, it was only about 7:30pm or so, it seemed like no one was home. In my dream, where the girl got attacked, they start on the right and moved left, I wanted to do that here just in case it was the same place. Everything about this place screamed déjàvu to me, but my senses could be off because I was here with Cale the one time under weird circumstances. I just don't know.

As we were creeping around the corner of the house Tori tripped over a branch or root and fell into me taking us both to the ground face first. We both started to giggle on the spot, Nic tried passing us and Tori grabbed her ankle to bring her down to our level.

"Glad to see you're so serious about this Addie." She said sternly, trying to get up. Tori and I tripped her again. She couldn't help but laugh this time, the quieter we tried to be the more we laughed – tears and all.

We gained composure and rounded the corner. I stood totally upright taking it all in, even though it was dark it wasn't pitch black. I popped my flash light on. I walked toward the back of the yard down the right side of the property line and stopped halfway. There was a river birch tree centered in the back yard just off of the deck. This is where I was watching the girl get attacked in my dream, I could sense it, and I wanted to see more. I shined my light across the field in the path they took this summer. I got a chill.

When, Kaboom! I flew to the ground and tried to grasp my flashlight, the girls tackled me and pointed toward the house, I turned it off. People were inside. We were frozen to the ground for a bit, our anxiety growing stronger. I moved my head up slowly, I could see the guys at the far tree line waving us over and then they ducked. I stuck my head back in the tall weedy grass, it was itchy and all over. We were in a meadow-like area, the non-mowed part of the yard.

I looked back at Nic and Tori they lifted their hands to gesture what next. Like I'm an expert at this, I had no clue what to do. We were low to the ground so no one would notice us. I peeked back up at the house, the sliding door curtains were only drawn a bit I could see two people in the kitchen and one was helping the other to the table like they were injured or sick. I squinted my eyes to really focus.

"What do you see?" Nic whispered.

"Two people, one is sick or hurt. I don't know... oh my god!

Army crawl, army crawl, army crawl...." I said as we hustled near the boys who were camouflaged by the tree line. We crawled as close to the edge as we could when I saw something shine in the grass for a brief moment. Tori got up and started running which set the motion light detector off! Nic and I popped up and were hot on her trail. We ran right into the boys pushing them into the neighbor's yard. We were all laughing running as fast as we could to the car.

What's his face was fumbling for his keys. "Is this going to be like a horror film where..." The car started cutting me off mid-sentence. He didn't turn the headlights on until we got to the end of the block.

Nic said "Back to the bat cave Boy Wonder." Everyone let out a little chuckle. I looked back; no one was following us....

"Oh my gosh, my heart's beating a million miles a minute. " Tori said excitedly.

"Are you kidding me, I have to pee." Nic said and everyone burst out laughing.

Gus flipped his arm over the seat and said "we only saw mail for a Dr. Westman."

Under my breath I said "I saw it."

When we got back to our neighborhood and the boys reminded us it was there turn to pick the next adventure. We followed Gus and Boy Wonder into the foliage at the end of our street, it went right and left but we went straight. When we finished batting all the weeds out of our way we came to a secret clubhouse that was camouflaged by all the trees and brush. There we had our first Big Mouth Mickey's' beer.

After that we played Frisbee in the dark and then we all laid in the grass and looked at the stars. Here I felt I had more of a connection and more fun with this group than I ever had with Cale. Not that I ever dated someone seriously before, but if that was dating it wasn't for me.

CHAPTER 8

Nic asked me to be a wrestling manager with her. I hadn't even thought about doing it for the high school team but then I thought, what the heck, we had fun doing it last year. Only to find out that "Manager" is just a glorified name for slave girls – this year we have to clean the mats before every practice something we didn't have to do before, plus, we have to keep score and video tape all the meets, plus, girls aren't allowed to ride the buses to away matches. In junior high we only had to go to and keep score at the home matches and one tournament. It was a lot more work, it had better be fun.

After a few practices we got used to the routine, it wasn't so bad. I really didn't get why they needed us at practice. What I did like was Nic and I got to catch up on homework and all our gossip for the day. Today Nic told me that Mr. Meshko, our Algebra teacher, announced to all his classes that I have received the highest grade he has ever given out, that I was the only student to achieve a 100% in his class. I have gotten all of my homework, quizzes and tests 100% correct. I said "All his classes, ugh. I can't believe I'm doing so well in school this year, very unlike me."

After the second week we actually started to get to know the wrestlers and we were making friends and it started to be a lot of fun. I had more guys saying "Hi" to me in the halls, and more girls talking to me to find out how I knew this guy or that one. They'd even ask me to put in a good word for them, in turn; I made more girl and boy friends. My mom always said you can never have too many friends.

Hump day, Nic and I were waiting by the gym exit for our rides and were leaning up against the half wall by the doors, per usual. That's when he walked into the lobby. His hair was dark, messy and wet, he had a reddish-brown leather coat on and no shirt underneath. His skin was a soft golden brown, a couple shades darker than mine and smooth, his jeans were a faded shade of blue and the hems were tattered. His brows were thick and bold but his eyes were soft and dreamy, a deep caramel. He had wrestling shoes on that were unlaced and opened sloppily, but he wasn't on the wrestling team. I think I was staring at him with my mouth open because when Nic said something to me, she had to nudge me in the ribs with her elbow to get my attention. "What?" I had to ask her to repeat. I kept staring at him when Storm walked up to him and dropped his bag. They were talking and jabbing each other fooling around, then Storm's friend laughed. When he laughed his brilliant white teeth showed and his abs flexed showing every muscle in his washboard stomach. Most guys have a six pack of muscles but he looked like he had more of an eight pack, the way his whole stomach rippled all the way to his jeans. He was beautiful; the rays of heaven must have been shining down on me, to make me notice him.

Nic said loudly "Don't drool!" Jabbing me in the ribs again.

"What" I replied and started to laugh. "Holy crap do you know him." I asked in a whisper.

"Of course I do, that is one of Storm's brothers."

"His brother!" I was stunned.

"I didn't even know he had brothers or that they went to this school. What's his name? Do you know him? Can you introduce me?"

"You knew he had brothers because he told us at the wake. His name is Jett but I don't really know him, I just know he's Storm's brother. I think I heard he broke up with his girlfriend though, Lisa something. He is way out of your league though, sorry. Plus, you can get in line behind every other girl in school. Storm said all the girls like him. Plus, the girl he was dating, they like dated for a whole year and they were serious so Storm thinks the breakup is temporary. Lisa is real popular too. Besides you have Cale." I just gave her a hum drum look.

"Ha, ha but not for long... How come I didn't notice him before?" Nic explained to me that he was probably in another sport. I was going to have to figure out which other sport that was.

I was still staring at Jett; I couldn't take my eyes off of him. He looked over at me as I was staring at him and I just couldn't look away, he actually smiled at me. Nic nudged me again, I said loudly enough so others could hear "Oh sorry, I was star struck" – I hope he knew what I meant. You know how you stare at something whether you want to or not and you can't stop looking, you're in a trance, you want to look away but you don't. Not sure what it's called but I call it 'star struck.'

"Nic does he know what I meant? I don't want him to think I was staring because I think he's gorgeous. Although....he is...."

Nic looked at me again, "What's wrong with you?"

I told her "I'm in love..."

"Well, you need to take care of Cale first."

I shook my head, I wanted to tell her I saw Cale in that house that night but I just didn't.

"Don't you think he's awesome?" I said and nodded my head toward the new guy.

"So you're in love with all the brothers" she retorted.

"I'm sorry, but I don't even know who the other brother is... How do you know them and I don't?"

She turned to me and said "I just know their names but nothing about them. His older brother's name is Kyle, he is not bad looking either. Don't fall too deep, you may not be able to..." She tapered off. "What about Cale?"

"Oh good god, quit mentioning his name, I can't take it." I said with humorous agitation in my voice while rubbing my temples. Nic laughed.

I had to look again. The top button to his faded and tattered tight fitting jeans was unbuttoned. His hair still wet and disheveled, it looked good on him. Storm slapped him in the stomach and called him fat ass! And Jett laughed, took a swipe at him and said "Your ass, you're the one who's fat."

Storm replied "Get some pants that fit." They both laughed and I couldn't help but giggle about it myself. Some tall, dark and grumpy guy came out into the lobby and said "Would you two quit screwin' around, let's go." He held himself like the alpha of the group. It had to be Kyle, he was attractive in his own way.

None of them had an ounce of fat on them. They were a very good looking group of guys, they weren't pretty like Cale, but ruggedly handsome. Jett had a smile that just made me melt, he didn't have dimples but had this double crease at both corners of his mouth; it was adorable. Plus, nice straight white teeth, his skin looked soft and tan. I really wanted to run my fingers down his chest and stomach!

I turned to look at Nic, she started "Are you in love with all three of them? They are all brothers ya know."

I looked at her with a question on my face. "That's one good looking family I tell ya, they all have different physical charms, but no, not in love with all three, just in love with Jett." I said subtly and let out a breath of air. Just as the last word came out of my mouth Jett pushed the door open and turned around and glanced in my direction with his sexy smile showing all his straight perfect pearly whites.

"Oh ----- my ----- gosh ------! Did he hear me Nic?"

She laughed "I doubt it, I barely heard you. However the timing in which he turned around was spooky, like he did."

"Nooo." I said covering my mouth. "He couldn't have heard me he was pretty far away.... If he did hear me, I'm sure it's nothing he hasn't heard before. I'm sure lots of girls have said it to him or about him. Just look at him," I sighed, yet another incentive to get this Cale thing over with. All I knew was I'd fallen in love at first sight, I watched him walk out into the parking lot, and thought about his sculpted muscles that showed when he flexed.

Nic immediately said "Snap out of it girl, you need to focus on breaking up with Cale so you can move on."

"I know Nic, I tried but it just wasn't the right time, plus, he makes me nervous now. I'll do it tomorrow and if I don't tomorrow I'll do it over the phone, okay?"

"Good." Nic agreed.

Tall, dark and handsome. I couldn't get his smile out of my head all night. I couldn't study and I certainly couldn't sleep. That night I dreamt that Jett asked me out. I was hoping that this dream would come true.

The next night my dream wasn't as pleasant. I was having a

myriad of dreams. I saw the girl losing her bracelet, the truck rolling, and someone getting cut. I woke up at the usual time 3:17a.m., and couldn't go back to sleep.

The night after, I found myself hoping not to sleep, and it didn't come until after 1:00. It didn't take long to start the damned dreams again. I saw only flashes of things, nothing making sense. Someone running through heavy brush and their face getting whipped by branches, another of someone hopping into a pickup truck and slamming a door, a tall guy kisses an older lady, and then a man putting a baseball cap on. Me running but not being able to run fast enough or scream, that being typical dream stuff for everyone, I think. Then another flash of me, I was lost. I wasn't able to find my way in the daytime. Weird, weird stuff. I woke again at 3:17a.m. That was it for sleeping that night.

I was exhausted. I got to Art class and Nic told me I looked horrible. At least it was Friday, maybe I could catch up on sleep this weekend. Halfway through class I finally lifted my head off my desk and in walked Cale. He glowered at me untrustingly, causing my heart to race a million miles a minute. I swallowed hard and felt the lump go down my throat. I put my hand on Nic's arm slowly and squeezed it, not taking my eyes off of Cale, he didn't look away from me either. "It was him." I said steadily to Nic. Cale walked over to Topher and started talking to him like nothing happened.

"What was him?" she asked.

"That night at the house, the injured guy inside the house, it was Cale. I wasn't positive it was him, at least not at first. I wasn't sure until now, did you see the look he just gave me? The only thing I could have done to deserve that look was spy on him and get caught.... One more thing, when we were doing the army crawl, I think I saw the bracelet."

"Why didn't you tell me? We could have gone back to get it."

"That's exactly why I didn't tell you. We can't mess with that, what if Cale's the one who killed Jewel?"

"He's a high school kid, he didn't kill anyone. Just because you think you saw her killed at that house doesn't mean Cale killed her, maybe they rent the house and the owners killed her."

"Doesn't matter who, you want to go back to a murderers house to get a bracelet, and then what?"

"Right, well we have to do something."

Cale walked up to my desk slowly and put both hands on either

3:17 a.m. ...the waking hour

side. My palms became clammy, my throat tightened and my heart raced instantly. "So how are you girls doing? Did you have *fun* last weekend?" he said stiffly giving us a more serious look than social.

"It was all right, we had fun, we hung out at Addie's house and stuff... and you?" Nic said cautiously. I just pressed my lips together and avoided eye contact, it's hard to avoid when you want to.

"We had some trespassers this weekend, it's always disheartening when your trust has been betrayed."

"I know." I said finally looking him in the eye. "I thought you rented," my voice said dryly, I cleared my throat "...an apartment?" He let the corner of his mouth flash a glimmer of felicity, and then it was gone. He turned around and left. I hadn't planned on saying anything but my mouth has a mind of its own obviously.

Nic suggested I break up with Cale immediately. No duh, I thought. When I looked up Cale was in the doorway peering at me and nodded his head toward the hallway. "Maybe he'll do it for me." I said to Nic as I slid off my bar stool.

He was leaning up against the wall sliding his hand through his hair, I thought I would feel frightened around him, and although I was very nervous I wasn't scared. If he was going to hurt me he would have done it by now. His shirt had two buttons opened, it looked good on him. Of course, the first thing I asked him "Where did you get the scratch?" pointing to the open part of his shirt and pulling it sideways a bit.

He knocked my hand aside and said "Who knows, I was skiing." He said a little defensively, but then softened his tone right away "Sorry I didn't call, not much time for phone calls, besides it's not your thing right? I'll call you tonight maybe we'll catch a movie". He kissed me on the cheek and left and I let him. I watched him walk away and I didn't say a word to him, like 'Right skiing, I saw you this weekend, or don't bother calling, I'm busy or even 'Hey, I don't want to date any more I'm breaking up with you.' All good choices but not a one of them passed my lips. I hate good after thoughts.

I went back to my desk and put my head down. Nic asked me "Did you break up with him?"

"No" I said grumbling into my sleeve. Nic and I started an accelerated chat about Cale, and she offered to let Cale down gently for me and we talked about how and when I would do it. We went over my past dating history with Cale. And the real reasons I am calling it off were: What is he up to? How and why did I fall asleep on that one date? Why did I have marks on my arm after? Why don't I remember anything from that date? And why was he at that house sick when he was supposed to be off skiing?

When I got home from school I found a note from my mom. "Cale said sorry but he can't go out tonight he had to go out of town last minute. He'll see you in a couple of days."

Thank goodness! I went and fell face forward on my bed and didn't wake 'til morning.

CHAPTER 9

That Monday at school I couldn't wait to see him, I couldn't wait to catch a glimpse of his smile and see if he still looked as good to me today as he had before, I was focusing all my positive energy on Jett. I didn't know how to find him during the day or how I would see him, but I was going to try. We just started our second quarter of school and Nic and I stayed in Art Class but this time it was called Design. Cale had moved on which was nice so I didn't have to see him in any of my classes.

This morning we both talked about Cale and Jett in the lowest of whispers. I not only wanted to catch a glimpse of Jett, but I was supposed to break up with Cale today. Even so, I kept daydreaming about Jett all day but never did find him, I was disappointed.

Nic and I got to wrestling practice and did our normal routine. We cleaned the mats, put everything away and sat up against the wall as we usually did. All the usual wrestlers started coming out of the locker room and were warming up when Storm came over and chatted with us.

"Storm, how come you didn't tell me you had two other brothers just as good looking as you?" I said playfully. He looked at us with his gorgeous green eyes and said "I was hoping to keep you two for myself."

"Good answer." I replied in a higher octave.

"How nice of you to say," Nic agreed.

"Which one of you likes who?" Storm replied nonchalantly. He looked at me and asked "You like Jett? Of course you do, everyone likes Jett." Storm snarked.

I was quick to answer "I don't like either of them I was just making an observation. Don't get in a huff."

"Besides" Nic chimed in "You're dating Shelby, you shouldn't care." And on that note he stood up out of his squat laughing to himself and walked away.

"Why in creation is that so funny, I'm good girlfriend material." I said while making an iffy face at Nic, holding my hand out, tilting it side to side.

She smiled, "Oh I bet you are," with a little sarcasm.

I let out a long sigh "I don't.... I haven't told Cale yet, he just got back from his trip today and I didn't see him, for your information."

Nic gave me a look "I know - - whatever..." she retorted and walked away.

I knew I had to break up with Cale tomorrow; it was the right thing to do. Cale, Cale, Cale, thinking about him and trying to break up with him was exhausting. I'm sure he knows it's over himself. I thought I should do it right after Algebra, because that class was on the same floor as his locker. Nic and I plotted, she offered her help.

To my surprise, when I walked out of Art class Cale was waiting for me; we didn't speak at first. I started walking, he grabbed my hand which threw me off guard. I told him I needed something from my locker so we passed my history class, and kept walking.

"I need to talk to you about something." I started off a little shaky. He let go of my hand and slid it up my back to my shoulder and said "Oh yeah," in a low soft voice. I was hoping I had the courage to continue as I choked back the lump in my throat, looking at the floor for wisdom. But standing right in front of my locker stood Jett and some of his friends, my heart plummeted. I just stood there, rooted, looking at Jett and his friends, Jett was leaning on my locker, I wasn't moving or talking.

Cale broke the ice "Uh, excuse us, we need to get in there." I thought I heard a growl. I looked around at Jett and his friends not sure who made the noise, not sure if anyone else heard it besides

3:17 a.m. ...the waking hour

me. They all moved. Cale put his hand under my elbow I turned around so my back was to my locker. Cale slid his hand to mine.

"Can we talk later?" He asked. I cleared my throat and sent back a shaky "Uh, yeah" and nodded. Thank goodness, because I couldn't get any other words to escape from my lips. He leaned in and kissed me on the mouth, pressed generously until our lips parted. I let my eyes fall closed, it felt cold and manipulative and I felt watched. When we were done I couldn't look at Cale so I looked over and noticed Jett was looking right at me, leaning against the wall opposite me with one leg bent and his hands in his pockets. As I caught his gaze he did a half nod of acknowledgment to me, and turned into the classroom he was standing next to.

I finally got to my class and sat down. My face was flushed, my hands were clammy and my heart still rushing at a fast pace. I could hear it pitter-patter, pitter-patter. I was a little too preoccupied to pay attention to the lecture. I had to figure out when my next chance would be to talk to Cale, because he now knew something was up, he kissed me, what was that all about. Algebra, I remembered was on the same floor as his locker. It'll have to be after algebra…

I thought Storm wasn't talking to me again, but he leaned over in his chair and whispered "I thought you weren't interested in Jett."

"I'm not interested in him! I'm trying to break up with Cale! What's it to you anyway?" I stammered. I was trying to figure out how he might know I was interested in Jett, interested is a strong word though, I was definitely crushing on him. I only told Nic and I was sure she wouldn't tell anyone else.

"Well, if you're not interested in him then I'll let him know."

"Let him know? Why would you need to let him know? Better yet, why don't you keep your nose in your own business, if Jett has any questions for me you can send him on over to me." That shut him up. He seemed to swallow that explanation hook, line and sinker. Although, *now* he wasn't speaking to me, I could tell by the way he was sitting. I had one thought, Declan. I had asked him about Jett and Declan was good for gossip that's for sure.

After Algebra, I rounded the corner to Cale's locker and there was Nic talking to Cale. I stopped cold in my tracks, oh crap, was she breaking up with him for me? I quickly turned around started walking back the way I came, as fast as I could and 'BAM'. I walked right into Jett. "Crap" I said quickly then stammered out a "Sorry." He smiled at me and said "In a hurry?" and everything stopped as we looked at each other. It felt like an eternity, but undoubtedly was only a few seconds. I was dazed by his gorgeous smile, dimples, not dots but that second crease running along his smile line; perfectly straight teeth and that twinkle in his eye. How embarrassing, my face flushed, I said a quick "Yes, excuse me."

I ran for the stairs and tripped going up them, dropping all my books. Someone helped me pick them up but I couldn't even look them in the eye. I said a quick "thanks" and kept going. I was mortified – I didn't break up with Cale, Nic did it (I think), I literally ran into Jett and then I tripped going up the stairs. Who does that? I hope Jett didn't see me in all my glory.

I got to the top of the stairs. My shin was killing me and I gave it a little rub, I could already feel the knot. I was almost running to Home Ec, Nic and I had decided to take Home Ec right before lunch so we could eat all the stuff we made. I got there and of course she wasn't. I sat down and just started fidgeting and checking the door every few seconds. I don't remember confirming the need for her help to break up with Cale for me, but why else would she be talking to him. Did I tell her it was okay to help me? Did I tell her to break up for me? Oh my gosh, I wonder if he's mad because she did my dirty work for me? Calm down a little. If she did break up with him for me, on the bright side, the task is done. I'm sure it's done and because for some reason I know she did it. Now I just have to worry about him being mad at me because I didn't do it myself. Worst case scenario, if she didn't tell him, I can do it right before lunch if I can find him.

She walked in the classroom and stopped at the first table to chat. I quickly went over there and gave her big eyes, nodding toward our seats trying to tell her she has more important things to talk to me about. She smiled and I walked back to our table and started pacing.

"So what were you talking to Cale about?"

"He called me over and asked me what was up with you so I told him you wanted to break up…. I figured why lie."

"That's what I like about you, you're so direct. What else?" I was talking quickly.

"He said he understood but his jaw got tight and he seemed real tense. And then he told me to tell you no hard feelings."

"I find that hard to believe for some reason. I tried breaking up with him this morning but we ran into Jett at my locker and I froze." So I told her the whole sordid affair, even the part where '*I ran*' into Jett after Algebra. She started to laugh, so I pulled up my jeans and showed her the huge mark on my shin; it was shiny and red in the middle and already beginning to bruise. Plus, it broke open the first couple layers of skin but wasn't bleeding. We both said "Ooooo," at the sight of it. Our Home Ec teacher, who was lecturing, came over took a look at my leg because she heard us "ooooo" and kept talking, turned around, got a bag, filled it with ice and handed it to me never stopping her lecture. It did help.

Cale didn't show up for school that Friday and he didn't call me either. I felt bad, maybe I should have still talked to him myself. Nic said that doing it over the phone was lame but I bet having your friend do it for you was even worse. Now I wished I hadn't chickened out – or I wish that Nic wasn't there after Algebra, maybe I would have still gone up to him. In any case, it's done.

My parents dropped us off at the football game, it was fun. No messages or any drama, just fun. After, at the bonfire, Storm offered to give Nic and me a ride home. All we had to do was wait for his brothers.

Kyle and Jett came out of the locker room, hair wet and bags in hand. They didn't look too happy when they saw us standing with Storm, and when he told them we needed a ride home, they were definitely pissed off. Jett was extra grouchy because he fumbled the ball once, plus they lost. Yep, Jett's on the football team which I hadn't noticed before. He still looked hot, bad mood or not. Storm, Nic and I sat in back and we acted like the other two weren't even there, chatting about this and that. I told Kyle he could turn around at the bottom of my driveway. So he pulled all the way to the bottom. It was large enough to park a few cars.

My parents and some friends were on the porch having a few drinks. I got out and yelled "Hi mom," our porch was one story up; my mom replied back over the railing "Tell those boys to get up here and eat this food so I don't have to put it away."

I asked Storm if he was hungry and he shrugged and nodded toward the other two. I knocked on the window on Jett's side, he looked very grumpy but he rolled his window down and I nodded toward Kyle in the driver's seat and asked "You want some food and beer?" That put a glimmer in his eye and a he gave me a half smile. "Come on we'll make you some plates" I said. Jett kinda grumbled. I didn't care about his attitude this second so I leaned through his window, across him, and turned the car off and kept the keys. Kyle got out lickedy split, I opened Jett's door and said "Come on grouch, maybe food will make you feel better."

I introduced the three boys, explaining that they were on the football team. Storm on the freshman team and the other two on varsity. My parents asked for my program and made them sign it in case they were ever famous. The boys perked up after they had some food, I put the keys in the middle of the table. My sister and Alec came walking up the steps.

My dad looked at me and said "You wanna play some ball with your old man?" I looked at him and shrugged "Sure."

Kyle and Jett looked at him like *"really."* "Don't worry boys, you don't need to play, I need you to polish Mrs. Gellar's food off so she, I mean so we, don't have to put it away. Nic, Tori and Alec get down to the field, I'll get Kit." My dad went into the house, turned on our flood lights that lit up our very large side yard and retrieved Kit. When we girls got there Storm was behind us. The teams were Storm, Tori and I against Nic, Kit and my dad. Storm complained "These aren't fair teams…"

"Don't worry, Nic stinks and I'm faster than my brother, plus Tori plays dirty" I said with a raise of my brow.

We played a couple of plays and Storm, Tori and I did well, we were winning. Alec came out a few minutes later, followed by Kyle and Jett. My dad chuckled and turned to the boys and said "This is touch football, do you know how to play *touch* football?" being facetious. They both smiled cheerfully and said "Yeah." Storm and I got Kyle and my dad got Jett and Alec. Storm looked at me, like he was going to say these aren't fair teams but I told him reassuringly not to worry. He gave me a crooked smile and I said "Trust me - -" all I could think was those damn McGaven boys have nice smiles.

We huddled up, the play was to pass to me so I got to the front line, Alec was covering Tori, Nic and Kit were on Storm, Jett was to cover me, I looked up and said "Hey! This is not fair..." Jett interrupted with "Chicken!" and a smile. The food must have worked.

"Look here boy" I replied "I bet you're really tired from all that

3:17 a.m. ...the waking hour

playin' you did tonight..."

"Hut1," Kyle exclaimed, "Hut2....Hut3." I shoulder checked Jett off the line and took off. Tori just grabbed Alec at the knees and he, being too afraid of hurting her, went down. Storm actually had Nic and Kit on him like glue and my dad was trying to rush Kyle. I ran up and then bolted two steps right and then rolled left losing Jett for a second. Kyle threw the ball and I made a touch down!!!!!

"Whew" we yelled and Jett just looked at me and gave me a slight body check walking by and I said "What do you think of that old man." Everyone laughed, Jett was smiling too.

We were up fourteen points and about to huddle up one last time when I noticed a dark truck driving by the front of our house, really slow. I stopped to stare, and then Storm came by my side and Kyle on the other. We all watched the truck and we started walking toward it - as soon as it came upon the driveway they must have noticed us and sped up, taking off down the road. Storm turned to me and said "Is that your lover boy???"

I shrugged my shoulders "I don't think so, he doesn't have a truck like that as far as I know. And he's not *my lover boy anymore.*" I said exaggeratedly. Giving Nic a high five saying "Yeah!" Nic said "It sure looked like him from afar though." I was a little wary of Cale ever since I saw him in that house. I looked at Storm with worried eyes and he gave me a dirty look back. "What?" I said and I pushed him. "I broke up with him! Sorry he knows where I live!" I ran up behind him and grabbed him around his shoulders bringing him down for a soft tackle.

"Addie" my dad said "Don't hurt the boys." Jett and Kyle of course gave a laugh and called out some names to Storm. I rolled on top, kissed him on the cheek and ran behind Kyle.

"Don't use me as a shield girl," Kyle said "You started it." He stepped left leaving Storm and I face to face. I held my arm on his chest holding him arm's length away, leaning forward. We were both laughing.

"Storm..." I warned, "My dad is here and this flirting... Shelby won't like it." He stood up, stopping the commotion, then grabbed me around the neck and knuckle rubbed my head. The game continued. We covered the same guys who covered us before, giving me Jett. The good thing was the boys were afraid of hurting the girls and Tori and I knew it, so we took full advantage. Tori and I gave each other a nod, we had a plan.

We lined up, I actually touched Jett's shoulder and said "I saw you limping earlier are you hurt is that your excuse for not being able to run fast." He brushed my hand off his shoulder "You can't touch me, it's illegal." I replied "You don't like girls." He straightened up. My dad yelled "hike." I tackled and rolled into his legs, Tori doing the same to Alec, both boys hitting the ground and my dad started laughing. Storm and Kyle were covering Nic and Kit. When my sister and I headed toward my dad, he started laughing more, and we two hand touched him right before he threw the ball away. My dad was laughing so hard he started crying, contagiously making everyone else laugh with him.

Everyone was out of breath and in a great mood. My dad called the game. We won! Storm was happy. "You didn't tell me *you and your* sister played dirty, glad you were on my team." I gave him a wink.

"Those boys sure can eat." My mom said as we got back to the deck, she was re-warming some food on the grill. We hung out and chatted all night, the boys ended up leaving around two in the morning. That was the latest any of my friends had ever stayed. Maybe things are changing because we're in High School now. As Nic and I walked the boys to their car, Nic pointed to the street across the way down a couple blocks. The same truck as before was parked with its lights off.

The wrestling room was a little more crowded than usual when they started warm ups today. It looked like they had more newcomers. Nic and I were conversing effortlessly when the coach startled us by yelling at a newcomer who was late to practice. We both looked up and to my surprise my stomach dropped, my face went flush immediately, and my heart accelerated. I felt weak. I had to get up "Nic, I'm going to the bathroom." Everyone saw me get up in a hurry and I darted out the door to the nearest bathroom, down the hall just around the corner. Nic followed. "What's wrong Addie?" she asked "What's wrong?"

I rinsed my face with cold water and dabbed it dry with a paper towel. "Was that Jett who came in the wrestling room? I swear it was him. I can't go back in there."

"Why not?"

"I don't know, as soon as I saw Jett, my heart started to race and my hands got all clammy."

3:17 a.m. ...the waking hour

"Girl you got it bad, but why are you acting so weird we just played football with him Friday?'

I paused, I had none of my usual come backs right now. "Maybe it was just because I didn't expect him...... so what is Jett doing in wrestling? He's never been there before." I asked Nic very concerned.

"He must not have been able to come before because of football. I heard the football players can either do weights, run or wrestling practice since the last game is this Friday."

"Ugh" Could this be true? Jett on the wrestling team, of course it could. Nic and I took our time. We chatted in the dim hallway right outside the bathroom, like I said, I don't like hanging out in bathrooms.

As we were talking all nonchalantly I glanced down the corridor and grabbed Nic's arm. There was someone standing at the end of the hall, a light was on behind them but the hallway between us and them was dark. We could see a silhouette standing with his feet spread and his arms held slightly away from his body. A second shorter silhouette appeared next to him, both seemed to be in hooded sweatshirts.

Nic said "I swear they are looking our way..." and backed up a few steps and so did I. Nic shouted "Hey!"

They started walking toward us "Did you just hear a growl?" I asked Nic as we took a few more steps backward. She grabbed my hand "Uh huh!" We looked at each other and ran, turned the corner and ran down to the double doors to the wrestling room. We tugged and pulled on the handles to the gym doors but they wouldn't open. Suddenly, one side clicked open. We pushed ourselves inside, pushing Declan aside, and we pulled them shut and held them closed.

There we stood holding the doors shut panting from being chased when I noticed how awfully quiet it was, I nudged Nic, we both turned around keeping our hands on the handles. Everyone had stopped what they were doing and all eyes were on us. Declan was smiling, like it figures, we were always getting into trouble. Nic's face was void of any color and I bet mine was too. We let go of the door handles slowly.

Coach yelled, "What are you two ladies up to?"

"Uh, they were, um, chasing us?" I said pointing my hand back toward the hall. "They growled at us." Nic added and I shook my head in agreement. There was a low rumble of amusement in the room. The coach walked over to us, we moved aside. He pushed open the door and stepped out into the hallway, he yelled "Hey, you two come here." He dropped his clipboard and was running after them. He was down the hall in a flash with Declan and Storm on his heels. I held the door open and a couple other wrestlers followed, including Jett. When they got to the end of the corridor they stopped, just peering down its end.

Coach threw his hands up and said "Back to work guys." By the time they trekked back up the hall, my hands were no longer trembling and I felt warmth returning to my face. When they re-entered the wrestling room they all gave us a look though, especially Jett.

We sat down in our usual spot and everything went back to normal, like nothing had happened, so we did the same. After all the wrestlers were in action coach came up to us and asked if we knew who had chased us. Unfortunately neither of us did, so we both said no. However, I had a sneaking suspicion…..

I went into a little bit of a trance just watching Jett wrestle; I couldn't really hear Nic either. I was just watching him swirl his body around his opponent and then locking his arms around the other wrestlers arm and neck until his grip was broken. Then he would move around again and try another hold. When his arms would lock they would flex and show every line of muscle. It was a thing of beauty. I could tell they weren't really going at it; it was more of a warm up wrestling match, trying different moves. I could still hear Nic mumbling in the background and I thought I better pay her a bit of attention before she gets mad. She said "I'll do it tomorrow." So I replied "okay Scarlet" so as not to hurt her feelings.

I was hoping I could catch a glimpse of him after his shower so I could see him in his leather coat with no shirt and his hair tousled again, but my mom picked me up before any of the wrestlers came out. I was disappointed, especially because my mom usually runs late. I said good bye to Nic and took off.

When I woke the next morning, I remembered my dream; I was running away from my wolf, this time we took a different route. It chased me in the woods, and then in the sand, I kept running and running. It was a never ending dream that wouldn't stop no matter how fast I ran or what I did. I was looking for the dirty slide to end

3:17 a.m. ...the waking hour

the chase, when I found it and ran half way up a man grabbed me from behind and tried biting my neck. My wolf barred his teeth and jumped on his back loosening his grip but not before we tumbled to the bottom of the ravine. I got up ran to the top of the slide. I looked back at them and I could see their eyes and fangs glistening in the moonlight. I didn't wake up at 3:17a.m. which was a relief. However, it was one of those dreams that left an impression on me, one I wouldn't forget, at least not anytime soon.

Things don't seem to happen in the dead of night they all happen just before dusk and when I wake from my dreams, the waking hour.

CHAPTER 10

I was proud of myself when I got through practice the next day without blushing or being embarrassed. When the wrestlers started to get up to leave, Declan, my supposed friend and confidant for the past two years, said very loudly across the practice room, "Hey Addie, I heard you broke up with Cale."

The hair on the back of my neck stood up, I was in a little bit of shock. How do rumors travel so fast? I stood up brushed off my pants and replied "Wow, how did you hear that already?" We walked toward each other, very grateful for any kind of distraction, even if it was walking toward the problem.

"Why did you break up with him?" Declan asked.

I shushed him "Can you keep it down. He really wasn't my type." I said in a softer voice and, now that I thought about it, he really wasn't. "Why are you so interested?"

"Just curious, since I got my own car I've been driving to school and we haven't really chatted lately."

"Hmm" was all I said and I started walking to the doors with him slowly.

"Did you know you are the first girl in history to ever break up with Cale Winters? It's awesome! A lot of us guys loved hearing it."

"I didn't break up with him because it's a game to me you know; I didn't intend to hurt him and I certainly didn't want to be the first one to break up with him. He just was sort of boring, so serious all the time." I heard a little chuckle behind me. I turned and noticed none of the other wrestlers were talking; they were all trying to chime in on our conversation. I said to all of them "Guys are the worst gossips I swear! Mind your own business, besides, I'm sure Declan will give you a full play-by-play in the locker room." I waved them on to pass us.

As the wrestlers were filtering out of the room, I happened to lock eyes with Jett just for a moment. Declan made sure everyone was out of ear shot and asked me straight out "Did you break up with Cale because of Jett?"

"What do you mean?" I asked "Why would I do that? I don't even know Jett, I've met him once."

"Well I heard you broke it off with Cale, and I noticed you around Jett so I put two and two together."

"You noticed me huh. That obvious?"

"Oh yeah, she's crushing on Jett." Nic said walking toward us.

"Declan, I really don't want to talk about this with you, I don't want rumors floating around the locker room. And I didn't just break up with Cale to go after Jett. I know you're going right back in that locker room to tell the guys everything, to give them the scoop." I felt a tingle at the back of my neck, my senses were perking up.

"I promise I won't tell them anything you tell me about Jett, and I apologize for that too.... *but*..... I gotta tell them all about Cale, it's just too funny and juicy to keep to myself. I'm asking as a friend, besides I'm friends with Jett. I can put a good word in for ya.... ya know he asked about you."

"What? What did he say? And what are you apologizing for? Is that how Storm knew....?" I asked slowly and cautiously. "Huh, Declan!" I put my hand over my mouth, I shouldn't have been shocked but I knew; he was my leak.

"I thought you liked him..."

I just smiled. "Well that doesn't mean you go tell the whole school, and shouldn't you have checked with me first. Maybe find out for a fact that I really liked him before blabbing to people."

"I apologized for that and from now on, I promise I'll check in with you first, but it wasn't like I planned on telling anyone. Storm and I were just having a conversation and it came up. I promise it won't happen again." Declan seemed sincere about it.

Nic added "If we can't trust you Declan, we can't tell you

anything and you won't get any more of these," she gave us a group hug. Declan crossed his heart after.

"So do you wanna know what Jett said or what?" Declan said grinning.

"Absolutely!" Nic responded.

My face lit up waiting for Declan to continue.

"He asked if I knew who you were and I told him you were dating Cale but I guess you aren't now so I could give him an update and I'll tell him anything you want me to tell him." He said quickly without taking a breath. I saw Nic shaking her head in the background.

Nic said, "That's all he said.... I guess, at least he asked about you."

"Well... because I don't want to come off as a little school girl that gossips all the time, kinda like you." I said as I looked at Declan squinting my eyes smartly. "You can tell Jett and all the guys that I broke it off with Cale because he just wasn't my type. And tell Jett, if he needs to know anything else about me to come right up and ask me himself, I won't bite."

Declan laughed and pleaded for juicy gossip one more time, but I didn't want any more rumors flying around than necessary. Even though I would like to tell him the whole low down on Cale, I have enough issues with him already as it is. I may be sarcastic, but I'm not a mean or vindictive person. I would never try to hurt someone on purpose.

Declan pleaded with Nic and she patted him on the shoulder and said "Sorry but that's all you get for now." As Declan headed for the lockers, Nic said loudly "But you can tell him she's nice...and funny too!" He just waved his hand back at us.

Nic came up to me "You handled that very well. Since our break up with Cale I think we have both matured." We laughed, locked the supply closet, locked both gym doors and went to wait in the lobby to give the keys back to Coach. He came out promptly.

That Friday I started feeling on edge and a little tense. Today is our homecoming game, but that's not why. This is the first year for it, but our school decided to sell roses as a fund raising event, I can't help wonder if Cale and Topher didn't help get this started. Guys or girls can buy a rose for a dollar and have it messengered to

3:17 a.m. ...the waking hour

any student in any class. Each color rose means something different, red meant love, yellow friends, pink sweethearts and white means you have a secret admirer. Nic received a pink one from Topher which I thought was sweet, since the two of them still talked from time to time. I thought they should date but they obviously didn't think so. I received one red rose in every single class, too bad they were from Cale. I have no idea what he's up to but he's making me feel uneasy.

After school, I showed Nic all eight of my red roses before I deposited them into the garbage. "You know I had a dream I got a bunch of red roses once."

"Oh yeah," Nic replied as we headed for the buses. What a good friend she was for helping me through all this, I would definitely have to return the favor.

Nic and I were holding up the fence near the end zone, as usual, during our last home football game of the season. We were finalizing our plans for the homecoming dance tomorrow; we were going with a group of friends. The field was pretty crowded, everyone we knew from school was at the game. Storm and Shelby stopped to chat with us when Cale and an older girl walked up to us; Cale asked if he could talk to me. I looked at him and shrugged a shoulder.

He led me toward the guest side, it was a little more secluded. I hoped this wasn't going to take long, of all places for Cale to show up – he never comes to the games.

The weather was nice, I had a t-shirt on and a sweatshirt tied around my waist. I noticed Cale was in long sleeves and now that I think about it he always wore long sleeves. He was still dressed cool – wearing the same type of clothes he did in school, so he looked good, unlike the grandpa I dated. His hair was getting darker, no doubt from lack of sun and his eyes were very blue today with a darkness encircling them. I never noticed his eyes being blue before, just soft tones of grey.

I crossed my arms and looked down at my feet. There was a bit of a pause and he finally started speaking, "I think we should still go out."

I looked up at him in surprise. "Really why?"

"Because I really care for you and we're good together."

I was shocked. "We're good together? Cale you and I both

know there is no chemistry between us, and sure, we're good as friends, but that's it."

"Why didn't you break up with me? Why did you have Nic do it?" I looked him right in the eyes they seemed a little wild tonight.

I dropped my eyes and said with no emotion, trying to keep the peace. "I tried breaking it off with you a couple of times and Nic was upset with me that I hadn't followed through so she said she'd help. Plus, I'm not a real fan of hurting people's feelings."

"I had no idea you felt this way." His face tightened, his jaw flexed. "I want you to come with me, I need to show you."

"Show me what?"

He stepped closer to me and went to kiss me on the lips and I turned my cheek. With a little more enthusiasm I said "You'll show me what? That you do everything better than me? Forget it Cale, we're done."

Under his breath, "No one's ever broken it off with me before!" He was hurt you could tell and he was getting agitated. He was upset I broke up with him sure, but only because I broke it off? Whatever!

Me and my mouth had to keep going "Oh, so sorry I was the first girl to ever break up with you Cale, but that's why you're mad and want me back!" I was almost yelling at him now. "I felt nothing from you, we have nothing in common, there is nothing between us Cale." I said pointing back and forth between the two of us. Trying to calm down with each word.

Well technically, I didn't break up with him, Nic did, but it was by my hand, my idea, I wanted it. Technically, maybe he needed to hear it from me, so maybe tonight would be it. "Cale we're done. I don't want to see you anymore. I'm sorry, now please leave. I know you hate coming to the football games anyway." I said shaking my head looking down at the ground again.

I didn't see him coming toward me right away. He grabbed my arm and said he wanted to talk to me alone, pulling me toward the gate. I pulled my arm loose and he tried grabbing both arms, but as he went to grab me I pulled away again. When he finally got hold of me, with his face so close to mine, he said under his breath, "You're coming with me!" He was gritting his teeth, his eyes full of rage and excitement. I pushed my hands together, up toward the sky and then outward breaking his hold on me. Without thinking about it I moved both arms back and with a huge sweeping movement forward, stepping into it at the same time, I shoved him right in the abdomen with such precision and fluidity you would have thought I had training. I had no idea what I was doing, it was purely an automatic reflex and adrenaline. I didn't think I pushed him that hard but he went flying back a few feet and landed on his ass. His friend lunged toward me but I stepped back and sideways, gave a little shove, and she stumbled into the fence.

I yelled at him, looking him right in the eyes, getting closer with each word. "Tell me why you still want me! Tell me why you were so distant when we dated! Tell me what's different now!"

Cale, as he pulled himself up said "I'm glad to see Logan didn't break you, you still have a lot of fight left in you. And in the eyes of death, even as a human, you were fearless."

I swallowed hard and looked at him in confusion. "What?" came out of my mouth, weak and exasperated, I was confused.

"I didn't push you," Cale said "I was going slowly for you, but I see I was wrong. You're stronger than I thought. Even though your brother saved you, I wonder if you really needed the help. I was going to step in but Kit saved the day."

"What? What are you saying? You were there?" I asked, shaken by the possibility that he knew all along, or that he witnessed *it*.

"I have feelings for you now, I need you for more than just love." Cale said tapping his heart with his hand.

I turned around, people were starting to gather so I wiped my tears and backed up. I felt Nic put her hand on my shoulder. I looked back at Cale, and out of the corner of his mouth glimpsed a look of sheer devious pleasure, it sent a cold, revolting feeling down my spine. I took Nic's hand and she weaved us in and out of the crowd as quickly as possible until we were almost to the other side of the field, yet still with a crowd of people to surround us.

Nic said "What did you do?" She sounded upset and froze for a minute and said "You knocked him down and now he'll be maaaad..." She started to cry, no, wait a minute, she was laughing. "You knocked Cale Winters on his ass!" She laughed some more and it was contagious! As upset as I was, I couldn't help but let loose with a chuckle.

And my laugh then turned into tears. "Did you hear what he said? Did you tell anyone? I never told anyone about..."

"No Addie! I never told a soul, I never told anyone. Logan may have told people he was in love with you but I highly doubt he told anyone that he sexually assaulted you." There was silence between us. "What I do know is that Cale is one messed up crazy person and he is obsessed with you for some reason." Nic explained.

I put my trembling hands to my face and wiped away my tears. "That night there was someone on the front lawn, do you think...." was all I said. This has turned into such a nightmare.

I leaned on the fence trying to spot Cale and his girlfriend, or whoever she was, but I didn't see them. So I scanned the parking lot hoping they were leaving and straight across from us, behind the guest side bleachers, I saw them and they were kissing! He backed her off right away, but I swear I saw her kiss him. They got in a truck that I knew, that I'd seen before, it looked very familiar. It was dark, black or navy blue, and old, with big nubby tires and it was all dented up.

Nic touched my shoulder and I just about jumped out of my skin. She scooted up next to me and I nodded toward the parking lot, pointing. "That's Cale and that girl, I think she's his girlfriend, I saw them kiss."

Nic covered her mouth "The truck from your dreams…" I nodded, she's very smart and catches on quickly "If that's his girlfriend then why did he feel the need to come looking for you, I mean why would he need you as a girlfriend? "

I looked at her and said "Exactly!"

"Maybe that girl wants to be his girlfriend and he has no interest in her, but then again I didn't get that feeling."

"Weird, very weird." I murmured.

They hadn't pulled out yet, they seemed to be arguing. He grabbed something from behind his seat and put it on his head, it looked like a dark colored cap. I got that eerie feeling I get when a dream I've had was about to come true. It was so intense it knocked me back a few steps and my knees went weak. "I know that hat." I don't remember thinking of saying that or how the words passed my lips, but it was true; something about that hat was familiar.

Halftime was about to start and I wanted to see the guys come off the field, so Nic and I headed back to the end of the field where the field house and concession stands were located. The gates opened to let the players off the field. Although, I didn't expect him to acknowledge me, I knew he would put me in a good mood just seeing Jett.

The whole team started jogging toward the gates, he didn't notice us and I barely caught a glimpse of him, he was in the middle of the swarm of football players. I was trying to play it cool, you know, not eyeballing the team directly, but looking at the stands and concession stand and then looking at the team and trying not to stare a hole through anyone. We went to get a soda from the snack bar and it took a while, I was glad for any distraction.

We ventured back over to the opening in the fence. I turned to Nic and asked if she cared if we held up the fence for a while. She knew why we were here; the good thing about best friends is you don't have to explain everything to them because they get you. She replied "Of course not, that's what friends do and you'll obviously have to return the favor someday." I said "Absolutely!" We stood there in silence for a bit when we were joined by Shelby. The three of us didn't move the entire half-time, we watched the hand-made floats the seniors made go by, the marching band and finally our cheerleaders who made the crowd go crazy.

As the team was walking back to the gate to enter the field I spotted Jett, his hair all disheveled just like the day I saw him in the school lobby. And it made me smile. Storm walked up behind us, put his hand on our shoulders and said half laughing "Good job Addie, way to end it with Cale!" As quickly as he said it he was gone. He had his brother's red leather coat on, and it reminded me of the first time I saw Jett. Storm had some room to grow into it. Nic had to explain the Cale thing to Shelby.

As the players were going through the gate Declan came up to us, studied me, his lips drawn into a thin line which grew into a smile, "Nice job with Cale, I heard you knocked him down."

"How did you hear that already?" Nic asked.

"You're the story of the night!"

"Nice!" Nic said in an upbeat tone. Then we gave him a quick version of what happened.

"Well, if you run into trouble you come get me or any of the wrestlers. You know your kind of *our girls* now and any one of us would help you out." He walked out onto the field, and stood behind the team. Yeah you know he was reporting back to them on what happened. I wonder if my parents were getting wind of this, as they were at the game tonight.

We found my parents in the stands, wondering what they would say about all this, and my dad started laughing. He said "I heard you're beating up boys again."

"What!" I retorted.

"Kit told me you hit a boy in the gut and he went flying." He was still laughing and holding his gut.

"Oh that..." I said "I think I just caught him off guard."

On that note, Nic and I went to walk over toward the entrance, "You were being a bit modest weren't you?" Nic asked. I just shrugged my shoulders.

Two Richfield police cars pulled up to the gate, one marked and one unmarked, no lights though. Four guys got out, two plain clothed and two in uniform to match their cars. They went to the gate and chatted up Nurse Melinda who was manning the booth at the entrance. We walked a little closer; Nurse Melinda came out and pointed to Nic and me. I wondered if they had questions for us or any 'ole students in general.

"I didn't think they'd come here." Nic said.

"Who, the police? You know why they're here?" I looked at Nic "Oh No! What did you do?"

"I told you at practice the other day, you know, after the hallway thing, that I was going to give the police all the info we could on Cale. I told you I'd do it the next day, you said okay, so I did. And I didn't mention it to you afterward because they looked at me like I was crazy. Plus, I thought you had enough on your mind – sooo – I didn't report back to you."

"What did you tell them?" I said out of the corner of my mouth as I watched them walk directly toward us.

"Just the clues, not that you dreamt it." She said in a panic.

"I didn't agree to this."

"Well, that's not what you said before!" She exclaimed.

I thought I would have been more nervous but found myself checking out the cop in jeans, cowboy boots, a black leather jacket and brown wavy hair. He was a big guy, tall, looked ruggedly handsome with green eyes, he looked familiar but I couldn't place him. It looked like he hadn't shaved in a couple of days but it definitely looked good on him. "Oh lordy is he hot." I'm not sure if those words passed my lips or Nic's, but he was hot.

He looked like he was just out of college. He walked right up

3:17 a.m. ...the waking hour

and introduced himself "I'm Detective Grey and this is Detective O'Connor." We shook their hands and said "Nice to meet you, I'm Addie Gellar and I guess you've met Nicole Newland," I said pointing toward her. They shook her hand and introduced themselves and said "No we haven't met yet."

"Do you ladies have a few minutes so we can ask you some questions?" Detective Grey asked. We both shook our heads. "We aren't charging you with anything nor do we plan to, so there is no need for adult supervision or a lawyer. We just want to ask some questions."

Nic and I looked at each other and agreed. I looked behind him, the policemen in uniform were chatting, looked pretty casual. Without moving his feet Detective Grey twisted around to see what I was looking at.

"Protocol." he announced.

"Hmm." I said. Checking him out as I said it.

"Detective Grey smiled and looked down, giving us an '*Awe shucks moment.*' "Ma'am....."

I interrupted "Ew, Ma'am is for my mom." My smart mouth said.

"Sorry," he looked down at his pad of paper "May I call you Addie?"

"Well that's my given name, so anything else would be inappropriate. And that's the last sarcastic remark I'll make." I said smiling.

Nic interrupted, thank goodness, "She's very sarcastic and just can't help herself, she gets that way when... well all the time." I nudged her.

They asked us questions for about half an hour and only finished with us five minutes before the game was over. However, they asked why Nic went in to the station to talk to an officer and not me.

Then they asked us if we were eye witnesses to any of the incidents we told them about, of course we had to say no, we weren't. They asked us questions that verified the information that Nic gave them. Since she looked at me for every answer and I answered most questions, I think they knew something was up. Another question they had for us was how we came about the leads and information that we gave them.

Nic nudged me "They said leads".

"So we helped you get leads on the investigation?" Nic said nudging me in the ribs again "Good job Addie." I let out an exasperated breath, now they're gonna find out I'm a whack job – I'll have to tell them how I know.

Detective Grey asked if he could talk to me alone and he put his hand on my shoulder and we walked only a few steps away, I turned around and gave Nic a wink, she gave me the thumbs up. Detective O'Connor just rolled his eyes.

"So Addie, I have a feeling you're the one who came up with all the information we received from Nic. I need to know your source so we can get to the bottom of our investigations." Now that I was looking at him, I realized, if he didn't have that scruff on his face he actually didn't look that much older than us.

I crossed my arms and thought for a minute, "Aren't I allowed to be kind of like a reporter who reports information to you and I keep my sources confidential?" I started talking slowly but picked up speed as my thoughts formed. "I mean, if I tell you my source maybe it'll dry up.... and I'm certain they won't talk to you. And then my reporting days would be over."

I was watching his facial expression and he didn't seem bothered by this too badly. He rubbed his chin with a finger and thumb on either side. "Are there any other details that we didn't cover that we need to know about?" Grey asked.

"Besides the location of Jewel's bracelet? No." I said nonchalantly and realized we hadn't mentioned the bracelet before. I quickly replied with "Do you know where Jewel was killed? A while ago the news said Jewel was killed in another location and then dumped in the park? I may have an address for you, I can ask my source..... Just so *I know*, if I give you an address and it turns out to be the wrong address, how bad would that be?" We hadn't mentioned Cale's name either but somehow I got the impression he was on their list.

Grey replied "As long as you give us the information in good faith and you truly believe the information is correct nothing will happen to you."

"Okay, I'll see if I can get you the address in question."

My dad came up and put his hand on my shoulder. "Can I help you officer? Has my daughter done something wrong?"

"No sir." Detective Grey replied and straightened up in respect for my father. "These two young ladies have given us some information on a couple of ongoing investigations and we were just asking them some questions. And we may need to talk to them more later."

"That's fine, you let me know if we can be of further assistance," my dad said shaking Grey's hand. And with that they left. But the look on my dad's face said it wasn't over.

My dad, along with my mom, grilled us with lots of questions on the ride home.

That night I had a dream where I remembered Tori losing her boot in the quicksand. When I woke up it was 3:17a.m.

CHAPTER 11

Saturday was the big day for the dance. Nic and I were going to get ready at her house. We were both asked to the dance by boys but since we weren't interested in them we decided to go by ourselves – well in a big group. I didn't hear from Cale, thank god, and though how he had never asked me I realized he didn't go to any school events, just another weird notch to put on his belt. I'm glad he didn't ask me though, because I would have had to back out of that one.

An hour before the dance Storm, Shelby, Tori, Alec, Declan and his date came over, their parents came too and we all took pictures and had some snacks. My sister even brought a bunch of mint gum to take with us. The parents trickled in and out, and finally it was just us kids left. We were waiting for Nic's mom to grab her purse while we were checking our make-up in the mirror and the boys were straightening ties when a car we didn't know pulled up.

Nic and I walked out to see who it was and out stepped Topher. "Holy shit." I said in a monotone voice.

Topher looked down and around "What? Do I have food stuck in my teeth?" He bent down to look in his side mirror, "they look good to me" he said, then retrieved a couple of packages from the back seat.

"Now that definitely deserves a holy shit." Nic said.

3:17 a.m. ...the waking hour

Topher walked over to us and said "Now you two knock that off."
Tori came out of the house and said "Holy shit."
Nic and I both said "I know!"
"Jinx"
"You owe me a coke." We both giggled.
He was holding two corsage boxes, and held them out to the two of us.
"How nice, thank you" I said. "Boy did I date the wrong guy. You're hot in school but hotter, like James Bond out of school." I pointed my hand toward him "and you're so considerate!" All the girls 'awwwed.'
He helped me take out my wrist courage and put it on. Then he helped Nic do the same, but when he helped Nic, I saw something in his eyes. They didn't have an official date but I knew they'd be dancing tonight. Topher gave us a ride, letting Mrs. Newland off the hook. Storm and Shelby drove with Declan and his date and the rest of us piled in Topher's Car.
The gym was all decked out with disco balls, balloons, streamers and lights. We had a DJ that was actually played good music. Everyone was congratulating me for turning Cale in for hurting me when really, I didn't. I guess when they saw the police at the game they assumed that's what was going on. It was too long of a story to rectify, so I let them think what they wanted because frankly I am glad I am done with him.
I guess now that Topher showed up I was a fifth wheel, but no one in my group left me alone. We all went out and danced together. Tables and chairs were set up around the perimeter of the designated dance floor. When we were sitting we would chide some of our fellow classmates for dance moves or the apparel they chose and we'd do the same to ourselves.
I can't help it, but every time Jett walks into a room I get all choked up. As soon as I set eyes on him, I couldn't talk or pay attention to anything but him. He looked sharp with a navy suit, light blue shirt, designer tie, shiny black shoes and a gorgeous smile. He walked in with a slutty looking chick, her skirt so tight I bet you needed a crow bar to get it off and so short you didn't need the crow bar. I doubt she could sit, plus, she had three pounds of makeup on.
Nic said to me "Jealous much?"

I replied laughingly "Absolutely, but I wouldn't be caught dead in that dress and I'd chew off my left arm before I'd wear that much makeup." I finished saying it as the happy couple got close to our table, and then I couldn't speak again. I caught Jett looking at me and couldn't look away and I didn't care. Declan tapping on my shoulder to ask for a dance snapped me out of it.

When our dance was finished I noticed Detective Grey standing in the doorway. I gave Declan a squeeze and thanked him for the dance and walked on over to him.

"Detective Grey, are you here for a dance?" He gave me a smile out of the corner of his mouth.

"No Addie, but any one of these young men would be lucky to have you. You do look very nice tonight." He replied.

"Why thank you." I said with a smile. When I am in a formal situation I am always polite and polished. It's from all the years of training my parents have drilled into our heads. My hair was up and I actually had full make up on – full for me. I had on a very simple black dress with lining which helps my lines, fitted but not too tight, long but not to my ankles with two thick straps making "x's" on my back. Black sandals and hose of course, topped off by a nice thick row of cubic zirconia's around my neck, earrings and a couple of bracelets to match. My mom always says "Less is more, k.i.s., keep it simple. Then again, not enough may have you standing on the corner and getting unwelcomed offers." She would always giggle after that second part.

"I have some urgent questions for you, and ah well, there's a missing person and we think there is foul play involved. Do you have time?" he asked, facing me and not backing up at all.

"Well, I just have to tell my friends we'll be back in a few minutes." I said as I was pointing back to our table. "Should we go get a cup of coffee?" I asked.

"Ah, no, I sent Detective O'Connor to get us some; he set something up for us in the hall."

Jett came over to our table. "Uncle Grey, you're not looking for me again are you? I swear I'm clean." He put his hand out for a shake as I was leaning over the table to grab my purse when his hand brushed along my arm. I felt a surge of electricity go through my body. Startled I looked him in the eye, he reciprocated and I knew he felt it too.

I turned to talk "Grey, Grey McGaven, I love that name, very nice. So you're Jett's uncle." He nodded. "Why don't they call you Detective McGaven?" I asked but as I pondered it Detective Grey does have a nice ring to it.

"It's less of a mouthful they tell me, they started calling me Detective Grey and it stuck."

"And it sounds cooler," he smiled as I said it "shall we go?" I turned back to the table told Nic I would be with Detective Grey in the hallway.

"Grey don't you think she's a little young for you?" Jett stated and put his hand on the middle of my back, I felt the same surge as before, it made me straighten up a bit. I turned my head to see Jett, his eyes locked onto mine and then they wandered all the way down to the floor.

To my surprise Detective Grey said "Afraid of a little competition."

By now we were getting a lot of attention. As I said, he was good looking and an older man meeting me at the dance. It was sure to get all sorts of rumors flying.

I turned back to Jett and I placed my hand around his bicep, he flinched and flexed it, I think he was shocked I grabbed his arm. I found the words to actually come out smoothly "If I go missing, tell everyone it was your uncle." Grey and Jett laughed. I told Grey "I'm ready, I'd like to get out of here, everyone is paired up but me."

"Shall we," Grey said. Giving me his elbow, I tucked my hand in the crook of his arm gently. "O'Connor went to get coffee and he said he set up chairs in the back hall for us. Sorry we're disrupting the dance on you... Also the crack about competition, I couldn't help but bedevil my nephew."

"Don't worry about it, I am done with the dance too, I made my appearance. Too bad O'Connor isn't picking up burgers, I'm starving." I said.

He laughed "Finally, a girl that eats... Should I call your parents?"

"Not unless you're going to ask for my hand in marriage, and since this is our first coffee, I would say no." He laughed again.

We didn't talk shop waiting for O'Connor who had set up chairs in a circle by the gym exit that Nic and I usually waited for our rides home after wrestling. We started talking and Grey told me he graduated high school early and just plowed through college so he could get to work. I had a feeling he was some sort of genius and I bet he could do anything he wanted to, so I wonder why he picked being a detective.

We actually had a nice personal conversation. I told him I liked to golf and swim but I wanted to go to school for fashion design. We talked about golfing a lot, "The older you get the more people you can find to play." Grey said. "Your right, it is hard to find people to play a round of golf at my age." I replied.

As we were talking Jett came into the hallway and glanced our way. I wanted to give him a little wave, but didn't. Not taking my eyes off Jett I asked Grey "Do you want to ask me questions about Jewel? I didn't kill her you know, and neither did Nic." And finally tore my eyes away and back to Grey. He let out a little laugh "I know you two didn't kill anyone nor do I think you had anything to do with either of the cases I'm working on. But my partner thinks we need to bring you into the station for questioning, and that can be really rough on someone as young as you. So I wanted to talk to you further to try and get a feel for what kind of information you've given us and where it may have come from. Maybe figure out how I, or we, should proceed from here."

When Grey saw O'Connor at the door he went and opened it for him, he actually brought coffee and donuts. I raised an eyebrow in pleasure. "Food, right up your ally, right?" Grey asked.

"Absolutely." I said. I grabbed a donut and a coffee; I could tell that Grey's mind was just ticking away trying to figure me out and what to do next. Now that O'Connor was there, Grey shared the fact that I liked to golf and we socialized a bit more. O'Connor was married and had two kids. Then they slyly started asking me the same questions they had the night before. I think they were satisfied with my answers; they had to be the same if not similar as I only knew the one side.

Students from the dance started exiting the gym, then coming up the stairs by us, making the hallway louder and a little more crowded. We were still in a circle with me in the middle of the hall and Grey and O'Connor were nearest the wall. I was about to scoot my chair in when someone bumped me and I spilled a bit of my coffee on my dress. I immediately stood up. Grey pulled me in and then pulled my chair up against the wall. I picked up the bag of donuts and placed them on my chair, so they wouldn't get trampled. "Gotta save the donuts." Grey said. "Of course." I replied.

Storm must have seen it because he charged up the stairs and asked if I was ok, "Do you need to go clean up, is your dress ruined?" I held my cup toward the middle of our circle and Storm took it, I got a napkin out of the bag and dried it, "Nope, my dress will live, it's fine, I knew I liked black." I crumpled the napkin and walked across the wide hall to deposit it in the garbage when I noticed them, Jett and his slutty girlfriend making out. I couldn't take my eyes off them as I was making my way back to Storm.

Storm announced he was going to Nic's and that everyone else was getting ready to leave. I looked to Gray and O'Connor "do you mind if I grab my coat now, before the mob comes?" They shook their heads and I went down the stairs past slut girl and Jett, past the drink table and finally to the coat rack. I looked over my shoulder to see if the two of them were still stuck together, when Jett brushed by me making contact. I just smiled. I found my coat when Nic and Topher came up behind me; he helped me put my coat on, such a nice guy.

We walked back over to the detectives and told them I had to get going and O'Connor looked perturbed by my comment. So I suggested they drive me to Nic's so we could talk more, I didn't tell them she was right up the road so they obviously wouldn't get much questioning in.

When we got to her house a party was hoppin,' they came in and met Mr. and Mrs. Newland and actually grabbed a soda. I grabbed a plate of appetizers and desserts. Mr. Newland was leaning on the counter. "I can't believe you're still eating" he said. "This is actually for you." I replied.

I nodded toward Mr. Newland and said "Isn't it mandatory to....." he interrupted "Yes, it's mandatory to grab a plate while you are here or Mrs. Newland will have your head," he said and Grey laughed.

"These are water chestnuts wrapped in bacon" I dipped it in barbeque sauce. "They are awesome," and popped one in my mouth.

Mrs. Newland came by and said "Good girl Addie, eat up."

"Grey put his plate on the counter, took a waster chestnut and then another. He chugged his drink and said "We ought to get going." O'Connor walked out and gave a nod good-bye.

I walked Grey out, "You didn't ask me any new or specific

questions about the cases, mostly just about my golfing habits."

"I know, I felt weird, I've never questioned anyone at a dance before – it was either that or bring you in. And now we're at a teenage party with my nephew giving me the stink eye. All just a little weird for me."

"Sorry, I actually feel comfortable around you, like I could talk to you, so I did what I would do with anyone – just chatted away."

He smiled. "I believe you Addie, and I think you're a sincere person, and both O'Connor and I are comfortable talking to you, too."

"Besides, getting to know me is being able to trust me, establishing a baseline in our relationship, right? That's why we talked tonight and we did that, right?" He didn't answer but seemed like he agreed with that. I had this aching feeling he wanted to ask me something important, maybe he knows about my dreams, but then how would he, "What can I help you with?" I blurted out.

I heard the storm door creak and turned to see Storm coming out of Nic's house. "See what I mean?" Grey said.

"I do, look at O'Connor" I said. Pointing to O'Connor leaning on the car with his arms crossed. "He's giving me the same evil eye." Grey looked over at him and laughed. "Tell Storm you need to talk to me on official business and we'll get this done now." I said a little more professional like. I liked Grey and if I was going to have dreams that come true and people getting hurt in them, he would be a great ally to have. Plus, I don't think I wanted to be brought down to the station for questioning.

Storm shook his uncle's hand and they chatted a bit. "Storm, I need to ask Addie a few questions, official business, and then I need to get going. Do you mind?" Grey asked. I got a little look from Storm but he left.

"Are you familiar with the neighborhood behind you? You're separated by fields, ravines and several acres..."

I interrupted. "Yes, I actually know it well, my cousin Peyton lives over there and I've hiked back there several times."

My cousin and I were always friends but I remember the day we became kindred friends. Both our families belonged to the same club and this helped us get into trouble. Stealing golf carts was one of our favorite things to do among other things, until this one incident. Peyton stole, well borrowed, a golf cart and I jumped into the passenger seat. We took off fast and went for a joy ride. If you have ever been on a golf course you know there are hills, ravines, sand traps, water and wooded areas. Well, when we went speeding down a steep hill and took a sharp turn it rocked the cart onto two wheels and I started slipping off the seat, the green grass was so close to me I thought I was going to eat it. Peyton tried grabbing my arm as she jerked the wheel the other way as my arm and leg were dragging on the ground. As she jerked it back, I hit my head on the back of the cart. The cart bobbled back and forth when it rocked back in my direction she let go of my arm and I fell out of the cart and rolled halfway down the hill before I could stop myself. I lay there still, feeling the cool cut grass all around me. I thought that was a good sign, feeling the grass. But could I move?

Peyton, came running down the hill completely panicked, her face all pale. I have never seen such a panic stricken look on anyone before. I looked down at my body, but all my pieces were still attached and I saw no blood. I looked back at her face and she still looked filled with horror, very grim. I tried to laugh, although just for a second I was momentarily paralyzed and couldn't.

Peyton had long brown wavy hair, she was adventurous and very, very social. She was just as popular as Tori if not more so. She's older than we are, but we all still got along. We used to be on swim team together. She had beautiful white, soft, skin and never got too tan and had these beautiful blue eyes. All the boys were always after her and my sister.

Years ago her brother was almost paralyzed from a senseless accident, and I saw that panic written all over her face. So I forced a laugh that came out horse at first. I wiggled my feet and legs they were fine, I started to sit up – everything felt okay. And Peyton began to laugh with me with tears in her eyes. It was much scarier than it sounds. Anyway, as soon as I was able to get up and walk, and it did take me a couple of minutes, we snuck the cart back and never took another one. Peyton and I had a closer relationship from then on. We had formed a bond that could never be broken. Like I said, some memories just stick.

Grey went on "There is a girl missing, only since this morning, but she's only ten. Her parents are friends of my boss. Can you ask your source?"

"Huhhh" I breathed in making a noise and held my chest. I remembered I dreamt running up and down hills, maybe it was our ravines! I looked down to the left and then to the right and up as if I were watching them run.

"You have got to be kidding me, you think you're a psychic?" He threw his hands up and turned his back on me.

"Hell no!" I replied, and laughed a little. "I mean no, I'm not a psychic. I was just thinking…" I exclaimed and immediately calmed myself. Nic and I rehearsed how I would react and what I'd say if someone ever asked. I calmly said "I do know a psychic, one just moved into the back of the Richfield Reading and Speech Center if you want one."

He turned around and looked a little aggravated. "I don't want a psychic. She isn't your source is she?" he said shaking his head.

"No" I replied and almost too quickly.

"…and you say you aren't one?"

"No." I said sternly, but then decided to try and lighten the subject. Thank goodness I didn't tell him, I almost decided to in the car. "I'm not a psychic, I'm a medium… just kidding! I'll ask my source if they know anything and I'll get back to you." We stood there in a bit of an awkward silence.

"Okay…" He said, sounding disappointed and took a deep breath. "Yeah that's fine, but the sooner the better." He replied pointing to me and in such a way that I think he didn't believe me, but he handed me another one of his business cards.

All in all it had been a good night. Topher hung around part of the time at the dance. Nic said she was glad for some of his absences; it gave her time to breath. But, as soon as he walked in her front door, she was there in a flash.

Nic's party was a blast, I can't believe that so many students can stay out past midnight. Topher stayed and helped us cleanup which took us an hour or so, but we weren't in a hurry either. After, the bulk of everything was cleaned up, I excused myself.

It was 2:15 when I got to Nic's room, exhaustion started to set in. I don't remember trying to fall asleep, I think I passed out as soon as my head hit the pillow. When I woke I was sitting straight up in bed. The bright fluorescent green clock screamed 3:22am at me. I put my hands to my face and rubbed and mumbled "thank goodness", at least it wasn't 3:17a.m. Hopefully this dream won't come true…. I must have woken Nic. I thought she and Topher would have still been sucking face. "What are you doing up?" I asked her.

3:17 a.m. ...the waking hour

She replied "I could ask you the same. Did you have another dream?"

"Yeah, but it's 3:22 so I'm not sure it counts," I whispered back to her.

She fell back into her pillow "My clock is five minutes fast."

I jumped out of bed and dialed Peyton immediately. "Thank God you answered, I'm at Nic's, can you come pick me up – it's an emergency." I hung up and found my satchel from that night. "Watch your eyes." I said to Nic, I had to turn on the light to read the numbers. "Detective Grey please. Yes, this is an emergency, I'll hold."

"What are you doing?" Nic asked.

"Do you remember the mud pit Tori got stuck in when she lost her boot?"

"Yeah."

"Well, there's a missing girl from that neighborhood. I had a dream and at first I thought I was just remembering what happened to Tori... but she's just a little girl I gotta check it out." I said as I was pulling my jeans on, with the phone tucked between my shoulder and ear.

"Grey, this is Addie Gellar, it's an emergency, meet us behind 2711 South Point Dr. Yes, now and go behind the house." I hung up the phone as he was saying something but there was no time for questioning me now.

Nic rolled out of bed and started dressing too. "I guess we can always sleep tomorrow.....I'll tell my mom we forgot to TP a football players house." I saw headlights flash through the bedroom window. "We need all the bandanas and flashlights you can find."

In the past, not all the neighborhood kids were ever ready to go hiking all at once, so we would tie a bandana on a tree to lead them to our location. If this girl was stuck we needed to find her fast and I wasn't going to wait for Grey to get there.

Nic and I piled in the front seat of Peyton's car, she was in her jammies and boots. We explained the situation to her and she sped the whole way back to her house. Everyone had paths in the back of their houses that lead into the ravines. We started at the one in Peyton's back yard. I drew a quick map in the dirt while Nic held the flashlight; I wanted to make sure we headed in the right direction. As it was I think we were closer to the pit from Peyton's house than mine. We tied off a bandana on the tree by the path and left one flashlight on pointing back at the house so Grey could find us and we headed off.

It was hard to navigate in the dark even though we had flashlights. I got hit it the face a few times by branches I just couldn't see – I tried to make sure they didn't fling back at Nic and Peyton but when you're in a hurry it's not that easy to do. I heard a few nasty comments from behind… Twenty minutes in we started yelling "Is anyone here?" I didn't remember Grey telling us her name. Just as dawn was breaking I knew we were in close proximity to the mud pit – visibility was still not good. I had to watch where I stepped. I turned around and fell to my knees, but no sign of a girl.

Peyton and Nic were back a few paces, I held the flashlight in the path to get to me.

"You found her!" Nic yelled and started running toward me. "What? Where?" I put the flashlight down and started patting the ground. I screamed. I felt her arm and it was stone cold. I started digging and digging, "Get help!" Peyton turned and ran, Nic and I dug and dug. "Is she dead?"

"No Nic, no, she can't be! You get her under her arms, I'll find her legs." My chin was sitting on top of the mud. I held my breath, turned my face sideways and pushed in the mud until I found her legs. "Pull!" I said. We did. Nic counted "1-2-3 pull, pulllll…" I felt something horrible and crunchy still in my grip, I felt it and it felt like bones from a squirrel, I panicked and shook them off my hand and wiped them on my jeans. I could see flashlights bouncing toward us in the distance and felt a little relief.

"We need water!" I yelled and one flashlight went the opposite way.

"Roll her on her side" I exclaimed. We swept fingers through her mouth, gave her a pat on the back a few times, rolled her back over and started CPR.

"Is she alive?" Nic exclaimed. I breathed in deeply and then exhaled into the lifeless soul below me. My hands were shaking uncontrollably, but my work and progress steady. Grey was there, flashlight in hand, asking "Is she all right?"

Nic started rattling off feebly "We found her only a few minutes ago. She's cold, not breathing and we couldn't feel a pulse," and she broke down and started to sob.

Grey moved me out of the way to take over.

3:17 a.m. ...the waking hour

"Quiet." I said to Nic who was sobbing "Quiet." I said strongly. I put my ear to her mouth "I swear I felt warm air....."

"I think I have a pulse." Grey retorted. He scooped her up and started running back to Peyton's house, we followed. Firemen were flowing down the hill as we neared; they took her from Grey's arms.

Nic and I were sitting at the edge of Peyton's patio. Nic's head was on my shoulder and my arm was wrapped around her sharing a blanket when Grey came over. "They have her stabilized and on the way to the hospital. Do either of you need to be checked out by a paramedic?" I mumbled "no."

"Are you two sure you're okay?" Grey asked.

"I'm fine." I replied, having to clear my throat. "You?" I asked nodding at Nic, she shook her head.

Grey squatted in front of me; he had mud all down his front. "It's okay not to be fine, this is very traumatic, but you saved her you know. You saved Samantha." He sat next to me "If it wasn't for the dirt on your face and the rivers running down it I may not have been able to tell you were crying..." He touched my cheek. And the river started again.

He came in for a group hug, it just made it worse. "She's fine, you're fine everyone's going to be fine." He purred. "Just one question Addie, how did you know where she was?" I could tell he was asking on a personal level not a professional one. He let go. In all sincerity, I needed him to know, to help prevent bad things from happening, things like this. "Detective Grey..." I started.

"Go ahead."

"Detective Grey, I'm exactly what you don't want me to be. I'm a freak, but I don't care, I'll tell you everything and you can believe me or not." There was a very long period of silence before Nic nudged me. "I have dreams that come true, and not all them are nice and fuzzy dreams either, as you can see."

He gave me another squeeze as he swiveled to sit next to me. "That doesn't make you a freak that just makes me a jerk for being closed minded that there is such a thing, someone who can foresee the future."

"I haven't really told anyone else about it but Nic and I'd like to keep it that way."

He smiled at me, not showing any teeth, rubbed my shoulder

and said "I'm not sure anyone else would believe us anyway. We'll keep it between the three of us for now. Do you need another blanket?"

"I could use some water."

"Girl you need more water than I could find." Then he let go, holding his arms out looking down at his jacket and the two of us chuckled.

"I can clean up at Nic's." Peyton came out of the house with glasses and a pitcher of water. She looked terrible. I could just imagine what we looked like.

CHAPTER 12

Life is good as long as we obey; in school, at home and in life. Otherwise, there are always consequences.

Just as Nic and I had finished mopped the mats and closed up the closet, Coach came up to see us and told us that he needed us to coordinate the 'Lil Sis Wrestling Program.' Then he turned around and asked for a volunteer from the wrestlers. No one moved a muscle, although not everyone was there yet. A few seconds passed and still no takers, until thankfully Storm volunteered and had to explain the program to us.

The Lil Sis program is a group of girls we needed to put together, one girl per wrestler. Each girl makes their wrestler a snack before each wrestling meet. We could ask girls from any grade to sponsor a wrestler. They could bring any kind of treat they wanted, and they would give it to their wrestler Friday at school. It was up to each wrestler to decide when to eat it; most of them had to wait until after weigh-ins at the wrestling meet, since many of them were dieting to make their wrestling weight. Of course, the heavy weight didn't have to wait for weigh-ins so I thought it would be fun to get him; the whole program sounded fun. That was our project for the week. Nic, Storm and I wrote down a bunch of girls names we could ask. We would ask all the girls in all our classes, too.

Practice was starting, the whistle blew and Jett entered the room. The coach looked at him and yelled "You're lucky today boy, but next time you better be here before I blow the whistle!"

"Okay coach" he yelled and smiled his adorable little smile.

Nic looked at me and said "Do you need to go to the bathroom?"

"No, why?"

"Your face is all red."

"Okay, I'll go" I said. Sitting on the floor Nic gave me a hand and helped me up. "What is wrong with me, I can't even look normal around him." I rinsed my face and said "I'm ready to go back."

"Really, because you don't look ready."

"Nic, it's obviously a crush and I know he's never going to ask me out. So I just need to regain composure and I'll look for another boyfriend to keep me preoccupied. No biggy."

We got back to the wrestling room and worked on our Lil Sis list a little more, which took up about twenty minutes. We drafted a flyer to post and hand out with the details about the program and how to sign up. That took another ten minutes.

"Nic, let's make a list of possible boyfriends for ourselves, I won't include Jett, I'll start fresh. What are your criteria?"

"Taller than me and funny." Nic said.

"I'll say tall, dark and handsome, into sports…. "And I added "a sense of humor, no one too serious for me." She gave me a seriously dirty look.

"Hey!" I said "Now I know what I like, I'll just find it in my league." So we wrote it down on the piece of paper. We doodled, checked out the wrestlers and every time my eyes went back to stare at Jett, Nic would ask me another question to break my trance. We kept ourselves pretty occupied and I think we looked busy too.

I walked in the front door when I got home. My mom was sitting in the living room with a lady I didn't know, there were two huge bouquets of flowers and a box of chocolates on the table. As I was taking off my shoes and coat they both stood, and the lady just started crying. She came over to me and hugged me and didn't let go. I looked at my mom and she too started crying. I got all choked up myself. The lady said she couldn't thank me enough and how could she ever repay me. "I babysit" I replied, she laughed and let go. It was Samantha's mom, the girl I saved from the 'not quicksand' fiasco. She held me at arm's length and smiled and replied all choked up "I could use a babysitter." She pulled me back in for a hug. This time I reciprocated and told her I was glad to have helped, every action has reaction, consequences. And in that moment I knew I was placed on this earth with my dreams to help people.

Wednesday, Coach asked how our planning for the Lil Sis program was going and we told him we'd have plenty of girls making snacks by Friday. It was fun trying to find girls; I've even made a few new friends in the process. It was a good program just to get to know more people. The girls, I'm sure, do it to meet the guys.

By weeks end my embarrassment and heart flutters were manageable, but my heart still leapt every time Jett came into the room or looked my way. At the end of practice we pulled all the names for the Lil Sis program, Nic and I were both going to sponsor two boys because we didn't have enough girls for all the guys.

Nic was like the fifth name pulled and she got Storm, which I thought was convenient, and another boy named Ron. I, on the other hand, was called last; very convenient since I didn't remember hearing Jett's name called yet either. I felt something brewing, some shenanigans were definitely going on. The Coach had to be in on it to. I was conveniently the last Lil Sis pulled from the bucket and since I got two names I got Randy's and of course Jett's as the second one. I turned red when Jett's name was called. The team all gave out a little laugh, obviously, everyone knew I had a crush on him. So I decided to cheer and lifted my hands and said "Yes, I got the hot guy!" Everyone laughed a little harder.

My crush couldn't be helped, sometimes, no matter how hard you try, you just like who you like. Well, Jett didn't think it was too funny that I got his name. He had to know I was crushin' because he glared right at me, got up looking really pissed, swept his towel off the ground and headed right for the locker room. I felt a little abashed by my cheering. I did that to myself on a daily basis so normally I wouldn't care – but what I really felt bad about was the fact that Jett was upset and may resent me.

When he came out of the locker room he was alone, so I took a deep breath and walked up to him. I told him since he was so upset that I got his name, I could switch his name with anyone else's on the list. I also explained to him that I had nothing to do with me getting his name.

"Just let me know which girl you would like me to make the switch with and I'll make it happen." I went to walk away and he caught my arm. I felt a little tingle go through me, nothing I could control. I turned around and he let go. I smiled at him and said "Yesss" a little goofy like. He smiled back at me, we made eye contact, there was a slight pause. I just waited; normally I'd have my mouth spouting off something sarcastic. It was a good quiet moment though.

"No, it's fine. You and I will get along just fine, besides Declan said you can cook." I laughed.

"Time will tell won't it?" I said "Actually, I'm a good baker but not a real good cook, but I could feed the masses."

"The masses?" He questioned.

As I was backing up to grab my coat and bag I said "My mom likes to cook big and entertain –I help cook, we cook *a lot*. You talk to Declan a lot?" I asked.

"Yeah he's my best friend and has been since the seventh grade." He said smiling. I knew that fact but was dumbfounded, I had no idea what else to say. A first for me.

That weekend Nic was at my house. We were bored so we went up to The Akron Reading and Speech Center to get a candy bar. I didn't go there often but every now and then we would run in for some chocolate. There was a small moving truck around back. A new tenant, we figured, was moving in. Rumor was she's a real psychic.

We stepped inside the lobby and there were two ladies talking; Marge from the Richfield Reading and Speech Center and the other lady we had met briefly before. How Marge remembered our names when we visited impressed us because, as I said, we only came in once or twice a year, but we always did chat with her.

As soon as we got to the counter Marge put her hand on the counter to acknowledge we were there. She took a few seconds finishing her conversation, and turned to us and said "Girls this is our new tenant, Shelia. She is a psychic and will be renting the back office."

Shelia shook our hands and asked if we wanted a free reading and pizza in return for helping her empty the truck. We shrugged our shoulders and said "sure." Sheila had dark hair with big wavy curls. She was wearing jeans and a t-shirt. She was shorter than the both of us, she wasn't skinny but not fat either. She looked totally normal, like someone you'd meet in the grocery store, she didn't look crazy psycho at all.

There weren't that many boxes and it went quickly with three of us. When we were done she called for pizza and sodas. She dug around in a box marked "IMPORTANT" and pulled out a large deck of cards in a tattered card box.

"Who's first?" she asked. I let Nic go first. As she was shuffling her tarot cards she told us "Sometimes you need a couple of readings to get the gibberish out and the truth pulled forward." We knew there would be a sales pitch somewhere. Then she said "But sometimes we just nail it on the head the first time, depends on how open you are to the reading." She gave us a sincere smile.

Nic got cards like love, the queen, the sun and she was told she would travel a lot. So I thought, piece of cake. Sheila reshuffled the cards, I cut the deck and she started laying them out. "You have an admirer" she said to me.

She flipped an evil looking card "You have another admirer; this one is upset with you." She continued. "You are destined for a great love very soon." Then the death card came up, then the fool card and then she stopped. She said it doesn't necessarily mean death that it could also mean illness, or a loss of a job and not necessarily to do with me but someone around me.

She pushed all her cards together and cleaned them up. She suggested to me that I was an emotional reader and asked me if I had any experience, meaning '*could I*' read cards. She didn't press the issue – Nic and I just gave each other a wide-eyed look. She said her gift was handed down to her.

I looked Sheila in the eye and asked why they moved here and about her history. I was curious and really wanted to know. Shelia started talking slowly about her past. "In the early 1900's there was a man by the name of "Dr. Sal Rewtnic." He's not in the history books, but should be. He was what we would call, these days, a 'mad' scientist. He did experiments on humans to try and cure diseases such as leprosy, auto immune disorders and the like. He would use strange things such as animal parts, bone marrow, blood, saliva, magic potions, spells and other sorts to try and cure illnesses. That's how my ancestors got involved...magic and spells.

Rewtnic's son was ill and he experimented on him along with his nephew until he was forced to institutionalize both of them. Rewtnic continued his experiments on others and some of his patients went crazy and that's how the rumors came about that there were vampires and werewolves during that time period."

"In one instance, a man that was being experimented on, began to grow hair all over his body and went mad. When people tried to capture and help him he was outraged and became unhinged. Some people got hurt and one man was killed trying to commandeer him. Hence the rumors of werewolves coming about at that time. After his newest experiments other such rumors entailed that, he cured people of their diseases, but they would burn through their blood cells quickly, needing transfusions every few days. They would grow pale, become sensitive to sunlight and then need more blood. A couple of them that had agreed to multiple experiments were brainsick and went around trying to suck people's blood. They weren't vampires just ill, but that's how these rumors started. This all happened in the early 1900's. However, in these instances of seeing the so called werewolves and vampires, our groups recorded them as rumors because that's exactly what they were, rumors. And our group hasn't recorded seeing werewolves or vampires since, rumors or real." We looked at her in awe and just listened intently.

"When the authorities found out about his experiments, his books, journals and all his notes were confiscated and burned. Even his patients were burned at the stake for fear they were evil, contagious or would turn into vampires or werewolves. But not everything or everyone experimented on was destroyed. My family took on the role as "watchmen" when he started his experiments and were witnesses to his work. It was my great great great grandmother who fell in love with Sal and started our watchmen duties." "Before they destroyed everything she took some of his books that listed patients and experiments. Authorities thought they had destroyed all evidence to do with Dr. Sal Rewtnic, but they hadn't. The reasons why the gypsies were so interested in his work was because his last tests had shown great results of curing people, and that group of people never got sick for the rest of their lives. Some even gained the gift of psychic abilities and foreseeing the future."

"Most everyone who survived his treatments that didn't go mad has now passed on, but we are tracking their offspring. The only two remaining from his time are his son, Sal Rewtnic the third and his cousin Neil Royce. However, they are in their 70's now." She shook her head and we all snapped out of our trance. Shelia said "I cannot believe I just told you all that. I haven't shared that story with anyone."

I looked over at Nic and she looked just as freaked out as I was. We got up wanting to leave but the pizza came. We ate as fast as we could and got out of there, laughing all the way home. I hadn't shown Nic any of my notes about my dreams about my wolf, but I was a little freaked out by her story and my dreams and I had a feeling they had a connection. I was wondering if I should tell Nic or would she think I've gone off the deep end.

That night I had a bad dream. It started with the wolf running after me, I tried losing him but I just couldn't run fast enough. I recognized where I was, the ravines behind me, but just couldn't put my finger on the exact location when something else started chasing us. I ran down a hill and through trees and brush. I jumped over the creek and then back up a hill. I stopped to see where I was and got knocked down, it was pitch dark and I couldn't see a face. With the weight of his body on me I was fighting to keep him from biting my neck. Flashbacks and horror entering my mind, my wolf jumped him from behind. I felt a slash across my arm, and scrambled to break free. I picked up a branch and started backing up. As I got to the top of the hill, the tree line broke and I was on someone's lawn; the grass was cut and manicured. There was another tree line to my right probably a property line, as I was walking backward, I was surrounded by darkness.

I kept backing up, I looked down and I was on the street standing next to a four door car. Looking up I saw someone backing out of the woods wearing a white shirt, my heart was thumping and my eyes tearing. I woke so horrified, my eyes were actually wet. I was glad it was just a dream. I was exhausted and relieved it was only a dream. I looked at the clock. It was 3:17a.m., I started writing.

I woke the next morning still unable to shake that feeling from my dream. It was leaving such a strong impression on me, more so than seeing a really good movie that just stays with you. I tried thinking of other things just to shake the unpleasant vile feeling coursing threw me, the dream was so intense I was having a hard time.

Brushing my teeth I realized I hadn't had a dream I remembered in a couple of weeks. I wonder if Shelia was able to push me to dream or if it was a coincidence.

CHAPTER 13

That Monday when I walked out of art class, I spotted Jett across the hall with his hands in his pockets and one foot bent backwards leaning on the wall looking very cool. It didn't matter how he stood he always looked hot, of course Cale fooled me with his 'in school' looks. I wonder how Jett looks after school or better yet on a date. As I looked at him he looked right back at me, I squeezed my eyes together ever so slightly and gave him a nod, I turned right and started walking to history.

From behind me I heard "Hey Addie" I turned to look over my shoulder not stopping and it was Jett catching up to me. I stopped and he almost ran into me. "What's up...?" I said, and then I remembered he may not want me to be his Lil Sis anymore and said, "Oh, who do you want as your Lil Sis?" I turned around and started walking again, he caught up.

"That's not what I wanted to talk to you about, I don't want to switch, I'm cool with it." Jett said. He had a fitted t-shirt on under a flannel shirt and work boots that were unlaced.

"So, what's up?" I said very slowly because my heart started to beat so hard, like it wanted out of my chest and my face started to flame.

"I uh... I wanted to see if you wanted to go out Friday."

"With you?" I replied questioningly.

He laughed "Yeah, with me. You told Declan if I had anything else to ask you, to ask in person." He slid his hands back in his pockets. I did say that but I didn't expect this.

"Friday? For what?" I was confused. I swore he was mad when I got his name as his Lil Sis so I thought he didn't like me, at all.

"Here I thought you would have been excited." Jett said. I started walking slowly, trying to make the blood circulate again, because my brain wasn't really working. He followed alongside me.

"It just seems weird you asking me out." I said. He laughed again. I stopped and had to smile at him. He had a smile that shined, and when he smiled, I had to smile.

"I need a date for Friday, dinner and a movie." I stopped in front of my classroom, thought about it a second, then shrugged and said "sure" and walked into my classroom and sat at my desk.

"Hey," Jett said leaning on desk, startling me. "I'll, ah, pick you up at six o'clock."

I looked up at him and said "K". I watched him walk out.

I had a smile on my face, ear to ear. I didn't care why he asked but as I sat through class I realized I should have gotten more details out of him. I looked over at Storm, my face still warm, with a shit eaten grin spread across it, and he just snarled at me again. I didn't care.

Since Jett didn't wrestle last night, I was anxious to get a glimpse of him today if I could get one, I wonder if that's being stalker like. Sure enough I came down a different stairwell to go to Algebra and I noticed Jett leaning against his locker in his 'locker pose'. Knee up, hands in pockets and a sexy smile on his face. He had his work boots on again, untied, just my thing.

I glanced at him then turned pretending not to notice him. I heard his friend say "Hey, isn't that your little freshman friend?" all snarky-like. I was walking slow, trying not to run away but not too slow to make it look obvious either. Jett caught up to me and tapped me on the shoulder. I turned around smoothly, right in the middle of traffic - across from the elevator where it always gets jammed up and immediately people were crabbin' at us to move, so we moved toward the windows. I think I said it pretty coolly "Oh, hey Jett, what's up?"

He cleared his throat "I wanted to confirm our date for Friday night." He continued and said we were going out in a big group, my jaw must have dropped because he laughed and asked me if that was okay.

"Who is *the group?*" I asked. He rattled a bunch of names off including the name Lisa; I didn't know any of them.

"Lisa, isn't that your ex-girlfriend? Why would we go out with her?" I asked and swallowed hard. It felt like an apple went down. I just looked at him weird and focused on his face, yet not looking him in the eye. I couldn't think Lisa's name was ringing in my ears. I heard she wasn't even nice. My heart began racing, its thump so loud, I could hardly make out what he was saying. I swallowed hard again. What was he saying? "Sure, that's fine" I said with regret.

He said "Great, I'll pick you up at six."

I was so excited yesterday and since I hadn't thought to give him my number the first time, I thought I would do it now, with short instructions on how to get to my house. I had written them down on a piece of paper in class as I daydreamed about him. I handed it to him. My hand was trembling, so as soon as he grabbed it, I put my hand in my pocket and kept the other tightly on my books. "I guess I'll see you Friday" he said.

"I'll guess you'll see me tonight." I replied.

"What?" he jerked his head up.

"We'll that's if you'll be at wrestling."

"Oh yeah" he said softly and smiled out of the corner of his mouth.

I walked away slowly. I wish I could say I was having déjàvu and had had a dream about this, but that wasn't the case. I just had a bad feeling. This wasn't a good sign. Why was our first date with a big group of people? I could see a double date, but with a big group and his ex, ick. I bumped into someone and almost dropped my books, my concentration was gone. I finally got to class with no other thoughts in my head.

I took a deep breath and figured it didn't matter why. The important thing was he had asked me over a thousand other girls he could have asked. Plus, it was Wednesday so he was planning ahead and giving me details which were good to know, I felt a little better, but underneath I had a harrowing feeling I was being ambushed. Me and my tingly senses; I wish they weren't working today so I could just enjoy the thought of going out on a date with Jett, instead I was all worked up about it all day.

By Thursday, I was so worked up I needed to blow off some

steam so I went to wrestling after school, helped Nic clean the mats and went down to the pool to do some laps. There was no swim team practice on Thursdays, just some swimming lessons with a couple of lap lanes open, so I was actually looking forward to it. When I got there the pool was empty.

Water and swimming were second nature to me, it relaxed me. I stretched a little before getting on the starter block, and then got in place with both feet on the edge, toes wrapped. I placed my hands to the side of block, placed my right foot back, leaned forward and held tight pretending to wait to hear the pop of the cap gun go off, and dove in.

It felt good to hit the cool soft water; I raced down to the end and back in freestyle. Then two laps of breast stroke, backstroke and then butterfly. It felt good to swim. I started doing all my favorite drills from practice; I had the pool to myself for the moment. It felt like I was cutting through that water like there was no tomorrow.

As I turned back doing fly, I noticed someone standing at the shallow end of the pool. My eyes were blood shot from the chlorine and I couldn't tell who it was. When I got to the end, they were gone. I headed back for another lap of breast stroke and someone was standing at the deep end now. I slowed coming to the edge and before I reached it they pushed me under, I got loose from their grip but they dunked me again as I came up for air. When I broke the surface again I thought I was in the middle of the pool so he couldn't reach me but he did and this time I took in water, making my nose and throat burn awfully. I grabbed his hand on my head pulled him in the pool with me we were a tangle of arms and legs as I was trying to break free. I was trying to come up for air but he was fighting to keep me down. We both finally came up for air and I gasped for air loudly but didn't hear a thing from him. I swung, hitting him in the nose. He dunked me again and this time I couldn't get loose, I felt like I was under water for quite a while. I was on the verge of hysterics but instead I told myself I am not afraid of the water, let some air out through my nose and tried to relax. He loosened his grip and I kicked him in the stomach and swam to the bottom of the pool, let out my last bit of air and held my breath. When I came to the surface he was running into the guy's locker room.

A swim class was entering the pool area, so at least I wasn't alone anymore. I stood at the end of the shallow end and just shivered trying to figure out what to do. I had lost all reason to a rational thought. I couldn't concentrate. I heaved myself up out of the pool, my arms burning and my legs felt like jello; I grabbed my towel and noticed someone staring down at me from the top of the bleachers. He was in sweats and a hoodie that hid his face, how brazen of him come back. I couldn't get myself to move to do anything about him, a few more girls entered the pool area, I was focused on them, no words passed my lips, I pointed to the bleachers however, when I looked up my ominous figure was gone.

Unfortunately, I was proven right to be worried about my date with Jett. Nic came up to me before first period Friday morning, she was with Declan, they both looked somber "What? What's wrong?" I asked mystified. She and Declan explained to me that he overheard Jett and the guys talking in the locker room last night and Jett said he'd show Lisa he could get a girl anytime he wanted and that he could get laid Friday or any other night! And then someone else added "Especially since Addie is easy, she dated Winters." So Storm was right, everyone thinks I'm a slut because I dated Cale even though nothing ever happened.

"I thought you and Jett were best friends, why are you telling me all this?" I asked Declan pointedly. He explained that I was his friend too, and that he didn't want me to hear it from anyone else and that Jett is a standup guy and it was all just locker room talk,

"I knew it, I knew something was up." I replied. Nic asked if I was going to cancel. I said "no" but it wasn't a convincing no. "I don't know what I'll do but.... he sure isn't getting lucky with me. If we're going out in a big group it shouldn't be hard to keep my distance. Maybe I'll sabotage the date myself."

"Don't worry Addie, Rae and I are going so you'll at least know two other people in the group."

"Rae?"

"Yes Addie, my girlfriend, try and keep up would ya." Declan and Nic started an in depth conversation about it when I noticed Topher at a locker just a few down from mine, which was strange, because his and Cale's were on the first floor near the gym. I walked up to him and leaned on the locker next to his. "So Topher, whose locker are you breaking into?" I said with levity.

I startled him, he looked a little ragged to me, he had dark circles under his eyes, he gave me a labored smile. "I uh, actually changed lockers.....mine... uh... wasn't working, they couldn't get the uh....lock fixed."

"Mmm, I see. Are you sure you just aren't stalking me?"

"What?" he replied surprisingly, with shock in his voice. I touched his arm, he flinched, "I'm just teasing Topher. You okay?"

"Oh" he said with a little laugh, more of like a sigh of relief. He started fiddling with some books in his locker. "I am glad to see you're ok." What does he mean, about our break up?

"My locker's right over there," and I pointed back over my shoulder. "As a matter of fact Nic's is near mine too." I turned a little "Right where she and Declan are standing." There was a little bit of a pause, I detected some sadness in him. "I'm going on an awful date tonight. Do you want to come so you can laugh at me?" He didn't respond. He closed his locker and we started walking together "Why are you going on a date if you know it's going to be awful?"

"Well, I'm not sure it's going to be awful, but the rumor is that Jett's just going out with me to get his ex-jealous and he thinks he can get lucky." I said with air quotes.

"You know, it could just be classic trash talk guys do in the locker room, they all do it, or it's a rumor that started differently and grew. Just be real honest with him, don't play games like other girls do, it makes them petty."

"You know, you're a pretty nice guy. Thanks for saying that." I felt a little less apprehensive.

As we walked I said "You and Nic should go out again. I thought you guys got along really well." He turned and nudged me with his elbow, and said "You know we did, maybe I will."

After school Tori actually sat next to me on the bus. She asked me what was wrong and why I wasn't more excited about my date. I told her the whole story and she listened, this was a new experience for her and me. She asked if I was going to cancel and I told her no. "I'm not afraid of him and if he lies to his friends about what happens I'll call him out on it, in front of his friends." I told her.

Tori backed me up, "I cannot believe he's such a jerk. I thought he was nicer than that, he seemed like a decent guy."

I think I was still trying to be an optimist "You know, it may

3:17 a.m. ...the waking hour

just be rumors and I plan on asking him before we go to dinner."

"You're so brave" Tori explained, "he could still be hung up on his ex-girlfriend and mad that she broke up with him. If that's the case be careful.... I'll help you get ready for your date if you want." I gazed at her for minute "That would be great."

When we got home she asked our mom to pluck my eyebrows. My mom was excited about the endeavor; she's been asking me to let her do it since seventh grade. It took her a good 45 minutes to finish, because every time she pulled one out I had to rub my eyebrow, it hurt and itched! When she was done with me, my eyebrows were so red and puffy I had to ice them. I thought they looked worse. I gave Tori one evil eye because I had an ice pack on the other.

"Don't worry," she said, "The swelling will go down and the red will go away."

"By tonight!" I exclaimed. Tori rubbed fresh aloe on my brow, it felt cool, soothing, better.

She chuckled, amused by my discomfort. "You'll get used to plucking them, it won't bother you so much after a week or so." I gave her an even dirtier look, like I was going to do this again.

She had me do her "getting ready ritual" she does before going out, starting with a shower. She instructed me on the shampoo and conditioner to use and she made me shave my legs even though I protested because I was going to be wearing jeans.

When I got out she put stuff on my face and in my hair. Then she blew it dry part way and put my make-up on before she did hers. Then we both curled our hair. I looked pretty good and I didn't look like Herman Munster anymore. My eyebrows were nice, not too thin, but shaped, it made me look different. Mom said it elongated my face and gave it more shape. "Hmmm" was my only comment because I kind of agreed with her.

I was amazed I looked so good. I peeled off my robe and started looking in the closet for a top. I asked Tori what I should wear, my wardrobe was more basic than hers. I could see I would have to make some improvements. She pulled out a sweater of hers that I loved and she let me borrow it. I looked at her and said "I like this much better."

"Like what better?" she asked.

"I like it better when we get along." She laughed, smiled at me and said "Me too."

The sweater came just below the waistband on my jeans I thought it was too short but Tori said that's how it should be. "But if I lift my arms my stomach will show."

"Exactly" she replied. I didn't like the idea but hoped she was right.

The bottom half of the sweater and from the elbows down were a deep sky blue and the top a dark pink. It was hand knit even though we bought it at the department store, really thick with an elementary house and flowers stitched on top; it was my favorite sweater of hers. She made me change my jeans so I had a fresh pair on; she was pulling out a pair of boots for me when we heard someone knocking on the patio door. "You go ahead and change and I'll get the door." Tori said quickly.

I looked at the clock and it was 5:50pm, he was early. Don't tell me he was going to be a *grandpa* like Cale. I grabbed my coat and walked into our eating area. There he stood in cowboy boots, nice jeans, a black thermal shirt with a couple buttons opened and that reddish brown leather coat. He looked smokin' hot! I checked him out up and down and turned right back around and headed straight for my bedroom.

Tori came flying into the room, I was laughing. She said "What's so funny? "

"I should have known he didn't want to go out with me, he is sooo hot!"

We both laughed and she said "He is... hot, and you totally deserve to go out with him, you look hot yourself, now go set his ass straight and tell him like it is." We hugged.

"Awe..." I said "We just had a sisterly moment!"

Tori replied "It is better." I smiled.

"Now what do I do?" I asked her.

"Pull your ID out of your pocket, hold it up when you walk in the room, say you almost forgot it and then stick it in your pocket." I did just that and he wasn't any the wiser, smiled to myself and thought it's nice having an older sister.

Jett was looking at me, smiling, full eye contact and didn't look away until my mom and dad came into the room and started drilling him on the details of our date. They asked him to have me home by eleven. He looked at me and I just shrugged and he winked at me. My mom looked out the window and said, "Is that your big sedan out there? Hope you're picking up friends."

3:17 a.m. ...the waking hour

"Mom! I can't believe you just said that! Cale picked me up in a van and you didn't say anything to him and by the way, it was empty!" I took a deep breath and said "Let's get going." I smiled; this is how it was supposed to be, not the other way around with Cale chatting up my parents before each date and them just trusting him.

We got down to his car and my mom was right; it was a big stinking sedan and no one else was in it. I looked at him with a look of disappointment because I knew where he thought this night was going. I got in, he started the car slowly. "You look really nice. You look... different." I said "Thanks," really short, and we were off.

We were silent for what seemed like forever, but then he looked over at me and tapped my arm with the back of his hand "What's up, is something wrong?" I looked at him and said, "It's just hard being the crash dummy." He laughed and said "What's that supposed to mean? "

"I can't even believe you asked me out – so what's the deal?" Oh my gosh do I ever know when to shut up? It's my curse, I speak and then think.

"Excuse me?" he asked, his voice strained.

I said "The whole school thinks you asked me out just to sleep with me and if you knew me, you would know that getting lucky on our first date or at all, is not part of the deal." There was silence that was deafening, but I'll be darned if anyone is going to use me. "Just because I dated Cale Winters doesn't mean I am any more experienced than I was before I dated him either, pal."

I paused momentarily but started again. "It means I don't know why you picked me to make your ex-jealous and I'm not sure why you told your friends you could get lucky with me either, because I have done nothing to you! I am not a dumb bimbo like your precious little stuck up ex-girlfriend. Is she even your ex? Or is this just all a contest or some weird bet?" You know I couldn't stop me and my mouth. We pulled in front of a fancy restaurant and he parked the car and we just sat there.

"Sorry" was all he said. "My intentions may have been different when I asked you out and I may have shot off my mouth off in front of my friends but I have never taken advantage of a girl before and I don't plan on starting now." There was a pause and then he continued, "I really am sorry, I never meant to hurt you."

The way he said sorry was cute it sounded more like "soary." He cleared his throat "Do you want to go in? Or do you want me to take you home?"

I let a long silence linger "What is this place?" I asked somberly.

"They are supposed to have great Italian food."

"Everyone picked this place to eat?" I asked.

"No, I thought you and I could have dinner alone. Like I said, I may have asked you for one reason but then I changed my mind."

"What changed your mind?"

"Well, I thought you were too young for me at first but then my mom pointed out that she is three years younger than my dad and you're only 2 years younger than me. And then I saw you swimming this week and I like that you're interested in sports. I've never dated a girl into sports before."

"So you were the one standing by the pool when I was swimming?"

"What? No, I saw you from the top of the bleachers. That was you, right? I'm supposed to run the pool bleachers to help me make my weight – it's warmer and more humid in the pool area making us sweat more and lose weight faster."

"Yeah that was me..... I'm actually really hungry and I bet their plates are small and fancy here. Can we go somewhere else? Do you want to go to Papa G's?"

He laughed "So you're hungry. I don't think I've been on a date with a girl that actually admits she's hungry and eats her dinner."

He started the car, backed up, and said "We can't go to Papa G's, that's where the rest of the gang is." Cars were going by us flashing lights into his eyes illuminating the copper flecks in his irises.

"We can sit at a separate table." I'm not sure why I pushed it but I did, I think I figured that I may as well meet everyone now and get it over with.

He looked at me, pursed his lips, and said "Okay, I could go for some pepperoni pizza."

I looked at him with wild eyes and said "Pepperoni *PAN* pizza!" excitedly.

And he said "That's right baby, nothing but! " We both laughed.

I said "Awesome! But were getting a large, I'm starving."

"Me too." he replied. "Did you really call me pal?" he glanced at me and we both chuckled.

3:17 a.m. ...the waking hour

We talked the rest of the ride, telling each other what classes we had. I told him all the sports I was in and I even mentioned golf, he thought it was cool and wanted to learn. We laughed a little about this and that and to my surprise he was very easy to talk to.

We got to the parking lot and didn't say another word until he parked. The parking lot was a little icy in spots, he came around my side and gave me his arm until we reached the restaurant door, when he opened it for me I let go. I was really nervous and I must have looked it. The hostess came up asked us how many, when his friend came up and said "I thought you were going to Luigi's? Our table is over here, come on."

Jett looked at me, slid his hand into mine and said "No thanks, we'll get our own table." His friend knocked him in his shoulder and said "Whatever."

Jett gave our hands a little jiggle, leaned over and whispered, "Is this okay?" I nodded with a half-smile, his warm, strong hand felt really good in mine.

"You okay? You look mad." he said to me.

I smiled a cheesy smile and said "No, I'm fine. Sorry, I was just trying to spot your ex and see who's here." He pointed slightly to the right. "She's the one with too much make-up on and too much hairspray, in the black sweater." he whispered in my ear.

"I have makeup and hairspray on too, so does that mean you think I look like a hooker too?" I asked sarcastically. He kept holding my hand and led me through the crowd after the hostess. She sat us at a booth. I took off my jacket and threw it to the end of the booth. He did the same with his on the opposite bench and I scooted in on my side, mid table. I could see the big table where everyone was, I had the good seat.

Jett came over pushed himself in with me, he hip checked me and said "Scoot over fat ass!" - - he totally froze and said "Ooo, I'm so sorry. I didn't mean it, it's a term me and my brothers use, a good term, like a term of endearment....I didn't mean it." He looked really concerned. "I... I think I just said it because I am so comfortable around you...please I didn't mean it." I started to laugh and said "No way am I fat or sensitive. You're lucky I could care less what you think."

He laughed a little and said "You don't look like a hooker either."

"You mean a fat ass hooker." We both started laughing so hard

my eyes started to tear. I noticed his friends at the big table taking glances at us. We settled down a bit and he said "I think you look beautiful tonight and you look good with or without make-up. You don't have two tons on like most girls wear either."
"Thanks, my sister did it for me. She wanted me to look good for when I turned you down and told you off tonight."
"Oh really…." He said and we both laughed over it.

He started pointing out all his friends when Declan and his girlfriend came over and sat across from us and introduced Rae to me. She started right in the conversation with "How come we have to sit with the bitch when you two are having all the fun over here?"

"I like her already." I said.

Jett leaned into me and said "Rae has always hated Lisa." Declan chimed in and said "I second that."

Jett looked at me. "I think I was the only one that liked her and now that I think about it, I'm not sure what I liked about her either." Everyone laughed louder than it was funny and I caught a glimpse of Lisa looking over.

The waitress came over and Jett ordered our pepperoni pan pizza and then ordered two sodas and he asked me "Do you want anything else? Soup or salad?"

"No thanks, but make it a pitcher of pop, probably cheaper right? I'm thirsty from our workout in the car." Declan's eyes popped open. They were so wide I thought they'd pop out of his head. Rae just said excitedly "What?" Jett and I just laughed again and they joined in. "She's just kidding." Jett said, and everyone laughed more and I said "Not really."

After everyone's laughter subsided I told them "You guys don't have to try and make me feel better, it's fine. I'd rather eat over here because I'm sure to get my equivalent in pizza, I'm hungry." Everyone chuckled a little, and Declan said "So you're an eater huh? I didn't know that. Good match for Jett, but you could never out eat him."

"Maybe not, but I could give him a run for his money."

"So little girl, you think you could eat a large pepperoni pan pizza all by yourself?" Declan said.

"Sure I could, but not tonight."

"Oh, I see how you are, copping out all ready."

"No, that's not why." I said giving 'em a nervous laugh.

3:17 a.m. ...the waking hour

"Really, then why?" Declan said.

"If I tell you I'll probably put Jett off."

"Not much will put this kid off; now tell us why you can't eat a whole pie tonight."

I looked at Jett and he made an upside down smile and shrugged, like who cares, tell your story. So I went on "First off is because I ate before I came......" with a little unsurety of what they would think of that, I continued "I ate because I thought we were eating in a big group and sometimes you just don't get enough to eat. Since I'm the new girl I wasn't going to say anything if I didn't. You know, just like eating before you go to a wedding." No one said anything.

Then Declan chimed in "...and the second reason."

"Oh, well my jeans are tight now, if I stuff myself they'll be even tighter and I'll want to pop my button. I don't think that is good first date stuff." They all chuckled.

"Oh my god, Jett!" Rae said, laughing excitedly. "I love this girl! She's a perfect match for you." Everyone at the table chuckled again and Declan agreed and said "no kidding."

Jett put his arm around me and gave me a squeeze. "It sure seems that way doesn't it, I ate before I came too." I looked at him, smiled and asked "What did you have?" I said excitedly. Rae interrupted "Who cares what you two ate. Let's talk about something else."

She seemed genuinely happy I was there. Maybe she didn't get along with the other girls. "No more talk," Jett stated, "You two run along because we aren't sharing our food." They sat there with puppy dog eyes and looked truly upset they had to sit with the others, they didn't move until Jett made a thumbing motion toward their table. They got up begrudgingly; Rae turned and stuck her tongue out at Jett, Jett returned the gesture.

"I like her, she's cool." He took my hand in his slowly and said "they are cool... is this, too much?" as he twisted our hands above the table. I pulled them under the table and said "Only if you don't mean it."

"Well, I'm having fun so far which is not what I expected. I'm not sure what I expected, but this is all right." I kept holding his hand.

After the waitress delivered the pizza he moved to the other side. I looked at him and said "Do I smell?" sarcastically.

"Nooo.... I need elbow room when I eat, because we're piggin' out right!" he said with a big fat grin on his face.

"Absolutely," I told him.

"Piggin' out 'til we have to pop the button on our jeans." He said and winked at me.

"That's what I'm talkin' about" and we both laughed. That's when I caught an evil look from his ex; I didn't care though. Hopefully our date would keep on going well, even if we only ended up being friends in the end; it would be good enough for me.

I didn't finish my half so Jett did. I was stuffed. Declan came over told us they were leaving for the show. Jett gave him a twenty and said "Get us two tickets, we'll be right behind ya." I got up tapped my belly and stretched, forgetting the sweater I had on, and said "I am so full, I may just need a nap." Jett reached over and touched my belly and I flinched and pulled my sweater down. He moved his hand to my waist.

"You must not be full enough, your jeans are still buttoned." I smiled and took his hand. I don't remember laughing at all with Cale, I wonder why that was? I pondered through all our dates on how serious they were and then realized I felt like they were all controlled or very well planned somehow, and just boring. I was quiet in the car contemplating all this.

Before we got to the movie Jett asked "A penny for your thoughts."

"Where's my penny?" I asked. He dug in his ash tray and handed me a nickel.

"You better be sure you want to hear what's on my mind before you ask, because I always have a lot to say." I replied.

"That's fine, talk away..." He reached out and I slid my hand in his.

"Well, I was just thinking about Cale."

"Oh." he said disappointingly and loosened his grip. I scooted closer and put my other hand around his so he couldn't let go.

"No, no no no not like that. I was just thinking, here I am on a date with you expecting to get used and thrown away and to have a terrible time, but I have laughed more with you and have had more fun on one date with you than I ever did with Cale."

He let out a sigh of relief and squeezed my hand. "Me too."

"So you dated Cale too? Just kidding.... Hey, are we here to

3:17 a.m. ...the waking hour

make your ex jealous or what?" He didn't respond right away.

"I don't know" he responded with sincerity "We made her jealous at the restaurant. Making her envious was fun but I have moved on, starting with you. The more I hang with you the more I realize she wasn't such a nice girlfriend." He jiggled our entwined hands.

"I think it would be fun if we had a plan." I said. "Something to make her jealous but nothing too obvious, she may already be provoked by us from the restaurant."

"What do you mean?" So I told him I caught her giving me "an evil eye" a couple of times during the evening, he enjoyed that.

We didn't make a plan which was fine since I'm not that vindictive of a person. The ride to the theater was short so there wasn't a lot of time to plot and plan anyway. We had to park in the back lot because the front lot was full. Jett shut the car off and I slid myself out. As I was straightening my coat and shirt someone grabbed me from behind. A gloved hand covered my mouth, pressing my head back firmly onto him so I couldn't move it and the other around my arms and chest. I couldn't scream. I looked for Jett, he was on the other side of the car. When he finally looked back he did a double take. I could tell he was confused, shocked. I saw him saying something but couldn't make out his words.

My feet were dragging on the ground as I was being pulled backward. I tried to dig my heels into the snow and ice but it didn't help. I lifted both feet up hard and pushed off of the car, we fell back, hit one car and bounced off another and then we both hit the ground. I was on top trying to get up but he was pulling on my coat, I turned around hit him, got up, kicked him and started running toward the building but not before he grabbed my ankle. I fell right into Jett, he grabbed both my arms, whipped me around releasing my ankle and asked me if I was ok. He sounded a million miles away. I nodded, I had a hand on his car holding me up, he took off running but not very well as the parking lot was slick with ice. Once he hit the snowy field, though, he really took off.

As I turned to look at the building, I saw Declan and Rae walking toward me. I yelled and pointed, "Jett just took off after this guy who attacked me!" Without even flinching Declan took off in the same general direction. I stayed leaning on Jett's car, I was trying to get my bearings. Rae yelled my name, she was standing by the building, she waved me over. She was holding her coat closed, carrying the biggest purse I have ever seen, she looked cold. I let go of the car, my legs were shaking but managed to make my way over; as we walked to the front of the theater I told her what happened.

"Are you okay?" she asked. "What kind of maniac would try something on you around Jett? If he gets hold of him he'll tear him apart." I didn't say anything, I was just shivering, not sure if it was from the cold or the fact that I was totally freaked out.

"Let's go inside, get you warm plus it's probably safer inside." Rae said as she led me around to the front of the building, after we turned the corner and stepped onto the sidewalk we saw Jett and Declan, they were walking toward us. They jogged over to us.

"We lost the guy, he had parked his truck on the side street" Declan announced thumbing to the street behind them "...and took off." I didn't stop, I just kept walking until I was inside the theater doors. When I stopped inside Rae fixed my hair straightened my jacket; she had me turn around looking to see if I was alright.

I shivered "Ah Jett, I panicked and kicked your car, I'm sorry, I'll pay for any damages." He smiled and came over, put his rough warm hands behind my neck and under my hair and pulled me closer. I put my hands on his chest, they were still shaking.

"We've had girls do crazier stuff than that to our cars and never once has any of them apologized nor had a good reason for it, please, don't worry about it." Then he kissed me on the forehead and gave me a hug. "Are you okay?" He rubbed my back and it warmed me immediately and I felt safe in his arms. I pushed back gently, "I am fine, don't we have a movie to see?" I asked, giving my fake cheesy smile. Jett pulled me in for another hug, I could get used to this.

Rae questioned my efforts, "Don't you want to go home or call the police?" I knew I had 24 hours to report a crime, since Nic and I had researched it after my other incident this summer. When I told them I could wait to file a report; they seemed amazed I knew that information.

"Let's go see the movie, and after, if all of us think we should call the police we will. But I'm sure it was someone just playing a prank on us...." Not that I believed for a second it was meant for anyone else, but I thought it sounded good.

We entered the next set of doors. Rae gave us our tickets. "We're getting popcorn, you guys getting anything?" I looked at

Jett and shook my head. "No, we're good," he said. I saw a wall and thought I'd hold it up while we waited. Jett came with me, stood across from me, his hands in his jean pockets. He looked solemn, serious, he looked into my eyes "Are you sure you don't want to leave?"

"I'm fine." I said, shaking my head, "A little shaken up maybe, but fine."

He came even closer to me, put one of his muscular arms on the wall next to me and leaned into my ear. "Are you sure, you look like you're trembling to me." His hot breath permeated around my ear and sent a definite tremble through my body that sent a warm feeling right down to my toes. I turned my head only a smidge and my cheek touched his "I'm fine." I whispered back. He touched my face and pulled back slowly until our lips made contact. We released and I opened my eyes and held his gaze for a moment when I noticed Lisa standing only a few feet away, giving me another dirty look. I looked right back at her and gave her a nod. Jett turned his head slightly, spotted her then turned back toward me and said "Sorry, I didn't know she was there." He straightened up, stood next to me and took my hand.

Jett sat on one side of me in the theater and Rae on the other. She handed me a bottle, I handed it to Jett, he opened it and handed it back; it was beer I could smell it when he handed it back to me. Rae said "You deserve it girl, drink up, it will settle your nerves." She gave one to each of the boys too. The girls in front of us, which were part of the rest of our group, including his ex, giggled and talked through the entire movie, knocked over bottles that rattled all the way down to the front of the theater and were just utterly obnoxious. Thank goodness I didn't knock any over because I could tell Jett was annoyed.

CHAPTER 14

Before we got to the end of my block I asked Jett to pull over and park. He laughed and said "I thought guys were always the one to ask the girl to park."

"Really, I wasn't sure how that worked because I've never parked before."

"Now that I don't believe" he said "You and Cale never..."

"No, I told you we never had fun and we only kissed. He was boring and acted like my dad more than anything else. Now that I think about it I'm not sure why I dated him." I paused then continued "Oh yeah, I dated him because he was good looking but looks can only take you so far in a relationship, obviously."

He put one hand behind my waist and slid me across the bench to him. "Nice." I mumbled.

I started "I don't want to..." and he pressed his lips into mine before I could say anything else.

"THUD!" Both of us stopped and froze, then tried looking around outside. Jett got out of the car and I followed suit. Something was on his trunk. We inched toward it slowly. It was a big rock with lots of mud on it, like someone just dug it up and decided to toss it. "That wasn't very nice" I said, "They didn't even leave a note."

In a split second Jett took off, I saw it too, the movement between the two houses. He ran fast, I yelled "Jett don't...."

3:17 a.m. ...the waking hour

I stood, my body locked in a still position, just outside his car. We were on my street, in my own neighborhood where I normally felt comfortable but tonight I got that peculiar eerie feeling. I looked at my watch and thought I would wait right here.....then I thought if he doesn't return in five I'll get in the car and lock the doors, and if he doesn't come back in ten I'm running home .... Since this summer's incident, I scheme and pre-plan exit routes all the time.

I looked at my watch again, it hadn't even been a minute but felt like five. I started pacing and looking around to see if anyone was sneaking up on me. I saw nothing. One thing about being out in the country is when it's dark, it's dark. I felt like my eyes were opened wider than possible. This had to be someone playing a prank, I told myself. Crap, I should have gone after Jett. I looked back down at my watch and only two minutes had gone by.....I ruffled through his glove compartment looking for a flashlight, nothing. I started nervously walking in the same path that Jett took behind the houses. There was a tree line a few feet wide dividing the neighbor's yards. Behind the houses and yards was the same ravine that connected to mine. I heard nothing standing next to the neighbor's house, still nothing when I got to the back yard. My heart felt heavy and my hands clammy. The backyard was pitch dark, the owners were either in bed or not home.

I heard some rustling in front of me. I kept walking; I stumbled on a big branch and decided to pick it up. I heard something again as I approached the ravine. I raised the branch over my head and I said quietly "Who's there?"

"It's me", Jett whispered. I saw him bend down, he picked something up, it was a piece of wood. "Get back to the car." he whispered loudly.

Oh no, dammit, déjàvu. I know this, I know it! "Jett," I said in my normal voice as he walked backward toward me. "He's gone, I'm sure of it." Jett said.

He turned to look at me and he said "Nice branch." He held up his, mine was three times bigger. "What were you going to hit me over the head with that?"

"No, what were you going to do with yours, write a message in the dirt?" We both laughed.

"I thought I'd conk the other guy on the head with it." Jett dropped his and I threw mine like a spear into the black abyss and we heard a grunt and then a bunch of rustling. Jett and I ran to the car.

We were laughing, he started the car and headed down the street, "How do we get to your house from here?"

"Just up four houses on the right" I said.

"We're awfully close to your house to be parking aren't we?" He asked and chuckled.

"I didn't want to park, park. I just wanted to talk to you alone." He pulled to the bottom of my driveway, put the car in park and turned off the engine. "What do you want to talk about?"

"Oh, not like that, I just wanted to talk since we couldn't during the movie and if we're here we'll probably get interrupted." Our outdoor lights went on and they cast light and shadows into his car, there was just enough light to catch a glimpse of the blood trickling down his arm onto his hand. "Holy crap, you cut your arm! Are you okay?" I looked closer, "Do you need stitches?"

"No, I don't think so." He pushed his sleeve up and the cut was pretty big, I touched it "Are you sure?"

"No it looks fine." Jett said as cool as a cucumber.

"You better come inside, I'll take a look at it and clean it for you....." He hesitated. "Come on don't be a baby, I don't bite."

I led him into our basement through the garage, and over to the bar, which reached across the width of the room, it was big. "That's a nice bar," he commented.

"Thanks, my parents entertain a lot so it's fully stocked too. Grab a seat." I pointed to the bar stools. I went behind the bar and grabbed our first aid kit. I grabbed the bag next to it as well. "What's in the bag?" Jett asked.

"My mom overstocks gauze and first aid supplies ever since my brother slid down a tree." He looked at me with a puzzled look.

"Well, let me tell you my brother's story." I helped Jett take his coat off while I was talking. Then I rolled his sleeve up. "After swim team, two summers ago, we came home and my brother wanted to play outside, so no big deal, he did. The problem was he had his Speedo on, no shirt and no shoes. If you've ever seen a Speedo you know they're like underwear." Jett nodded in agreement. "He was climbing a tree near our fort and was pretty high up. It was one of those skinnier trees with very rough bark and no branches for at least 12- 14 feet in the air. When he got up really high, the tree started to bend, you know flex. And I think it

3:17 a.m. ...the waking hour

freaked him out because that's when he lost his grip and slid all the way down. He still has the scars on his chest to show for it." Jett made a noise like he knew it hurt.

When I was done cleaning and bandaging his arm I noticed his jeans were torn on his thigh, he had a cut there too. I just stared at it and he said "What?" he looked down. "I didn't know that dog got me on the leg too. You ought to have your parents call animal control."

"It was a dog? I thought you said it was a guy?"

"I don't know, I didn't see much. When we tussled I thought I heard a growl, maybe it was a dog and a guy. Or a really hairy guy," he said laughing.

I asked Jett again, "Are you sure you don't need stitches?"

"No." He said ripping his jeans a little more. All I could do was stare at the muscular leg – he was perfect. "I'll be fine" he murmured. I couldn't believe we were on a date. This beautiful boy asked me out, but would he ask me out again or was I just supposed to make his ex-jealous? Plus, this date had been overly chaotic, one incident after another. I'm not sure I would want to date me.

I managed to get another piece of gauze out, he took it from me and cleaned his leg. I managed to get the bandage on him without embarrassing myself, although, the touch of his skin made my heart race. It was hot and smooth and I didn't want to stop touching him, so I smoothed the bandage on really well, leaving my hand on his leg and it felt very serene just touching him, I was in heaven.

He let out a little laugh and said "What are you doing?"

"I'm sorry, but you have very nice skin." My eyes almost popped out of my head and I quickly asked. "Are you gonna tell me what happened? You ran into the ravine after a guy, then you were attacked by his dog? Do you know who it was?"

"Let me see your other arm." We pushed his other sleeve up and sure enough another cut on the back of his wrist but not bad at all. "Oh, that was from before the movie." I looked at him, concern in my eyes. "It's fine," he said pushing his sleeve back down, "I'm fine. I didn't see anything it was too dark but I heard a growl and the bite felt like a dogs so I assume some guy sicced his dog on me"

He turned to me and said "Thank you – I don't think anyone has ever complimented me on my skin before." he half laughed.

"Are you kidding me? You're gorgeous."

He looked a little abashed, but it didn't keep him from talking. "No one has ever told me that before."

"Now that, I don't believe."

Why did I have to say, you have nice skin.... Why couldn't I have said nice smile, nice eyes, anything but nice skin – although, it was smooth with muscle underneath, when he flexes I can see every muscle. I have got to stop drooling over him, get it together girl.

"You seem to be pretty honest and you speak your mind." Jett said. As he was talking I went back behind the bar and grabbed a couple of sodas and glasses. "So if I asked you anything, do you think you'd tell me the truth?" I froze before setting the last glass down, giving him a nervous smile, not showing any teeth.

"I assume I would, I guess it depends on the question......no, I take that back, I'd either tell you the truth or tell you it was none of your business."

"Fair enough," he said. "Why did you ask to park, with me, really?"

"Of course," I replied, "I wanted to talk alone....I didn't know if my brother and my sister would be home and..... I wanted to...to see if...." He looked at me not believing my story – I squinted my eyes at him "Fine, maybe I wanted to see if we could duplicate our kiss from earlier." I let out a breath and said "I wanted to see if you were a good kisser." I walked around the bar, wanting to run away but instead I sat on the bar stool next to his. He had a goofy look on his face so I added "Because if you weren't, and the theater was a fluke, then I wouldn't go out with you again" ...and I grinned because I knew that wasn't true.

Laughing he said "Oh really?"

I, of course, couldn't keep my mouth shut, so I retorted "Just because you're mister good-looking doesn't mean you're good at anything else. .... Oops I'm sorry Jett, I'm sorry." He continued laughing. "I say what's on my mind and I'm very sarcastic. I get that from my dad, but he's actually funny."

"No, no, I think you're very funny and the reason why I asked you out was because I heard you were interested in going out with me. I had no idea you were sooo..." He sat forward on his bar stool and said "But if you're not interested and I'm not a good kisser, I guess I'll just leave."

3:17 a.m. ...the waking hour

I almost choked! Did I talk him out of going out with me? What am I stupid? I quickly retorted "I never said you were a bad kisser, I said I wanted to test the theory which if you recall we did….." He grabbed my bar stool and pulled it as close to him as he could get it to him, with our noses almost touching. I didn't breathe and I didn't move. I was trying to stay quiet.

He said in a low soft voice, "The reason why I asked you out was because you seemed different. You don't wear a lot of make-up and I think you're pretty without it. And I actually thought you liked me." I leaned in for a kiss and he pulled back. I let my hands rest his legs gently and looked in his eyes, they were so dreamy they made me melt. They were a warm butterscotch with light gold and copper flecks and I whispered "Please don't leave, I'll be nice." My voice was a little shaky. There was a long pause, almost too long, but he kept looking at me. "I promise that I'll try not to be so sarcastic," another pause, I held my breath again.

He pulled back. "I like sarcastic – and a sense of humor. The other girls I've dated are way too serious, and by the way, most girls ask me out and make the first move. So even though I have a reputation, I didn't make it all on my own. It was sort of made for me. I'm actually kind of shy." He turned his chair and stood up.

Okay, now what do I do? "Would you like more soda?" My voice was still shaky and nervous. I wished I was Tori right now she would know what to do; she'd have him wrapped around her little finger.

"No," he replied and put his coat on. I quickly retorted, "So you asked me out to get close to my sister then? Because she'll never ask a guy out, you'll be waiting a long time!" He turned and gave me a dirty look. "Crap, I said I would try……sorry."

"You sure do say sorry a lot, and I have no interest in your sister, I wouldn't do that I have two brothers so I know how that can be. I should be the one that's worried. You dated Cale, one of the best looking guys in school. I should be nervous on where I stand."

"I usually don't screw up a date this bad, you just make me nervous and as for Cale he's more of a pretty boy and we had nothing in common, so nothing to worry about there." I went to push myself off the bar stool, putting my hands on either side of the seat to slide off, but instead Jett leaned toward me putting his hands over mine gently. His hands were warm and felt nice. I held my breath, trying not to move. His lips touched mine ever so softly, barely brushing mine. I was waiting for a panic attack, but nothing happened. Please don't stop, please don't stop, was all I could think.

He moved one of his hands off mine slowly, I let my hand wander up his arm. He slowly moved his hand onto my knee and I kept my eyes closed and my head down. Jett swooped one of my legs to the side and then the other in one smooth sweeping motion and wrapped his arms around me, pressing me into him. His whole body felt warm, I could feel the heat radiating from him. I had no clue what to do, my hands were idle. Should I move them? Should I open my eyes?

He pulled my chin up with his hand. His lips touched mine and I could picture his smile in my head, his lips a soft cherry red and his butterscotch eyes. His lips were soft and warm, when he pressed them into mine, I didn't know when to breathe.

He stopped; and pressed his forehead to mine so I figured I ought to breathe. He moved in again pulling my hips closer to him. Freeing my other hand, I put my arms around his neck as we moved our lips slowly and softly. The kiss deepened and our lips parted. I felt a heat wave come over me. He was done kissing me and my eyes were still closed.

He whispered "Your eyes are closed." I opened them slowly hoping to look like I knew what I was doing and said "I know, weren't yours?" He smiled and went to say something but I interrupted and kissed him again. I put my hand on his cheek and slowly moved it to the back of his neck. His hands on my hips moved slowly to the small of my back and touched my skin, I winced a little and the other moved up to my mid-back almost touching my bra and I started to squirm, I broke out of the kiss and just looked at him. He stared back, waiting for me to say something.

"I thought you didn't have any expectations for our date?" I replied.

"No I don't, I thought we talked about that." he said with a slight inflection in his voice. "Why? Did you?"

"Just one.....I was, well, I no...."

He leaned in and kissed my neck, "You can tell me."

"I wanted to...the first day I saw you, you had your jacket on with no shirt" I said wavering

"Yes, and?"

"I always think about it." I replied.

"So I didn't have to take you to a dinner and a movie."

I giggled and said "nope" softly.

He took my hand and kissed my palm. I looked down at our hands, he pressed mine firmly on his waist at the hem of his shirt; I flattened it and slowly pushed upward until I felt flesh. It sent chills through me, I felt him quiver; I moved my other hand to his stomach. He was very warm, his skin soft as silk, I slid both hands further up across his abs and then onto his chest and back down. I pushed them around to his back and lightly scratched him, pulling them up and forward and up again. I looked into his eyes, they were closed for a second and then he looked down at me. We kissed, I pushed my hands up to his chest, his nipples were dense, it was angelic. I moved my lips to his jaw and then his neck and breathed him in letting my hands move down slowly out of his shirt and down to his butt and then I stopped. I kept my eyes closed and then started to think and hoped he wouldn't try to go any further because I'm not sure if I could resist him. He leaned in and kissed me on the cheek and dropped both hands to the small of my back and pronounced hoarsely "I should get going."

I let out a deep breath, a sigh of relief. He pushed back a little and said in surprise "What, I'm not a good kisser? I thought that went well."

"I thought that went very well..... I'm just nervous around you until, you, touch me, then I'm....not, and that makes me nervous." I said slowly as I snapped out of my trance. "Are you sure you don't want more soda? Did I mention I'm a little nervous? Why don't we have a soda and you can tell me about yourself – I know you wrestle, play football and have a great smile but that's about it." I was impressed with myself, I think I recuperated quickly and sounded very adult-like with no sarcasm.

Jett replied "Do you know what time it is?" I looked at the clock behind him and wanted to lie because I didn't know his curfew. But I told him the truth, "It's 12:15 what time do you have to be home?"

"Well..." he said.

"Please stay, I'm just a little nervous. I'm quite normal, trust me." There was a moment of silence I couldn't take so I added "We can sit and chat for one soda...."

He took his jacket off and I saw all the muscles in his arms flex, I could daydream about him for days now. I caught a glimpse of his arm and noticed blood seeping through his bandage; I went to touch it; he didn't flinch and reassured me "I'm fine, don't worry about it." And sat back on the bar stool and rested his arms on the bar. "What'll ya have?" I replied "Soda only, my parent's mark their liquor bottles so we can't drink from them."

He replied "Of course, I would never touch your parents stock. I wouldn't disrespect them or want to make them mad at me for any reason, and I wouldn't let you drink it either."

I hopped off my bar stool and went behind the bar, I took a couple of Pepsi's out of the fridge, opened the bottles, sat on the counter behind the bar and handed him his soda. "So you're saying that I'm not allowed to drink my parent's alcohol the next time you're here?"

"That's right. I don't want you getting me in trouble with your parents".

So I of course replied out loud instead of to myself "So there'll be a next time - -"

Jett said "Well I was hoping, of course, if I'm not a good kisser....." he laughed, I smiled too.

"Jett" I said "I think we're going to get along just fine and if you ask me out again I may just say yes. And don't worry about me drinking, I don't." He laughed and showed me his great smile, which I absolutely adored.

"You did tonight. You had a beer that Rae smuggled in to the theater, actually a couple."

"I was just settling my nerves and I only had one, okay two, one to settle my nerves the second one was a social drink." I said sarcastically, using my hand to talk. "Ok maybe you're right."

"I love your sense of humor, if you're lucky I'll call you."

We talked and talked. It was easy to talk to him and he had a good sense of humor. I hoped we would have a second date. My dad called down, "Addie you better wrap it up." I quickly looked at the clock and I couldn't believe it was after one already!

"Oh my gosh, are you late? Do you need to call your parents and let them know you are on your way home?" I asked.

He laughed at me again and said "No, that's alright, I don't have a curfew. I'm a junior so my parents don't give me a time to be home. I just didn't want to stay out too late because I have to work out tomorrow before our wrestling match – coach likes us in early."

"I have a curfew, my parents wanted me home by 11:00, I tried talking them up to midnight, but..."

Jett quickly replied, "Of course you do, you're a freshman and a girl."

I replied back like whiplash... "What does being a girl have to do with anything?"

He laughed. "Addie, it's nothing against you, it's just how it is. My cousin has to be in by 10:30 so you should be happy with 11:00 it's a reasonable time and it's long enough for dinner and a movie. Your parents are just trying to keep you safe. I have to get going Addie." And with no hands he leaned over for a short kiss, but I put my hand on the back of his neck and gave him, hopefully, a kiss to remember. As he pulled away, he said "Your eyes are closed again." I opened them.

"If you keep on commenting on how I kiss, I just might get a complex." Geez laweez I told myself, please shut up!

Jett replied, "Well, we wouldn't want that to happen."

CHAPTER 15

Monday on the bus, to avoid giving Declan further date info on Jett, I told him about Topher and his locker because it had been bothering me all weekend. Declan thought it was curious too, "Normally they don't move your locker, they just fix them," he told me. In return, I told Declan I would ask Topher why he moved his locker again and see what he said. I knew how to set the trap for Declan to go digging for more information, and he took the bait. Declan said "I have a class with him third period, I could see if I could get the *'dish'* on him.

"Sure" I agreed, "let me know what happens at wrestling."

"Okay, I'll give you a ride home."

"But how? You rode the bus like me, duh…."

"Long story short, my car will be at school later."

"Ok, then I say awesome." I replied and with that we didn't have time to discuss my date. I betcha he forgot to ask.

After school Declan was the first one in the wrestling room, he looked like he had a big story to tell me and couldn't wait until after practice. He was even pacing a bit. "Declan, what's up? Did you talk to Topher?" There was silence, it wasn't like Declan not to say anything and he was pacing right in front of me, concentrating on the floor.

I caught his arm, and he stopped.

"I talked to him." He said solemnly still looking at the floor and started chewing on a finger nail. He put the heel of his hand to his forehead. "It can't be all that bad Declan, just give me the heads up, it is what it is, it won't change by you telling me."

Nic was mopping the mats, making comments, making fun of Declan, "Not now, I have a headache," she giggled. "Can't we just be friends...?"

Declan turned to me he looked so serious and said "I am going to tell you but I don't want you asking any questions or interrupting me when I tell you. Then when I'm all done you can ask me as many questions as you want and all the way home. Okay?" I expected him to start but he was waiting for me to agree.

"Fine. Okay" I said.

He grabbed my arms and said "I'll help you with whatever you need."

"Help me? Okay...." I replied again. Now he's scaring me.

He took a deep breath and started with "I saw Topher third period. I was going to ask him the scoop about the locker change and I noticed he looked bad, depressed, not his usual self. He looked sickly almost. So I went up and talked to him. We had a sub so we got to talk the entire class, and let me tell you, I barely had to grill him to get info. He was primed and ready to tell someone about it and he just started spilling everything he knew." He took a deep breath and let a long pause linger.

So I said "Okay..." with a tone like what does this have to do with me? I smiled at him thinking he was being overly serious.

He started again, "He said Cale and he started hanging out this year, because their lockers were together. Cale only started going to school here his junior year....last year. I'm trying to tell you everything in order." Declan said a little panicked, looking at me incredulously. He paused again, but then continued. "So at this point I was thinking Cale and Topher did something bad and one of them doesn't want to fess up to it. And he verified my fears when he begged me not to tell anyone, but that this was too big and he needed to tell someone."

He took both my arms again and said "Listen to me, listen to every word I tell you!" He shook me out of my thoughts and I looked at his face and burrowed my eyes in complete concentration on him.

"Cale has been...has been ...stalking... you, since... this summer...." He said very slowly with a pause in between every word. He was still talking but I heard nothing, it was like being in a tunnel and everything and everyone was getting further and further away. "Addie, Addie can you hear me." Nic was right in my face.

"Of course I can hear you." I looked around, I had a crowd around me and everyone was looking down at me. I felt the floor, I was on it. "I knew I shouldn't have told her." I heard Declan whisper to Nic, "This is way too crazy, we need to tell the police."

"What did you do to her Declan?" Nic snarled and her hands were balled into fists. I propped myself up on my elbow, I meant it to be funny but instead it came out weak and more serious. "Boys, girls relax. I fell, I'm very clumsy when I get my period." All the guys in the group went "ugh" in disgust and walked away.

"The things that come out of your mouth girl." Nic replied. I scooted up against the wall. Declan plopped himself on one side of me and Nic on the other. "At least now I know how to clear a room."

Coach came over "Declan get to work."

Declan whispered "We have more issues over here other than her just having her period." Coach "ugh-ed" turned on his heal, blew the whistle, and walked away to start practice with everyone else. Jett came in right when he was blowing the whistle, just what I needed.

"Well, I guess it was good that I was on the mat when I passed out. The floor would have hurt more."

"Addie, can you take anything seriously? I mean really, if you could see your face right now, you are whiter than a ghost." Nic had real concern in her voice. Jett was just looking at the three of us, I gave him a little wave. I'm sure the other wrestlers would fill him in any minute. Just what I need, him thinking I am a weenie who passes out when she gets cramps.

"Declan can you tell me everything again? I have a feeling I may have missed some of it."

Nic gritted between her teeth and said "Yeah, what did you tell her to make her pass out?" She hushed her voice at the end. If she thought we were going to talk about my period (that I didn't even have) I'm sure she'd want to keep it quiet. Not much embarrassed her, but that would.

Declan started off "This is bad, really bad. We need to tell your parents Addie and probably report it to the police." I put my hand over my face and rubbed it, then pinched my cheeks tryin' to get some color into them.

"Please just start again. The only reason I fell down was because I forgot to breath, you know such a silly thing. I am breathing now and sitting down so let's hear it all and then we'll figure out what to do next."

"Yes! Let's hear it!" Nic agreed.

"Cale never wanted to be your boyfriend, he's been setting you up since this summer!" Nic and I were silent so he repeated himself, explaining it in a different way like we didn't understand. "He's been following you around and stalking you since this summer!" Declan exclaimed.

Nic had doubts "Come on! Why would he do that? That guy could have anyone, he doesn't need to be a stalker." Declan looked across me and over to Nic in disgust for her interruption.

I replied "It's kinda startin' to make a lot of sense to me, the truck, the baseball cap, the dreams..." I tapered off.

"I tell you what, Topher was shaking in his boots and I believe everything he told me.... Plus, after he told me what he did, I know he regretted it but I told him I wouldn't tell anyone but this secret can't be kept. Topher said he was at Cale's house one night testing new sound equipment. They had a few drinks and Topher passed out. But when he woke up, Cale and his girlfriend were fighting, and that he knew it was his girlfriend because of what they did after the fight...." He stopped because he was waiting for me to verify that I was with him or that I knew what he was talking about. I think he was being cautious with me. So I let my eyes go wide and said "Yeah. Like I said, I only passed out because I forgot to breathe... nothing Cale does scares me that bad he's just a high school boy, please go on."

"It all makes sense Addie!" Declan continued. "You told me he only kissed you on the forehead and weird stuff like that and that you thought he acted more a like a dad. It's because everything he did with you was planned and set up! The only thing Topher didn't know is why, except for that he's a sick bastard."

"So maybe I was a stupid bet or something" I replied and Nic agreed.

"Unfortunately, I don't think so not by the other details Topher mentioned."

Nic jumped in while I was rubbing my face "There's more?"

"Oh a lot more and I still don't even think he gave me all the details or that he remembers them himself. He started getting sketchy in some parts and it gets really weird."

"Just what I need, to be involved in someone's sick and twisted stalking routine. I guess this is my year for atrocious and weird incidents."

"No kidding" Nic agreed. "Like you need anyone else attacking or stalking you for that matter."

"Someone else attacked you?" Declan said "Did Jett do something to you? You never did fill me in on your date." I gave Nic a dirty look, she slapped her hand over her mouth, I know she didn't mean it.

"No, my date with Jett was fine, kind of, someone tried grabbing me before the movie and then after someone tossed a rock on Jett's car when we park.... ah... later that night."

"I've been thinking, I have noticed that I have been getting that 'eerie feeling' a lot since this summer and I thought it was because I was attacked but maybe it's because someone really has been stalking me. But stalking me just doesn't make sense, why would anybody be interested in me?"

"True." Nic said. Everyone was amused but not enough to laugh. She went on "Maybe when you started winning all your swim races was when Cale noticed you, and then started watching and got obsessed with you. I mean who quits after you get really good anyways." I just gave her a ferocious look, not sure about which part, maybe all of it.

"Whoa, whoa, whoa!" Declan said really loud, loud enough to get half the wrestling team to look over at us. I started to say "Oh, I have such bad cramps" but before I could finish Nic covered my mouth. "Addie you got attacked and by whom? Was it this summer? Because Topher's ramblings might make sense then." I was in deep thought gazing at the ground in front of me when someone's shadow came over me.

I looked up and it was Jett. He squatted in front of me and asked "You okay?" He had his wrestling uniform on and I could see all his muscles. It was the best part of my day watching him, looking at him, in his tight little uniform.

"Ohhh, yeah." I said "I'm fine, we're just trying to figure some stuff out. How are you doing?"

"Fine" he said with his double creased sexy smile. I took a deep breath. He put his hand on my knee, I just looked at it and he asked "Do you need a ride home?"

"Thanks, but Declan's driving me home today." Declan cleared his throat and said "Well I do have to go to run an errand, so it would be better if you could get a ride home." I gave him a surprised look. Jett used my knee to stand up and said, "I'll see you after practice."

"Now what? I have to explain to him I don't have my period.... yeah, that should be fun." I said sarcastically.

"Would you please stop saying that word?" Nic said, annoyed, and went on with "You should explain to him why you think you got attacked on your date." Nic replied and Declan agreed.

"And we need to tell someone of authority, possibly Detective Grey." Nic replied.

Declan started his story about Cale again as if there had been no disruption in our conversation. "So Topher was getting more nervous as he told me details, but he said he definitely overheard him say 'When he first found you this summer, you were his missing link and he thought you would have been an easy mark, but he has no 'mind control' over you at all, so he has to come up with a new plan. Plus, he thinks you know too much.' Or something to that affect. He was complaining that they couldn't find his father's journal that made up the serum and that he has no idea where it was lost since it's been 85 years since his passing. And something about your blood being the key." No one said anything. I grabbed the crook of my arm, so he took blood from me that just sounds crazy.

Declan began to continue....but I interrupted, "what, that's not enough, pfff, give me a break."

"Cale thinks you know who killed Jewel and thinks you're a threat and he can't control you, whatever that means and after the final test results, if they are negative, he'll just have to get rid of you because you know too much."

I grabbed the crook of my arm when he mentioned my blood, this all just sounds insane. "Who the heck is Jewel? I don't know any Jewel, and we're already broken up, so what's the big deal."

Nic nudged me "Jewel is the girl from the wake earlier this year. Right Declan?" "

"I must have had a brain cramp, I remember."

"And remember when he came up on us in the hall when we were talking about that dream? When he startled us? We were worried he overheard us. When he says get rid of you...what if he means permanently? Plus, your letters went missing after that."

I just started laughing "You watch way too much TV Nic..." No one said anything for a minute.

"Oh yeah," Declan said "He also said he wished some guy, he told me his name but I can't think of it right now, would have gotten a taste of your blood straight from the vein to see what would have happened! Weird, right? So other people need your blood too??? Anyway, the next time Topher said he opened his eyes he had an IV in him and they were taking his blood, but passed back out."

Oh...oh...oh....I was starting to put all the pieces together in my head. "Holy crap... nooooo, it can't be all that serious, can it? Was his name..." I swallowed back the nausea in my throat..."was his name Logan?" I asked sluggishly, I was finally getting it.

Declan nodded "Yeah, maybe, is he the guy who..." and he stopped. "This is very serious. Cale is delusional and needs help. We have to go to the police." Declan exclaimed. His hands were shaking and he had such a serious look on his face.

I looked at Nic "What do you think?"

"I think we need to write down a time line listing all the facts we know - compile everything into a file and then give it to someone, most likely Detective Grey. Maybe we can write down all the dates they need to check Cale's whereabouts." I just shook my head, everything seems so surreal.

"So I'm a psycho magnet huh....the questions is, is Jett a maniac that I should stay away from too?"

"He's not, he's a solid guy, plus I've known him since pre-school and we became best friends in seventh grade, really, he's a good guy." Declan stuck up for him.

At the end of practice coach's closing line was "I hope I don't have to remind you that what happens at practice stays at practice." He glanced over at me, and then rest of the team glanced my way, wonderful, they all know what he was talking about. I was exhausted and not at all ready for my ride home with Jett.

Nic and I stood in the lobby, I was actually pacing. "This is weird, should I tell Jett that I think it was Cale Friday night? Maybe we should think about it over night before we say anything to anyone."

"Sometimes sleeping on it sheds a whole new light on things; at least that's what my mom says." Nic rattled off.

"Yeah, maybe I'll wait one night." I agreed with her, my head hung low. "Our date didn't go that well, if you look at it as a whole. We got attacked by someone twice, dinner was good, the movie was good, the kissing was amazing." I just shook my head, biting my thumb nail, looking at the ground.

I turned around to face Nic and said "Oh my God!" loud and aggravated. Jett was behind her, of course, I could never seem to do anything right around Jett. He looked at me, "Did I take too long?"

"Of course not, I'm just glad this day is almost over – it was a rough one." I looked at Nic and shrugged a little.

"Do you have your stuff? We should get going. Storm is coming out any second." I grabbed my bag and coat.

"Ugh, I'm ready." He walked past me and I was still looking at Nic and I mouthed "Storm" and shrugged my shoulders walking backward. Then I gave her a goofy face and put my hand up to my ear mimicking a phone and mouthed 'Call me later.' She nodded.

As I went to turn around, Jett stopped abruptly and I bumped right into him. "Oops, sorry I was trying to get a better look."

"A better look at what?" He asked, "oh nothing." He laughed "You really are something aren't you?" I turned around and gave Nic two thumbs up, then quickly followed Jett to the car. He opened the trunk to put his stuff in. "Who else is coming besides Storm?" I may have said it with a little inflection in my voice. He had one hand on top of the trunk looking toward the school, he slid his other into mine. Storm was on his way and he looked grumpy as usual.

"What, you and Storm don't get along?" Jett asked.

"No, we get along fine, depending on his mood, of course."

He chuckled "Right, no kidding, you can sit up front." He said to me as Storm was throwing his stuff in the trunk and I got another dirty look from him so I stuck my tongue out at him. "We have to drop Storm off at his friend's house, it's on the way to yours.

No one said much when Storm was in the car. But as soon as he got out, I felt like I could finally breathe. Until Jett asked "So are you okay, I heard you passed out in wrestling right before I got there. You don't have to be embarrassed either, I have lots of cousins and they stay at our house all the time, so I know about girl troubles." I sat there and thought for a minute, if I tell him I was faking 'the girl thing' would it sound bad? Probably, but decided to just tell him the absolute truth "I don't get embarrassed about too much, no I didn't pass out from my period but I hear girls have before; I knew saying that would get everyone out of our hair." I took a deep breath. "Declan had just told me some weird and very disturbing news and I think I just forgot to breath. I had an off day, didn't eat much lunch. You know... got bad news... didn't breathe... I passed out." I explained nonchalantly.

"So you don't want to tell me the bad news then." Jett replied.

"Ah... no, I don't like complaining about stuff, but once I resolve it in my head I could probably talk about it." I thought about it....and said "You know teenage stuff can be so dramatic and trivial." He chuckled a little again and I said "Okay, tell me about your day, it had to be better than mine."

He started telling me about some of his classes and then asked me if I was going to college and banter like that. It was nice to have no major turn of events to talk about, not my silly dreams, stalkers or anything dramatic, just pleasant straight talk. I wondered if he appreciated it as much as I did.

When we got to my house he pulled to the bottom of my driveway, our garage door was open. It was dark outside but there our outside lights were on casting light and dark shadows into his car. I wasn't sure what to do next, but I looked at him with my hand on the door handle and said, "Thanks for the ride," and gave him hopefully a nice smile.

"I should get your bag out of the trunk." He said and we both got out.

He had trouble with the lock but jiggled it around a bit and then got it open. "You almost didn't have to do homework tonight." He smiled his sexy little smile and flashed his bright whites.

"Almost" I replied "Do you wanna come in for a drink?" I said and started to shiver.

I wanted to say something important, and I was thinking about telling him about Cale just to keep him here talking with me, but then decided against it at the last minute. I wondered if I should ask him out on a date. He closed the trunk after retrieving my bag and leaned on it. I was shivering a little more. He looked in my eyes and gave me his crooked little smile, "Are you cold?" He asked putting his hand out to grab mine.

He pulled me close to him, between his legs. "I'm always cold."

"Always?"

"Always" I told him. He nudged me closer by putting his hands on my waist, and his lips met mine, a gentle kiss. I stopped shivering.

The wind was whipping around the corner; I turned my head away from him so my hair would blow away from our faces. He slid my bag off of my shoulder and led me into the garage, setting my bag down by the door.

He pulled me into him; since his coat was open I dug my hands under it and around him. I buried my face in his shoulder and breathed him in. He smelled so good and he was so warm. I wasn't worried about anything anymore, I just couldn't seem to care right now.

I left my head tucked against his shoulder wishing he didn't have to go. I thought of nothing to say, I just felt safe and warm. I didn't want to move.... and then, finally, I lifted my head and his lips came down on mine with the softest touch, I felt very connected to him. He took my breath away; then he kissed me more urgently, as if it was our last.

A slow, burning fire coursed through me, and I knew I wanted to be with him. I wondered if he felt the same way. His muscular arms encircled me, securing me to him, just as I've dreamt of so many times. He released me and said good night. I just stood there in the dim light from my garage and watched him pull away. My chest felt heavy and sad and I knew he wasn't going to call.

I was running and running through foliage and trees with my wolf. In the ravine behind my house, I knew exactly where I was going. He was chasing me. I looked back he was gaining on me, I turned right and ran as fast I could. I looked again and saw nothing. I high tailed it up our dirty slide. As I was running up, I flashed back to the pool with the freezing water and the creepy guy looking at me, next I was in the lobby and the guy on the shiny payphone turned to look at me, at the Monaham's after my attack I stood up and saw the stranger in the front yard, all the eyes were the same and glowing at me, just like my wolf's eyes did. I reached the top of the dirty slide and after I cleared the brush Cale was standing in my yard. He was smiling at me with his arms crossed and sunglasses on; some guy was lurking behind him in the distance. I yelled "Hey" at him. Cale took off his glasses, glanced back at the guy behind him, he didn't seem too concerned with the ominous figure and then back at me, his eyes were glowing. I woke up it was 3:17a.m.

CHAPTER 16

I had been having strange dreams all weekend and I only remembered bits and pieces of the one I had last night. They weren't particularly scary, but I still felt panicked when I woke up. Something bad had happened, someone was injured but I'm not quite sure who. I remembered getting an ice pack out for something urgent but didn't know why and then tying off something, not sure what. It was confusing, nothing made sense. Maybe because my last encounter with Jett didn't make any sense. The kiss felt real, but it also felt final. If it was final why bother taking me home? He could have just let everything lie and that would have been that, we wouldn't have dated again. Why drive me home, lay a couple on me, make my heart flutter and never call again?? What's with that?

    I rode the bus to school with Declan and he tried to bring up the Cale situation but I stopped him and we didn't talk the rest of the way to school. I felt numb about the whole situation; I was hoping last Friday was all just a bad dream. The bus pulled into the parking lot and Declan said, "We should probably talk at lunch to try and decide what we're going to do." I was too tired to argue. We got off the bus and went our separate ways.

    I didn't see Jett at all that day. Wrestling practice was over until after the first of the year, although the wrestlers were supposed to run and do stairs every day while on Christmas break. I thought of

Jett running in my head, he always looked good and made me feel relaxed, happy. Two more days of school and then I could sleep in for two weeks. All I had to do was stay awake today.

I didn't catch Jett at all this week. I even took the stairwell next to his locker but didn't see him. Declan and I never did talk at lunch about what we were going to do, I was hoping it was all blown way out of proportion and we could just let it go.

A week into our break and still no word from Jett, pretty much what I expected but I was hoping. I was worried too much had happened, and that night he dropped me off was a jumbled mess in my head.

I was trying to focus on other things at hand like our Christmas party at the Club tonight. Tori knew what had happened with Jett to date, because we were confiding in each other more and more these days. Since she felt bad for me, she told me she'd do my hair and make-up for me. She even had me polish my nails and give myself a pedicure. We spent the whole day getting ready. I didn't mind because I had nothing else to do. My mom had made me a dress just for the occasion.

When I was finished getting ready, I thought I looked too dressy for the occasion. However, Tori reminded me my look was just fine for the Club, you could always find someone dressier than you there. Plus, they hosted lots of weddings and black tie events, it's not like I was going to change at this point.

When you looked at the dress from the front, the top looked like a mock turtleneck and it buttoned with two buttons behind the neck. Below the collar in the back, however, it was bare to my waist. The shape came down in a "V." The skirt just passed my knees and buttoned all the way down the back. It was long sleeved. I had a black belt with some silver charms and jewels on the buckle. The fabric was black with a silver pattern of un-perfect shapes throughout. I had continually told my mom I could use something a little sexier, but I felt bare. It covered everything it should, but I still felt au naturel, but it looked amazing. Tori even said she gets to wear it next, so you know it had to look good.

We always carried our coats to the car. Styling your hair, pulling on tight hose and putting on make-up can really make you warm. My dad always valet parked so we were let out at the front door.

We were ready, although I was thinking about wearing my coat all night after I've cooled off. My mom asked my dad to stop at

7/11 so we could pick up some aspirin. He didn't ask why, he just did it. When we got there, I knew she would ask me to run in, Tori never wanted to and Kit was too young. I was always the gopher, but didn't mind.

Of course, some obnoxious boys were saying stuff to me when I went in. I knew I should have thrown my coat on. "Oh baby you are smokin'!" One of them said as I reached over for the aspirin. I turned around ready to say something smart, but stopped myself because low and behold, it was Jett McGaven in person, with his friend Declan and some other guy. The other guy was the one yappin' his jaws, I believed his name was Brett.

Declan gave off a whistle and laughed, walked toward me and said "Addie you are smokin' hot!" He put both hands on my elbows gently and gave me a kiss on the cheek. I saw Jett moving forward in silence, just looking at me.

"Where are you going looking so fine may I ask?" Declan sounded like he was trying to be cool in front of the guys. "The Club." I replied.

"Oooh, the Country Club." he said whistling again, "going to a wedding?"

"No, it's a Christmas dinner."

"Wow Jett, you didn't tell me your girlfriend was rich! Aren't you gonna say hi to her – it's not like you're sick anymore." Brett snarked.

"We're not rich" I looked at Jett concerned "You were sick? Are you okay?" I squeezed by Declan and leaned in to give Jett a kiss on the cheek and said "Merry Christmas." I was in formal mode. In my family, we greeted everyone with hugs and kisses. Jett had put his hand on my waist and gave me a peck on the cheek back and whispered "You do look really nice" and let his hand linger there.

He cleared his throat and asked "Are your parents outside?"

"Ah yeah, they're waiting for me." I held up the bottle of aspirin and went to purchase it. The three of them went out to my parents' car.

"Nice Caddy Mrs. Geller" Declan stated as she rolled down her window.

I walked out and heard my mom asking "Where have you been Jett? You must come over again you know I love to cook big and I know you're a big eater." He smiled and introduced his friends; I saw them shaking hands with her through the window. Jett replied "I'll come back again, I just had the flu recently."

"He was way sick, too." Declan commented. "He was hospitalized, had blood transfusions and everything."

"I'm sorry to hear that dear, but I'm glad you're better. I'll see you boys soon then." She put her window back up and I said, standing behind Jett, "Is that a promise?" Jett just smiled and opened my door for me.

The next few days were very restless for me. I wasn't sleeping well and I was having dreams that made absolutely no sense. I couldn't even piece anything together in order to write them down. Jett wasn't calling me but neither was Nic. I knew Nic had lots of holiday plans. We on the other hand have no family in the area, so now that Christmas Day was here we had no more parties until New Years. Tonight is our family dinner, just the five of us, but mom still makes us dress up and set the table formally.

Our dinners are always fun. Last year my Grandma was with us and we ended up playing poker, which I never knew how to play until then. We also hung spoons on our noses, Grandma was pretty good at it, she'll be missed.

Tori and I got ready and wore nice jeans with a dressy top. My mom didn't say anything to us when she saw us, we swore she'd make us change, but she didn't. Tori and I gave each other a high five when we went into the dining room to set the table. Kit came in with a jacket, pants and a tie on, looked at us and said, "I'm telling mom!"

"Go ahead, she already saw us bird brain," Tori retorted. His eyes went wide and he went running for his room. When he reappeared he had on a pair of jeans, no jacket and no tie. We got a little giggly.

Just then, I heard my mom yell to my dad, "It's 3:00!" Three o'clock on special occasions around our house meant cocktail hour. Shortly thereafter she would call us kids to help carry food into the dining room, dad was in charge of opening the wine. I noticed my dad never had more than one drink, he mostly just drank diet soda. Today he was pouring wine for everyone even my brother. Of course, it was a very small portion, only a sip or two. The legal drinking age in Ohio was 18, but they have been talking about changing it to 21, just like in the big cities, I hope they wait to change it 'til after Nic and I turn 18.

My dad ordered this special salt cured ham and he was very excited to try it, so he was in a good mood, hence the wine for everyone. We were staying home tonight and we would probably make popcorn later. We said grace and my dad jumped into carving the ham up straight away. My mom made a small turkey too, in case the salty ham didn't go over well. As the conversations went on, I just stared out our window, looking at all the snow, then wondered if I could see any kind of prints or tracks in the snow by the dirty slide, curious to know if some of my other dreams may be true.

My dad started "Now everyone has to try a piece of the ham, it's from Alabama and supposed to be very good. However, if you don't like it, don't waste it, send it down here and I'll eat it. "He said with a big grin rubbing his belly.

We dished out food until all our plates were packed. My mom stood up and announced "I would like to offer up a toast to thank Santa Claus for all the wonderful gifts, to a great family and to another wonderful year! Oh and the ham, and the wine to drink first, before trying the ham!" Everyone giggled a little bit, and then we all clinked glasses. My whole family had a sense of humor and I liked it. "Would anyone else like to make a toast?" My sister shouted out "To sex, drugs and rock-n-roll!" Us kids laughed and my dad said "Here, here!"

My mom didn't like it at all, "Tori! Sean! You two are terrible and that better have been a joke Tori!" She even stomped her foot. "It was mom! All the rock stars say that – it was a joke." My mom pursed her lips together, letting herself be beat.

The ham was not bad at all, it was actually very tasty. My sister chugged her first glass of wine, I had only drank half but she poured more for both of us and our mom. Kit put his hand on top of his glass, shaking his head and scrunching his face notifying us he didn't like it at all.

I'm not a good joke teller, but when everyone told a joke I tried one too. My delivery was just not good. After the joke telling we all proceeded to hang spoons on our noses. Tori finished her wine and then switched glasses with Kit and finished his, then emptied the bottle in her cup. My dad poured some of the second bottle in his glass and poured more for Tori. He said "Make sure you eat," and gave her a little wink. My brother told another joke that made

Tori start laughing so hard she couldn't stop, which in turn made all of us laugh more. She picked up her glass of wine to take another drink and my mom went to grab it from her. Still laughing, she had tears running down her face, as did we all, but Tori snatched it back and said "No way!" My mom got up and chased her around the house trying to get the wine out of her hands.

We were all laughing. My sister went through the den and out the sliding door, but my mom paused to put her shoes on so Tori got ahead of her. Tori chugged her wine, slammed her glass on the rail and ran down the porch stairs to the side yard, no coat, no shoes where she proceeded to do snow angels - face down. We all started laughing harder; my sister always did crazy stupid things that would make us laugh uncontrollably. I bet our parents thought she was drunk, but I betcha she wasn't, she was just being Tori. My mom made Kit and I go collect her. We laughed for a long time about it. My sister had to change her clothes, they were soaked. Before I headed back up the porch stairs I looked over to the entrance of the dirty slide and noticed someone or something had been over there and my heart began to race, as I walked a little closer to investigate, I began to relax because I realized it could have been Kit or anyone for that matter. I found nothing substantial to connect anything to my dreams.

That night I had another 'makes no sense dream' but some things were clearer, so when I woke up at 3:17a.m. I wrote down the clues I thought I remembered; Sand Run Park, walking path, rocks that formed a huge cubby hole big enough to take cover under, a blonde girl in a red coat and a guy in a white hooded sweatshirt.

I didn't want to have another boring day so I called Nic and asked her to meet me at Sand Run Park. I thought I could look around and see if I recognized anything, hoping I would stop having this weird dream that kept me from sleeping. She agreed.

I brought a bag with some food and a blanket and got there about Noon, or close to it. Nic wasn't there yet, so I was surprised when my mom didn't wait with me. I plopped my bag that was slung over my shoulder down on a table under the covered pavilion, it had a great stone fireplace in it and several picnic tables that looked worse for the wear but still sturdy. I looked around and saw a path that had an immediate curve going around a steep hill. I

3:17 a.m. ...the waking hour

thought I recognized it, so I walked over toward it. A directional sign looked familiar; after I read the sign 'Valley Trails' I felt the onset of déjàvu. My body shivered thwarting me into the eeriest feeling I've ever had, I didn't like it but knew what it meant.

There were trees all around the path; I noticed a sign at the start of it that warned you to stay on it for safety reasons, and to watch for mud slides. They had a water fountain and bathrooms off to the right in the distance. Sand Run Park was nice, they had outlets and was equipped for family picnics, so people had them here all the time. They had several choice spots to choose from.

I was bundled up, hat down over my ears, a warm winter coat, my winter boots, mittens and a scarf. I started walking down the path and noticed some movement in the wooded area to the left, probably a raccoon or something. Up and to the right I saw a steep little hill that went down to a bridge then up around a curve. It was the same bridge I know I saw in my dream. So I took it. In the distance, I saw two people walking to my left, one in a red coat the other in a blue coat. I sucked in a deep breath. I was about to turn around to follow them....

* * * * * * *

I woke up and sat up quickly, but felt woozy; Nic grabbed my arm and Storm the other. My head was pounding, when I looked at Nic it was like I was watching an old TV turning off, the edges getting black first and circled to the middle until it was almost all black. I laid back down. When I looked up Storm was looking at me funny, so I gave him a look back.

I held my head "It's pounding." I announced...then remembered "Did you see him? Did you see Cale? Did you get him?" I asked.

Storm looked at Nic and said "I think she hit her head harder than we thought." Storm moved so my head was on his lap and I could feel heat radiating from him, it made my head and neck feel warm.

Nic said "Do you have ice in your bag."

"Just get snow, I have baggies in my pack." I said and Nic replied, "Well she didn't hit it that hard. I'll be right back."

I looked at the surroundings around us and there was a bridge with a cubby hole looking type of cave under it - just like in my dream. I told Storm "I just don't remember... how did I get over here?"

He looked down at me "Nic and I dragged you over here, more tree coverage and we're off the path. We found you over there, passed out," He pointed to the open area. "What do you have your period again?" He looked down at me and half smiled. I tried laughing but stopped because it hurt my head.

"You know, you have a really nice smile." I said to Storm. As soon as I said it, he stopped smiling.

"We need to take you to the hospital, you obviously shook your brain." Storm said jokingly. "No, but we should get you back to the pavilion. Can you stand yet?"

I tried pulling the letter from my front jean pocket but a searing pain went through my right shoulder and I was shivering so much I couldn't quite get it out.

I told Storm, "Get it would ya" and I put my glove back on. I glanced up at Storm, he just stared back at me with those green eyes...."It has information on it." When Storm put his fingertips on my hip I could feel the heat radiating from his hand. He slid his hand into my pocket real slow, it was a tight fit. I felt him slide one finger under the note and the others on top, pulling his hand out slowly. When he handed it to me I noticed he was holding his breath.

Nic came back, "Good thing you packed a blanket," she said pulling it from the bag. "Body heat will help you too. Can you sit up? Storm can sit on one side of you and I on the other. My mom will be here in about thirty minutes."

I started to scoot up and felt Storm put his hand on my back to support me. "Storm you're hot, just like my electric blanket." Of course I had to mention it; but I think Storm took it the wrong way because he started to blush.

I pulled my glove off and took Storm's hand. "Nic, feel how warm he is." Nic took his other hand and said "Wow, you are hot!" and gave him a wink. "The only thing that would make someone this warm in this kind of weather would be someone who's part werewolf." She looked at me and smiled with her eyebrows flexed and put her hand over both Storm's and mine. "Addie your hands are ice cold, you know vampires are cold..." We all chuckled, but I gave her sort of a warning look not to say anymore. I didn't want her telling Storm about my dreams especially the one I kept having

3:17 a.m. ...the waking hour

about a wolf.

I put the note between my teeth, pulled my other mitten off, held his one hand with both of mine and sat really close to him trying to get warm. He let go of Nic's hand and took both of mine and sandwiched them between his and rubbed my hands quickly to make them warm, it was working. Nic pulled the note out of my teeth. "If we are vampires and werewolves what does that make you?" I asked.

Nic replied, "Well, I am of course normal, everyone has to have their sidekicks." Storm remarked that we were crazy...

She unfolded the note and read it, "So you came out here to meet Cale?" she said very slowly not giving out a clue in front of Storm that it could have been one of my hair brain dreams. "Soooo did you meet him?" she asked.

Thank goodness I had written a note and called Nic to meet me here so I wasn't alone. "I didn't expect to see Cale. When I got here Cale and his friend must have already been here, getting ready to attack a girl or something. I saw the girl in the red coat. I hadn't even spotted Cale when he came at me full force, knocking me into a tree and then I woke up here with you guys." I explained.

Nic asked "Following up on a dream?"

"Ah, yeah."

"What?" Storm asked in confusion.

The picnic area was just a few yards away. Storm helped me up, I was a little wobbly and fell into him a bit so he readjusted his grip and put his arm around my waist, his face was close to mine. He had a different scent than his brother. He still smelled good - just not the same. As we headed back to the pavilion Nic explained my dream to Storm and then handed him my note. We made it to the picnic table, they sat me on the bench and I leaned on the table so I could rest. Storm straddled the bench next to me, continuing to warm my hands, I thought it felt very personal and I felt bad that I was still shivering.

"How come you can't move your arm?" Storm asked.

"He tackled me; he came so fast, I didn't know what hit me."

Nic exclaimed, "He tackled you? Take your jacket off, let's take a look." Storm was just taking all this in sitting next to me on the picnic bench warming my hands and sitting close. He took my hand, put both hands around mine, and then Nic covered them and me in the blanket. Nic was good at taking care of people, especially me, Storm wasn't bad at it either. I tried pulling my sleeve up to see my shoulder but it didn't push up far enough without removing layers. So she pulled my collar over to take a peek "Holy crap Addie."

"Just leave it" I mumbled.

Storm asked "Should we take her to the hospital?"

"No" I snapped. "I'm not going, it's just a bruise. He hit me two seconds ago, give me a minute, would ya?"

Nic replied "Ahhh, what do you mean two seconds ago? You were knocked out when we got here!"

Storm started getting protective all of a sudden and said, "Addie you had to be knocked out for at least five minutes. If Cale did this, you should call the police on him, he had to hit you hard to knock you out. I'm sorry, but I hate that guy and he needs to be put in his place."

Nic had made more snow ice packs, Storm felt the back of my head, found the knot and put the ice on it. "My head is pounding." I said.

"I hope you don't have a concussion."

He took out his pocket knife and said "Can I cut your shirt?"

I started to whine "Do you have to? It's one of my favorite sweatshirts."

"It's either that or you're going to the hospital!" he got a little sharp with me. I held the ice pack to my head with my other hand and he cut, "I don't know what the big deal is." He just gave me a look.

"Fine" I said sardonically. He cut a slit on either side of the neck, it allowed him to pull the shirt down over my shoulder.

"Ow, ow, ow, STOP!" I squealed.

He stopped "Do you see anything?" I asked Storm. Both Storm and Nic's eyes were wide.

"Addie you are.... I was going to say black and blue, but there is no blue, just black."

Storm said "We need to ice this up and get you warm. Are you sure you don't want to call the police or go to the hospital?" I nodded. "Nic, can we go to your house?"

"Wow. A man who takes charge, glad you brought him Nic."

He helped me put my coat back on my arm, I still bumped it on the table and I let out another little yelp.

It occurred to me that I had no idea why Storm and Nic were

here together. "So why are you guys together, are you together?" I said as my teeth chattered. Nic looked up quickly at Storm. Storm just gave me a squeeze around the waist helping me up as Nic's mom pulled up in the lot. I told them not to help me so Mrs. Newland wouldn't know but couldn't help but limp. Nic told her I slipped and fell on the ice, I told her Nic pushed me and laughed. Nic denied it and we were bantering like normal all the way home.

When we got to Nic's house, she started telling me that Storm was worried about Jett and he needed someone to talk to; Storm finished her story and told us "Jett's been really sick again. I think he's having a relapse, because I can see all the symptoms happening again. If he loses his temper he gets sick even quicker, so my mom is trying to keep him happy all the time now – he gets whatever he wants. We used to fight a lot, now I just keep my distance." Storm explained his symptoms, "he gets sick with a fever, then his temperature drops, he gets real pale looking and shakes a lot, says he's in a lot of pain that it feels like all his bones are breaking. Each time he gets sick it gets a little worse. He even lost a couple of teeth but the doctors think it's unrelated to the rest of whatever he has. They don't know what's wrong with him either. However, within 24 hours after receiving a blood transfusion last time he seemed to be fine. Quickest recovery they have ever seen." I didn't know what to say to him.

CHAPTER 17

It's freezing cold outside and going back to school was a drag. I never did hear from Jett, but maybe he was still sick or just busy with the holidays. People with big families always have lots of plans, and I got the impression his family was big. I guess I'm trying to make excuses, maybe I just have to get over Jett and move on. Besides, it's not like I was having the best of luck; I still have the issue of Cale possibly stalking me but it's been quite lately, maybe he's over it. In any case, I'm glad I have all new classes so I can avoid Cale altogether.

Third quarter gave me a new start. Too bad my arm was still really sore, and I still had a small knot on my head; at least neither were visible.

After lunch, Nic and I got to chatting so much I was almost late for my architecture class. I ran in the room just as the bell rang. I glanced around quickly and all the seats were taken but two. At least they were at the back of the class. Then I noticed Declan was in the row in front of the open seats. He's the one who suggested I sign up for the class. Plus, I thought it sounded like fun so I did. I noticed someone's stuff on one of the chairs so I took the desk next to it. The teacher announced "Take your seats." I plunked my books down on the desk and I noticed Jett walking toward me, he smiled moved his items from the chair to the desk and sat down. My eyes were about to pop out of my head

It figures! I had to arrive late to the only class that I have with Jett and the only empty seat was right next to him. I'll just have to get here early tomorrow and grab a seat elsewhere. I betcha he never sits in front. The teacher started talking "Where ever you are sitting today is where you will sit for the rest of this class!"

"Pffff" I let escape from my mouth. The teacher and our wrestling coach started walking down the aisle between the architecture tables. "Do not raise your hand and ask if you can move. You can't. I don't care if you are dating the person next to you," he touched my desk and looked at me. "And then you break up, I don't care." All hands went down. "I repeat, do not ask me to move you because I do not care," Mr. Landry announced. He's why Declan picked the class, I bet all the wrestlers took this class; I looked around and noticed quite a few.

"The only nice thing I will do all year is give away this packet of architecture tools to whomever comes closest to the number I am thinking in my head." He held up a package of rulers, T-squares, specialty pencils, led and other supplies. He continued "The number is between 1 and 100!" He said as he headed back to the front of the room. I immediately thought of the number 27, because it was my favorite number but it was also Jett's football number, but I'll be darned if I pick it. So I decided on the number 54, 27 doubled, as long as no one else chooses it first.

As he pointed to students they guessed at the number. He did it methodically, the first row right to left, and then the second and so on. The good thing about going last was you could pick something no one else had. Nobody else even picked a number in the 50's so I held fast with my number, so when he pointed to me I said "54". Jett gave me a dirty look when I picked it, I just gave him a look back. "I have a winner!" He kept pointing at me "...and she was only two numbers away from the number I picked which was 56!"

"I won!" How fun was that, I looked at Jett and scrunched my nose. Declan turned and said "Good job Addie."

"Why thank you Declan" He turned back around, I didn't even look at Jett again. Coach started to lecture, but only for about ten minutes. He told us all the supplies we needed to purchase, told us about the class and after we got up to get our books and syllabus at the front of the room. He also had supplies for students to purchase today.

I was lucky, since I only had to grab a syllabus and book.

Declan and I were first back to our seats. He leaned on the front of my desk and asked "Are you and Jett fighting?" I just shrugged. "What are we going to do about Cale" he continued, I shrugged again.

"Ugh, I can't think about that right now. My head and shoulder are still killing me." As I'm finishing my sentence Jett came walking right towards our desks and bumped into me on purpose, hitting my bad arm sending shooting pains throughout my shoulder. I stood up so fast my stool flew back. I grabbed my bad arm and leaned on my desk. It was now throbbing hard, uncontrollable tears flooded my eyes.

"Dammit Jett, can't you watch where you're going." I gritted through my teeth as the whole class and Declan just looked at me.

"I'm sorry Addie, are you okay? I didn't mean to hurt you." Jett said.

Declan interjected "She has a bad shoulder, really bad. You okay Addie?" I looked at Declan, "I am fine, I'll be fine." I said sternly. I had explained to Declan earlier about my run in this weekend and how I thought it was Cale who tackled me....

"Addie, I'm sorry I didn't know you were hurt, are you okay?" He said "sorry" again the same way he always says it "soary." It was cute and made me ease up a bit, plus, it looked like he meant it.

Trying to fight back the tears I told them I was fine. They were both hovering at this point and I didn't want to draw any more attention to myself. Jett went to the front of the class and then disappeared by then everyone else had gone about their business. I felt relieved; I didn't want to show him any weakness. Jett came back in minutes with an ice pack. He said "May I?" Holding it up so I knew what it was. I let go of my shoulder, he pulled the stool back up for me, as I sat and tried to relax, I looked him in the eye; he did look soary. He took the edge of my sweat jacket and pulled it back carefully. The bruises weren't totally hidden under my tee, but it looked better. "Holy cow Addie, what happened?"

I looked down and pulled my sleeve up to show the remnants of the very large green, yellowish and brown bruise. "Oh, this looks good, you should have seen it two days ago."

"My God" Declan said. "That's what Cale did to you?"

I snapped my head in his direction, gave him a dirty look. "You mean when I fell." Jett pulled my sleeve down and put the ice pack over it and put my sweat jacket back on my shoulder and held the ice pack in place.

"Cale did this?" He said in almost a whisper.

I let out a breath of air in a huff. "Ya know Declan, you have a big mouth." But I knew that when I told him, so maybe I wanted Jett to find out, maybe I was looking for him to tell someone because I do need help but it's too much for me to figure out right now, especially with the searing pain in my shoulder.

"Addie that isn't even the half of it and you know it. And if you don't do something by this Friday, I will." Declan said with authority, I gritted my teeth with annoyance.

"Gee Declan, what do you think you'll do? Tell my mommy?"

"Sure I will, at least it'll be something." Declan smirked back.

"Maybe I can help." Jett interjected. "Maybe Declan is right, you should tell someone. I mean, you did get attacked on our date, twice."

I looked at him and said "How do you know it wasn't someone after you."

He and Declan chuckled. "Because no one in their right mind would mess with a McGaven, they have a reputation you know." Declan said.

"What reputations, all I know is they are moody and have no follow-through." Jett switched hands with the ice pack and put his free hand on my back, laughing at me. "I'm glad you think it's funny." I said looking at him trying to soften my tone.

"I do think it's funny. I was sick the entire Christmas break so between that and family plans I had no time to myself. Besides, my phone wasn't ringing either."

I looked at him with a little smile and a glimmer of hope. "I shouldn't have to call you, not until after the third date, isn't that the man's, I mean boys job? You're supposed to do the asking and chasing. Ask your parents I'm sure that's how it goes."

Declan started laughing, "I guess you have met your match!" After the two of them stopped laughing at me, Declan took charge "Addie you need to start by telling Jett your story, because whether you two are boyfriend and girlfriend or not, he's got a point, no one messes with the McGaven's." There was a slight pause. "We have to come up with a plan because Topher was obviously right, Cale is stalking you."

Declan came back and said "I'm not overreacting and by your

arm and your head you know I'm not. We should call the police or at the very least have Jett take care of him."

"Cale's stalking you and he knocked you on the ground hard enough to make you pass out? That's how you got your bump on your head and your shoulder so messed up?" Jett said exasperated. I looked at him and blew air through my pressed lips, it made my bangs ruffle.

I explained to them that I actually sought Cale out; I was the one that went to the park to find him. "Yes, when he tucked his shoulder and ran into me I got knocked off my feet into a tree and landing on the ground before losing consciousness," trying to make the topic sound much lighter than it was. "We can't exactly go to the police because I never saw Cale's face, it's just he's the same size and shape and I am pretty sure it was him. And I don't want Jett *'taking care of him'* either. I don't want anyone else getting hurt."

"What an ass" Jett replied and Declan agreed with him.

I put both my hands to my face and rubbed it. Jett's hand was rubbing my neck and moved down to my back and I felt a tingle go down my spine. "I rather it all just goes away," I murmured.

Jett started talking to Declan but was replying to my statement, "Cale is scrawny and I could take care of him easily, but I'd bring back-up just in case."

"No, no, no." I said "Declan is right. If all this weird stuff is happening we may as well go to the police and try to have him put away so no one else gets hurt. The last thing we need is for one of us to get arrested over this." Declan smiled at me like a cat that just ate the canary because I finally agreed with him.

Declan started filling Jett in on all the details. Class was a bust with everyone jabbering. I tapped Jett's hand and he took the ice pack off and put it on the desk, my shoulder was numb. He and Declan were still talking; he was still rubbing my back with his one hand, just small gentle circles; after he put the ice pack on the desk and pulled my sweatshirt back on, he moved behind me and rubbed my neck with both hands. The bell rang.

At wrestling when, Jett came in the room, I caught his eye and looked at him and he nodded at me with a smile. So at least I know we are on talking terms, what I want to know is why his big muscular hands were rubbing my neck in class today. He did it like he had known me forever and we'd been dating for years. Maybe he was a playboy and just knew how to get all the girls to lust after him.

Declan came up to me "I'm driving you and Jett home after practice." I nodded and smiled, as he walked away, I shouted a little "What about Nic?" He turned around putting his head gear on and gave me the thumbs up.

Nic, the poor girl was cleaning the mats again, so I thought I would empty the bucket. There was a low sink in the utility closet, I could dump it no problem. She was just about done so I got up and rolled the bucket toward the closet, Jett came running over. "I'll do it." he said.

"Are you sure? You wouldn't want the other wrestlers to think anything was going on." I held my arm across my waist like it was in a cast. I held the door open so everyone could see what was going on. He dumped it, I'm sure I could have managed, but it was nice seeing him bend over to dump it. I tilted my head and watched him walk away when Nic walked in and said, "It is a nice view."

"I know isn't it? I think my arms going to be sore for a while."

Jett just stood up, rolled the bucket to the back of the closet, and looked me up and down smiling and slid his hand around my waist as he exited. I just took a deep breath as he walked by, he didn't wear cologne but he always smelled good. He didn't notice, but Nic did, "Girl, you are bad."

"I know."

As Nic and I waited in the lobby we wrote down all the dates we thought Cale had hurt someone, including all my incidents. No one knew about my dreams except Nic, oh and Detective Grey, and darn it possibly Storm too, but no one else and I was planning on keeping it that way. We had no idea when Cale first spotted or started stalking me, but I would guess around the first dream I had about the shiny pay phones – with the guy at the phone with a baseball cap on.

When we got in the car, Nic and I sat in the back and the two guys in front. As soon as the doors closed, I just started talking. I had decided to look at all this as if we were figuring out a mystery and it wasn't really about me; I was thinking it would make it easier. "Nic and I made a list of all the dates we would like to know the whereabouts of Cale. We also think that maybe we should go to the police, tell them I was attacked several times and that we suspect Cale, and that he may be responsible for other incidents. We could give them our timeline and maybe someone could question him about the dates and see if anything comes up."

Nic continued from there "Of course like on TV, if he's really good and pre-plans all this he could have fake alibis, so this may not even help us."

Declan said "You watch way to much TV."

I looked at Nic and said "I forgot about the raccoon date, let's write that down." She took her pen out and said "Do you remember the date."

"You dated a raccoon?" Jett asked laughing.

"Ha ha ha. No, I heard noises like someone was on our deck and found a dead raccoon, well it actually wasn't dead yet." I said.

"Seriously?" Jett replied.

"I know it was on a Thursday and in September...where's your calendar?" She pulled it from her bag. Looking at it I knew it had to be September 17th.

Jett turned around in his seat "This guy's been stalking you since September?"

Declan replied, "We think June or July."

I looked back at Jett, held his gaze, shrugged my shoulders as best I could and said "I guess I'm just so irresistible he can't....."I laughed at myself mid-sentence and then continued, "or maybe he has too much time on his hands.... We only think that because of what Topher said and because of the weird things that have been happening to me, like on our date. Weird, right?"

"Hmm" he said "We should ask my Uncle Grey the detective what to do, maybe he can help us. What do your parents say?"

"Whose, mine?" I replied, "I haven't told them anything because I'm not sure what to tell them, but I guess I should just in case Cale comes around the house again." I said it but I wasn't sure I meant it.

We arrived at Nic's house, as she was closest to the school.

"Jett, I think you should pretend you and Addie are boyfriend and girlfriend because she can't afford to be knocked around anymore. You should also introduce her to Kyle so everyone thinks she's a friend of the family. This way they'll think if you mess with her, you mess with the McGaven's." Declan schemed. Jett chuckled "True."

"I think that would be a good start, and Addie you shouldn't go anywhere alone until we know for sure what's going on." Nic added. "Plus, we'll tell Detective Grey."

"So you, Jett and Declan will be my bodyguards then, and we aren't going to tell anyone else about this until we talk to Detective Grey. If he thinks it warrants other actions, I'm sure he'll let us know, right?" I questioned.

"Yeah" Jett explained "I forgot you've met him. He's a really cool guy and has always helped us out when my brothers and I have gotten into trouble."

"How do we schedule a meet with your uncle?" Nic asked.

"Good question my dear Watson!" I looked at her with a smile. "What?" I said to Declan and Jett who looked back at me funny. "I don't think I'm Sherlock – I was just jokin'." I blurted out.

"Oh I know! Jett and I will go *'park'* when your uncle's on duty and get caught!" I said with enthusiasm.

"What?" Jett exclaimed.

"I meant necking, you guys are perverts."

"Oh boy" Nic said "We better get her home before she really gets slaphappy."

"Oh I know what if Nic and I break..." Nic interrupted "That's it, I'm outta here." I started laughing.

"Yes, I'm feeling a little slaphappy. Hey Nic?" She turned to look at me before closing the door "I gotta stalker and you don't." She slammed the door in my face. She waved and Declan backed out of her drive.

I put my bag at one end of the seat, laid down and put my head on it. Detective Grey had given me his business card, if I can find it, he told me to call anytime. Jett started talking to Declan "What's up with her? She seems awfully happy," in a low hushed voice, pointing his thumb back at me.

"This is how I get Jett, deal with it, I sometimes get slaphappy!"

On my behalf Declan told him "She's actually pretty funny sometimes. It doesn't happen often though; not the funny part, the slaphappy part. Plus, she's pretty sarcastic. Like I said, a good match for you."

"Why thank you my dear Watson, I appreciate the compliment." I was losing it. "My dear friend, stop at the nearest bar I need a drink." I said with a little accent on it. Sometimes I just couldn't stop myself. Jett and Declan chuckled a bit. Declan floored it over a hill and I rolled off my seat onto the floor which would have been funny if I hadn't hurt my shoulder again.

"Damn it, that's twice in one day." The two of them were

laughing, I would have but it just sent more shooting pains up and down my arm.

"That's twice you fell off a seat." Declan said.

"No, that's twice I fell off my shoes. Hardy, harr, harr, no that's twice I hurt my shoulder." He slowed down, "Ooh sorry, I forgot about that. You okay?" he asked as he turned his head as much as possible to check on me.

I sat up "Declan are you taking me home first?" – That finished my slaphappy mood. "I was going to take Jett first" he came back.

"Fine" There was a bit of silence in the car. Then Jett started "I'll call my Uncle to see when we might be able to meet with him. We should all be there, I'm afraid I don't have enough details for him, plus if your shoulder still looks bad he can see that."

"Well, if the two of you keep beating me up, I'm sure it will."

"What, are you grouchy now?"

"Well yes. I'm female, a teenager and hormonal! Plus, my shoulder, shooting pain, lots of fun." I said sarcastically. "I definitely need a drink now". I said under my breath.

We turned into Jett's driveway. "I'm getting in front." I announced and Jett gave me his hand to help me out of the back. He pulled me close to him and asked "Do you need an ice pack."

"No, I'll be fine bodyguard," and I slid into the front seat. Jett squatted down by me and put his hand on my thigh, I could feel the heat radiate from him; how could someone be so warm all the time and it's winter.

I looked at him "Sorry, I'm in a bit of a quandary today, my shoulder hurts, I supposedly have a stalker and now I have a bodyguard. At least he's good looking." I turned my head toward Declan and winked.

"Hey!" Jett retorted, "Oh yes, I mean two good looking bodyguards." I said. He laughed a little and slid his hand off my leg, slid it into my hand as he stood and held it lightly until it fell out and closed my door.

"Take me home James." I said to Declan. "I'm exhausted."

"I believe this has got to be an emotional roller coaster for you." Declan suggested as he pulled out of Jett's driveway. I turned my head toward him and gave him a subtle smile.

"An emotional roller coaster, huh. It just makes no sense Declan, why me. I never hurt anyone and I'm not special." I closed my eyes.

"Crazy obsessed people don't do things for any rhyme or reason. You were probably in the wrong place at the wrong time and he has honed in on you ever since."

"I guess" I said. "The only good thing to come of this is I get to pretend I'm dating Jett. Good idea by the way." I was slumped down in my seat a bit, I was always very relaxed around Declan.

"Yeah well, he likes you." With that I sat up in my chair.

"How do you know?"

"Well, for one, he was rubbing your neck in architecture."

"You noticed that huh? Why else do you think?"

"I like you and he has the same taste in girls as me."

"So you like me?" I squinted my eyes at him.

"Well, not like that, but I think we would be compatible."

I dropped that subject quickly "Maybe he's dating around, playing the field, I'm sure he has plenty of girls interested in him."

"He does have girls after him, but I don't think he's interested in any of them."

"So you know something you aren't supposed to tell me."

"Maybe."

"Why doesn't he just ask me out then?"

"Maybe he will. Don't forget he was really sick over Christmas break and it really freaked him out he told me he thought he was going to die."

I closed my eyes and scrunched back down in my seat. "He was that sick..."

The next morning, I was in a good mood. Jett was flirting with me plus we were pretending to be boyfriend and girlfriend. Even though that's all it was, pretending, I was fine with it. Since we were all about staying together Declan picked Nic and I up for the wrestling meet tonight, which was at Copley. It's where I used to have swim team practice during the winter months before I was in high school. I was glad to be here; a familiar place with good karma, at least for me.

One of us needed to keep score, and the other needed to video tape the matches. While all the guys were weighing in Nic and I were in the gym lying on the bleachers. We were alone except for the custodians setting up the scoring tables; the main mat and team chairs were already in place.

Some boys from Copley came up to us and started chatting. I'm always a flirt; well let's call it social, I love to talk to people. It's not my intention but Nic tells me I'm always overly friendly. Of course, she's the same way. There we were talking to a couple guys and everyone was being 'overly friendly.' I had my arms and legs crossed casually sitting on the bleachers and Nic was standing casually next to the Copley guys when in came Storm and Declan.

They didn't look too happy when they came up to us, they looked glum, so I introduced the other guys to them like they were good friends of ours. They were short in conversation, darn right rude and acting all grumpy until the Copley guys left; Storm and Declan stayed. They stood there with their arms crossed and acted like they were going to ground us or something.

"What do you two think you are doing?" Storm replied. I shrugged and Nic said "Making friends, you didn't like Jace, Ryan or Sam."

Storm looked at us like we were crazy. "What?" he said.

"They were nice and if you guys hadn't come along I'm sure Addie and I could've gotten dates," she raised her brow. The rest of the team was trickling in along with people sitting in the bleachers.

"You two, of all people, aren't allowed to flirt with the opposing team," Storm stated, Declan nodded in agreement.

Nic excitedly told them. "They aren't on the wrestling team..." We glanced over at our team, they looked upset with us.

"You know what we mean" Storm said quietly through gritted teeth. "You're making us look bad like 'our' girls need to stray. You're supposed to be on our side."

"If you guys want us to be on your side then you're all going to have to at least acknowledge us and chat with us once in a while. A little flirting wouldn't hurt. Everyone can come and talk to us a little before and after their match and help us video tape and score. It's pretty boring sometimes." Nic explained and I agreed.

I hope we got our point across and I think we did because Storm pushed his bottom lip upward contemplating what we said and replied "I hadn't thought about it that way. You guys just waiting out here doing nothing until the match starts and videotaping alone, I've done it, and it can be very boring."

"I guess you're right." Declan looked at me and squinted his eyes at me.

"What Declan? I mean body guard? I wasn't alone, Nic and I

were together." I talked towards him as he walked away.

Nic didn't have a boyfriend, at least not yet, I couldn't believe she didn't have one because she was tall and gorgeous. I would kill to have her long legs. She was tall enough to be on the basketball team just not coordinated enough. She laughed when the basketball coach asked her to try out.

She and I got so chatty while setting up the video camera that I forgot to look for Jett when we heard a "hey" behind us, startling us both. It was Jett all dressed in his wrestling gear, coming toward us. We were at the top of the bleachers in a second gym setup for gymnastics that over looked the main gym floor. He didn't look happy, Nic said "I'm leaving, I need to go keep score."

As soon as she turned around, I begged "Don't go Nic, he doesn't look happy."

"I'm not mad, just in wrestling mode." I smiled a Cheshire cat smile, all my teeth showing, but Nic kept going.

"Can I talk to you a minute?" Jett asked.

"Sure." I mumbled. "I have to start recording as soon as the first match starts, so you actually only have a minute." I continued setting up the camera and Jett took one of the wires and unwound it for me and plugged it into the wall. I looked at Nic below and noticed one of the wrestlers had pulled a chair up next to her to help keep score. She was introducing the other teams wrestling manager to him, who had nothing on Nic.

"So what's up Jett?"

"I like how you say what you want and you seem to be yourself around me. Other girls can seem fake." I looked over at him and nodded. My heart started to race a bit; this was either going to be good or bad.

"Hold that thought," I said. I pointed the camera in the right direction, focused the lens and started to record. Once in place all I had to do was start and stop the camera between matches so the wrestlers didn't have to fast forward through a bunch of nothing. Plus, it saves tape. We walked away from the camera and watched the match; Jett started telling me about the other wrestler that he was really good, so it was important that our guy win, because they were both fighting for the number one slot at this point.

I held a hand up and rechecked all the settings to make sure everything was on and in focus and I walked back over to him. I thought he was going to break up with me even though we weren't dating. Maybe the fake relationship isn't working for him. My hands started getting a little clammy; I thought I was over all this nervous stuff, I wish Nic or Tori were here to run interference. I was looking at the floor, then the walls, anywhere but at him. I had my arms crossed waiting for the bad news to come.

"I only have a minute Addie, I saw you talking to several boys earlier...."

"Sooo, you were checkin' them out huh!" I said sarcastically, I always had something smart to say.

"Okay smarty pants, I only have a minute."

"Sorry" I wanted to say it's been like five, but I didn't.

"This week, you know us pretending to date? Well, when I saw you with those other guys.... well, I didn't like it..... I didn't think you were interested in anyone else."

I interrupted, "I'm not."

"Would you just let me finish. Wait, what did you say?"

"I'm not interested in anyone else."

"So you were talking to those guys to make me jealous?"

"No, we were talking to them to be nice and we had nothing else to do. It's not like any of our team is social with us."

"Yeah that's what Storm said. Can you maybe not flirt with anyone else until I wrestle, maybe the rest of the meet? I can't concentrate when you do that." he pleaded.

"Okay," I said with a soft smile and took a step closer to him. When I did he took one back and put his hands up. I squinted at him, he explained "I don't think so, I have to go wrestle with a guy, in this..." he said pointing to his bibs, "so we'll talk afterwards."

I agreed "We'll talk later then." A lot more things came to mind but I didn't say any of them. I walked back to the camera to put it on pause. When I turned around he was gone. I looked at the gym door below and he was walking in, he looked up at me and gave me a half smile. I smiled back, he started stretching.

A couple of minutes later our 98 pound wrestler, Jim, who had just finished his match, came by me.

"Hey" he said.

"What's up?" I said back. "I taped your match, it was a good one – does this mean your number one?" I turned around to turn the tape recorder back on.

"Yes, I think it does. Too bad I didn't pin him though."

"But you won." I replied. We both started chatting and the next thing I knew Brad, another wrestler, was up talking to us. I looked at Nic and a new wrestler was talking to her too. It was nice, they were keeping us company. I was leaning over the rails along with a couple of other wrestlers cheering Dean on when I heard a very soft "hey" from behind us. It was one of Copley's wrestling managers, she had a t-shirt on that said Copley Wrestling.

We had all turned around and said "hey." I walked up held my hand out and introduced myself and I turned to watch the match so did she. "So.... your guys are really nice to you two girls, and I think it's really cool."

"Thanks. Our guys are very nice to us and sometimes too protective," we all laughed a little.

"Well I think it's nice. Our guys just ignore us."

Jim leaned over and chimed in "That's too bad. You two seem so nice."

"Oh, I'm Susan and that's Leah," she said pointing to the score table.

"I met Leah earlier, she's very nice and a good score keeper." Jim was flirting and fine by me. They chatted through an entire match. Throughout the match the wrestlers on our team rotated keeping Nic and I company. "I like your shirt Susan, did you have it made?" I asked.

"Oh yeah, the whole team had some made." she answered.

"Nice, I'll have to see if I can get one made for Nic and me." We talked a little more before she left.

Our wrestlers kept coming and going, rotating by me and Nic, I wondered if they would keep on supporting us the rest of the season. I hope so, because it made the meet more enjoyable, and I bet they just might. Two other girls from Copley approached us from the bleacher side. Two of our wrestlers squatted down by them and chatted them up.

Storm came up by me since his match was done and I told him "I don't think it's fair that you guys can flirt with 'the other team's girls' but we can't flirt with the guys."

"Sure it is" he said "This way none of our team feels jealous, plus, their team is now getting their undies in a bunch." I looked over at the Copley team and, sure enough, they were checking out the girls who were chatting with our guys and looked a little envious.

Storm put his arm around me "you guys have us" I shrugged

him off right away. "What, are you kidding me? Your brother will get all mad." He just laughed.

"Who cares? It's not like you're dating."

"Well, I told him I wouldn't flirt any more today. It seems like he's all worked up about something."

"Whatever" he grumbled and went over to talk to the other girls.

When the match was over, Nic and I waited in the lobby with the camera equipment. As we were waiting we had some more girls come up to us and ask about Storm and one of them gave us her number to pass on. For some reason, I think the girls approached our guys tonight because they were talking to us and being nice. It's easier to talk to guys when other girls are around.

Storm, Jett and Declan all came out in a group. I handed the piece of paper to Storm. He opened it and laughed "Which one was this?" Nic described her to him.

I took a bill out of my pocket and held it up in the air and said "My mom gave me $20 for pizza. Who wants to go?" Declan swiped the money out of my hand and said "I do." Jett swiped it out of his hand and said "We'll all go. Nic and Storm can drive with Declan and you can drive with me." Jett instructed. I liked that plan.

"So, are you two still pretending you're dating or is this the real deal? Because you know she isn't dating anyone else." Nic said and continued. "As a matter of fact Jett, the first day she laid eyes on you she broke it off with the guy she was dating." I jabbed Nic in the side for saying that. "Oops" came out of her mouth.

"Good" replied Jett; he stuck the twenty bucks back in my jean pocket and picked up his bag, he put his arm around my neck and said "Let's go *Honey*," sarcastically. Everyone laughed and followed us out to the parking lot.

We took about ten steps into the parking lot and I got that eerie feeling, I started to look around the perimeter of the parking lot. I put my hand on Jett's, the one around my neck. "Does it seem creepy out here to you?"

He looked down at me. "No, why?"

"Ah, nothing." We got to the car and he flipped his bag in his trunk and I got in and locked my door. He got in and looked at me. "Everything okay?"

"Oh sure," then I leaned over to his side of the door and

3:17 a.m. ...the waking hour

slammed his lock down. He stopped me, my hand pressing on his thigh and his hand on my hip. I moved slowly to meet his face and he covered my mouth with his. Our lips parted and I slowly sat back on my side. Jett smiled and flashed all his teeth, I relaxed and almost melted. He started the car, not saying anything. We were in his brothers Trans Am with the gear shifter between us. When he went to put it in reverse, I put my hand over his and said "No way pal, we aren't' going anywhere." I could feel my cheeks were rosy and my heart was a flutter.

"Excuse me." he said laughingly.

I swallowed hard "Not until you tell me what that kiss was all about and this whole week." I started out strong but ended with a whimper.

His hand found mine, he spread his fingers apart and I slid mine through. "I thought we were on the same page."

"And what page is that." He turned his hand over and we intertwined our hands again. "That we're dating."

I took a deep breath "So we aren't pretend dating, we're actually dating, dating. When did this happen?"

"You sound mad." He replied

"I'm not mad at all, but when you're dating someone it needs to be mentioned. You can't just assume that we're dating."

"Okay, then are we dating...will you..." I cut him off with a kiss and he reciprocated and said. "I guess we're dating now." My face was on fire, it was zero degrees outside and I was burning up. I wonder if he noticed how red my face was. Not sure I cared. I had a smile on my face, ear to ear. I looked at him and realized he did too.

We walked into the restaurant and the others already had a table. We were hand in hand and both grinning ear to ear. Nic gave me a look and I gave her a wink, she knew what I meant. Nic was just as bold as me with speaking her piece so she asked Jett "So does this mean you'll ask her out on another date or what?" He laughed, "This means I don't have to ask her out on another date." He pulled a chair out for me.

Boys are big eaters I tell ya, I thought I ate a lot but the three boys put away everything we ordered. Storm started to say something but a big *'crash'* sound overwhelmed him. I jerked my head up and looked at Nic wide-eyed, "déjàvu" I whispered. "The manager is going to trip and hurt his ankle." I whispered to Nic and pointed in his direction. But I didn't whisper soft enough because Jett said "What did you say?" Nic shook her head like she remembered my journal.

I looked over his shoulder and felt like everything was happening in slow motion. The manager was walking behind our table toward the kitchen but before he got there, he tripped and fell.

Nic let out a gasp and covered her mouth. She looked back at me and said "Now what?" I just sat there motionless. "Addie what happens now?" I just looked at her with my eyes wide.

"Umm, what? Ah, I guess we pay the bill and get out of here." I gave her the evil eye. She knew I didn't want to tell anyone about my crazy dreams.

I rubbed my arms 'cause I had a shiver running through my whole body. I waved my hand in the air and yelled real loud "Ah, waitress!" and waved her over. I looked at Nic and said "Done. In my dream, she backed up not looking where she was going and stepped on his ankle spraining it as she tumbled to the floor." The boys just looked at us like what were we talking about, but no one said anything. Jett took his coat and put it over me, I just breathed his scent in. He scooted closer to me and put his arm around my chair. I think he thought I was cold.

When the waitress arrived I asked for the check. Too bad she didn't know I saved her and her manager from further embarrassment and injury. If she did, I'm sure she would've thanked me. When I got up I handed Jett his jacket back. "Why don't you keep it" he asked. "I like it on you better, especially without a shirt."

"Get a room!" Declan chanted.

CHAPTER 18

No school on Monday and I was just moping around the house. My mom said "Shouldn't you return Jett's jacket, what if he only has one coat?" she paused "I thought he was picking you up today?"

"Yeah but not 'til later, he doesn't have a car 'til then." My mom was putting her coat on "Why didn't you ask me for a ride?" I just shrugged my shoulders. "I can drop you off now if you want." I called over there; no one answered, but went with my mom anyway.

It took us thirty minutes to get there, running an errand in between. The sun was out, the sky was blue, it was a nice day. The closer we got to his house the more nervous I became. I rang the doorbell once and waited with his coat in hand. No one answered, so I rang one more time.

I turned around to go back down the steps when Jett whipped the door open, his hair all wet and only shorts on. He had one hand on the door and the other on the door frame. You could see every ripple of every muscle he had.

My mom rolled down the window and said "If I leave her here, you gotta promise not to walk around naked." She was being facetious. I turned toward him laughing and tilted my head and spoke so only he could here "It doesn't bother me a bit," and raised one eyebrow.

He laughed "Of course not Mrs. G, I just got out of the shower," and he pulled me in and closed the door. Then opened it and my mom hadn't had here window quite closed, "I'll a... drop her home later." My mom just waved.

I got inside, handed him his jacket. I went to pull mine off when I knocked a vase off a table that was close to the door. I turned around with my arms still in the sleeves and caught it with both hands before it hit the ground. "Sorry, so sorry." I exclaimed.

"What are you sorry about? It didn't break. I could tell you stories of the things my brothers and I have broken." He turned and walked toward the kitchen. I put the vase back and finished sliding my coat off carefully and left my shoes on the mat.

Jett turned to me in the hallway and said "Has anyone ever told you, you have quick hands?"

"As a matter-o-fact once, a semi-pro baseball player told me I did."

"Did you break his vase?" Jett chuckled.

"If he thought I had quick hands, do you think the vase would have broke?" I said sarcastically but then continued. "I knocked a salad dressing bottle off the table with my left elbow and caught it before it hit the floor. And then he made me do it a bunch more times to see if I could do it again, and I did."

"No offense but that doesn't seem *all* that hard."

"No, it's not, but try doing it without looking at the bottle at all, plus, I'm right handed. Don't look at me that way, not sure how I did it nor if it's all that significant either, just know that I'm quick." As he headed back toward the kitchen, I gazed at Jett's back. It didn't look or smell like he was just out of the shower but his scent was still intoxicating to me as always.

"So why are you half naked and not showered?" I asked. He sat down at the kitchen table, rolled his chair over to me and pulled me onto his lap. "Do I smell?" I let go of my coat and pressed my lips into his. We maintained that position for a while. I slid off his lap, picked up my coat and said "Well I got what I came for, I guess I'll be going."

He pulled my elbow back; I fumbled over one of the casters on the chair but caught myself on Jett, one hand on the back of the chair and the other on his chest, our faces so close I didn't bother to say anything. He pulled my face down into his hot lips, his skin was warm to the touch. I breathed him in and pressed back.

"You're right that was much better, now I can go."

"No, actually you can't. My Uncle Grey is coming over for dinner and you're stayin'." He pulled me back into him.

"I guess if I have to." I mumbled while our lips touched.

"You're very sarcastic, aren't you?"

"I do try. If I stay, you'll owe me, I do have places to go and things to do you know."

"Oh really, that's it?" He said, stood up, ducked under my arm and waist and lifted and hauled me down to the basement.

"You're going to hurt yourself! Put me down!" I yelled. "I'm telling your Mother!" He just laughed and tossed me onto a tattered worn plaid couch, you could tell it was the one they used previously in the family room upstairs and now it was on its last leg in the basement. He wedged one leg between the inside of the couch and my hip, he kept the other planted on the floor. He leaned forward and put his hands on either side of my face. I pushed my hands up on his bare chest, his skin felt toasty, his skin a beautiful shade of melted caramel. He bent over to kiss me, I took one hand with all my nails spread and gently dragged them up the center of his back.

He pulled up and said "Damn, don't do that..." I pulled him close again "sorry" left my lips and his next kiss told me he really liked it, maybe too much. I broke away and pushed him into the couch as I slid out.

"Wew. I didn't, ah, come here for that." I said as I fanned my face then fixed my clothes and hair. "Are you actually going to take a shower sometime today?" I headed back toward the stairs, he caught up in two steps; put his hand on my hip and I just felt the warmth come over me.

He turned me at the bottom stair and kissed me while his hand slid from my hips to my butt. I could do this all day I thought. He pulled away and then kissed me on the neck. "I gotta help my mom," he said as he took two stairs at a time to the first floor.

"What?" I replied following him, thank goodness, His mom? Then I heard someone by the front door, Storm and she had their hands full, I on the other hand never heard them coming. He took the bags from his mom and I took the bags from Storm, who gave me a piercing look. It took a couple of trips to get everything in.

His mom came into the kitchen and seemed frazzled, yet tired at the same time. "Hi" she said to me "You must be Addie."

"I am" I replied. "It's very nice to meet you." I said with a smile as we shook hands. I started unpacking the bags and folded the empties and laid them on the table. She looked up at me, took a deep breath and said "Thank you for helping!"

"Jett, finally a girl who has manners. Go get in the shower. Storm, go clean the family room." I interrupted "What would you like me to do."

"Oh, nothing honey, you're our guest."

I replied "If a guest doesn't hold their own then they aren't invited back as much, besides I am a great sous chef."

She pursed her lips together, looking at me "Really? Since I'm running behind I'll take you up on it."

"Great what are we making?" She rattled off the menu and I came back to her with "If we par-bake the Italian sausage we won't have to grill it as long. If you have a crock pot we can heat up the sauce in it and add the sausage after it's cooked on the grill to give it more flavor and that way you're done and no one has to cook while your company is here. I'll cut up the veggies for the salad and the peppers and onions to sauté. Then we can sauté veggies, cook pasta and cut rolls 10 minutes before dinner. Or we can wrap the veggies in foil and cook them on the grill."

She looked at me, mouth opened, not saying anything. I inquired "Too pushy?"

"No, no, very helpful as a matter of fact."

I continued "Actually, if you point out where a broiler pan, crock pot, cutting board, and a chopping knife are I can get everything started....." I let that sit for a second before continuing. "If you need to get ready or something - - I got everything under control for now." I looked in the oven and then turned it to 350.

"Storm, I need the crock pot from downstairs and my big metal pot." His mom announced. He looked up at me kind of grumpy like, I guess I just made work for him: I followed him into the basement. Storm handed me the pot, by the time we got upstairs Mrs. McGaven had everything out. She took a deep breath and looked at me with dubious eyes. "Storm and Jett can help you with anything else you need."

"Awesome, my mom always says the more cooks in the kitchen the faster things get done."

Storm replied "I thought too many cooks in the kitchen spoils the pot."

"I think I'm gonna like you and your mom." Mrs. McGaven replied.

Storm was still looking at me funny, "What? I'm not a good cook, just very organized in the kitchen, don't worry, we can't mess this up."

"I wasn't worried about that. What are you trying to do? Kiss my mom's ass to get on her good side."

"I can't even believe you just said that, don't you always have to help out with dinner and cleaning the house?" I asked.

"Ah no, my mom does that." Storm said.

"Well, that's just rude, especially with the way you guys put away food. Rinse that pot and fill it a little over 3/4's of the way and put it on the back burner on medium." He just looked at me. "D o I h a v e t o t a l k s l o w e r?"

"Talk slower for whom?" Jett said walking up to the kitchen.

"For Storm, he's mad I'm helping out." He came up behind me squeezed my shoulders.

"What do you want me to do?"

"I heard you've never helped out in the kitchen before, at least that's what Storm tells me."

"Not so much, but I'll start now." Jett stated leaning on the counter. He had no socks on, jeans and a t-shirt that looked like it had been washed a thousand times but definitely looked good on him.

Talking to both Storm and Jett I said "Don't you find your parents give you more, let you do more and give you less flak the more you help around the house?" They both just looked at me with their mouths open, dumbfounded. It must be a McGaven thing. "I'm just saying..."So I gave Jett instructions on putting the sausage on the broiler pan; when he opened the pack he pulled his face away from it and wrinkled his nose said that the sausage was really strong. I smelled it and didn't think so. Storm did the water and then I had him setup the crock pot. By the time their mom came back down we were all sitting at the table cutting vegetables and breaking up lettuce.

She stood in the doorway "So they are capable of working in the kitchen." The timer went off and Jett looked at me, "Start the grill and I'll set the timer for 15 more minutes." He actually got up and did it.

"Wow, I'm impressed." Mrs. McGaven said.

"Oh thanks, I'm actually not a good cook, but I can bake. Your oven is warmed up if you have rolls or a cake or brownie mix we can pop it in after....." "I looked up at her, "...if you want......"
"Feel free to keep it up. It'll be nice if I don't have to think." I just smiled at her. "Box cakes are easy..." she said grabbing a box from the cabinet.

She sat down and took a deep breath and ordered Storm to get a bowl for the peppers and onions.

"If you have a big frying pan we can just throw them in there and save a dish."

"Storm, get our big frying pan out instead."

"So, I see you've done this before."

"Yeah lots. Usually on very big scales, my mom and dad entertain a lot. We have a great basement for it, plus, I don't think my mom knows how to cook a small meal."

Jett chimed in "She does have a great basement, they also have a huge stocked bar." We were all done with chopping the salad by the time the timer went off. I got up and took the sausage out. Jett volunteered to grill and, being competitive, Storm said "What should I do next?"

I looked at Mrs. McGaven and she shrugged her shoulders and said. "Your show."

"We need a mixing bowl, eggs, oil and a baking pan."

Everything was moving and going. "Oh honey, did you already put the water on?"

"Yes, we over filled the pan and put it on medium so the water will be preheated and boil faster when we're ready to start pulling everything together."

"I don't know why I asked."

"Because I'm a teenager and you should be checking up on me?" As I realized I was talking out loud she gave a little laugh, "Right you are. What next?"

"Music, bake the French bread and set the table."

We had a great time, I even washed the dishes and Jett and Storm dried. "My boys have never worked so hard in the kitchen before" Mrs. McGaven stated, "I'm going to have to kick up their allowance if they keep this up. " I turned to the boys and raised my eyebrows in complete satisfaction as in '*I told you so.*'

After dinner, Jett got his Uncle to come into the living room by himself. Since I didn't have my paperwork, I had to go off memory but told him everything I could remember, dates times and places. He asked us questions jotted some stuff down and then we gave him Cale's name. He sat back in his chair and put his hand through his hair. Jett was silent, listening intently, like he was trying to remember everything I told him verbatim.

Grey had a serious look on his face "Cale Winters huh," he said grimly and leaned forward rubbing his face. "This guy Cale Winters, stay away from him," he said in his deep raspy voice. "He is slicker than you'd think. We have checked on him and he's suspected in foul play...." I interrupted "Like for Jewel Ann Richardson's murder?"

He just gave me a dead stare which felt like forever, then he shook his head a bit and continued like I hadn't interrupted him and glanced away "...his alibis..." then said and cleared his throat making eye contact with me again " ....he always has one but they seem to be too convenient and he always has the right answers. We haven't got him on anything yet but I don't like or trust him and neither should either of you."

He finally looked away, thank goodness, because I couldn't have held his gaze much longer. I let out a breath. There was a bit of silence until Jett broke it. "Should we file charges against him or some kind of report?"

"Well if you saw his face and could identify him then I would say yes. But from what you've told me, and if it was Winters, then I doubt you saw his face because he's too careful, every move he makes is calculated. I'll record this and put it in my report in case anything comes of it later. That way it will be official, but right now there's nothing else we can do without evidence."

"So this guy can turn into a werewolf or a bat, that's how he makes a quick get away at the first sign of trouble," I remarked. Jett laughed and got up to stretch and his uncle looked up slowly at me, he looked mad, stared me down again with his piercing eyes and mouthed to me 'What do you know?' I raised an eyebrow at him and said quizzically "It's in a book I'm reading." I was so startled by his response that I lied.

He slapped his knees and stood up, Jett and I stood up too. I shook his hand, he grabbed mine firmly. "Nice to see you again, please keep me updated on anything, no matter how inconsequential it may seem." Grey said it as though he was talking in code and I was to decipher the message. I blurted out "Did you ever find Jewel Richardson's bracelet?" He paused shaking his head saying "I don't remember any reports of a bracelet."

"It's in the field where she was murdered; it's silver and shiny with a bunch of charms on it." I said in a very neutral voice. "Nooo…" he said suspiciously, "We haven't found the location of the murder as of yet." He didn't ask me how I knew that bit of information, but he knew where it came from. Jett on the other hand didn't even question it which I was glad for, because I shouldn't' have said that in front of him.

Jett added "Were you able to check Cale's house?" His uncle looked at him shaking his head. "We checked out his apartment and we didn't find a thing, it was spotless, looked like no one lived there, as a matter of fact. We don't have a record of Cale living in a house, just an apartment, what makes you think that?"

"I think Cale lives in a house," I announced. The fact that when I woke up on our so called date and we were outside a house means nothing, anyone could have owned it, maybe his friend lived there and he just visited. But for some reason between my story and Topher's and seeing him there sick, it seemed as though he lived in that house.

"Don't look at me, I don't know all the details, just that it's right off of 77 in Brecksville and it's a white ranch with green trim. " Jett looked at me like I was crazy. Grey said "Don't ask." I took the pad of paper from his hands "Do you know what a river birch is?"

"Yes, but I'm surprised you do."

I drew the house and then the backyard which looked like a wavy shaped oval or "U."

"This is a river birch with four trunks." I had drawn a stick tree and pointed to the right of my oval, then pointed to the field. "This isn't a really big hill but it slopes downward, and here is where, I believe, she was killed and where the bracelet was dropped." I marked it with an 'X'. "I've only seen Cale's house once, the other time I was half asleep so it doesn't count. Maybe it's Cale's very own back yard." I volunteered the information because if it was Cale, I wanted him caught.

Jett looked at me in astonishment or was he looking at me like I belonged in a Looney bin, not sure which; I shrugged and handed Grey his pad of paper and pen back. "He isn't registered to own anything in the area, but I'll check into this." Grey said. "I'll get in touch with you if I need you for any reason, but by all means call me if anything else happens and please keep me updated. Maybe we'll put a tail on one of you to see if anything turns up." Grey seemed like an alright guy.

After Detective Grey left Jett turned to me and asked, "How did you know some of the stuff you were sharing with Grey? I mean was that what you and my uncle were talking about before when he came to the school?" So I told him that Topher and I put everything together from conversations we overheard from Cale. Jett and I got in his car shortly after that, so he must have been satisfied with my answer, in any case, I didn't talk I just looked straight forward. I couldn't shake the feeling his uncle knew a lot more than he was telling us. Of course I didn't tell Jett about my dreams, so he was being left in the dark twice, however, I did say more than I should have. "Jett did you get the feeling your uncle was holding back info?" He turned to me and shook his head "I felt like you both were. Maybe there's information he's not allowed to give us, maybe they don't want anyone else knowing certain details yet." I gulped at his comment and there was a short pause, "I know you'll tell me more when you're ready." I smiled at him and shook my head.

The sky was fire reds and pinks as the sun was about to go down and the clouds looked like popcorn making our moods brighter, Jett took my hand. I was very relaxed and happier now that we let Detective Grey know all about Cale. I felt like I could finally breath and I let a smile slowly come across my face.

Even though it was dusk and the sun was at our backs Jett still put his sunglasses on, which I had never seen before. I asked him about them and he told me ever since Christmas break his eyes and all his senses had been overly sensitive, the doctors thought that was normal though.

Jett asked. "The house you went by that you think is Cale's..."

I didn't even let him finish because I knew where he was going with it. "I don't know the address but I know how to get there, it's off of the Brecksville exit. We can try and go by there now."

"Awesome. Tell me what you know."

I rattled off all the information that I knew about how to get to Cale's supposed house. As Jett pulled down the street he drove slowly, it felt very ominous. I pointed to the house and as he passed it I ducked. "What are you doing?" Jett asked laughing. "I'm hiding, of course." He handed me a rumpled envelope and pulled a pen from the ashtray "Here, write down the address "2620 Shea Ct." I scooted on the floor, put the paper on the seat and wrote it down. He turned the car around, in the next driveway when Jett said "Oh shit!" and floored the car back onto the street and sped all the way back to the highway.

I got back in my seat, "Did you see him?"

"No, but I saw someone coming out of the house. I'll get that address to my uncle right away."

Right before I got out of the car Jett asked me again how I knew some of the stuff I did. I told him that was a whole other conversation, and we were both so tired he left it at that for the moment. Something was still bothering me about Jett not expecting more of an answer out of me. Maybe he wasn't telling me everything either making it acceptable for me not to have to tell him everything myself. I should have tried to get some more information out of him about his senses and his illness, not sure I know how to go about that though.

I got a personal call from Detective Grey the next day. He told me they raided the house that morning with the address Jett gave them, and I was right. They found the bracelet with traces of blood. They are testing it to see if it matches Jewel's. The house was being rented by a woman named Dr. Cassandra Westman. The landlord thought she had a couple of guys living with her too. One was thought to be her boyfriend and he gave them a similar description to Cale's. The house is locked up and under further investigation. I asked if they arrested Cale and he said no arrests were made, no one was there and it looked like they packed up in a hurry.

A week went by and I hadn't heard from Jett nor seen him in school, and then, another week; he wasn't returning my phone calls either. Finally, I saw him at his locker, I always took the routes that passed by his locker if I could. When I saw him my heart leapt, and panicked all at once. I practically froze, I didn't know what to do and before I could decide I found myself walking up to him like some mystical force forging me forward. I said "Hi" and his senior friend made a smart remark, something to the effect of "Look your little friend is back, she's been looking for you every day like a little lamb." I didn't look his way. I looked right at Jett, who was staring back at me until he turned to regard his friend and tightened his jaw "Brett don't be an ass, if you talk to Addie like that again we're going to have issues."

    I couldn't believe my ears, all I could do was smile ear to ear. Jett looked back at me and said "Sorry Addie, I don't have time to talk I'm late for class, we'll talk later." He got his books out, kissed me on the cheek and he was gone. I turned around and Brett smiled mutinously at me, he puckered his lips and made a smooching sound in the air, what a jerk.

CHAPTER 19

After wrestling was over and the guys were walking toward the locker rooms I said "Hey Jett" but he didn't hear me so I said it louder and I added "Can I talk to you?" Of course all the guys went "eeeww" in unison. I turned a little blush, not because I was embarrassed for me, but for Jett.

He turned and started walking toward me. His bibs were down and his chest was bare and that's what I was looking at, but then I averted my eyes up to his. I raised my water bottle up to him; he took two steps back and casually leaned against the wall next to me using one arm to hold himself up, crossed one leg and downed some water from my bottle, not putting his mouth on it, just pouring it in. We both watched as the other guys filtered out of the gym and then the coach.

Nic was putting everything back in the closet. I looked at Jett, "So are you okay? Were you sick?" He inched a little closer to me leaning forward and giving me a peck on the cheek. "I was really sick and all I did was sleep for two weeks. Mom was threatening to take me to the hospital the whole time. Glad she didn't because I'm fine now, actually, I'm feeling *really* good now."

"So then you were sick and that's why you didn't call me?" I said.

"Yes, that would be why I didn't call you, but you have a phone too." he said smiling.

3:17 a.m. ...the waking hour

"I did call once.. Storm took the message, since you didn't call me back I didn't want to bother you again. I didn't want to seem like a stalker." He just laughed...

"One or two phone calls are not too many, after four maybe. I'll have to talk to Storm; I never got your message."

"So did you need another blood transfusion?" I asked. He said nothing back, but looked at me with concerned eyes. I changed the subject right away, knowing he was annoyed with my question. "Are you feeling good enough to do something this weekend? Maybe a movie.... with me?" I bit my lip. "Or you could come over and we could just hang out."

Even though he smelled of sweat he still smelled good to me. He turned placed both hands on the wall on either side of my face and leaned in and gave me a sweet full on kiss. His lips were warm and soft, when he pulled away he replied "Sure let's do something, but I really have to catch up on all my classes, so we'll talk more about this later."

I placed my hand on his chest, it felt like he had a fever he was so warm, I pressed my face to his and our lips parted. He grabbed my hand on his chest lightly and said "None of that here."

"Excuse me, you started it" I replied. He gave me a peck on the lips and walked toward the locker room. I stared at his backside the whole time, Nic walked up to me, "Nice view."

"I know, right."

I didn't want to screw things up with Jett, and bug him about this weekend but my parents were going to be out of town and our babysitter was Peyton for the first time, so I bet we could get away with doing stuff we normally wouldn't. And if Jett wouldn't do something with me, then by god I was going to make plans. Nic was tired of hearing me whine about it so I asked her what I should do. We decided to make plans that Jett could be included in; I thought it was brilliant.

I talked to Tori to see what she was doing and we decided each of us would invite a couple friends over and have some pizza and snacks. When Peyton heard our plans she was fine with it and asked if we cared if she invited a couple friends. We all pow-wowed and decided as long as we all invited no more than four friends each and told no one it was a party, we'd be fine.

Jett had been acting distant and weird, so after practice on Thursday I told him the plan for Saturday and he acted like it was a boring idea. I got mad and snapped "whatever, your welcome to come by if you get really bored." I turned on my heel and walked away.

Saturday, Tori and I woke up and started cleaning the house like we did every Saturday and Peyton asked us "What the hell are you two doing? You don't clean before a party, you clean after."

Tori chimed in with "I thought we weren't calling it a party."

"That's right" Peyton replied "We're just having some friends over." She winked at us and grabbed the car keys off the counter "Now, let's go pick up some snacks."

By 7:30 all our friends had arrived, by 8:30 it had turned into a party – I just wished I could have invited everyone I wanted had I known this was going to happen. However, just about everyone was here, except for Jett. Cale even showed up, I turned immediately and looked for Peyton so she could give him the boot but instead I found myself trapped on the driveway by the garage. His arms were twitching nervously by his sides, he was staring me down and demanded "Where's Jett?"

I replied cautiously "Not sure, he's around." I lied.

"No he's not," he accused, his jaw tightening. "Why would you lie to me?" He took a step closer, I stepped back.

"Cale, what are you doing here? You're not welcome." I crossed my arms in front of my chest. He stepped so close to me it was uncomfortable, so I pushed him gently backward. He grabbed my wrists so fast and pushed me back up against the brick wall. He scrunched his nose, squinted his eyes and gritted his teeth.

"My you have big teeth." My smart ass mouth said and he shook me and slammed me against the wall again. I was trying to get my wrists free but he was holding on really tight. I thought I saw Jett out of the corner of my eye coming down the driveway. Whomever it was stopped as he saw us, he just stood motionless. I put my head on Cale's chest like I was going to surrender, relaxed my arms and I felt Cale ease up, then I heaved my knee up as hard as I could between his legs and whipped my head up hitting him in the chin. I twisted and turned my wrists trying to get them free.

"Let go!" I roared in a voice that projected so loud and so deep I wasn't sure it was really me. I shook loose, I shouted "Someone help me!" but that gave Cale incentive to surge toward me again, his eyes watering and a look to kill on his face, I kicked my foot in the middle of his chest, he snagged my foot making me lose my balance but caught myself on the half wall before falling. Cale stumbled backwards into Jett; Jett grabbed him from behind and threw Cale to the middle of the driveway like he was a ragdoll.

"Damn it!" I retorted. Jett was in front of me in a split second, protecting me. Cale got to his feet, specifically looked at Jett gave him an approvingly sly smile and left. Jett turned toward me and I put my face in his shirt and breathed him in, "thank you." I put my hands inside his opened jacket and around him. He put his hand on my head and caressed my head. "You okay?" he asked, his voice cracked. "You know for a minute I thought you and Cale were getting back together, my heart felt like it dropped out of my chest when I saw the two of you, but then you proved me wrong. Anyway, I'm glad to see you can defend yourself." He kept stroking my hair.

"I can't defend myself, I can't and if I hadn't seen you coming I'm not sure what would have happened." I started pacing back and forth a bit. "And I'm not sure what's wrong with me, I seem to keep attracting freaks and getting attacked! I need to learn self-defense."

Jett laughed, "one freak, and he just won't leave you alone. I should call my uncle."

"Well..." I almost told him about Logan but then I didn't. "I had no idea what to do, I saw you and a few seconds later I was defending myself. I need to know what to do all the time."

He was just looking at me with a half cracked smile, arms folded in front of him in a wide spread stance. Yeah, he was a bit of a bad ass.

"I haven't seen Peyton in a while do mind helping me find her?" I asked.

As we looked around the house I headed toward my parent's bedroom, Peyton and her boyfriend were just coming out, their corduroy pants filled with white fuzz, the same color as my parent's bedspread. She acted all cool like nothing had happened I gave her a look and glanced down at her pants. She stammered she lost an earring and I just gave her another look. "So the two of you were looking for an earring... while rolling on the bed??" pointing to their pants. Obviously we knew where it came from, they were definitely busted. They both started to laugh – "Shhh" she said "Don't tell anyone else..." she stumbled away pulling her boyfriend with. I looked at Jett and we both said simultaneously "She's drunk."

"Do you want a drink?" I asked Jett as we turned into the kitchen. He leaned up against the counter and crossed his arms and legs almost like he was still upset. I opened the fridge and looked in "Do you want a beer or a soda?" I closed the fridge part way and saw his face and said "You need a beer." He replied by saying "No, I'll take a soda."

I opened two bottles and handed him one and sat on the desk across from him.

"So were you grouchy before you got here or after you saw me being assaulted by Cale?"

There was a moment of silence "I was just wondering if you wouldn't have backed Cale off if you didn't see me comin'."

I rubbed my face and replied "Probably not..." he stood up and went to walk away. "Seriously, would you let me finish." He stopped for a moment and I continued "As I was saying, he had such a grip on me I didn't know what to do. He was hurting me bad, but when I saw you, I knew if I fought back and it didn't work, you would have backed me up." He leaned back up against the counter. "I was way panicked before I saw you but when I did, I felt the urge to defend myself. I'm not even sure where I learned those moves but thank goodness I did them...... If you hadn't come along, I probably would have just screamed and if I got loose I would have tried running. I'm really glad you came though... and not just because you helped me out of a jam either, because I wanted you to come."

Nic walked in "There you are! Oh, hey Jett. Your sister is hilarious and she isn't even drinking yet. You guys gotta come down stairs." I looked at her and said "Okay we'll be down in a minute."

"So should I call the police – if I do, I think I need to break the party up first." I got up and walked over to Jett and stood in front of him.

"So Cale is sick in the head huh. We should tell my uncle, since he knows the rest of the story." He pulled on the hem of my t-shirt and I let myself fall into him, putting my hands on his waist and I'm not sure if I planted one on him or he on me, but we kissed.

I grabbed his hand and pulled him downstairs to see what was going on. The party had grown; our basement was large so it held everyone. My sister and Alec were playing music and dancing, everyone was having a good time. The only one that was out of control was Peyton... dancing like a mad person. I'll have to make sure she doesn't drink anything else tonight. Her boyfriend and other friends seemed to be outside, they started a bonfire. Nic, Storm and Shelby were at the bar. We went over to chat with the gang.

"Hey, nice to see you guys!" As we made our way to the bar, drunken Peyton fell into Jett, "Crap, I should take her upstairs" I said.

"I got it." Jett replied.

"Really?"

"Yeah I got it. Your parents room, right?"

"Yes please" I replied, turning toward the gang. "So did you all get a drink?" They all lifted their sodas.

"Hmmm. Well, I'm going to have a beer does anyone want to join me?" No one said anything, so I went and grabbed a few from the cooler – "Who's driving?" Shelby raised her hand. I told her "You could spend the night so you don't have to drive," her eyes lit up. I handed Storm and Nic a beer and grabbed two more for Jett and I. "Shelby there's a phone upstairs in the kitchen. Why don't you call home before you start drinking," she ran.

Jett came down as I was telling Nic and Storm the story about Cale, Nic hadn't even known he was there. I told them my wrists were still very sore, that he's crazy and Jett and I were going to call his uncle.

After about one in the morning I broke the party up, started getting people out of the basement, then put out the bonfire, threw stuff in the garbage and did a quick mop up. Nic and Tori crashed in our room, Kit and his friend in his, Shelby and Storm in the living room when I suddenly realized it was just Jett and I.

He had a beer in hand, his jacket on and I noticed his t-shirt was fitted, well it was fitted on his chest and a little loose everywhere else. I turned to him as he fished his keys out of his pocket. "You aren't going anywhere." I said.

"I only had two beers." he said.

"I need to check on Peyton and you're sleeping here.. Don't argue either." I grabbed two more beers from the cooler and headed into the basement family room, turned on the TV. "I'm going to check on Peyton and make sure all the doors are locked and I'll be right down – do you want some sweats to sleep in?" He nodded and opened our beers, I took a sip and left.

Peyton was in my parent's bathroom on the floor; she'd gotten sick and mumbled something unintelligible to me. I got her a blanket, flushed the toilet and left her there. I checked all the upstairs doors, went downstairs checked the garage door, it was closed, thank goodness. Then I checked the door by the bar. We were all locked down.

When I returned to the family room Jett was sprawled out on the couch. I picked up my beer and took another sip. He patted the couch by him. I threw a pair of sweats to him. "I'm going to change into sweats." I said quickly to him and ditched out into the laundry room, changed and was back in a flash. When I got there he was already changed. "Damn that was fast I was hoping to catch you in the act."

He pulled me down into the couch with him. I was warm so I peeled off my sweatshirt. Jett startled me by his comment "Holy shit!" He made me jump but then I laughed "What, I'm more beautiful than you thought?" He didn't say anything so I said "I have outstanding biceps and you're jealous." He was fumbling for the lamp and I heard it click, click, but it didn't turn on....He got up and took my hand gently leading me into the hallway, I glanced out our picture window and saw a pair of eyes glowing, Jett gave me a tug under the light, I leaned over to look out the window again but I saw nothing. Jett flipped on the light, it stung my eyes for a minute. He put his hand under my elbow and held it up lightly caressing my arm. I looked down at my wrists. "Crap, I knew they hurt but they look worse."

"You're going to be sore tomorrow." Jett stated. I walked further down the hallway to the bathroom and turned on the light. Sure enough both arms matched. They had bruises, some in the shape of fingers, from Cale earlier. Jett and I just stared at my arms in the mirror. "You should probably put ice on them."

"Does ice help bruises?" I asked.

"Not sure, but most injuries you treat with ice, it helps the swelling, numbs it a bit and helps. Why didn't you say anything?"

"I was trying to ignore it and they really didn't start hurting until just a little bit ago – so I had a beer."

"Aspirin would have been better Addie."

As we climbed the stairs I peered out the picture window again - still nothing. Upstairs I packed a bag of ice and grabbed a towel.

3:17 a.m. ...the waking hour

Peyton was still on the bathroom floor sleeping, the rest of the house was quiet.

By the time we got back downstairs my arms were throbbing. We tried lying on the couch together but it really bugged my arms. There was an antique dresser in the room my mom kept filled with blankets and pillows, so we spread a comforter on the floor and one on top then tossed four pillows and a couple more blankets on the floor. Then I got inside, Jett laid next to me. He propped his head up with one arm and used the other to hold the ice pack on my wrists. He leaned toward me and kissed me with the lightest touch and brush of his lips to mine; I could feel the warmth radiating from him.

When I woke up the next morning, Jett, Storm and Shelby were gone. I peeked in my room and Tori and Nic were still sprawled all over the beds. Kit and his friend were up and dressed. I went into the bathroom to check out my arms and they were black and blue, they looked worse to me. I put on a sweatshirt so I wouldn't have to explain it to anyone else. Got out my notepad and started writing: I was in my backyard and everything was spinning, Cale was there with his arms crossed, sunglasses on at dusk and a figure behind him the same height and build. As I spun in a full slow circle Jett appeared behind me. I came back around and Cale and the other guy disappeared and another guy in a dark cloak stood in their place. My wolf was at the ravines edge I saw his eyes glowing and as the man in the cloak raised his hands in the air the wolf ran. I felt Jett squeeze my shoulders from behind so hard it started to hurt. When I had woken up, it was still dark.

I checked on Peyton, she had moved to the bed but not before puking on the bathroom floor. Of course, she didn't clean it up. She was going to be of no use to us today. My parents were coming home later, so I started looking to see if anything else needed cleaning up. I did a pretty good job last night, the coolers were left and maybe I'd have to mop the basement floor again.

When Peyton woke up for a few minutes she paid me $20 to clean up her puke and went back to bed – I don't think she could have done it because she was in bad shape. Plus, she knew she wasn't getting paid for watching us either.....even though we wouldn't spill the beans to my parents I'm sure the rumors would fly somehow. They always did.

When I finished cleaning the puke that was half dried on the floor and almost made me spew myself, I hopped in the shower, a long hot one. After, I pulled some clean sweats and my favorite zip up hoodie on and although the style for the socks were to wear them pulled up I always had them pushed down around my ankles.

I woke up Nic and Tori, they were half awake anyway. And I went into the kitchen to cook some breakfast, my favorite meal of the day, when the doorbell rang.

It was Jett with coffee, donuts and a Valentines card. It was Valentine's Day and I hadn't even realized.

I took the box from him and kissed him on the cheek "Good morning! I didn't think you were coming back..."

"I remembered you telling me your dad used to pick up donuts before anyone woke, and..." I cut him off with another kiss that led to a better kiss. He put his face in the crook of my neck with my wet hair. "You smell good."

"Are you sure you just aren't smelling the bacon I'm cooking?" I said with a little laugh.

"You're cooking?"

"Ha ha ha," I said pushing him away gently and went to the kitchen to put the bacon on paper towels and turn off the stove.

Every once in a while my dad would wake up before anybody else on a Sunday – well he always woke up before everyone else – but sometimes he would go get a dozen Amy Joy donuts which was always a treat, and he always remembered to get everyone's favorites. I remembered sharing that info with Jett. It was very nice he remembered.

He grabbed the back of my sweat jacket and pulled me to him. I turned around "I'm sorry I didn't even get you a card, I forgot about Valentine's Day. Thank you for the donuts..."

I felt his eyes, like he was looking right into my soul. He bent down and kissed me gently. His thick hands moved slowly down my side then onto my butt and he squeezed, and pulled me up. I wrapped my legs around him. He turned us around and set my bottom on the counter. I kept my legs around him. He pulled away and I started to kiss his neck and bit him lightly. He picked me back up and carried me downstairs to the family room where the blankets lay crumpled on the floor from the night before. He stopped and I slid my legs down slowly and I pushed my hands up under his shirt, and pulled it off.

We both kneeled down while still having our arms and mouths caressing each other. His chest was bare and I couldn't stop touching him. Jett put his hand under my sweatshirt onto my back wear my bra should have been, but I wasn't wearing one, I thought it was just me and the girls today...He let out a soft moan when he felt my bare back. He laid me down gently, unzipped my jacket only part way and slid his finger down from my neck to my breastbone. It sent a shiver right through me.

His hand slid over my jacket to my waist, and he pressed his lips on mine. His hand under my waistband; he traced the line of my sweats and then slid his hand on my hip bone. He let out another gasp. I bit his lip and pulled him closer to me. He pulled away and rolled over onto his back.

I stopped, his whole body was trembling but other than he wasn't moving....... he didn't say a word. "Are you okay?" I asked as quietly as I could. Still, he didn't move except for the tremor going through him..........his eyes were closed, you could tell he was fighting something, his jaw severely clamped and all the veins showing in his neck. I sat up staring at him wanting to touch him but somehow knowing I shouldn't....

After our wrestling meet on Friday, Nic and I got a ride home from my other Lil Sis wrestler, Randy, who was also driving four other wrestlers home. But instead of going directly home, we decided to stop at Skyway's first. Randy was driving, I was in the middle, Declan was on my right and in the back were Dave, Nic and Jim.

Randy pulled into the parking lot and as soon as we got a few cars in, he said "Now" and everyone in the car ducked except Randy and me. He put his arm around me while we cruised the parking lot, I laughed the whole time. Everyone laughed and thought it was funny too. After the cruise I even said "Ooooh, Jett's going to be so mad at you....." and everyone laughed even more.

When Jett came to pick me up on Saturday to go to a movie, he was late and when he got here he didn't come in, he stayed on the deck. I walked out there and he was leaning on the railing next to the stairs that led down to the driveway. He looked serious.

I walked up to him and asked if he was all right. "I'm fine." he said. "What'd ya do after the meet last night?' he asked looking right at me, and when I looked back at him, he looked down.

"You have got to be kidding me" was all I could say because I knew it was about Skyway, even though it wasn't a big deal at all. "It wasn't a big deal. Randy was just joking around and I had no idea they were going to do that, besides we all laughed so hard about it we had tears in our eyes. Then I told them they were in trouble with you and we all just laughed again.... It was just for fun."

"Yeah well, I didn't appreciate it and I didn't appreciate hearing about it from someone else either."

"I was going to mention it tonight," he just gave me a look like he didn't believe me. "Whatever Jett, believe who you want. There were five other people in the car you can ask about it including Declan." There was a little pause. "I bet it's your good buddy Brett stirring this crap up, right? He's always trying to get between us and making crap up about everyone's girlfriends. Am I right?" He had no response. "Yeah that's what I thought." I looked over the rail, just what I thought, Brett was sitting in the car.

"Brett is a good friend and he would never lie to me about something like that." Jett still leaning against the railing, he still looked sexy to me even though I wanted the railing to give-way right now.

There was a long silence. I had nothing more to say, I was cold and just wanted to go back inside. He stood there motionless and silent. "So Jett, what's going on?" I asked.

"I don't know. I need some time to think."

"Fine take all the time you want, but just remember, I can be trusted and I'm probably the most trustworthy person you'll ever meet." I said.

"You brought this on, not Brett." he said.

"Brett hates me and can't stand seeing you with me. Did he tell you he asked me out before we started dating and I turned him down? Ask him about that – oh and by the way Jett, you're looking a little pale, it looks like you need another transfusion. Please take care of yourself." I said and walked away, I was hoping he would have stopped me, but he didn't.

Jett turned and went down the stairs, got in his car and left. I watched him from the kitchen window, I didn't yell anything through it but I really wanted to call Brett names and flip him the bird. Maybe next time.

For some reason, I had a feeling it was because Jett and I were on the outs that Storm started hanging around Nic and I more. I was fine with it as long as we all stayed friends, besides we were all getting along.

That was until Storm started sitting a little closer to me and putting his arm around me, I tried getting him and Nic together but no, he didn't sway. One night Storm made movie plans for the three of us, at least that's what he told me, but of course Nic didn't show because she didn't know about it, since it was all last minute I didn't call her either, I should have known. However, if Storm was all I had to worry about lately, I welcomed it, versus Cale and the drama with him. He's been incognito lately, maybe it's all blowing over.

Almost a month had gone by and no reconciliation with Jett; the bad thing was I couldn't get him off my mind. Today I entered the lunch room with Nic; we got in line, got our food and sat down by Storm, our usual routine as of late. We were several tables away from the windows but facing them. I heard loud laughter by the windows, when I looked up I noticed Jett and a bunch of his friends. I couldn't look away even though I wanted to, he caught my eye, my breath hitched in my throat. He nodded at me then waved me over. I was taken aback but then stuck my tongue out at him. I wanted to go over there but he's been avoiding me for weeks and now he wants to talk in front of his friends - forget about it. His jaw dropped and his eyebrows raised looking surprised and waved me over.

I looked at Nic and she said "Go on, if you don't go you'll wonder what it was about all day, if not longer, and you'll bug me about it for weeks." There was a slight pause and then she said "And be bold."

I looked at Storm, he looked enraged "he's treated you like crap, forget him" he stammered.

"I think I'm done melting over him every time I see him, I can handle this." I announced proudly and walked over to his table and I nodded at Jett. He was sitting at the edge of the bench. I said "Scoot over." He did a little but I hip checked so he'd move some more. "Give me a little room, would ya." I said.

His friend across from him chuckled. It was silent "Sooooo whadya drag me over here for, you gonna set me up on a date." Jett looked at me like I was crazy and his friend laughed and said "I told ya you didn't have to ask her permission."

"Permission for what?" I asked.

"Oh, so you want to know who you should date... If you plan on dating him…" I said pointing to the guy across from us, "I don't think it's a good fit. On the other hand, that one right over there is more your type, more submissive." Jett nudged me, laughing.

"Stop it, I told you we were just on a break." Jett said.

I froze and one of Jett's friends said "What, cat got your tongue?"

I looked at Jett and said "Really, this guy's your friend?" Then I turned back toward his friend "did you come up with that all by yourself?" There were hoots and hollers from the rest of the clan. I knew these guys were all pro's at being sarcastic and I was hoping I didn't go too far - I could have said a lot more, but so could the rest of them.

Jett introduced me to a guy across from us, his name was Smith, who was 6'5". He grabbed my hand and pulled me over to him, I went reluctantly, he put his arm around my waist and said, "Hey baby your break is done with that schmuck over there, you're my kind of women."

Everyone at the table roared with laughter. He pulled me down on his lap. I let loose with a giggle when Cale strolled by, I stopped laughing cold and went and sat back by Jett. "Hey honey, where you goin'? You ain't gonna let little ole Cale intimidate you are you?" Smith gloated.

I folded my hands together, elbows on the table and rested my hands on my right cheek, trying to look relaxed. I don't think it was working. Agitated, my cheeks were blushing and warm. My cool hands felt good on them. I looked at Jett and in a hushed voice said "How much longer are you going to torment me like this?"

He laughed and put his hand on my back and rubbed it. "These knuckle heads over here, want to go on spring break.

"No," I said.

"No, what? Jett asked.

"You didn't let me finish. No way, I don't want to go, not with you guys."

"Oh sorry honey, that wasn't the question," Smith responded.

"Thank God" I replied.

Jett continued..."The guys want to go on spring break and I wanted to know if you would mind if I went with them."

There was an interlude...I regarded Smith with scrutiny and said "Good time for your line now." I contemplated the loaded question, looked at Jett and said "So if you're asking me if you could go on spring break with these guys, then we must not be on a *break*." And I put little quotes in the air as I said the word break. "So therefore, you want permission from me, the *girlfriend*, to go on spring break." I did the air quotes again when I said girlfriend.

"Yes. Declan told me it was the way to go." Jett said.

I leaned over to look at Declan and he gave me a wink. I continued slowly and said "Well, if we are now dating and you want something, then so do I...."

"Oh you do, do ya? What do you want?" Jett said laughing.

"That my friend, will have to be discussed in my private quarter's thank you." And I got up to walk away, Jett stopped me.

"No, you can ask me now."

"No" I said, "then my answer is no," and walked away. As I was telling Nic all about it, I looked up and there was Jett, smiling down at me with that glimmer in his eye.

As Jett sat down, Smith came over and leaned on our table. He let his head sink between his shoulders and said with a bite "Well, can he go?"

I replied "Of course he can, I'm not his mother." He stood there a little dumbfounded at first but didn't leave. I looked at him and said "What else could you possibly want? Why are you still here? Are you gonna ask me for permission so he can pick up girls too? If he does, all I'm saying is whatever happens on spring break stays on spring break. And all of you better practice safe sex, buy a box of condoms."

"Dude" he yelled pushing off of the table and punching his hands in the air. "I love this girl!" Then gazed back at me. "Are you sure you want this guy?" Thumbing toward Jett "...for your boyfriend, because honey, I will treat you like gold."

I replied "No you wouldn't, you're a man whore."

He contemplated and then humorously said "Yeah you're right, but I still love ya!" He palmed my head messing up my hair and finally left.

I looked at Jett and took a bite of my sandwich. "So you're really gonna let me go." He asked.

I looked at him incredulous and said "Yeah, why wouldn't I?"

"Some of the guy's girlfriends are giving them a hard time," he started.

"Well, what comes around goes around, right? You would let me go, right?"

"Hell no, at least not without me! Spring break is all about drinking with the guys. Plus, girls don't fare well at these things."

"They must fare fine, otherwise no girls would ever go and spring break would be a bunch of guys on vacation and what fun would that be?"

"I guess you're right. So, you're saying I can go and flirt and if anything else happened you would be fine with it."

"No, I didn't quite say that. You're really going to act like we haven't spoken for the past month?" I asked.

"No."

"So, are you still mad at me for the Skyway thing?"

"No, I'm not."

"Well that was three words, more than your last statement." Nic got up quietly and left. "Do you trust me? Because if you don't, that means I can't trust you, people with trust issues are usually the ones telling the lies. And I know this for a fact because 'I know' I'm not lying about a darned thing."

He looked me in the eye and put his hand on mine. "I actually really do trust you, implicitly. You were right about Brett, Rae pointed that out, and you were right about my blood being low too. By the time I got home that night, I had dark circles under my eyes and I was craving a rare burger – a tell tale signs of getting sick again. So I went to a free clinic the next day and while I was there, I met another doctor who is studying people with my unknown illness. We drove to her office and she took some blood and she gave me a transfusion. She said she can help me and that I actually need a transfusion every 30 days or so to keep me healthy."

"Wow, that's great! Someone who knows what's going on." I picked up my tray and dumped the contents in the garbage and returned it, Jett followed and grabbed my hand.

"So we are officially dating again. I'm taking you out this weekend! And, just to re-iterate, you said it's okay that I go on spring break and that I should have fun, I can do whatever." He said pretty happily and kissed my hand.

"That's not what I said. First, I said I wanted something in return. Second I said you can have fun and I hope you don't go out there looking for anyone or anything... you know with another girl, but whatever happens out there, I don't want to know about it especially if it pertains to a girl and you. And the very worst scenario, if something does happen, I hope you are smart enough to use protection even if the girl tells you she's on birth control or clean. You need to protect yourself against diseases. You may not get another chance to go on spring break, so go and have fun."

"Really, that's it? Have fun and use protection."

"I mean, yeah, we're in high school" I like watching him and his reactions when we're talking "I really hope you don't meet any..." He interrupted me with a kiss.

"I'm not going for the girls. The guys need enough of us to go to cover hotel costs and gas. Plus, I think it'll be good for me to get out of town and blow off steam, it should be fun."

"Well then" I said with a great big grin "I want you to buy me a t-shirt." I said.

"Any shirt I choose?" Jett said with a devious look on his face.

"Sure as long as you wear it and I actually want you to wear it a lot and after you've worn it a while then I'll steal it from you." He looked at me strangely but agreed. I always thought it would be cool to wear my boyfriend's shirt, so here's my chance. Plus, it'll be from Florida. He got up to walk away and I said "Hey! That's it?" He turned to me and smiled "I'll give you a ride home tonight and we'll talk more then." He started to walk off then turned "You could ask me for one of my shirts, I have no problem with that." I smiled.

On our ride home I turned to him and asked "Along with needing blood transfusions are there other treatments for you and what other symptoms are you having?"

"Excuse me?" he retorted.

I re-asked the question I really wanted an answer to. "What other peculiar symptoms are you having? Like, that night in my basement, plus, I noticed you seem to be even better at wrestling; quicker, stronger. If you're sick why wouldn't you be weak and fatigued?"

He took my hand and was hesitant but then asked... "Can we

talk about this later? I am sick to death of my illness right now."
"Sure." I said and didn't ask him anything else about it..

CHAPTER 20

I woke up at 3:17a.m., got my pad of paper out and started writing. I had a very strange dream. It was about the Incredible Hulk slamming his hands into the dirt digging a hole, no shovel or anything, just his hands. He was mad, just digging. I can't imagine this one will come true, why would I dream about this? I really thought that maybe I had been watching too much TV, but wrote it down anyway.

It was my dad's idea to invite our boyfriends over to help him with yard work. When I had asked Jett he seemed to be okay about it but when he got to our house Saturday morning, dropped off by his father at the top of our driveway; he looked like he was in a *baaad* mood. I was waiting anxiously for him to come over today, but when I saw his face getting out of the car, I was ready to run the other way. I watched him closely from the bottom of the driveway. I started walking slowly toward him, giving his dad a wave as he left, he probably couldn't wait to get out of here. I mean he really looked cranky, in a horribly rotten mood, although he still looked hot as all hell. He had on a white tank top that fit him with a t-shirt flung over his shoulder. His tan broad muscular shoulders stuck out, I wanted to touch them and run my hand down his arm. He had on painter jeans that were baggy but no matter what he wore they still showed his very nice butt. He also had on work boots to complete the bad boy look.

Jett met me half way down the driveway and I leaned in to give him a kiss but from the scowl on his face I decided to plant it on his cheek. He didn't reciprocate and he didn't say anything. His face was cold and rigid, what did I do now? I guess I'll have to figure it out because I'm not asking him. In any case, he was in *a mood*.

We walked down to the bottom of the driveway in complete silence where Tori and Alec were standing, I think the birds even stopped chirping afraid they'd rub him the wrong way. Alec was cute but not my type at all, my sister and I don't have the same taste in boys, thank god but at least he was in a good mood. I wondered if she wanted to switch for the day; I looked at Jett again and laughed I knew she wouldn't nor would anybody else for that matter. Alec was holding a beer, he was 18 so he was legal to drink.

Jett looked perplexed and spoke rigidly, "Alec did you drive?"

"No" he said and laughed. "My parents dropped me off. Mr. Gellar said he'd drive us home, this way we can drink and not have to worry about driving. Do you want a beer?" He said with a chuckle, meaning dude have a beer. He could tell Jett was in a mood, everyone could.

Jett looked at me with mean little eyes and I said "Dude, it can't make your mood any worse, but if it'll get you in a better frame of mind please drink." And Alec tossed Jett a beer. He chugged it in no time but still didn't say a word.

My dad came around from the front. He's an intimidating looking type of guy, at least my friends tell me so. He has broad shoulders and a belly but it doesn't distract you from his masculinity. He exudes great confidence and talks with it as well, making him come off very daunting. All of our friends and any kid in general were quiet around him and tended to listen to him intently.

My dad said "Boys, you're going to help me take down some trees today. Obviously, my girls don't have the strength it needs, so I recruited you – actually I forced my girls to ask you for your help." He laughed and slapped, then rubbed his belly "We have beer, sodas, chips and sandwiches in the cooler, help yourselves. The bathroom is just inside the garage, you don't have to take off your shoes. The first thing I need done is to have the big old birch tree near the road dug up." He pointed to the street up the hill where the birch rested, he handed the boys gloves, Jett turned

around, still agitated, and walked off toward the tree taking very large steps up the hill. I hustled behind him but struggled to keep up without running. "What is wrong with you, are you mad at me?"
"No!" Jett said giving his encrypted answers again.
"Do you want to go home?" I asked.
"Grrrrr."
"Leave if you want, I don't care. My dad thinks this stuff is fun to do and if you're gonna be all pissy, it's going to make it much worse."
"He wants this damn tree out! I'll take it out, but it's going to be a pain because it's still alive."
"No it's not. Go do something else – go away. Do you want me to get my mom to drive you home?" He didn't respond.

He stood on the street side, pulled his gloves on and tossed his shirt to the ground. He took one of the tree trunks and grasped it with both hands, pulled back and forth and heaved up on it the whole while I could see every muscle ripple and his face turned brick red, until we heard a loud crack. He looked up at me and said "I told you it was still alive." It sure looked that way, where it cracked at the base it looked healthy. He let the huge branch fall partially into the street, part of the roots were up-heaved from the ground. I could hear my sister and Alec mumbling with laughter from behind as they walked up next to me to see what Jett had done.

Jett took the tree trunk by one end and rolled it onto our yard.

"You couldn't wait for everyone else? It's more fun to do it in a group, and easier, that's why my dad asked for your help" Tori exclaimed. I looked at Tori and Alec and in a hushed mumble I told them I had already mentioned that to him, and shrugged.

He looked at us and walked around the other side of the tree. He kept his eyes on me, not saying a word. He raised his arms higher than his shoulders and pulled his arms down hard fast into the barely disturbed ground. Then pulled up, gritted his teeth, veins popped on his face and neck. He repeated that motion again and again, until he had pulled up the rest of the ball of roots. Some of them held fast to the ground and deterred him from pulling it more than knee high. He let it plunge to the ground. I gazed at him; he looked bigger, his tank was messy but also stretched across him like it didn't fit. I couldn't look away, his muscles gleamed with sweat.

Alec, behind me, started laughing – Jett stomped on the

remaining trunk that was still partially intact, and it too, collapsed to the ground. There was a long long pause, no one said a word. We stood in astonishment for a while.

Tori said "Impressive Jett. Let's get that man a beer." Alec ran to the cooler parked on the sidewalk, charged back up the hill and tossed Jett a beer. Jett opened it and chugged it faster than the first one.

"Do you feel better now?" Tori asked.

Jett walked up to Alec slowly they held each other's gaze silently, Jett reached over slowly took Alec's beer from his hand , opened it and took a swig, the two of them started to laugh. Jett took his tank off and I could see his "V" the transverse abdominal muscles, his lines were beautiful, his abs incredible and his chiseled chest smooth.

I was definitely staring, my mouth must have been open because Tori commented sarcastically "Addie you're drooling – use his shirt to wipe your mouth." I turned to her embarrassed, still not closing my mouth and said "No thanks, I'll use yours" and pulled her shirt and pretended to wipe my mouth. Everyone laughed. Jett tossed me his shirt and actually smiled at me – as the shirt flew into my hands I could smell the scent of him on it – he definitely wasn't getting this shirt back.

Jett and Alec pulled the tree into the yard. My dad came up with chain saws, pics and shovels in his wheel barrow; the boys smiled at that, my dad stared in wonderment. "I guess we won't need the shovels. How did you two do that?" My dad asked bewildered. They both just looked at him and smiled, Alec pointed to Jett.

My dad ordered Tori to get three beers. They cut the tree up and tossed the good parts into one wheelbarrow and bad parts in another. We had two fireplaces in our house so the wood would go to good use, Tori and I stacked it onto our wood pile and we dumped the bad onto our compost pile in the back.

Alec peeled his shirt off too – I think it was a guy thing – and although he had a nice physique I was not as impressed. He was really white and had to catch up on his tan to look as hot as Jett.

It didn't take long to finish, Jett went up to my dad with the chain saw resting on one shoulder and said "What's next Mr. Gellar?" My dad grabbed his shoulder and explained "The next one will take some doing and pointed to the largest tree on our lot, it also had four trunks but each of them were very large, the whole tree had to be over forty feet high, it was a lot taller than our house.

Jett looked back at him and said "Do you have some rope? We'll have to use it to make sure it doesn't hit the house".

My dad replied "Well, all right then." And Jett followed him over to the cooler where my dad handed him a sandwich, got one for himself and they paced down toward the garage for some rope. Alec, Tori and I continued to wheel barrow and stock the rest of the wood.

All three of them got along very well, and they included Kit whenever they could. They ate all the sandwiches by noon, so my mom made an early dinner for everyone. We ate at the picnic table in the grass rather than on the deck. The boys enjoyed another beer and Jett asked me "Aren't you going to have a beer?"

I replied "I'm not 18 yet."

"Still, jailbait" my dad retorted "...and don't forget that son."

"Absolutely sir." Jett replied, which made us all laugh.

My mom set a beer in front of me and my sister and said "That's the only one you're getting, and you don't have to drink the whole thing either." I smiled at my mom and took a sip.

When we were done eating Jett and I went inside to the downstairs family room and sat down on our old orange leather couch from the 60's, it was built so rock solid it just wouldn't fall apart. Mom said she was going to re-upholster it someday, but the leather wasn't worn in the least bit. The TV I clicked on was really old I couldn't believe it still worked but my parents always said things were built to last.

The couch was cool to the touch which felt good after being outside all day. We hadn't had a conversation to ourselves all day. "I'm glad to see you're feeling better. Is there something you want to talk about? Are you or were you upset with me?"

He looked at me oddly and said "No." That was it, another one liner, although he didn't look mad or anything and I didn't want push it but I needed to know where I stood.

"Hey, if you don't let me know what's up I won't be able to stop myself from ticking you off again. I thought we were friends. Friends are supposed to talk and help each other out." There was a long pause I just waited and waited. He said nothing I could feel him thinking so I laid down and put my head in his lap and stared at the ceiling.

It wasn't a comfortable silence but it wasn't totally uncomfortable either, somewhere in the middle. So I laid there thinking what it would be like if Jett liked me as much as I liked him, but that I was happy to be with him. He started to shift so I lifted up my head and he pulled me up and over so I was sitting on his lap.

Sarcastic me said "So what are you so excited about?" I don't even know if he was, but he smiled and laughed and asked me "So do you like me or what?"

I froze and looked into his eyes. He scooted over on the couch so my back was against the arm of the sofa, my butt slid off his lap and hit the cushion, my legs still crossed his – I didn't know what to say. He said "Well" and I said "What's not to like..." He moved his face closer to mine, I didn't move, he moved in even closer until he brushed his soft warm lips across mine. He pressed a little deeper and our lips parted...we stopped.

I said "...Besides your horrible mood swings." Jett swung his legs out from under mine so he was vertical on the couch and pulled me down so I was laying on it and he was on top of me kissing me again. He was very good at this, I wanted to know if he practiced that move, he did it fast and smooth. Is he a player? I stopped kissing him back and squinted my eyes at him and said "Are you playing with me?"

My dad yelled down the stairs "Are you ready for dessert?" Faster than he had said it Jett was off of me and onto the floor with one arm propped on the couch pretending to watch TV.

I heard the door shut and looked down at Jett and said "What are you doing" He pulled me off the couch on top of him and we started where we left off.

When we finally came up for air I said "I need pie, how about you?"

He asked "With ice cream?"

"Is there any other way to eat it?"

"I like you Addie, a lot."

"Good because I'm having your baby."

He had to do a double take, the look on his face was priceless. Of course, we hadn't but it took him a minute to register. "Psych" I replied.

"You are so sarcastic, but it's all good" he gave me a hand up off the floor.

"I'm glad you think so. And by the way I'm having twins!" He chased me up the stairs.

Jett was a little tipsy by the end of the night. I had to help him into bed, Kit offered up his room for him. He was like a big fluffy teddy bear – without much control either. I tucked him in.... I couldn't believe my parents asked him to sleep over and that he actually did, it could have been because he lived 40 minutes out, in any case I was excited about the whole ordeal.

When I woke at 3:17a.m., I wrote down another one of my silly dreams, this one seamed sillier than the night before. I remembered Jett at the top of the hill today; he almost mimicked my dream. Crap. Now I was nervous recording this one, I wrote: 'I had a dream that Dracula was sucking my blood.' I looked at the ceiling and laughed at myself and thought I'd keep this one to myself. 'He sucked the blood out of my neck while I was sleeping but I woke before he was done and ran after him.' I thought that was unlikely. Everything in the room was dark, all the walls and comforter matched, I had never seen the room before but felt familiar. The dream cut off and picked up again, the second time I met Dracula, I was awake and I went to him willingly and when he took blood from my wrist he turned veiny then back to normal.'

CHAPTER 21

The next morning Nic came over early, she'd do that sometimes; she always fed her horses and lets them out every morning and afterward she'd get her mom to drop her off at my house. My mom was making a huge breakfast since Jett had slept over and we knew he had a good appetite. I answered the door in my pajamas and Nic asked me how last night went, so I dragged her to Kit's room, cracked the door and we peeked in at Jett, who was adorable even when he slept – Nic's eyes almost popped out of her head.

We went into my room giggling and I quickly grabbed some clean clothes, one of my notes and Nic's hand and we flew into the bathroom and locked the door tight. I told her all the details of Jett being a grump and how he pulled the tree out with his bare hands and how I thought he was like the hulk in my dream and his shoulders, arms and whole body bloated; they amplified.... and then I handed her my note. I gave her a minute to read while I brushed my teeth and hair. She looked at me with her mouth open; I told her we could talk about it later. .... and I continued my story about my night with Jett and the great kiss after dinner. I also told her how totally fun it was to put him to bed. He was so relaxed and funny, he was like a huge teddy bear.

"Did you strip him naked before you put him in?" Nic giggled...

"*No!*" I said "He borrowed a pair of sweats and that's what he went to bed in - - but no shirt."

"Yeah I noticed that." Nic gave me a wink.

After I finished dressing, Nic and I went to check on Jett again. He looked so cute his hair was tousled and the blankets tossed. He moved and Nic and I closed the door quickly and bolted to the kitchen.

While we were chowing down on scrambled eggs, fluffy pancakes and some crisp bacon, my mom asked if we would both head up to the Richfield Reading and Speech Center with her, she was going to have coffee with her new friend who had a daughter she wanted to introduce us too. I looked at Nic and rolled my eyes, but she immediately said yes for the both of us. I gave her a dirty look, she said "Where's your sense of adventure?"

"In Kit's room of course" I whispered.

We had just finished eating when my mom walked back in the kitchen with keys and purse in hand and said "You girls ready?"

"Now mom? But Jett's still sleeping I feel rude just leaving him here."

"We won't be but an hour; I'm sure he'll just be waking up by then – write him a note."

So Nic and I wrote him a note and hustled my mom out the door to get this party started.

The good thing was we could walk there but we took the car so it only took us a minute to get there. My mom pulled into the empty parking lot but kept driving until she reached the back where there was a separate entrance. On the window it read 'Shelia's Future Diagnostics' and underneath in small letters read 'Fortune Telling and Horoscopes'. We went in and there she was; she looked different today then I noticed she had straightened her hair, she was wearing nice pants and a blouse. My mom immediately gave her a friendly hug and introduced us.

Sheila said "We've met, how are you two doing? Thanks for your help by the way."

"Where's your daughter Shelia?" My mom asked.

From behind us another girl walked in, she was slim and had long dark wavy hair. She was pretty but looked like a burn-out by the way she dressed and wore her make-up. Sheila introduced us to her daughter as Catalina; she was carrying in boxes of pastries. She acted like we've never met, so I went along. She seemed totally normal, at least from the outside. A couple other ladies walked in too.

Catalina handed me the boxes "We're running a little late. Can you two help me set up the pastry table?" She asked eyeballing Nic and me.

"I have two more boxes in my car."

"Sure," was all I said and she dumped the boxes into my arms and disappeared outside. Nic followed. I walked over to the table and started setting it up. My mom was helping Shelia set up the coffee table.

Nic walked up next to me holding some folding chairs, "Too bad we didn't know there would be food, we could have saved some room." Nic said. I looked at Nic and then at the sweets, they all looked good. Catalina returned with two more boxes, she set one on the table and the other behind. We set up the table as quickly as possible, in silence, as others were coming in the door.

"Catalina" I said "I guess this is an open house, since you're new in town."

"Yeah" she responded "Promise free food and coffee and people will come, it's from 9 – 1 so people can come before or after church so tell all your friends." She said happily, "And by the way just call me Cat." She stuck her hand out to shake Nic's hand and then mine. I held tightly and stared right at her and asked "You were there that night. Weren't you?"

She gave me a cocksure smile, "I was, I overheard you were going to try a spell and I wanted to see if it would work."

"What did you think?"

She smiled like she knew it did but her mom called her so she walked away without answering my question.

I was satisfied with the look she gave me. I popped a pastry in my mouth, they were scrumptious. Nic gave me a crazy look, I just winked at her.

We finished setting the table, the room was crowded with ten of us in it, Cat motioned for us to follow her outside. Nic got really into it and started asking Cat all sorts of questions. "Can your mom really read fortunes and horoscopes? How much does she charge, what happens if she's wrong?"

Cat stopped by a car and opened the trunk. She took out some chairs and we took them from her, she pulled a small card table out. We set it up near the building under some shade and we all sat down.

Cat started talking and I thought it sounded more like a sales pitch for her mom "My mom is actually very good at fortune telling, we won the lotto recently from her predicting the winning numbers. She's not supposed to use her 'gift' for herself, so when I turned 18 a few months ago I paid her and asked her for lotto numbers. She got five out of six of them correct so we won a hundred grand. We used the money to move here, and re-start her business. I also took some money and invested it for us."

"Why don't you keep on playing the lotto, have your mom keep predicting numbers for you?" I asked.

"My mom doesn't want to *jinx it.*' If we win too much, or use her gifts too much for our benefit we'll be jinxed, she thinks her gifts will dry up or something bad will happen. Plus, she says we won't appreciate life if we don't work for it. She said we need to struggle a little to live a good life and enjoy what we have. She'd like to keep her good 'predicting' for her clients. We'll see though, we are trying the investment angle to try and keep our money working for us."

"So how do you get the gift? Do you have it?" Nic asked.

"My mom and I are from a very long line of original gypsies, some call us witches, depending on what a person's beliefs are. I don't have any psychic abilities yet, but my mom said I can develop them at any time. It usually happens around the age of thirteen but they can develop as late as your twenties. She has told me all the family stories *'that must be handed down'* generation to generation." Cat was a dandy smooth talker and I'm sure it came from the experience working her mom's business.

"We actually picked this location, my mom said, for two reasons. She's predicting in the next ten years that this area will grow and will be the perfect town for us. But most importantly, a person, I mean a relative, actually a couple of relatives moved to this area that she'd like to be closer to."

I scrunched my eyebrows together in confusion. They followed someone here not relatives but they want everyone to think they are relatives.....?

Nic asked "What kinds of stories are you to hand down?"

"The accurate history according to us gypsies." When she said gypsies she made her fingers scrunch in the air like quotation marks.

"Stories about witches, fairies and leprechaun's?" Nic asked with a grin.

"Can you tell us the accurate history according to the gypsies?" I asked squinting my eyes at her.

"Well there are stories of what happened to people that were thought to be witches, or fairies but most rumors were about vampires and werewolves. As far as our tales go on vampires and werewolves they were all killed by one vampire in the late 1800's and then he killed himself. In this century, they haven't been witnessed by our group, but rumors did fly around in the early 1900's. Our legend says a scientist went insane, and did experiments on people that went "wrong." She said with her air quotes again. "These stories were kept in secret and not published in history books or anywhere, it was scandalous and a huge cover-up."

"Sounds interesting" I said looking her in the eye, I like having direct eye to eye contact with people. My dad says it shows strength and honesty. "Can you tell us more about them?"

She let a slight pause go by then said "they, this scientist, was trying to make the perfect human or one that wouldn't get sick but the experiments didn't work the way they were intended. They were supposedly ahead of their time trying to heal lepers and other diseases. Some experiments changed appearances physically, and they didn't go back to normal either, for better or worse. In some instances, some were cured, but they grew hair all over their face and body and were unstable afterward – hence the werewolf syndrome and stories."

"Anyway" Cat continued. "The rumors became vicious stories and the people became afraid of the so called monsters, vampires and werewolves, creating huge chaos in the cities. In the end, they were hunted down like animals. The scientists, all his notes and subjects were destroyed; everything was burned until every scrap of evidence was gone."

"So although the stories of vampires and werewolves may have had some truth to them centuries ago, nothing really exists like that now. Nothing scary, like in the movies, has been documented in our journals this century, just rumors exploding. Rumors don't get out the same way they used to either, my Great Grandmother tells me. There are lots of new ways to communicate and get the 'word' or truth out. Now-a-days anyone slightly insane or considered mad are institutionalized pretty quickly or put in jail."

"Well, that's the really fast version of the "history" I've been told a million times." There went her air quotes again. She seemed really nice and her stories even make a bit of sense.

As Nic and I were walking home, we saw Jett's brother's car pulling out of my driveway, they stopped in front of us. Jett asked me if I wanted to hang out at his house later. Of course I said sure, not even checking with Nic or my parents first. I looked over at her quickly and she said not to worry her family had plans and her mom was picking her up by Noon. "You better have eaten some food..... " I started to say to the boys when Jett interrupted me by showing me the very full bag between his legs on the floor.

Jett replied "Tori gave us enough food to feed us all day." I smiled and said "Good, what time should I stop by? "Any time after 1:00." He pulled his arm in the car like he was ready to leave and I went to walk away but then pulled me back and said "What, no kiss?"

I was in high heaven on the way back.

"Sooo....." Nic said....

"I know, she told us some odd stories, but then again not so odd according to my dreams." I was thinking out loud.

"And what about the comment that they moved here for a person and then she changed her story and said it was a couple of relatives." Nic commented.

"You caught that too" I said. "Weird, right?" I paused then closed my eyes took a deep breath and said "I got one more 'weird' thing for you, there's been like a series of dreams I've been having that I haven't told you about..." I told her all the details I could remember. She sat there contemplating what I just told her and concluded with "Did you write them down?" I shook my head.

"Well you better get them and I'll read and sign them."

My mom dropped me off at Jett's house just after 1:00p.m. Before we got there I realized I never met Cale's parents and never heard him talk about them except when he told me they went out of town, which isn't normal now that I thought about it.

When I arrived no one knew where Jett was, his mom called around and sent me in the basement after him. I went down and found him working out. He was in fitted shorts and no shirt bench pressing some weights. If he was down there lifting weights to impress me, it worked because all I could do was stare. If he was lifting five pounds or a hundred I had no idea. I stood at his feet watching him and finally startled him with a "Hi."

Clank! He dropped the weight down and said "Holy shit!" and sat up. "You scared me, is it one already?" He scooted himself to the end of the bench and grabbed his shirt from the floor and wiped his face and threw it on the stairs. "I'm sorry I was hoping to have taken a shower by now."

I was thinking thank goodness he didn't, my heart was racing a little and my face went flush. I remained silent admiring him.

He looked at me and smiled, reached over and grabbed one side of my jacket and pulled me toward him. He put his other hand inside my coat and around my waist and pulled me down onto his lap. Facing each other, neither one of us spoke, I felt like he was giving me time to back out. I broke the silence in a hushed voice and asked him what he wanted to do today. He pulled my legs on top of his and then wrapped both his arms around my waist. I thought I would panic and squirm but the panic didn't come. He pressed his lips into mine parting them as we kissed. My face turned hot and my body was tingling. I slid my hands up his bare arms to his smooth bare neck and through his hair. He slid his hand up my back under my coat and the other slid down to my waist while pulling me closer to him pressing his chest to mine. One hand slipped under my shirt and touched my skin.

I immediately pushed him back. I felt claustrophobic with the onset of a panic attack and I tried to talk but what came out was barely audible. "I thought we were hanging out today." He pushed back, he looked relaxed, however, I was still a little freaked out. He backed me up onto the bench next to him and he leaned back and crossed his feet and said nonchalantly "I need to take a shower, possibly a long one." He kissed me on the neck, his lips were hot. "Come on" he said reaching out for my hand, I took it; his hand was very warm and masculine and felt good in mine.

His mom was at the kitchen table, she asked me if I was hungry. My face was still flush and I was a little embarrassed but sat down. She offered me a drink, I accepted. She was awesome to talk to and before I knew it Jett was done with his shower and dressed. His mom complained that he worked out but hadn't hauled the hay from the truck to the barn yet.

I chimed in "We can do that now" he looked at me very strangely and said "No way, I can do it later." If our chores weren't

3:17 a.m. ...the waking hour

done at my house we weren't allowed to do anything. "If we do it now, it's done, then we have all night to hang out."

"All night, huh." He said to me, narrowing his eyes.

I shrugged my shoulders with a smile and said "All night..."

He didn't grab a jacket, I swung mine back on and we trekked out to the barn. When we got there he pushed me slowly against the barn wall bringing himself with, I couldn't move. He whispered in my ear "So you just wanted to get me alone." He kissed my neck and then moved to my lips.

I put both hands on his sternum and pushed back. "No, I actually thought that the two of us could get this done faster than by yourself."

"Hmmm" was all he said. He grabbed the key from above me and started up the tractor and signaled for me to get on. There was a trailer on the back, I hoped he didn't mean for me to get on that because I hopped on the seat behind him and grabbed him around the waist. He pulled up and around to the driveway. He stopped the tractor alongside the other trailer attached to his dad's truck and I got off. It was too wet to drive the truck down to the barn. Jett asked "So, you can pick up a bale of hay and feed huh?"

I said "Hell no, not the hay anyway, well maybe. You need to turn the tractor around so both trailers are back to back. "He looked at me quizzically.

"Trust me, Nic and I have done this a million times. Just do it" and to my amazement he did. I made sure the tractor trailer was lower than the trucks by pushing it down with my foot.

I hopped up on the truck trailer and told him to come up with me. "Now what genius, I do all the work?"

"I'm glad I'm not the only sarcastic one. Now, we flip the top row end over end so it's on the trailer bed." The hay was stacked two rows high and three rows deep. He went to grab one, and I showed him. "No do it this way." He moved his hands to mimic mine, he looked at me thru his eyelashes, "Now just slide." He slid it so hard that it went off the tractor trailer. "Pure genius Hercules, try to be a little gentler. If we slide together it will go right to the end of the trailer." We got three bales of hay on the tractor trailer and straightened them. It was a little awkward and not as easy as when Nic and I did it but I hopped back on the truck trailer and nodded for him to come up, he didn't look really impressed but the rest went easier. He jumped down and I slid the feed bags to the end of the trailer where he was standing. He plopped them on top of the hay. He smiled at me.

"See, not so bad" I said. "Now we're half way done." We got on the tractor and I got on behind and put my arms around him.

Another ten minutes at the barn and we had the trailer emptied. I turned to him and said "Now that you know how to do it right it'll go faster next time."

He laughed "Really? I don't know how to do it?" he said mocking me.

"Well you do now," I replied. "I bet you and your brothers try and toss each bail by yourself seeing who could toss them the farthest or lift it the highest and hurting yourself in the process."

He laughed "Just about."

"You and your brothers could get it done superfast this way and without hurting yourself. Plus, Nic and I use hooks to hook the hay - it's way easier." He shook his head in satisfaction.

I walked outside the barn to check out their yard. We owned an acre and a half which I thought was a lot but they had ten. They had a small pond just beyond their barn and a perimeter of trees and brush surrounding the property. I was scanning the woods nearest us when I swear I saw something large move.

"Dammit!" I was pissed! How was this guy stalking me when I didn't even know I was going to be here today? I started walking toward the woods, slowly at first. Then I saw the movement again but it stopped behind a tree. I yelled "Hey!" Jett came out of the barn and asked me "what?" I glanced at him and back at the stalker or whomever it was and they started running, I took off after him. Come hell or high water I was finding out who the heck has been following me today. I heard Jett yell "Addie" I just kept running in the direction of the stalker, he was running toward the street. I lost him so I slowed down. The trees were dense and suddenly I was knocked onto the ground and then I was being dragged by my arm, but he stopped, looked back and let go of me. I couldn't tell who it was as he had a ski mask on, but I swear I saw sandy brown hair hanging down from its edges. He looked tall enough and his build looked the same. I laid there frozen not sure what my next move was.

He started running for the street again. Jett jumped over me flying toward the guy, Jett was running fast! Although Jett seemed to be just as fast or faster, he couldn't catch him. The guy jumped in a dark navy banged up pickup truck, someone was waiting for him, "Did you get his license plate?" I asked Jett as he offered me a hand and helped me up.

"No, his licensed plate was covered up."

"So this was all planned." I said. "I think that's Cale's truck" or his ladies friends truck I thought.

Jett looked a little panicked but he wasn't breathing all that hard, I was still winded and had been on my butt for at least a minute or two. I asked him "What's wrong?"

Jett started pulling some leaves from my hair and jacket.

"What is it with you and weirdo's attacking you?" He asked.

I stood there and stared at him in rapt. "How do you know it wasn't the boogie man and he was after you?" I said trying to be funny. The sky started to turn dark and ominous, we headed in.

CHAPTER 22

We took our shoes off inside and Jett helped me peel my coat off. We went to his room, I stood in the doorway. He peeled off his shirt and put on a new one and asked "Not coming in?"

I shook my head no. He met me at the doorway and I asked "Aren't your parents' home?"

"Yeah, why?" He replied and unbeknownst to me I let out a sigh of relief a little too loud. "What you don't want to be alone with me?"

I replied shakily "Not that alone" but smiled. He looked concerned, he leaned on the other side of the door jam and asked me if I wanted a clean shirt. I tugged on the one he had on and I said "I'll take this one."

"I wore this for a bit this morning, it's not clean." I just raised my eyebrows. He took his shirt off right in front of me. As he did, I put my hand on his chest and let it slide down six pack. He almost shivered.

He handed me the shirt and pointed to the bathroom and he disappeared into his room again. What I don't get is why this gorgeous, super talented, intriguing guy liked me. When he reappeared he had a new shirt on.

"I could use a sweatshirt, it's a little chilly." He gave me a peck on the forehead. When he returned, he smiled at me and said "I'll need that t-shirt back in trade for the sweatshirt. He stepped even closer holding the folded sweatshirt just off to the side. I'm not sure why, but right now, at this instant I wasn't a bundle of nerves, I felt safe and warm, steady. I couldn't imagine being anywhere else, I wanted to be here. I couldn't take my eyes off of his dark and full lips, he moved in closer, slid one hand behind my neck, I closed my eyes and let our lips part.

I pulled the sweatshirt out of his hand and whipped into the bathroom shutting the door behind me. When I came out Jett wasn't in his room so I went to the family room, he was watching TV on the floor and his mom was in the kitchen. She was only there for a minute and disappeared upstairs.

"So you don't trust me" he said as I sat next to him. I leaned up against the couch and held my knees up to my chest casually, I started getting nervous. "I do, why would you say that?"

"You said you didn't want to be alone with me so that must mean you don't trust me."

"Do you always think everything is so black and white?" There was a slight pause, a laugh and a "No" escaped his lips.

"Have you ever thought that maybe I have morals or that I'm not as experienced as you think and I just don't want to go jump into the sack with you? Maybe I'm not interested in having sex at all, it's not like we've even talked about it. Maybe I don't trust myself around you. Besides it's not like we are even dating exclusively, are we? What do you want from me? I mean we haven't talked about that." I went on so long I'm not even sure what I said. I almost felt mad though, I was waiting for him to respond.

"And there is the fact that you're hot and cold - your mood swings are killing me."

Jett was looking at the TV now, how long could the silence last. After what felt like forever, he scooted closer to me lying on his side and rested his head on the couch. He broke the bond easily between my hands and put his arm over my legs pulling me closer to him. I let them fall limp to my sides. Softly so no one else in the house could hear, he said "I like you a lot and I feel a lot when we touch or kiss. I would like us to date exclusively, I'm not interested in anyone else."

He kissed my shoulder I felt a little relieved, but still a little tense. "And for the rest of it" he continued "we can go as slow as you want. If you tell me no or to back off I'll stop, no pressure, I promise, you can trust me."

And somehow I did trust him and began to relax, my shoulders fell away. He pulled me down so my head was resting on the couch with his, it was uncomfortable and he whispered "I know something else is bothering you and I wish you'd tell me. Maybe I can help."

He got up slowly and pulled me up and held on tight to my hand as he led me downstairs. This time he pulled the door shut making me flinch and he felt it, he turned to look at me. The basement seemed to be a place we went for privacy. I sat on the old gold velvet couch that matched the tattered love seat and Jett sat across from me on the stained and faded coffee table. They didn't look nice enough to sit on but that's where we sat. He waited for me to talk. I waited not knowing how to start.

I knew he knew some stuff but how much? I asked him "What did Nic tell you?" I asked with no particular tone.

"What does Nic have to do with this? Does she know?" he looked down and fiddled with his hands, scratching a callus he probably had from lifting weights. He looked back up at me with compassionate eyes and I looked back. "Of course she knows" he said. I felt uneasy and started to squirm in my seat anxiously. I'm not sure if the fact that I was assaulted by a guy bothers me more than the thought of Jett knowing or anybody else for that matter. To me enough people knew and I wanted to keep it that way; but then again if Logan wasn't going to leave me alone then I'm sure more people were going to find out. Plus, who knows how many people already knew and God knows what Kevin, Logan and Lucy have told people. I just assumed everyone was keeping it to themselves but now I'm not so sure. And maybe he's talking about my dreams, I'm so confused, it's gotta be about the latter because I keep flinching...

I started to feel a bit dizzy. Maybe I wasn't remembering to breath. My eyes started to gloss over and I pulled my knees up to my chest. "I really don't want to talk about it, I'll be fine."

He sat next to me and put his hand on my shoulder and I flinched again. Chill out, I told myself chill out.

"What did this guy do to you? Maybe I can help. Maybe I can get this guy to leave you alone. Is he the one trying to grab you? Your ex-boyfriend?

"Ex-boyfriend! Hell no, I don't even know him, he just ups and......" I exploded, but stopped myself mid-sentence, I may have opened a can of worms I can't close. I think Logan needed to shut his mouth, but maybe I needed to shut mine too. Was Jett talking about the guy who tried to grab me today or on our date or both? Did he think it was Logan? I've always thought it was Cale, but I have no proof either way. I looked at him mortified, what does he know and what is he expecting me to tell him.

"Declan, you know, one of my good buddies, plays basketball. He had a tournament at Baskin's School last week and ran into this guy named Logan." I let my head sink into my knees and mumbled crap, he continued. "Declan said this guy Logan was talking matter-factly to him and asked if he knew you, when Declan said yes, he asked to pass a message along to you."

I had a complete look of utter horror and disbelief on my face, I didn't say a word. I wiped a tear and looked the other way. I put both my hands up to cover my face and said "I don't want to hear it."

He waited a minute and said "His message was to tell you that 'He's in love with you and that he cannot wait to be with you again.' " He kept looking at his hands.

"What a bastard" I mumbled.

Jett said "What did you say?" very slow and calm.

I repeated myself and said "I don't even know him Jett." I could tell by the look on Jett's face he wasn't happy.

"Then how does he know you?"

"He's a friend of one of my parent's friend's kids." As soon as I let that sentence out I knew I was going to have to explain. Maybe messages from this guy were the reason why Jett has been so distant and moody.

I couldn't look at him as I spoke… "We were over at my parents friend's house this last July and I ahh…….met him……." I took a deep breath. I felt my eyes welling up and turned so he couldn't see me cry.

I was going to continue but Jett told me more, "Declan said he went on and on about you how you're so pretty and that he thinks you like him too, and he's sure you two will see each other again but he didn't have your phone number. He made it sound like you had a one night stand with him."

"Did you have sex with him?" he asked.

"No! No!" I shouted. "I don't even know him!"

"Then why are you so upset? You can tell me, I won't tell

anyone. I'll beat the shit out of this guy if that's what you want, at the very least I'll get him to shut his mouth." I couldn't help but laugh a little with relief. Jett putt his hands on my shoulders and said "You really can trust me."

Calmly, I turned, looked into Jett's warm attentive caramel colored eyes and told him "The thing is he's not my boyfriend and never was, I only met him the one time."

There was another long pause, he was waiting for me to pour my soul out to him, he wrapped his fingers in mine. Just do it I told myself. I cleared my throat and said "He keeps sending me messages to people in our school that he's in love with me and we'll be together soon and all sorts of crap..." I trailed off a little thinking this isn't going to cut it either. "It's not something I have ever talked about to anyone and I really don't want to." I put my forehead on my knees, I'm conflicted whether to tell him or not. Will he think less of me, will he think it was my fault, will he even drive me home when I'm done telling him or will I have to wait for my mom out in the cold to come pick me up?

"Addie, I really want you to trust me. Since we are dating we should trust each other, and we need to tell each other everything. Otherwise how am I supposed to help or understand? I can't defend you from this guy unless I know what's going on."

I looked at Jett again and I knew I wanted to be with him and I guess I needed to just trust him. So I took a deep breath..... I started out telling him about where we were and that everyone was sitting in the living room, including Logan.

I told him EVERYTHING from start to finish. That it started in the middle of a conversation we were having in the living room, then this guy came flying across the coffee table at me. I left out no details, except I did summarize some of the details of exactly *how* he touched me, but that he did have his hands all over me and ripped my shirt and tried 'other things' was all I said. I continued "I didn't even remember his name until Declan gave me a message back in September from him and I knew it had to be him. I don't even know if I would recognize him if I saw him again." I realized it was so quiet you could hear a pin drop. I know I must have had a horrified look on my face, my eyes were welling up more and more, enough to drop tears and they did. I was crying in front of Jett, just the thing I didn't want to do.

There was such a long lapse of silence, I almost got up to leave but not before I looked at Jett, he looked a little choked up himself. He sat up like he was going to say something and then bent forward and rested his arms on his knees and continued to pick at the calluses on his hands. The tears started to flow and I felt ashamed and like a baby, I couldn't stop crying.

When I was done I just kept my legs up and my head down, I tried taking a couple of deep breaths to calm myself down. Then Jett started asking me some questions "So you never met the guy before that night?"

"No."

"And you didn't kiss him or flirt with him at all before he attacked you?"

"No! We were in the living room, the guy rang the doorbell and Kevin answered. We were all talking, I wasn't even looking at Logan, I was drawing pictures in the carpet. Tori said something and that started it!" I said with my voice strained; now I was getting mad. "If you think this was my fault or that I asked for it...!" I got up and he caught my arm.

"Addie no, it wasn't your fault, you should have called the police or at the very least told your parents. That guy...that guy should not have touched you for any reason, even if you did flirt with him – and you just met him and his messages just mean he's insane. He violated you as a person.... you need to tell your parents." His voice was quivering with anger.

"I can't, I just can't, especially not after all this time." A very long awkward feeling was in the room with us. "I'll take care of this Logan for you, don't worry about that. If you don't want to tell your parents, well that's up to you, but I think you should."

"Jett, I don't want you beating him up, I don't want to make things worse!"

"Worse! How could they get any worse? You think someone is following you and it could be him and you flinch every time I touch you!"

"It's not you." I said softly.

"What? I know, I know now."

"I mean I'm just jumpy. Sometimes I flinch, but it's not as bad now." I hunched my shoulders toward my ears. He put his arms around me giving me a big hug.

"That's everything, right?" Jett asked in a low soft voice.

I laughed a little and said "That's everything I know about

Logan......" Wiping away my tears, hoping not to cry again.

"That's all you know about Logan, so there is something else you aren't telling me?"

I looked up, dammit and replied "Well, we think Cale is the guy attacking and following me, but there no way to prove it. I am really baffled why he's after me in the first place."

"Mmmhmmm." He mumbled in agreement, looked up at me, raising one eyebrow. I said "I have no idea why Cale is so obsessed with me." I gave him a quick rundown on Cale being cool at school and then a geek on dates and that we only kissed even though his reputation is different. I also told him he acted more like a dad than a boyfriend. So I really didn't get his obsession, I also told him about the time I woke up in front of the white house and how Topher told Declan the weird story about Cale and his girlfriend and everything we hadn't told him before. And that is why I thought it was Cale in the woods today.

"*Really!*" he said. Jett pulled me on his lap and we hugged for a while. It was nice. I felt safe and I actually *knew* I could trust him. "I'm so sorry Addie, no one should ever have to go through that. Please know that you can trust me." I nodded my head while my face was still buried in the crook of his neck. "Is that everything?" I didn't break the silence "If I was to tell Nic you told me everything, and I mean everything, could she shock me?"

I cleared my throat. Damn he's good. I let myself slide off his lap, but first, I leaned against the couch and just looked at him and squinted my eyes a bit.

"Welllll" he said...I looked at him in astonishment - déjàvu - -I shook off the eerie feeling I was getting. I remembered my dream from last night...and him saying "Welllll" and everything about this moment. Now I know why I was crying in my dream. Should I tell him about my dreams or would he think I'm a freak. Maybe, I could just tell him what happens next and tell him the short side of it..... make it humorous....

"Dammit Jett," I got up and started pacing. "I have one other inconsequential weird thing, I don't expect you to believe a word of this but go ahead and read this." I took out my note from the front pocket of my jeans and handed him the folded up piece of paper. "I don't want you telling anybody any of this ever, not what I just told you or what you are about to read! You got it?"

I handed him the note but held on tightly to it so he couldn't get it out of my hand the first pull. "I mean it, no one!" I threatened.

"I promise." He said with a smile and I released the paper.

"It's not a big deal but Nic might tell you about this if you told her you knew everything. It doesn't happen all the time and sometimes it's just about little things and sometimes big. It's just something fun I thought I would do - write them down and see if they come true – and they seem to; my dreams come true." I was rambling but I got it out, I think.

He looked at me in confusion "What? What are you talking about?"

I put my hands to my face and said "Just read it." My voice muffled, "That's my dream from last night." He didn't stop reading my note so I got up and went upstairs to go to the bathroom to check my makeup. As I opened the door I saw Storm scooting around the corner and up the stairs.

Dammit, what am I, stupid? I should have remembered and known not to tell Jett unless I checked to see if we were alone. I went in the bathroom and started to half cry again and then I told myself to knock it off. I locked the bathroom door and washed my face in cold water several times and thought of the worst scenario, if he thinks I am a nut job then I go home. The best scenario is my dream comes true. Maybe I should get the note back from Jett, maybe this wasn't such a good idea. One story was good enough for the day.

A smart, normal person would have never told him about it and avoided the conversation. I should have ripped the note out of his hand and said never mind and then eaten the evidence. I smiled inside thinking that; but then I thought the more freakish my whole story started to sound. I should have kept my big mouth shut. I was obviously very nervous and unsure of myself – I found myself headed back to the basement in a hurry.

I darted toward Jett he was reading the last page, I went to grab it from him but he moved quickly and I missed. I tried it again and said "I changed my mind, can I have that back."

He looked at me and said "I'm almost done." I folded my arms, then threw them down, I couldn't watch him and walked back up to the kitchen. I was mad at myself for giving it to him....and then realized Storm just possibly overheard everything I told Jett. So the two of them now know, I felt myself getting madder, humiliated, distressed... and I couldn't undo any of it, I started pacing. When Jett is done reading my note he'll know Storm overheard us and me being pissed. Plus, he knew what was going to happen next...

The dream I had the night before, I almost didn't write it down because I thought I had the dream about Jett because I was in love with him. Plus, we had just spent time together and he slept over my house, so he was obviously on my mind. And not all my dreams come true. The dream started with him looking right at me and saying "Wellll." And here we are and now he knows about everything I dreamt about last night.

The clock chimed six. I sat and stared at him he turned the letter over. He looked at the clock, his mouth opened and then looked at the letter again, then looked at the clock and then at me and he scrunched his eyes in confusion. "Here goes nothing." I said

"Jett!" his mom called down, I just about jumped out of my skin even though I knew it was going to happen. "You have a phone call" I put my hands over my mouth, Jett pulled me up, put his hands on my waist and 'like a train' pushed me up the stairs. We stopped in the kitchen where he picked up the phone. I already knew who it was and that Declan and Rae were coming over with a pizza. He got off the phone and reviewed my letter again and I asked him "Did Rae get her hair cut?" He was still re-reading it when I saw a pen on the counter and told him he had to sign and date it. I explained why and he did.

He wasn't saying anything though, so I decided to "People make phone calls all the time and "wellll" is such a common word. Even if Rae got a haircut, people get them all the time and maybe she said something to me last week about it. As far as the rest, I had forgotten what I wrote in there otherwise I would have never have given it to you," rambling again. I really wanted to know what he was thinking - if my dreams does come true then I knew what he was going to do next but it just seemed weird....of course I wasn't going to tell him the only time I spoke to Rae was on our first date and that we hadn't spoken since.

I was pacing in the kitchen. He stopped and turned me, planted a soft kiss on my lips and said "Come on," and he took my hand and we were off. "I didn't dream about that kiss" I retorted but I knew where we were headed, upstairs and I knew exactly what was going to happen.

Upstairs we found Storm, of course, Jett asked him if he

was listening in on our conversation and of course he denied it. I caught him at the top of the stairs so I know he was lying, plus the dream caught it. Jett gave him a warning to stay out of our business and that he'd better keep his mouth shut! We left, I chuckled "following the letter to the tee I see." I felt a little bad for Storm, I wonder if he heard everything?

We paused in the hall and he stopped and turned around "I don't think this is in there." Jett said and bent over and pressed his soft warm lips to mine and the doorbell rang.

"That is!" I said.

When we got to the door I took my letter from Jett, folded it up and put it back in my pocket. He didn't say anything about it but I knew he still had questions. Declan and Rae came in, and Jett and I both looked at each other in awe. Jett took the pizzas from Declan and said "nice haircut Rae."

"Why thank you Jett, Declan didn't even notice" she said snidely.

"If he's so observant have him tell us what else you had done!" Declan said giving Jett a look.

Jett replied "Looks like it's lighter right?"

Rae hit Declan in the shoulder.

We headed to the kitchen and I whispered to Jett "that wasn't funny you just got Declan in trouble..." he laughed "he can handle it." Declan snarled at Jett.

We played a game and watched a movie and after Rae and Declan left Jett got real serious. I was hoping it wouldn't get weird.

"So you're telling me that your dreams come true?"

"Not all of them" I replied.

"And why do you write them down?"

"I don't remember some of them if I don't write them down. It started because I had a couple I did remember that I swore came true and long story short, I wanted to find out if they did... so Nic and I came up with this system. I write and she reads, signs and dates them...it's a simple method."

I explained to him about having a lot of "déjàvu or eerie moments" and then told him about my shiny silver pay phone dream... and that it actually came true on our vacation this summer. I told him the whole story. I also told him about the dream I thought it was about Jewel, he thought it was a little farfetched.

"That's why Nic and I came up with our little note system. We thought it was fun, of course, at first we didn't really think they were predictions, we thought they were just dreams but now....."

I continued, "If you don't believe me why don't we go check your tire, if it's true I'll have to call my parents to let them know we're going to be late."

"I thought your note said you were spending the night," he said and raised his eyebrow at me again. I could see a sparkle in his eyes.

"Well, I figured we can't jump the gun until things actually happen, besides I'm not sure this one wasn't wishful thinking." I said with a bashful smile. "Plus, they're usually not about me so I'm not sure how accurate this one will be or how accurate every detail is either."

"Hmmm" was all he said and headed toward the kitchen to get his keys.

"Don't forget to turn on the outside lights so we don't scare your mom." I said right behind him. He turned to me and said, "This is weird."

"I know, but fun right?"

"Yeah..... A little mysterious."

I leaned against the passenger side of his car and he took the flashlight around the other side checking out the tires. "Sure enough," he said "it's flat." His mom and friend pull into the driveway. In my dream we hadn't turned on the outside lights, and when Jett popped up from checking his tire he scared them half to death but that didn't happen because we turned on the light.

His mom's friend rolled down her window and Jett went over to chat and told them his tire was flat and he couldn't take me home. So his mom asked her friend to take me home as she lived out near me. She said no problem. Jett and I looked at each other, I shrugged - so now I know my dreams are riddled with half-truths.

His mom spoke up, "I promised Emily a cup of coffee. Addie I'll call your parents and see if they mind if she takes you home after."

"That would be great Mrs. McGaven." I didn't care, because the more time I spent with Jett the more I liked him.

"Let's finish our architecture project then." Jett stated so everyone could hear. I looked at him like what project - - then smiled and agreed with him and asked "Do you have extra vellum paper?"

"Yeah, I have extra." He smiled his crooked little smile at me and pulled my hand all the way to his room. He closed the door when we got in. He didn't even turn on the light.

He pressed me against the wall and whispered "You are so beautiful."

"Really? Because I thought you'd think I was..." he pressed his lips against mine for a second and then released, I gasped letting out "...crazy." I put my hand behind my right wing and flipped the light switch on that was digging into my back. "So do we really have architecture homework?"

"No, I just wanted to get you alone before you have to go." He flipped the light off.

"Yeah, I told you it was just a theory that my dreams come true." I turned the light on.

"Well it was a little farfetched but then again Rae did get her haircut and my tire is flat."

I heard the phone ring, Jett kissed me and rolled me onto his bed. After, I got up pulling his hand, he gave me a bit of resistance but gave up and we headed for the kitchen. His mom's friend was putting on her coat, "Yes." she said, "I'll be there right away."

"Addie, I'm sorry but I have to go, Carly will explain, I'm sorry..." And she left in a hurry not taking me with. We turned to Jett's mom, she explained to us that her friend's husband had to take their son to the emergency room; she was so calm telling us I even mentioned it. "You're so calm, aren't you a little worried?"

She and Jett just laughed, "Honey, I have been to the emergency room so many times with my boys and husband, I can't even tell you. So I'm not going to get worked up about it until we have more information. I better get your mom back on the phone and tell her you'll have to sleep over, Mr. McGaven won't be home until tomorrow."

I turned to look at Jett, my eyes and mouth wide open in a very happy surprise! He very silently waved me over to him and we went into the basement. We were laughing, "Can you believe this?" he said in excitement and I said "No!" in hushed tones of excitement.

"Give me that letter, I want to see it again," he said.

I said "No way."

"Give it." He started chasing me around the basement, not that there were many places to go. He had me cornered fast. His mom yelled down "Jett!"

"Yeah mom!" he said keeping me pinned in the corner, I was wriggling to get the note out of my pocket.

"Addie!"

"Yes, Mrs. McGaven?"

"You can sleep in the guest room, okay?"

"Okay" I said trying not to giggle as I was trying to squirm free.

"We'll take you home in the morning."

"Okay thank you." I said getting the note from my pocket and shoving it in my shirt.

Jett totally released me "That's not playing fair"

"I never said I played fair." We both laughed, I couldn't stop laughing. He picked me up over his shoulder and dropped me on the couch, I scooted up so my head was on the arm rest. He was looking in my eyes and I was searching his, he held my gaze for a second or two. I didn't move. His lips touched mine lightly and then our tongues met. My lips felt as warm as his, I didn't stop or slow the movement. I didn't want him to stop. He put his arm behind me and slid himself between me and the couch. His strong hands were warm and rough, but they moved gently. His hand went under my shirt and slid up toward my breast. He slid it around to my back, and had my bra undone in seconds. Then he slid his hand back out from under my shirt, I felt chills go through me... he grabbed my letter!

CHAPTER 23

That Monday I met Jett at his locker before my first class. He looked like he was in a good mood, he was leaning on his locker with a tight t-shirt on under a fully open flannel, tight jeans and boots; he looked hot as usual.

"What's up?" I asked with a smile and a nod. He stood up and walked right into me, giving me a hug with his feet on either side of mine, he couldn't get any closer. He turned me around and leaned me up against his locker and kissed my neck; it sent chills right through my whole body. He grabbed my butt with both hands and ran his hands right up... to my pockets...

"What are you doing?" I asked excitedly. "Are you feeling me up to get personal or searching me for notes?" He had a calm low laugh and that sexy smile to die for, I couldn't help but smile.

He shoved his hands deeper into my pocket and with a smoldering voice said "I was feeling you up because I love touching you and for an extra bonus I thought I'd check for notes." I didn't really care because I liked it when he touched me, he always made my heart flutter. However, me being the sarcastic person I was, I had to say something "Would you like to frisk my whole body or do my pockets suffice?" He took my hand and pulled me under the stairs across from his locker and kissed me hard and excitedly.

I pushed him back with my hand and actually had to hold him

there "You're in a really good mood today..... I think since we have class, though, maybe we should do this later..." ...he slid the note out of my front pocket and smiled.

Jett had asked me if I wanted to go to a family picnic with him over the weekend. I decided to go, meeting new people is never a problem for me and my calendar isn't full by any means. He told me they would pick me up at 1:00pm on Saturday. I asked *"Who are they?"* and thank goodness, it was Declan and Rae. Groups are always good, especially when you don't know where you stand with the boy you are going with, although I'd saying it's going well. However, he still gets moody and sick once in a while and that worries me and I know it weighs heavily on his mind.

They arrived a little before one and Jett came to the door, my brother Kit, answered. They were sitting on the porch talking when I came out. I was glad to see Kit getting some attention, I think Jett actually liked him. I started walking to the car and Declan asked me on the down low if I knew what was up with Jett. I told him "Frankly, I'm not sure. Maybe he's getting sick again – or maybe his doc has him on experimental drugs or something."

He asked "What is with his mood swings anyway?" I explained to him I wasn't sure, but I had a feeling it had to do with when he gets sick once in a while.

Jett came back to the car all smiles "Your brother is a good kid. I told him I would take him on his raft in the pond next door sometime."

"Awesome, I'm sure he'd love that," I replied. Declan turned around and looked at me and shrugged his shoulders, suggesting Jett was in a better mood now and everything was fine.

We got to our designated picnic area and there weren't many people at the park yet and Declan immediately started to complain – "Jett why did you make us come so early."

Jett said "Because I volunteered us to set up rather than clean up, otherwise we would have to stay until the very end of the party. This way we can leave anytime we want and not come back."

"Hmmm, that's my boy, always thinkin'!" Declan gave him a hearty slap on the back and was now very eager to help set up. "You two ladies sit down while I help Jett." They left to empty Jett's mom's car.

Rae and I sat down at the table with Mrs. McGaven and

another lady she was talking to. "You are lucky you don't have girls, my girls are so emotional I can't even tell you, mood swings all the time!"

"Are you kidding me?" I started "The McGaven boys act like a bunch of girls. I have never seen anyone as moody and hormonal as Jett and Storm in my life! Trust me - my sister and I would be a cake walk compared to them."

Mrs. McGaven and her friend started laughing, and then Rae and I joined in. Mrs. McGaven was laughing so hard she had tears running down her face; she obviously agreed with me. Mrs. McGaven, in the middle or her rant said "That is so true, oh boy, I haven't laughed that hard in years, I almost wet myself." She came up behind me and hugged me. "You're so right Addie, my boys are a mess."

She was wiping away tears when Jett and Declan reappeared with a couple folding tables. And then Mrs. McGaven and her friend just burst out laughing again. It made everyone else around smile even though they had no clue what was going on. She pinched Jett's cheek and said she's a keeper, nodding toward me.

Jett introduced me to his dad and took off to unload his car. His dad asked me "Are you Jett's new girlfriend?"

Mrs. McGaven replied like whiplash. "I don't think that is any of our business Hank!" and she gave me a wink. I smiled.

"Oh sure it is. Whoever is dating our son, we should get to know!" He said with this deep raspy voice.

I glanced his way and said "You're right, parents should know, most days we're dating, but between him and his mood swings....I'm not sure half the time, but you keep me posted if you hear anything different." Mrs. McGaven gave a little chuckle.

Mr. McGaven and I kept talking, even though he seemed like the quiet type I was focused I kept him busy with all sorts of questions. He was a ruggedly handsome sort of guy, I could see where his boys got their looks. He was built but not too. He had *MUCH* dark, short brown, wavy hair and scruff on his face. His eyes were even more piercing than Jett's or Storm's and very blue. I didn't expect him to say much to me; I thought he was like my dad, the strong silent type, but he was very friendly and talkative.

"I'll have a serious chat with Jett today to find out about your relationship status and I'll report back to you." Mr. McGaven replied.

"Really," came a loud sardonic voice from behind me, totally startling me. It was Jett with a great big smirk on his face. I could feel myself blushing, but as I'm quick tongued, I rebelled and said "Absolutely pally, your parents are on my side."

His dad winked at me and his mother looked at her husband and said "I like this girl more and more – I knew I liked her the first time I met her too, she has a lot of spunk."

"Great, I have spunk..." She cut me off mid-sentence and said "Of course your gorgeous too, Jett wouldn't pick a girl who wasn't."

I looked at Jett and told him "I like your parents!" and I really did like both his parents. They were very nice and fun. His dad actually sat next to me with two drinks and Jett said "Ah, what are you doing dad?"

"I'm talking to this young girl, now run along, would you." He laughed and Declan and he were off to set up a canopy. We talked for quite a while about sports, business, school, their property which I loved. Later Jett confessed that his dad never talked to any of his friends and Declan confirmed that, so now I was feeling pretty good about myself.

After a while, I had noticed that Declan and Rae had disappeared and Jett was off helping someone carry a cooler to the picnic area. I started thru the park, weaving in and out of everyone looking for them and started toward the parking lot when I noticed the two of them sitting in the car. On my way over I noticed a group of guy's two cars down playing hacky sack when I saw him from behind; somehow I knew it was him. He stopped me cold in my tracks where I stood petrified. It was Logan, that horrific night came flooding back to me.

Declan was saying something to me but I couldn't quite hear him. I turned my head and looked at him my feet wouldn't move. He said "Are you all right?" I breathed in and out and looked back at *them*. My eyes started to burn, I choked down a swallow. I could see someone coming toward me out of the corner of my eye, I wanted to move and carry on but I couldn't. Rae touched my elbow and asked again if I was all right. Not looking away from *him*, I choked out with a quivering voice "Do you know where Jett is..." My voice was shaky and crackling and it didn't come out very clear. My hands were trembling so bad I spilled half my drink. When I really meant to scream help me, please help me.

3:17 a.m. ...the waking hour

Declan hollered over to the two of us. Did she hear me? Did I tell her I needed help? He waved us over and Rae was holding onto my elbow trying to get me to walk. I wanted to take a step but I don't think my legs moved, they felt solid, like cement holding fast to the ground. My arms fell to my sides and so did my cup. My eyes felt like there was grit in them, they were about to tear. Declan was saying something. My face felt like the sun was burning it, I was mad at myself for recalling all the memories of that dreadful night at the Monaham's..... I was trying to block them out. I was trying so hard to forget them, but they were back..... *I was flat on my back and couldn't move, he licked my neck and was kissing me again....* I told myself to forget him, forget him, forget him...

My eyes squeezed shut, Rae jiggled my arm, "Addie, honey, what's wrong?" I was remembering everything that had happened and I was terrified all over again. I thought I was moving but when I glanced back to Declan he had this look on his face, he looked further away than before like he was in a tunnel... "Addie, Addie..." I could hear him faintly, "Addie, are you okay?" My face scalding, my eyes and ears burning. Everything sounded muffled, everything was blurred. I think I was breathing; I tried not to hold my breath. Declan was still saying something to me, what does he want from me? I can't do anything, how I wish I never came, I wish I wasn't here, I wished that night never happened. Just move, leave, ask Jett to take you home, where's Jett?

I turned my head and saw Jett; I exhaled slowly telling myself to breath, I watched Rae meet him and talked to him before he started walking toward me with a sense of urgency. Jett took notice of the obnoxious group Logan was in. I looked over where *he* stood and behind him stood three others. I had to swallow back the bile that rose in my throat. I wanted to think, think, try to think of what I should do. My legs still not listening to me, they were still tree trunks rooted and not moving but I was glad they were holding me up.

More than anything, I wanted to be somewhere else. I closed my eyes hoping it was a dream. When I opened them nothing had changed and I was still here, not dreaming. And then I heard the voice of an angel, Jett's, he was in front of me, he took my hands "You okay?" He said in my ear ever so softly "Take a deep breath, you're okay. I've got ya. Did you drink too much?" I shook my head. He said "What's the matter? What's going on I've never seen you like this before?" In a sigh of relief, I knew Jett would help me, I felt a tear run down my face that felt cool against my skin and I wiped it away quickly, my legs felt lighter.

Logan started shouting "Hey baby it's me, where have you been?"

From behind me Declan put his hands on my shoulder "Is that your ex-boyfriend, is he giving you a hard time?" Declan questioned.

Logan said as he was coming closer "Baby it's me, Logan, come on I'll show you a good time!" He turned and said to his friends "Boys the party has just started!"

Jett straightened up and said "You're kidding me, who's this joker?"

Declan took a few steps closer to Logan and his friends and told them to back up or else, Logan didn't budge. Jett let go of my hands and they dropped to my sides like jello and he gave me a hug which was really holding me up. "Close your eyes take a deep breath and think of something positive, going to the beach, dating me," he gave me a big grin and kissed my neck just below my ear. "Do you feel better yet?"

Rae came up behind us with water. "Do you need to sit, I opened my eyes. I still saw *him*, he and his buddies were standing in front of Declan. "What is the matter Addie? Do you want to go sit in the car?" Rae asked.

"No," my voice crackled. It was urgent they knew I didn't want to get any closer to *him*.

Jett was being so patient, I needed to relax, pretend I was at the pool. I'm always relaxed in the pool, breath in breath out. I wanted to speak but it wasn't that easy. I was able to produce the words "I'm sorry." My voice crackling again. I couldn't seem to move my feet.

I saw Declan walking in Logan's direction.

Jett immediately said "For what, what are you sorry for –" and I let out a deep breath and said "I'm being a baby" voice still crackling, I took a sip of water and tried clearing my throat. "I don't... I can't move... I don't want to be here..." my voice trailed off. "Away from here. I wasn't ready for this, I thought I was, but I'm not."

Jett said, "I'll drive you anywhere you want to go." I turned away from *him* breaking his hold and got my balance and started walking in the opposite direction of *him*, Jett followed. I couldn't even think of his name I was so distraught. "I can't help you if you don't tell me what's going on....."

I cut him off mid-sentence "I just don't know what to do or how to act and I can't believe I'm crying in front of you and everyone. I'm confused, I don't know what I'm supposed to do, I don't want to 'cause a scene I just want to go home."

"Ah baby, where are you going? I missed you!" Logan yelled in my direction. Right when Declan reached him and said something. I turned to look, the body language wasn't good.

And that did it, I broke down and started to cry, which I never wanted to do. I couldn't control myself. I was mad and upset and because I hadn't seen *him* since...I just didn't know how to react. "Let's go to the car I'll take you home, it's no problem" He said in a very stern voice. "I can't go over there...." I said as I feebly pointed toward Logan. "That is the guy..." I cried and sniffled "that... I told you about, he's the one."

I stood there with my legs shaking and my heart pounding. Jett slipped his hand into mine. It felt so safe and warm. He gave it a little squeeze and gave me a hug, he had never held me like this before, I felt like we had a connection. He gave my neck a kiss, his lips were soft and warm. "Let me help." He said softly. I thought of the two of us in my basement after our first date. I wished we were back there in that awkward moment versus here.

I wasn't prepared to ever see *him* again. What were the chances I thought? Grow up, stop shaking and stop crying I told myself "I'm trying to stop, I just can't" I said.

"I can leave you alone if you like, I'm not sure what you want or what I should do, tell me something." His grip loosened, Jett wiped my tears.

Declan trotted over and said "I think she's upset because her ex-boyfriend is here, you know Logan the one that gave me the messages for Addie and he is saying ... never mind." I let out a huge gasp of air I felt relieved he knew, the tears subsided.

There was a long pause; I turned to look at Jett "Logan, you mean *'the'* Logan?" Jett asked me, I shook my head and his hands dropped. "I'm sorry I freaked out. I'll be okay in a minute, I didn't mean to be such a baby, I told you it was stupid." I explained.

Jett replied, "you aren't stupid, please don't say that, you have every right to be upset. Which one is he?" He took my hand and we started walking back to the car and as we did I saw Logan walking toward us and he said "Addie every time I see you, you're crying, you're such a baby, but I still love ya." He grabbed his crotch and gave off a wretched little cackle. Declan warned him he was looking for trouble.

Jett left me and walked over to Logan "So you're the guy who tried to have your way without her consent aren't you? You think you're such a big man who has to assault an innocent girl to get sex. You're disgusting! If you ever go near her ever again....."

Logan cuts him off. "She's a tease and she was asking for it, she's a whore," and gave out a larger cackle than before.

"You better watch your mouth." Jett retorted calmly. Maybe it what too reserved like the calm before the storm.

"You can just go to Hell!" Logan exclaimed pointing at Jett.

Jett took a deep breath and said "After you!" When he took his next breath all his muscles flexed and I swear his shoulders and arms grew in size; Jett went right up to him and put his left hand on the back Logan's head like he was going to force him to head butt but something else happened instead. Jett pulled his arm back around by his ear, he looked like he was scratching him, but then I realized Jett's whole body was trembling, like the night I was with him. He kept pulling arm back and forth, shaking, holding on to Logan's ear. Logan was hitting Jett in the stomach and ribs every chance he got. Logan finally smacked Jett's arm off him and took a couple of jabs at Jett. Jett straightened up, hit Logan in the stomach with such force and velocity it jerked Logan's head and upper body forward and Jett kneed him in the face. Jett shuddered again. I yelled "Stop!" As Logan's body flew back from the force of Jett's knee, Jett swung his arm at him, holding his hand like he had claws, and tore thru Logan's shirt like it was paper. Ripping it from him and slicing through his shorts. I yelled at Declan "Do something!" but he was holding his friends back. Rae was by the car her mouth wide open in disbelief, staring immobile, in shock.

Jett put his hand on Logan's shoulder and the other one on his leg and lifted the guy up over his head in one swoop, and I swear I heard a growl. He turned and threw him onto the hood of the car next to Declan's. All the flesh on Logan's body shook as he landed and bounced, it's like it happened in slow motion; he looked lifeless and rolled back and laid there. It looked like he was dead. All his friends ran over to him in complete horror and astonishment. They shook him trying to get him to regain consciousness.

Jett stepped toward us, he didn't look like *himself* anymore. All the veins in his arms, neck and face were showing. His eyes were blood red and dark circles under them, his skin looked pale and grey.

I screamed "Jett stop, stop, don't! You'll make it worse. Don't" I screamed so hard my voice hurt. People were running from every direction, and Logan's friends looked at him in terror trying to keep their distance, they gathered Logan up after Jett turned away. There was a huge indentation left in the hood of the car. Logan and his friends started walking in the opposite direction as fast as they could dragging Logan with them. I was breathing hard and my eyes started tearing all over again. A few more people came running over.

Jett looked bigger to me. His shirt was so tight it rippled around him, his breathing was hard and uneven, veins popping out all over and his skin a sickly shade. His friends were patting him on the back saying "I can't believe you picked that guy up!" But when they saw his face they backed up. Declan and I looked at each other in astonishment. Jett didn't say a word to anyone. He glanced at me, backed up, walked away, and finally took off for the woods.

CHAPTER 24

Declan met me at my house. I was surprised when he showed up, but that means he knew there was something really wrong with Jett too. Since I'm the not-so-shy-girl I said what was on my mind as soon as Declan got out of his car "So I really think Jett has something 'wrong' with him" I said with air quotes "and I'm not sure what, but if it is something *weird,* I think this psychic Shelia, can help."

Declan responded "Yeah, I'm not so sure about the psychic thing myself but I'm thinking it couldn't hurt to talk to her – so I figured we could give it a try....... I don't want you going around telling all the guys we went either."

"Of course not – I'm thinking we won't tell anyone." I walked toward his car and passed it up.

"Where you going?" he asked me. "It's just across the street, at the Richfield Reading and Speech Center, Sheila's place is in the back. We can walk."

Declan started talking again "Addie, I'm not sure you get how worried Jett has been about all this stuff, he isn't talking to anyone about it. That's how he is, usually when he gets sick or hurt he doesn't talk about it with anyone until he figures it out or feels better. And the fact that he hasn't talked to me or anyone else about it makes me think this is really bad." I looked at him with concern and agreed with him, however, maybe it's worse than I originally thought. "I'm very worried about him to, that's why we're going to see Shelia."

As we were crossing the street, my brain started ticking away. I remembered the stories Sheila's daughter had told us. They've been gnawing at me since, and I have a sneaky feeling they would help us. Especially, since the doctors had tested Jett for everything else under the sun and they haven't come up with a thing. When I'd try and apply her stories to Jett, nothing really clicked, at least not yet.

"If anyone asks what we were doing - just in case we are seen together - we walked across the street to get candy bars while we discussed gift ideas for Rae and Jett. I was hoping you'd know when Jett's birthday is...."

"So you've done the snooping thing before, huh?" Declan replied, "No, but I feel like something is definitely up since you're worried about Jett too. So I came up with a back story for us. If we have to use it we're going to have to buy gifts and come up with something good.

"Rae does have a birthday next month, late July, so you can give me some thoughts on that and Jett's birthday is in August, so it's not a bad back story then." Declan winked at me.

"...Oooh I know, concert tickets! I just got my concert calendar in the mail. We can pick one out and get concert tickets for a double date kind of thing. We can check it out when we get back to my house!" I said excitedly – maybe too excitedly, I've never been to a concert with a boyfriend before, it's something I have wanted to do.

"That's a good idea. Rae's been asking me to take her to one, we'll just have to see what's coming up." Declan said nodding his head and pushing his bottom lip up in satisfaction.

Declan had a smile on his face, so I think he was feeling better about our trip to the psychic or at least I got his mind off of it; that was until I opened the door and he tensed right back up...

I went in first and Declan followed. Shelia came out of the back room as soon as the bell jingled. I started out with "I guess the question is, did you come to the front because you heard the ding or because you're a psychic and you knew it was us?" I stopped and Declan bumped into me, so I stepped forward exaggerated, we looked like an act.

"Declan, Addie follow me." We did "Take a seat." Shelia said holding her hand out palm side up pointing to a couple of chairs.

"How did you know my name?" he turned to me "Did you tell her my name?" I shook my head and he smiled, like this might be worth something.

She never did answer that last question, not answering them made her seem more mysterious that way. Declan started again "Sheila doesn't sound like a gypsy name or a psychic's name, it just sounds normal."

I was almost embarrassed he said that but she replied. "First of all, I am normal," we all gave a little giggle and it eased Declan a bit. My full name is Tshilabo (pronounced sheelaba) meaning seeker of knowledge. But since my daughter was a baby all she got out was Sheila, hence the name, not that she called me by my name but during business hours she would hear it often, anyway one of my customers heard her call me Sheila and it stuck, besides I like it." She said with a smile. My daughter's name is "Catalina" which means the pure one and our names represent our souls.

"That's cool. I don't think my name means anything." I said.

"What's your full name?" Sheila asked.

"Adele."

"Adele is an easy one, it means "a noble sort" and Declan means "to heal". She said raising an eyebrow at her expert knowledge.

"My friends name is Jett, what does that mean?"

She turned around and grabbed a book, its binding was tattered and torn, it looked very old. She flipped through a few pages and read "JETT: English name meaning "jet (the mineral), composed of inorganic elements other than human matter." She stared at the page, no one spoke.

"And your girlfriends name is?" She looked up at Declan and he replied "Braelyn."

"Hmmm we don't have that name, do you have a short name?"

"Yeah, and she definitely prefers to be called Rae" he laughed and looked at me, I smiled.

"Looking back down at her book and flipping some more pages she stops and read: "RAE: English name, possibly derived from the vocabulary word *ray*, meaning "sunbeam." Declan responded "well, she's definitely my ray of light."

Sheila snapped the book shut and said "That's always fun, I love looking up and knowing the meaning of names. Not everyone lives up to them, but some do. When our culture picks a name we have a process we go through to *find* that person's name because we believe the person becomes the name, it will help show its truth in the person."

"Interesting" I told her.

"So what do you have for me today Addie?" I liked this women, always gets right down to business. I didn't hold back, I told her about the 'Jett story' and the scratches he got on our first date that we thought they were from Cale. Then we described him being sick, his extreme mood swings and the physical changes we saw. Declan would intervene every now and then to add some detail or remind us of another event that happened. While we were describing everything to her I somehow knew she believed every word we told her. More than that, she was intrigued by our story and yet not surprised to hear all the things we were telling her either.

When we were done, Declan and I looked at each other and I think we were both relieved to get that off our chests, and glad that our stories were the same. Shelia got up to get all of us some water. I looked at Declan "I think we ought to write all this down so we don't forget any details. I hadn't realized all the facts we had and now that we said it all at once, I'm really convinced something weird is going on with him." He shook his head in agreement as Shelia came back with three glasses of water.

She started talking as she set the glasses down on the table between us. "You should write it down because you could forget some details that may be important later, and it may make for a good story one day." She gave me a wink and handed me a pad of paper and pen.

I was taken aback about the story comment, I was sure she believed every word we said, I just felt it. Declan jumped in "So you're saying you don't believe us and that you won't help?" We were both looking her straight in the eye.

"Declan, I also said to write it down because the small details may count." I relaxed a little "And I got us some water because I have some facts to share with you, a story if you will, and it may take a while because you may not believe me, like last time you were here."

Declan looked at me, "What happened the last time you were here?"

"I can tell you all about it on the way home." I said, but secretly

I wasn't planning on it. I thought she was weird after she told me the stories, and I didn't want everyone running around thinking I'm a freak so I kept them to myself. And I wasn't sure I believed her myself, I only knew the history I've been taught but now….I'm not so sure what's true…

She smiled at me, I truly believed she knew more of what was going on in my head than I did. "Before I start on the history of what I know" she said looking at me and I returned a smile, "If both of you spend a lot of time with your friend Jett, I could read your cards for details that may help you." Shelia had a very soothing, yet strong voice; it made you believe and trust her. But I looked at her and shook my head no and pointed at Declan. I didn't want a reading of me to freak Declan out like it did Nic and me the last time we were here. Maybe I just didn't want to get freaked out about myself again and hear some other bizarre things I can do, besides having dreams that come true.

Declan said "Sure" even though he didn't sound it; she pulled out the cards, had him split the deck. "I'll tape this for you so you can remember everything we say." She said pulling a recorder off the shelf from behind her, set it on the table and pressed a button. Declan and I looked at each other and shrugged.

She flipped over a few cards and said "A guy with light colored hair is a good and trustworthy advisor and his name begins with a 'T' but not a common name like Tim or Tom." We looked at each other and said "Topher." She also said he had more to tell. She went on, "You have already found your soul mate." Declan agreed and said he already knew that. He blushed a little too. Then the death card came up – she told us not to worry though, it doesn't necessarily mean death. She was having a hard time reading the card but had a feeling it was about Jett and that he would continue to change and struggle. She also told Declan he'd be going on a cruise in the near future, you'll also get married quickly. Declan raised an eyebrow at that one intrigued. After that she cleaned up all the cards.

She looked up at me "We're going to have to read your cards too." Sheila put her hand on top of mine. "Don't worry I'm not going to tell you anything you don't already know," raising an eyebrow as she said it. She pulled her hand away. I felt calm and thought she's right, what's the big deal? "I'll see if I can get a better read on you regarding Jett. Since you're both connected to him, signs or messages about him will show on your cards as well."

Declan said "So what we're done? He asked pointing his finger back and forth between Sheila and himself. "Aren't you going to tell me I'm going to be successful, what college I'm going to, how many kids I'll have and all that stuff." Shelia started shuffling the cards. "It doesn't work that way." She looked up and to the right "an in-state university not too far away. You asked me about a specific endeavor so that's what we are looking for and I can't see that far into the future, plus I would have to read your palm for more personal information, if you'd like." She pointed to the sign that told us how much everything was "at least you know who your soul mate is." She said with a calming smile. "...and to book a cruise."

She went on and explained that all we needed was a needle, thread, a sharpened pencil and a steady hand to find out how many kids we would have. We looked at her puzzled "You haven't heard about that yet? Probably because you're not thinking of having kids yet. All you do is put a threaded needle in the end of the eraser side of a sharpened pencil, wrap the thread around your index finger, not tightly either. Then someone holds it over the palm side of your wrist, the wrist you write with, and not your own, someone has to do it for you." She pointed to the most tender part of her wrist nearest the joint.

She continued "You hold it so it's completely still and the pencil will start to move on its own; if it moves back and forth in a line it means a boy and if it swings in a circle it means a girl. In between kids it will stop and twist and then start swinging again and when it's done moving – there are no more kids. It's a fun activity to do at slumber parties and it works on men and women."

"Hmm, that's interesting I'll try it sometime." I looked at my watch and it had only been twenty minutes but felt longer. This was intense stuff. Declan looked at me and said "Your turn."

"Okay, okay" I looked up at Shelia from the top of my eyes trying to tell her mentally let's not get into any psychic stuff about me in front of Declan. Somehow, I felt like she knew what I was after. She had me split the deck and started flipping cards. She flipped a lot more before she said anything.

Declan noticed too. "Aren't you going to explain any of those," he asked.

"Oh yes, sorry. I couldn't wait to see what happened next." She said slowly.

"You have a blonde admirer."

I looked at Declan and said "Shame on you." He laughed and put his hand on my shoulder "I do admire you Addie, but that's as far as it goes, you're like one of the guys to me."

"Ahhh thanks, I am teasing you don't even have blond hair." I smiled back at him and patted him on the shoulder. We both chuckled.

Shelia interrupted our chuckle, "Just because I said blonde doesn't mean he has blonde hair now some have blonde hair when they are kids and it turns to that dirty blonde color or brown later," she continued. "It is someone you know, and he's proud of you for doing something, breaking someone...breaking up with someone or breaking the ties – he is one of a pair. He is not alone and one of them is evil and the other is good, trying to help." She flipped another card – "You are going to fall, I think it's a physical fall it must be significant, I can't get a location or if you get hurt it's fuzzy." She looked up at me "Does any of this make sense?"

"I think so, the breaking up part does" I replied, I assumed she was talking about Cale and Topher.

"Sometimes a second reading at a different time can clear things up." She flipped a couple more cards, "someone gets lost or kidnapped, hmmmm, you don't know that person very well but you help them, her." She looked up "kidnapping seems harsh and rare so someone probably gets lost or they feel lost emotionally." She flipped another card and I could tell it was not good. "You know the person trying to take someone from a crowded location, like a restaurant or store." She said very slowly, I knew exactly what she was talking about, the last dream I had was about a girl getting kidnapped at a bar. Now I was freaked out.

She flipped over three more cards I didn't have a good feeling. "Wow Addie lots of action in your life. She started to explain that kidnapping and lost are big words that they may mean someone steals their heart away from you like a lovers quarrel, but I knew better.

I sat back in my chair and took a deep breath and then let it all out. I felt my eyes get big, looking at her. I glanced over at the cards again and then looked at Declan whose eyes were big too. We looked back at the cards saying nothing, I pointed toward a card and asked her what it meant. "Yes, yes your friend... is sick...or has been poisoned...." Sheila said so matter-factly. I looked up, I noticed a slight tremble in her voice like she was lying. She cleared her throat and continued. "I believe he's been poisoned, ingested something poisonous to him and it just has to work through his system." She cleaned up all the cards suddenly.

She got up and leaned on the counter behind her. She seemed to be nervous, worried all of a sudden. I think she just told us a white lie or didn't tell us everything she read from me. To keep her talking I asked her how her move went. She relaxed a bit and told us she was all moved into their house. The office was an easier move they had everything done in a day with the help from Nic and me. I asked her if she had tracked down her family yet, the ones they moved here for. She looked up at me terrified and said "Ahhh, as a matter of fact I am going to see one of them today." She wasn't smiling when she said it. She crossed her arms tightly across her chest.

"I would love to hear more stories or legends of your ancestors sometime." I told her. We were all standing around, things felt a little tense.

She crossed her arms across her chest tightly, "I heard my daughter told you about how the 'rumors' of vampires came about in the early 1900's."

"MmHmm, vampires and werewolves."

"Ooh, now that sounds interesting." Declan sat back down.

"They were really just rumors, like my daughter told you," she said nervously.

I looked at her seriously and said "Yes, it sounds very interesting, let's hear more."

"Well" she hesitated "Dr. Sal Rewtnic was a scientist that was never mentioned in the history books. He had the right intention but a few of his experiments on humans went badly. He was probably one reason why the FDA is so anal about NOT testing on humans. He had experimented on a man who had been ill his whole life and was already partially mad, living with an illness that long can make you that way. Dr. Rewtnic was way ahead of his time, at least a lot of people thought so then. Until this one man was thought to have been cured of his disease, the treatments seemed to have been successful for a couple of weeks. His illness and symptoms went away, he looked younger and was full of energy. A month after several treatments he became sensitive to light and his blood cell count started to diminish. Rewtnic started giving him weekly blood transfusions, which seemed to be working, but then the man went completely insane. Instead of showing up for his next blood transfusion, the man disappeared. He made his next appearance one evening by trying to suck the blood out of several people in town and inadvertently killing one young woman, he was acting like a succubus or vampire. That's how the vampire rumors started during that time period. They tried killing him but couldn't catch him. He was fast and strong, until they tracked him down in his sleep, during the day of all things.... And I know you know it as folk lore but vampires were real but killed off by an influential and famous vampire that found his conscience and knew his race and ours couldn't survive together and so he demolished his race and then killed himself."

"So you think Jett's a vampire." Declan said casually.

"There are no such things as vampires!" Sheila yelled. "Well there were but now there's not anymore, they were all destroyed a century ago, he promised our family!"

"So why are you yelling at us?" I yelled back. "Because werewolves and vampires do exist?" I said in a calmer voice. Calculating that Dr. Rewtnic's patients needed blood transfusions just like Jett.

Sheila shook her head and gave me the strangest look. "Well, I hate to cut it short but like I said I'm going to visit my relatives and I don't want to be late."

On the way out Declan said "That ain't right, it just ain't right... what just went on in there?"

"I have no idea..."

He asked me, "Do you want a candy bar? I'm buying." I gave him a weird look but then replied, "I sure need something but I think I need a Skyway cheeseburger, do you wanna go?" My voice more excited at the end.

"Not with you." he said "Isn't that what got you into trouble a while ago, cruising Skyways with other guys."

"I guess you're right but the whole thing was a big joke and you know it."

"Yeah, but if Jett really has poison in him, let's not get him any more excited than we need to."

"Good point." I opened the door for him to exit and I followed.

"You can pick it up!" ….." and we'll eat it at my house…if my parents are home they'll pay!"

"We'll let's hurry up then." Declan said excitedly.

I think he was mocking me but I didn't care I thought it was humorous. I ran across the street and he hadn't followed. So I yelled to him, "I guess I have a head start!" I ran all the way home, Declan caught up to me at the top of my driveway; we were both huffing and puffing. I had to put my hands on my knees.

"Are… you…always…this excited about …f…ood." He blurted out between gasps.

"Some…times" and we both started walking down the drive.

"Jett gets that way too." he said.

I was glad to see my parents' home. Declan flew to get us lunch from Skyway so I got on the phone and called Nic and told her the whole story about Sheila. "Do you remember when her daughter said they moved here for friends and then changed it to relatives?" I asked her.

"Ya, I do and I thought it was very weird."

"Well, Sheila told us that she was going to see her *'relatives'* today."

"What's weird about that?

"Nic, I can't come over today because I am going to my relative's house… Would you really say relatives, or would you say aunt, uncles or family?"

"Hmm." She said, "I think you may be right."

"Anyway, I think she's hiding something about her relatives and about the past and we need to find out what."

"I agree, let's make a plan." Nic suggested.

"Well, I'm sure Jett won't go to Sheila's voluntarily. So someone in our group should make an appointment to go see her. All of us will go in as a group, we'll say we're going out to eat right after." Nic thought it was a great idea. "And I'll check it out with Declan when he gets back."

Declan, Nic, Rae and I had decided that Rae would pretend to want to get a reading done for her birthday. We all met at my house, including Jett of course. We walked over for Rae's appointment late that afternoon there was a slight breeze, the sun was out and only a few clouds in the sky. It seemed like the perfect day.

We walked into Sheila's through the back door and she and her daughter were waiting there with their arms crossed. "I had a feeling you were up to something." Sheila said looking directly at me.

"Well, we need answers and I have a feeling you have them and we need to know everything you know about Jett's condition."

"I already told you, your friend was poisoned, I wasn't lying about that."

"Yes, but how? By who? And what kind of poison was it? I think the *relatives* you are watching may have something to do with it." I said making air quotes.

Her daughter dropped her arms and looked at her mother with concern. Jett must have gotten his feathers ruffled because he asked "What the hell is going on here? Is Rae getting her fortune told or what?"

Everyone replied "No."

"Who's been poisoned?" Jett asked.

"You!" Everyone said in unison, like he should have been clued in to our plan by now.

I looked at Sheila and with my most sympathetic look I told her "We need to know the whole story and who's behind Jett's poisoning so we can help him."

It worked, because Shelia told us that after her great grandmother passed away, her and her uncle took over tracking the *people* on their list. The people that were on the list were the offspring of people that had been experimented on by Rewtnic, the ones that weren't destroyed. '*Things*' had begun to stir with her uncle in Arizona while tracking them. She said it wasn't hard to track most of them, however, they believed if two of the people on the original list had procreated, they found that their children were very athletic and a couple of them actually showed to be gifted and exceptional in sports, almost defying the odds and limitations that a normal person should. One of them was even in the Olympics.

She stopped, closed her eyes tight… "Addie! Knock it off! Stop pulling that on me!" Sheila exclaimed.

"What? I'm not doing anything." I said holding my hands in the air.

"Honey, don't play dumb with me. You know you have compelling powers."

"Compelling what?" I looked at Nic and the others; I felt all the blood rush out of my face. I'm a bigger freak than they already know. Maybe Jett isn't the only one with something wrong with him. "What are you talking about?" My friends looked as dumbfounded as I felt.

Her daughter Cat translated. "You have powers of persuasion, you compel people to talk to you and they tell you things." She looked at her mom, "I don't think she knows she's doing it." She asked me "Have you ever noticed that everyone talks to you and they tell you things they wouldn't normally?"

"This is crazy, but you're right my dad never talks to any of my friends but he talked to Addie." Jett pitched in.

I shook my head, and Declan crooned "Oh yeah, she had Mr. McGaven talking forever." Jett chuckled. "And he doesn't talk to anyone."

Nic interjected "Everyone always seems to have no problems talking to you and confessing things, like all the time." She froze and sat upright, looked like she wanted to leave urgently.

"What? You guys are crazy, I'm just a likable person!" I said. I pushed the ends of my hair up pretending to fluff it up like I was adorable, trying not to show any frustration on my part. "We're here for Jett, can't we talk about Jett?" He gave me a look, it seemed he was happy when the focus was one me.

"You're right we're here for Jett and I don't need this to get any weirder." Declan said, then took a deep breath and turned his attention to Sheila and Cat "Who are you tracking and could they be the ones who poisoned Jett?"

"We are tracking, not that this is any of your business, Dr. Cassandra Westman. Her grandfather, Dr. Thomas Westman who has passed on, worked at the Dunning Hospital in Chicago and had taken care of Sal Rewtnic the 3rd, the doctor's son, and Neil Royce the doctor's nephew. They are the only two living relatives of Dr. Sal Rewtnic the 2nd. Cassandra's grandfather removed them from the mental institution a few years after Dr. Rewtnic was killed, quit his job, moved them to Michigan and home schooled them. Rumors were that the boys were crazy, or monsters, because no one ever saw them leave the house. We will to talk to them if we can track them down."

It was our job to track them but we're a little behind as my great grandmother lost touch when she became senile and let things go a bit and our family hadn't realized how important this was until we found out Sal changed his name and we've been unable to track him. Recently we found out he goes by the name Stew C. Neila, we think it's an anagram of his real name. Same with Neil Royce he now goes by the name Ben O'Riley. There is another note we don't understand yet, there is a key a celestial healer that has purified blood and we are thinking they can possibly heal your friend." She said gesturing her hand toward Jett.

She took a deep breath, "That's all I know. Except... Addie you need to look out for someone in your future that will leave a huge wake of betrayal in his path. He has an uncommon name that begins with the letter 'B' maybe 'C' it's a letter at the beginning of the alphabet." There was a long pause no one spoke. "That message has been screaming at me since you walked in the door. Good night." Sheila said.

We walked out of the building and everyone's eyes were on me.... So I wiggled my hands at Nic and said "Tell me everything you know," and started laughing and they all joined in.

As we were walking back toward my house Nic dropped back and so did I she looked at me like she was trying to tell me something with her eyes. I asked "what?"

"The tree, we have to check out the tree!"

"What tree?" I stopped and remembered Harriet's treasure story, everyone else eventually stopped too and looked at us. I started walking and stated "I think Sheila told us everything she knew, but I also think she and her uncle are panicked because those guys they are tracking changed their names must be up to something, they're just starting to piece it all together but until then I'm not sure the info she gave us helped or will eventually help Jett.... Maybe the healer part but how do we find that person. " I gave Nic a diabolical smile and shook my head, giving her the okay to plan another one of her perilous adventures.

We got to my house and Jett seemed to be in denial that he *has* something more wrong with him, more than he knows. So when he disappeared for a bathroom break, Declan, Rae, Nic and I decided that we needed to take pictures of Jett in his *state* for proof. Rae was taking photography classes and had a super-fast camera that we could use to catch him on film. So we just had to make a plan to catch him in the act. When Jett walked into the room, it was awkwardly quiet. So I asked "Who's hungry? And he didn't suspect a thing.

When we got to the kitchen Rae asked "What should we do tonight?"

Jett replied "I thought we were going out to dinner right after Rae's reading."

"Dude," Declan said "We were obviously lying."

Nic interrupted, "We could have a bonfire back by my company barn."

"I think that's an awesome idea. Her parents won't bother us out there so we could have some privacy." I arched an eyebrow at Rae and Declan to see if they were in agreement and get there approval.

"Can we cook out too?" Declan asked. Jett gave me a squeeze. Declan and Rae said they would bring drinks and they were going home real quick but they'd meet us back at Nic's at 7 or so. Nic said she'd bring chips and dip and asked Declan for a ride home. I volunteered to bring hot dogs and marshmallows as they were all walking out the door. I fixed Jett and me salami sandwiches and we headed back downstairs. Jett complained that the salami smelled and tasted really strong but I thought it was fine.

We ate on the floor by our huge old oak dining room table, my mom couldn't bear to throw it out so she had it converted into a coffee table by cutting down the legs. I took a sip of soda and Jett pulled me on top of him. He stared at me a bit and said "What else can you do, besides have dreams that come true and compel people?

"Well, we aren't sure I can compel people, but I can hold my breath a really long time.... Plus, you and Declan told me I have quick hands and I run fast...."

"You are fast... Make me tell you something."

I smiled, "Oh right, like that's going to work."

"You won't know 'til you try."

"How will I know you're telling me the truth?"

"Hmmm, well let's think of something I wouldn't want to tell you...but we could verify if it's true." I interrupted him. "I know, you refuse to tell me your middle name! I can ask you that...."

"Ugh, fine we'll know if it really works then because I've never told anyone my middle name and neither have my brothers."

He was lying on his back, legs up and I was sitting on him. I gave him a quick peck on the lips. I looked him in the eyes and said "Now what?"

"Well, ask me my middle name, but try and concentrate on me telling you the truth."

"Okay, okay." I settled my eyes on his, leaned forward and put my hands on his pecks to balance myself and said "What is ..." I smiled because all I could feel was his muscular chest under my hands..."your middle name?" and I laughed.

He rolled me over and told me I was supposed to be serious. I just laughed some more. "You really think I can get you to tell me stuff? Even if I can, I'm not sure I want to."

He planted a kiss on me and kept kissing me 'til my giggles were gone. I looked at him, I felt myself get real serious and focused and asked "What's your middle name?"

He replied "Agnew." He sat up, shocked he just said it. He looked at me mouth open and I asked "Do you love me?" and he said "Absolutely." He bent down and kissed me, I whispered back "I love you too."

And then it hit me, "Your middle name is Agnew!" I started laughing so hard my eyes began to tear. He covered my mouth, "You aren't supposed to laugh, that's just mean." I stopped and asked him how he got that name. Jett told me it was the name of the first Vice President for Nixon or something, his mom picked it out.

I told him "Hey, at least it's your middle name." I thought for a minute "Your initials spell JAM, I can always call you that."

"If you tell anyone, Addie Gellar, there will be hell to pay."

"I'm just teasing you, I won't, I promise.....So you're not mad about my second question?"

He shrugged his shoulders "No I'm not, because I do love you."

CHAPTER 25

I got to Nic's with the hot dogs, buns and a couple other things. Declan and Rae were already there. We got the fire started before we decided how to get Jett mad when he showed up with Storm.

From across the fire Declan and I were eyeballing each other thinking of something to get him worked up when a couple of other guys showed up with a twelve pack and before you knew a few more people showed and then some more.

By the end of two hours there had to be at least fifty people there. When Nic and I went back to the house to grab a sweatshirt, she met with a few other newcomers and showed them the way back. I went ahead to the house and grabbed the sweatshirts for us. On my way back out to the fire I ran into one of our wrestlers, Kevin, on Nic's driveway. So we started chatting and walking back to the company barn. When we were in the shadows and out of the direct light from the house he grabbed my arm and pulled me off to the side and kissed me. "Baby I can rock your world." he said in my ear and planted another one on me. He had a tight hold on both my arms, and when I squirmed to get out of his hold, his grip tightened.

"I... don't.... thi..nk... soooo. Damn it Kevin, Jett is here you know."

"What he doesn't know won't hurt him – I can give you what he can't."

"Let go of me right now or I'll scream!" I said with my teeth gritted he was backing me up and not toward the tree line, nor toward the house.

"All I need is an hour of your time baby. You know you want it."

"Please stop!" I pleaded.

My head was spinning and my arms and wrists both stung as I was twisting them trying to get out of his grip and he was re-gripping them when I got loose. It was harder to walk as the grass came up to our knees, I almost tripped twice. We had veered off the path Nic mowed to her company barn, when you own 150 acres of land you just don't cut it all.

"Kevin, let go!" I demanded. I can't believe he thinks he's going to take advantage of me when Jett is a little more than a hundred yards off. Or better yet, that he thinks I would want to. Maybe he's all hopped up on some kind of drugs.

"Owe" He had backed me up to the big tractor Nic cuts the grass with, the ones that the tires are as tall as I am. I got my wrist free and I said very sternly "If you don't back off now I'm going to yell for Jett and his friends and then we'll see where we end up. How would you like that?" I shoved him with my forearms, he let go.

Out of nowhere Storm appeared "Yeah Addie, I think you should yell for Jett and see what he'd think of all this."

I let out a deep sigh of relief and walked over by Storm and mumbled "Thank God you showed up." Kevin quickly started apologizing profusely, begging me not to tell Jett.

"You need to apologize to Addie and mean it." Storm said his voice deeper than I remembered. He did, he apologized then pleaded for us not to tell Jett over and over again. I started to feel sorry for him, not sure why, look what he did to me when no one was around.

Storm pointed to the tree line, "We aren't going to tell him you are." Storm had such a serious look on his face you knew he wasn't kidding. Kevin started walking toward the party and we followed shortly after. I picked up both our sweatshirts on the way back to the path..."Storm" I said very quietly and then stalled....

Storm waited then said "Yeah."

"Thank you but I ah, don't know if I want Jett to know."

He looked at me, put his hands in his pockets and gave me a

confused look "Why?"

"Well, I think I attract trouble or 'cause it all by myself."

He processed what I said and replied "So what did you say to Kevin to make him all over you, even though you were telling him to stop?"

"How much did you hear?"

"A lot, I wanted to make sure you needed help before I jumped in."

"Well thanks a lot for waiting 'til the last minute."

"So what did you do?"

"To who?" I snapped.

"Who do you think?" Storm replied sarcastically, and put his hands in the air while he said it. His down swing hit my wrists.

"Owwwww" I said more exaggerated than needed, it hurt but not that bad.

Storm grabbed my right hand I just shifted my weight to one leg huffed a little and looked toward the sky while he examined my wrists.

"Baby!" he retorted and tossed my hand back down by my side and started walking away.

I just laughed and he joined in. I pushed Nic's sweatshirt into his chest. "Hold this" I said and I put mine on....my favorite zip up, not in good shape but it was nice and worn.

I started to explain to Storm "I was on my way back out to the company barn when I ran into Kevin. And then he just grabbed me and pushed me off the path and planted one on me. So I didn't start it, but I was nice to him because I was in a good mood." I said the last part kind of full of pep trying to lighten the subject.

"Kevin's just an ass and I'm sure you didn't provoke him...I think he's high or something."

"Sooooo, are we telling Jett?"

"I told Kevin he had to and if he's high he might just do it."

We had the company barn and Jett in view; Jett started walking toward us, Kevin veered off to the right and neither Storm nor I said anything at all about our post problem.

"What took you so long?" Jett asked me but gave Storm the dirty look. Storm gave me the cool guy nod and walked over to the bonfire.

Jett looked me up and down. "I remember that sweatshirt. Are you wearing the same thing underneath as before?" He said with his soft sexy voice and bent down to kiss my neck.

"I'm sorry, I'm hospital ready today."

"What?" he said with laughter.

"Hasn't your mother ever told you every time you leave the house you should have clean underwear on in case you end up in the hospital or something like that?"

He laughed again "Something like that."

"Well I have on clean undies and a clean... well you know what I mean, hospital ready."

"Too bad," he said. He put his arm around me and we headed over to the bonfire and stood next to Storm, Storm handed Jett a beer. Storm grilled "So Addie, what kind of trouble have you been getting into lately," and gave me *'a look.'* I froze, stopped smiling and made my eyes into slits and returned a callous look back at him....Jett squeezed his arm that was around my neck, laughed and said "No kidding this girl sure does attract trouble, what did you do this time?"

"See Storm! I told you I'm a beacon for trouble so just shut up...." my teeth were gritted. I was steaming mad, I thought steam may have actually come out of my ears I was so pissed. I know he said it just to spite me too, but then again we were here to get Jett upset.

"Jeez, Addie I was just joking."

"Ugh. You know this is way too much drama for me, I'm going to look for Nic." I ripped the sweatshirt out of Storm's hands and gave him the stink eye and walked off saying "You tell him......oh, and don't forget to tell him the poor guy is all drugged up..."

I scrambled into the company barn where Declan and Rae were making out...."Ewww guys get a room...." I waited, when they came up for air I started again "I think Jett's about to get mad." That got their attention, they let go of each other and Rae grabbed her camera off the counter.

Declan asked me "What did you do Addie?"

I said "Nothing!" and crossed my arms "It wasn't me I just happened to be a person of, of circumstance!" I stuttered.

He grabbed Rae's hand and pulled her out of the barn and I followed and sure enough trouble was brewin.' "Well, it's what we sort of wanted right?" I asked uncertainly.

Declan said "Rae get your camera ready, and Addie, if he doesn't get mad enough we're going to have to help him along."

But then we saw some shoving going on between Jett and Kevin, we ran over. Rae stayed back, focused her camera and walked slowly toward them.

Kevin was enough to make Jett mad, Storm was trying to hold Jett back; I could hear Kevin say "Dude what's with your face?" I saw it too, but it was dusk and hard to see a lot of the details. The camera flash was freaky, it made the whole scene increase in intensity.

Declan had a hand on Jett and Rae was walking toward us slowly snapping pictures every few seconds.

"Kevin, get out of here." Declan gritted between his teeth as Storm and he were trying to hold Jett back and not very well I might add. They were pushing with all their might, it was like trying to hold back a bull.

"Is he mad enough Addie......" Declan asked, trying to hold Jett back. "You need to provoke him?" Declan turned his head and scrunched his eyebrows together at me.

"Why me? We should have let Kevin do it..." I held my breath and squeezed my eyes shut and shouted "it wasn't my fault he kissed me." I took a deep breath... "I was in a good mood and I said some stuff.... to him..." I said an octave higher than my normal voice. As I was trying to look at Jett's face to see if he was angry I shouted "Kevin started it..."

Jett roared and leaped out of their grips and he was on top of me. My hands were pinned to the ground and the weight of him had me pinned, immobilized. He growled really low. His face was in mine, his eyes were all blood shot, his cheeks had dark marks running along his cheek bones and under his eyes, the veins in his face and arms were protruding everywhere and his skin turned shades of grey-green. I squeezed my eyes shut. I kept chanting to myself "I love you, I love you, I love you..." Over and over again.

I noticed my breathing started to slow and so did his. "Addie...." he gritted between his teeth. I kept chanting "I love you, I love you..." I felt his face down by my neck...

And all I could say was....."*Really Jett.* You're the one on top of me, I can't move ya fat ass hooker," and then I just started laughing, I know it wasn't that funny but the moment was sooo serious and so intense I couldn't help but laugh and then Storm did too. Jett looked away from me and Rae snapped a picture right in his face. He growled again and quickly spun around and sat on the ground so his back was to everyone. He had his face in his hands that were large with veins pronounced, his nails looked like they were stained with ink. Rae's flash went off a couple more times. His shirt was stretched tightly across his back like it didn't fit, it looked two sizes too small. He got up turned to look at me still lying on the ground and walked away...I'm pretty sure he was missing a tooth.

We walked back to Nic's house and she and I stood in the driveway watching everyone leave when Peyton pulled in, she opened her trunk. She had rope, stakes, extension cords, work lights, flash lights, shovels, pics and she showed us her compass. She grabbed a helmet and turned it on it looked like something a coal miner would wear. "Nice" Nic said nodding her head in satisfaction. We got in the car, Nic's mom came out, Nic met her "Where on Gods earth do you think you're going at this hour?"

"The Winchesters, I asked Peyton to drive by her house on her way out and the cats escaped again, I'll tape up the screen tonight but we'll have to get a new one tomorrow."

"Oh ok honey, be careful." Her mother of course fell for that because the two of them had an affinity for animals and the screen really was torn but we had taped it up a couple of days ago. Nic got back in the car and we drove to Harriet's old place.

"I'm not sure why we couldn't wait until daylight for this" I moaned, I was exhausted and I wasn't sure what we were going to find or if I wanted to find anything at all.

"I didn't think I would sleep without looking for it." Nic said and Peyton agreed.

We went inside the house and Nic shined her flashlight on a picture on the wall, it was a family portrait under a huge perfect looking tree. "I know where this is," Nic stated. She probably knew the property well as she was the only person to cut grass and care for the ten acre property. I was worried this would take us *aaallllll* night long......

Peyton walked out strung her three extension cords together and connected the work light. Nic plugged it in. It lit up a section of the back yard pretty well. I wasn't sure I was seeing right but I saw a perfect looking tree in the back corner, the light just barely reached the outskirts of the shadow the tree would make during the day. Peyton picked up a shovel, slung the rope over her shoulder and tucked the stakes under her arm. Nic pulled stuff from the trunk too, so I followed suit, threw a helmet on my head and turned it on.

Nic stood at the base of the tree looked at her compass and adjusted herself, then paced off eleven steps and started to dig. I got a chill down my spine just thinking of what they might find. Nic and Peyton dug until the ground got so hard they couldn't dig any further. Nothing.

"Good" I said lying in the grass trying to ward off bugs. "Are you guys done now?"

"No" Nic pouted "I was sure after I found Dean and Sam looking for something suspiciously the other day that it would be out here."

I just started to laugh "So you think there is really some sort of treasure buried out here?"

"Yes" she replied wiping the sweat off her brow "I do."

"Well then you need to find the compass she used because it may not have worked right and it could send you in another direction, plus she was short, have Peyton pace off the steps. Of course, eleven may be a precursor for something else, it may stand for something like an anniversary month or birthday and you actually need to know the date."

"Genius, pure genius for that Addie, I will let your lazy ass lay there..."

"That is why you keep me around, besides my good looks."

Peyton knocked me with her foot "You wish." And she snort laughed.

Nic ran inside and about ten minutes later came up with a very old large looking compass, she pulled Peyton to the base of the tree. Their west was not Nic's first west, Peyton walked off eleven paces. They stopped, rooted to the ground, then they looked up at me slowly....

"What?"

"The needle is pointing toward you now" Nic stayed and Peyton left to get a stake and hammer and hammered it into the ground to mark *'the spot.'*

They looked back at me I sat up. "We need a date don't we?" I asked, Nic shook her head. She lent me a hand and I took it. We all headed back to the house. An old calendar was hanging on the kitchen wall, Nic took it down and paged through to November, the fifth was circled.

An hour later Peyton's shovel clinked.

The next day Jett picked me up, but we had to stop at Woolworth's first, so Jett could pick up some glue and he wouldn't tell me what for. He wasn't grumpy, wasn't smiling nor would he kiss me, he just seemed bleak.

We met at Nic's house to clean up from the party. We pulled in and chatted with Storm and Declan. Declan told us Rae would be here later and gave me a look, I nodded. We started walking back to the company barn and Jett told us he'd catch up.

It was hot, the sky was blue, it was a perfect day. Rae wasn't with us yet because she was developing the pictures we took of Jett last night and if he had known that's what she was doing I don't think he would have shown up today. I'm not sure how he'll take seeing the pictures either.

I was in a good mood, though, a bit nervous. I started cleaning the inside of the company barn, wiped off the furniture, counters and started to clean the floors when Jett came in. He was all smiles now. He came over and gave me a hug and kiss. I wanted to see his missing tooth, but the smile left him too quickly when he noticed me looking. He got on his hands and knees to wipe up the floor with me and I knocked him sideways. He laughed, all his teeth were in place. "I thought you knocked a tooth out last night." I said.

"You noticed."

"Well, yeah."

He waited a minute, "I glued it back in, that's why I had to go to the store...."

He got back on all fours and started cleaning the floor and we had it done in no time. "Wait a minute how did you glue your tooth back in?"

"You can't leave well enough alone can you?" I shrugged and gave him a minute. "About a month ago I lost both my eye teeth, so the dentist made me a retainer, he pulled it out of his mouth and attached to it were two teeth. I replied 'hmmm" I slid my hand in his other hand and we walked outside. I obviously had no clue what to say to that.

We came out of the company barn, smiling and hot. Hopefully the rest of the gang had finished picking up the garbage outside. I started in on them "You guys are bums, you're not done yet!" I flapped excitedly...I was in an overly happy mood. I had my favorite jean shorts and a tank top on with a flannel over it. The sleeves were cut off, it was open and I had tied it at the waist. I hiked the garbage bag over my shoulder and hauled it to the tractor and then let it roll off of me onto the trailer.

I put my hands on my hips "Aren't you guys done yet! Come on guys hustle up..." I said with a huge smile. Jett just looked at me wearily like he was so tired from washing the floor. Nodded his head upward, "What's that in your pocket?" he asked.

"What?" I touched my pockets, I felt my folded up note, it was peeking out a bit. My eyes got big, I smiled ear to ear and said "Ah, that's my grocery list." I shoved back into the bottom of my pocket.

Jett said "No it's not." Declan stood up "What is it!"

I looked at Jett "Why are you causing trouble for me crabby butt?" My eyes were wide and I was very giddy. Nic considered it and shrugged her shoulders. Storm perked up, he came over to me and said really softly "What's in your pocket?"

I just jogged to the other side where no one was standing as I was laughing, then stopped cold. I said very seriously "It's my grocery...." but then I lost it and laughed out "list."

Declan darted toward me and I turned and spun to the right to get away from him. "Jett if he touches me you're in deep......" Declan started chasing me. I ran under some evergreens instead of going around and started running for the dock. "Jeeeettt....you bett...er st...ooppp....him........"

I looked back and Nic had followed me, she darted under the soft evergreen trees like I did. The rest of them went around. I kept running I knew they'd catch up any minute. I kicked off my shoes at the sand and headed for the dock I jumped off it as high as I could and turned in the air so I could see who was coming. Jett was in the air with me....we both crashed into the water. He grabbed my waist and we went under water and Jett spun me so I was closest to the top. We came up and he was smiling again. I saw Nic crash into the water next, then Declan and Storm right on his heels....

Jett gave me a kiss on my lips and said "You're a dork." I just looked at him and laughed "I know...."

"The water feels good."

"I know not too cold."

"But you look cold..." I gave him a weird look like how would he know.

"White shirt," he said, my tank underneath was white.

"Crap" I turned around to button my flannel and he dunked me playfully, I was able to button it.

Nic grabbed some floats and tossed them in "Addie I can't believe how fast you can run."

"Yeah, no shit!" Jett replied. "I barely caught up to you and I'm fast."

Declan added "Yeah, Jett has gotten really fast this year and I bet you could give him a run for his money."

We were all lounging in the water when Rae appeared. Suddenly I recalled the whole reason why we were in the water, my note but no one else seemed too.....

I got out of the water and Jett pulled me back in and he kissed me on the neck. We floated for a second and he released me. As I was getting out of the water again, I checked all my buttons. "Hey Rae." I said.

Declan was already by her getting her wet, she was pushing him away. "Wanna take a quick dip?" He asked "No...I'm good." She grumbled, turned and walked to a nearby tree; dropped an envelope, her purse and kicked off her shoes. She walked back onto the dock, rolled up her three-quarter pants and sat at the end of the dock and dangled her feet in the water. I sat next to her when Jett swam over to us. Rae immediately complained she didn't want to get wet, but she got splashed anyway. Declan took a running start from behind us and jumped over us doing a can opener into the water getting us wetter.

Jett tugged on my legs and back into the water I went. It was a perfect afternoon. The guys all started doing all sorts of jumps off the dock. The girls stood at the end of the dock and held their hands together like a bridge and the guys jumped over them. Storm ran through them instead. Jett started getting some amazing height, it was awesome. After a while everyone eventually ended up lying on the dock or picnic table drying off in the sun.

I was almost asleep on the dock when I felt Jett roll onto his side and yanked the wet note out of my pocket. He hopped up real quick, I sat up fast holding my pocket which made everyone stir. Jett walked over to the picnic table and I laid back down.

I tilted my head sideways to check the scene out and Nic went over and straddled the bench next to him. The note was wet and folded up on the table, they were both looking at it. Then Nic stretched her arm over to it and pulled a corner and Jett assisted like it was major surgery. They opened it slowly. I laid back and closed my eyes.

The sun felt so good, it was so simple and care free laying here. I thought of Tori and I in our yard baking in the sun. Last year we bought our own six foot baby pool so we had a place to cool off. We would just lay in the sun, motionless and it warmed you to your core.

The curiosity must have been too much for Declan because I felt him take a step over me and I knew he wanted to see what the infamous note was all about. When they were done reading it Jett and Declan both looked majorly concerned. As I walked up to them I said "It was just a dream, it wasn't that scary."

They both looked at me, "If this" he held up my letter and shook it, "...is true...." Jett paused a bit and looked at Declan "and we don't do anything to stop it, I mean maybe we could have helped Jewel, and maybe we could help this girl!"

"So that means whoever's driving the truck intends to kill and has possibly killed before." Nic said to me.

"What, this hasn't already happened?" Declan was confused. We had to explain the whole dream thing to him. "Oh this just gets better and better," he replied.

There was a silence. Jett slid the note across the table and pushed it as though it weighed twenty pounds. The air felt like it weighed more, everything around me seemed more depressed and weighed heavily on us. Storm pulled the note over to him, when he was done he pushed it in front of me – like no one else wanted to touch it.

I noticed myself folding the note as though it was made of cardboard, hard to fold. I slid it into my front pocket as I always did and I could feel it sitting there weighing me down, it felt stiff, uneasy and uncomfortable. "While we are on uncomfortable subjects, I'd like everyone here to know that what we talk about here stays here, no one's to breathe a word of any of this to anyone else, please." No one said anything. I said "Alright?" Everyone mumbled in agreement, Storm just staring at me with his intense eyes, like he was looking into my soul and reading my every thought.

Declan asked apprehensively "Should we take a look at the

pictures?" As Rae went to get them Jett traced his thumb over the birthmark on my shoulder. "It looks like an angel, maybe it's my guardian angel." He kissed it. Storm scowled at that.

Rae sat down with the pictures and passed them around one at a time. They were passed around in silence. Seeing the proof in your hands was way more frightening than trying to recall what he looked like the night before when his emotions were heightened. Seeing these pictures made the situation all the more surreal and serious. This did not look like the Jett I know, he looked.... monstrous. I hadn't recalled that his eyes glowed. Jett looked at my face, dropped the pictures he had on the table and walked away. No one tried to stop him, or explain the situation away.... or said a word.

Jett drove me home I felt like there was iron curtain between us. He pulled down to the bottom of my driveway and we sat there for a minute. I asked "What's with the teeth and why did you hide it from me." He scrunched his eyebrows at me. I picked up his hand and put my fingers through his and then stroked the top of his hand with my other, shifting sideways so I was facing him. "You don't want to talk about it?"

I wanted Jett to know he could trust me. I know it's possibly only a high school crush, at least that's what my mom keeps telling me, but now in this moment, I feel like it's more. And since I have such an attachment to him, I really wanted to help him and I was very worried about him, I needed to know else he might be keeping from me.

"You know I can make you talk." I said sweetly with a smile.

"I think Sheila may have more answers for us, or I'm hoping she does. Why can't I dream what I want to know, that would be cool. Instead, I get these cryptic dreams never knowing who or when it's going to happen."

I walked in the back door of the Richfield Reading and Speech Center. I always loved the building. It looked like an old school house, red with white trim, very simple. When the door closed behind me Sheila jumped – I looked at her with my eyebrows raised and said "The real questions is if you're really psychic how come you didn't know I was coming?"

She couldn't help but laugh. "I'm not that kind of psychic" she said. "That's not quite how it works for me, I can read people when they are near me and I use tools to read them. I wish I was telepathic... What can I help you with Addie?"

"Can you look at me and tell?" I asked in a very subtle voice. I walked over to the counter and put my hands on the table where she was sitting, then clasped them together. I could feel the coolness the slate table had to offer. She laid her hands on mine, they were warm and the contrast between the two was pleasant, this moment reminded me of my grandma.

"I think our gift obliges us to help those in need, when we can," she said.

"I like that."

She removed her hands from mine "My relatives, I mean the people I'm tracking and the real reason we moved." She said grimly and hesitantly, I was hanging on every word she said. She continued "They...ah...weren't what I expected. When I saw them, they seemed... they were different." She seemed very nervous and unsure of what she was going to tell me next. "And well it scared me and I don't know what to do, not sure if there is something I can do or if anyone will even believe me." She stopped rearranging her books and her eyes began to search the table for the nothingness it provided. "But" Sheila said and paused "I have an idea about what's wrong with your friend."

Sheila and I jumped when Nic came in the room. We both looked at each other and snickered, "Thank goodness it's only you."

"How come you didn't..." I cut her off "she's not that kind of psychic... Good to see you Nic, the plot just thickened," I said. I reviewed what Sheila had just revealed to me.

Nic said "Addie knows a detective that didn't laugh at the weird stuff she told him."

I looked down at my shoes a minute and said "Yeah, Jett's Uncle is a detective I could call Jett and see if he could get his Uncle to come by."

"I have no proof of what he's doing..." her eyes searched the table again then she looked up "Can't hurt to call him and see if he'll listen."

I called Jett since I didn't have his Uncle's phone number on me. His mom answered the phone and I could hear her call for Jett and although her hand was over the receiver I still heard her tell

Jett "There's another dead animal in our back yard, make sure you clean it up before you go anywhere." Jett said something grumpily back to her.

When he got on the phone he sounded equally grouchy but seemed to lighten up a bit as I explained everything to him. "I'll call you back." Click, he was off the phone.

A few minutes later the phone rang. Sheila looked at me and shrugged one shoulder so I picked it up. "He's on his way so am I," was all the voice said on the other end, "click" he disconnected with me abruptly again. "Gosh darn it" I said "He keeps hanging up on me – but Jett and his Uncle are on their way."

Sheila went to her locked file cabinet and took out three old worn boxes and placed them on the counter carefully, they looked like they would fall apart any minute. They were only the size of a piece of paper and not very deep, like a photo box. One was marked "1911 – 1931" the other marked "1941 – 1961", the last was marked "IMPORTANT". She made a pot of coffee nervously, although she was trying to look relaxed, she was uneasy about something.

I broke the silence "Can you tell us what's wrong with Jett?" She looked at me in confusion.

"My friend that's been sick," I explained.

Twenty minutes later Jett stepped in and another five behind him was his Uncle. Nic said "You told me there was a family hotness but I didn't notice it 'til now, you're right." I looked at her smiling and blushed a bit "Right, I know – told ya." Sheila even gave us a smile of approval.

Grey shook everyone's hand and introduced himself and then shook Jett's hand and said "What's up?" and smacked him on the shoulder.

"Crazy stuff," Jett said and smiled nervously.

Shelia put cream and sugar out on the table and poured everyone a cup of coffee. Everyone sat around the table in silence. When Sheila sat down I took one of the pads of paper from the middle of the table and a pen and began to doodle. She started with "…as our history goes vampires and werewolves did exist but at the end of the 18th century one vampire realized the humans were in jeopardy and killed every last one of them with the help of our families. And then he killed himself. So nothing went on for many years and that's why it was such a scare for everyone in 1910. Her story that began in the early 1900' the one I heard before, or at least parts of it. She gave us the name Dr. Sal Rewtnic a familiar name both her and her daughter had mentioned before so I wrote it down.

She explained the experiments he was doing and the diseases he was trying to cure, and then she stated that they thought he was very close to a cure when his first staged experiments went crazy and the vampire and werewolf rumors started. Sheila also assured us that they were just rumors.

In any case the authorities extinguished everything and everyone involved, or so they thought. Her family took it upon themselves to observe and watch everyone that was experimented on and not destroyed. The second and third phase patients weren't killed and the police never found the last set of books with names and experiments that had taken place, her family hid those in a safe place.

The people they were to watch included Sal Rewtnic the third, Sal's son, and his best friend and Cousin Neil Royce.

I wrote those names down.

She explained that both boys were placed in a psychiatric ward in Chicago with Dr. Westman and he took custody of them soon after the death of Dr. Rewtnic and moved up to a place in Michigan. So our family moved and followed, well my Great Grandmother's family did.

She continued "My great grandmother became very ill and was sick for quite a while and she kept begging me to check up on this Sal guy and I kept telling her yes, okay, I will. She begged again on her death bed to follow up and for me to call my uncle for help. I didn't think anything of it, I wasn't into the stories like our elders were." Sheila had tears in her eyes. I looked around the table everyone seemed pretty engrossed in her story.

"We know we're supposed to track Sal Rewtnic the third the scientist's son and his cousin Neil Royce. The names of the other families we're supposed to track were George Grell, James Nelf, Matt Black, Charles Gellar," she looked at me as she said it "Shelly Falconer, Fred Labowski, Dena Castle, Lynette Coey," When she said that name I gasped and slapped my hand to my chest.

Jett replied "That's what your sweatshirt says, right? Coey?"

"Yeah, Coey's Crew is the name of my dad's hockey team. Coey was his mom's maiden name."

"Cool." he said.

Sheila continued "Elizabeth Nolan and Eugene White." The last name made Jett react. "Wait!" Sheila said grimly. "She pointed to Jett you know Eugene White? And Addie Charles Gellar is your grandfather and you know Lynette Coey?"

Shelia looked confused. Jett replied, Eugene White is my mom's father." I added "Lynette is my dad's mom and George Grell is my mom's dad." I explained. "How come so many of my relatives are on the list?"

She stared at me with a long gaze and mumbled out "Good question. Maybe that's why Cale is so interested in you." There was a long silence.

"Anyway" she said. "My uncle and I are tracking their family trees. Everyone on the original list should be in there eighties or deceased. However, he called me from Tucson, Arizona and told me that Sal Rewtnic's new name is now Stew C. Neila. It was a very bad connection but he said that Sal now Stew needed to be stopped." She took a deep breath "And then he sent me these boxes." She pushed one of the three boxes toward the middle of the table.

I don't think I want to hear this. I wanted to know what was wrong with Jett and I also wanted to figure out how to get Cale out of my life. I also wondered if he's the one I've been dreaming about being a wolf. So I wrote his name down and doodled some more.... I kept staring at the Sal Rewtnic's name on my paper and then Cale's. Nic seemed to be watching me intently. I crossed the letter "C" from Cale's name off of Sal Rewtnic's name, then the "A" and then the letter "L" and then the "E".

I sat up straighter in my chair and wrote 'Winters, then crossed the "W"' out in both names and then Sheila cleared her throat loudly, I stopped what I was doing. She began again "When I went to visit Sal Rewtnic's son whose name is Sal Rewtnic the third he should have been about 75 – 80 years old, but the man I found was not." She paused, "he looked much much younger. He looked about 18." I looked at Nic and we both said "Cale" in unison as she pushed a recent photo toward us.

"So you're telling us this guy hasn't aged at all." Grey responded. "I wouldn't say at all, but definitely at a slower pace than us, much slower. Doc Brown, my uncle, wrote me a letter that this box" she pointed to the one that was marked 1941 – 1961

3:17 a.m. ...the waking hour

"...was misplaced, because none of us were taking any of this seriously."

She looked at us but we were a little confused "The guy who's giving you a hard time?" she said. I wrote Stew C. Neila on my paper and underlined it then pushed my pad of paper near the middle for everyone to look at. Sheila immediately opened the box and took out pictures – sure enough they were old black and white pictures of Cale. "Doc Brown took these pictures of Stew a couple months ago." They were definitely Cale.

Nic whispers to me "No wonder he dresses like an old man – he is one...." and she giggled.

"What happened to the cousin? "Grey asked. She looked at him and her hands went lax on the table. "We're not sure. He usually follows Sal but he hasn't showed up in the area or if he has we just haven't found him yet." We asked his name again and Nic and I tried some anagram names for Neil Royce and Ben O'Riley. "However, Doc Brown says there are several missing people in Tucson Arizonian the last place we had tracked both Stew and Ben or Sal and Neil, we checked both names."

I looked at Nic and whispered, "So if Cale is really 80 no wonder he used to dress like a grandpa and treat me like his daughter, ewww," I got the chills all over.

As Grey was asking her questions she opened the box marked "IMPORTANT" and pulled out an envelope and set it down in the middle of the table. She got up and went back in her file drawer and pulled out an envelope, already opened and handed it to Grey.

"This all does sound absurd" Jett finally got in the conversation. I reached for the envelope in the middle and removed its contents. "Let me help" Nic said. We shuffled the photos around looking at them and Nic turned one over, they were all dated. "Let's put them in date order on the counter." Nic said. After we got up to put all the photos in order the rest came up behind us. No one had anything to say. We recognized Cale so the other one had to be his cousin.

I turned to Sheila and said grumpily "So this is Sal?" Everyone turned to look at her and she said "Yes, now I know this sounds preposterous..." she said with her hands held out in front of her, palms out and shaking her head "...and you probably don't believe it. I'm not sure I do, at least I know I don't want to."

"But you're psychic, can't you tell if it's him." Jett retorted. Grey said "Good point – if you are psychic what do your spidy senses tell you." He sort of snorted and dropped the envelope on the table and rubbed his face.

"She is not that kind of psychic" I started in "...she has to touch the person to read them or use some sort of tool to read them." She smiled at me and said "That's right, I can't just read someone because I want to or can see them. Just like Addie can't dream about what she wants they just come to her." Everyone at the table just looked at me, because putting the words psychic to my abilities for the first time was weird. I shook my head and said "No, I'm not a psychic I just have dreams that come true, sometimes." Saying that, was even weirder, I didn't want that title it seemed so odd. Everyone started talking at once back and forth asking all sorts of questions of each other.

"Hold it, hold it, hold it!" Grey said "We're missing the point or at least I think Sheila is missing the point." He pointed to the counter were the pictures lay. "That is Cale Winters, so Cale and Sal are the same guy. What was that other name, he uses, you gave us?" He nodded toward Sheila. She said Stew C. Neila, so Cale is his third name we need to assume his cousin has a third name as well, maybe that's why you can't track him yet. He wrote Neil Royce and Ben O'Riley down on my scratch paper and handed it to me and Nic, see if you can up with an anagram with these..."

"Ooh, good Idea" I replied and Nic and I grabbed the paper and started coming up with names, Nic immediately though of the last name O'Neil from one of our classmates. We doodled with the rest of the letters trying to get a first name.

"Cale being psycho answers a lot. Whatever experiments his father did on him could have made him crazy, and living for so long and not aging could also have an effect. If he's had to hide for so long and change his identity, it has made him crafty at being able to hide and aiding his ability to plan a killing spree all that much easier." Grey said in an authoritative voice.

"Do you have an address on him?" He asked Sheila, she responded "Not exactly, but I know he has a white house with green trim." He looked at me and said "What is it with women never getting an address… Well we know he isn't living there anymore and we found no evidence of any kind there, however the whole scene was peculiar." He walked back over to the pictures and studied them.

Jett saw the pictures, turned to me, squeezed my hand and said "I may be dangerous too, until I find out what's up with me I should probably keep my distance... I'm assuming Cale's the one who poisoned me or did what he did to me."

"Hell no!" I said. "We'll just keep people around us, you start isolating yourself it could make it worse." I said. "Ah...ah..." I said holding my hand up to him "I don't want to hear it! Does anyone think I'm wrong?"

"Nope." Nic said. Grey shook his head with his lips pierced.

"I'll need to research the new names you gave me, I'll verify all these sources, check into a couple other things and we'll go from there. If any of you find anything else out, write it down so you don't forget or if something else happens by all means call me immediately." Grey said and dropped some business cards on the table. "Does anyone have any questions? Good. Let's meet back here in three days, same time." My head was reeling and trying to process all the information we just found, too soon for questions, but I bet I'll have some soon.

CHAPTER 26

"I wish he could have Cale arrested, just throw him in the slammer." Jett said with anguish.

"I know me to," Nic replied. I stayed silent in the car and noticed Jett was taking us home. "Where are you taking us?" I asked "I'm starving I was thinking Skyway's, is that all right?" I leaned over and gave him a peck on the cheek, he passed my house and kept driving.

Nic said "Two peas in a pod." I smiled at her. As we were going through the parking lot Jett put his arm around me and smiled.

We got back to my house as Declan and Rae were pulling into my driveway. We were meeting to make a plan to catch Cale, based on my most recent dream. Declan and Jett were scheming on how to approach Cale. Jett told me and the girls that we needed to stay home, that we weren't allowed to go on their little adventure which was really my adventure, my dream, my thoughts. I gave him a dirty look, that's a bunch of malarkey. I wanted to go, we argued back and forth, I was so mad all I could do was stomp my foot.

Jett looked at me and chortled, "Did you just stomp your foot?" Pointing at me and looking at Declan and added "Don't two year olds stomp their feet?"

"Well yes Jett, I believe they do." Declan said sarcastically.

"Does the two year old need a nap" Jett asked in a baby voice. Of course, I couldn't help but laugh. We all did. I flipped them the bird grabbed my letter and said "That settles it, I'm going. Pick me up at eight. If you don't, I'll meet you there" and walked out.

I went to sit with Rae and Nic outside who had had enough of the situation, and I don't blame them. I was tired of talking about it myself. As I walked away I could hear the guys still laughing I was glad for it because everything else had been so serious lately.

My cousin Peyton had written me a letter, I sat next to the girls and took it out. Peyton decided to go on a five day river rafting trip before her college classes started at Arizona State, she was in Tucson hoping to go hang gliding. It sounded like Peyton, she was always looking for something adventurous to do.

I looked up, the girls were silent. Nic asked, "Can I read your last journal?"

"Sure, Rae have you read it yet? If not feel free." I replied. I handed the note to Nic and Rae sat closer to her. I had dreamt about a girl getting kidnapped in a bar, it had a dance floor and after I described it to Jett he said it sounded familiar, like a bar he's been to in Akron where all the young kids like to go. She gets put into the familiar truck I've dreamt about before and she is either dead or unconscious. We were hoping since I had this dream last night that it would take place tonight, and it makes sense since Saturdays are the most popular night to go to this particular bar called Angels of all things.

Jett and I arrived early and saw Cale walking into the bar. I was shocked because I remember everything happening when it was really dark and it was only dusk now, I guess it'll be dark soon and the fact that he could take his time looking for a girl could be a factor. We parked quickly and went inside; we didn't even know if the rest of the gang was here yet. I had never been here before but Jett had, we went up to the bouncer, Jett shook hands with him and he let us right in, didn't card us or anything. We walked in and there were people everywhere, to the right was a bar and a bunch of tables and as we walked forward there was a railing encircling a huge dance floor. When I looked up I saw a DJ with another railing that encased the whole second floor, just like in my dream. I think I was looking at the place in awe.

I took a place at the railing taking it all in. Jett leaned over "I'll be right back." The music was going and people were dancing, I heard a fit of laughter around me. The girl next to me nudged me, "Isn't that you?" pointing to a monitor mounted on the wall. It was a picture of me with the text "Never Been Kissed!" I blushed immediately, and they of course kept the camera on me. I spotted Jett across the way, he laughed too, nodded toward the monitor then back at me and gave me a wink.

Someone tapped me on the shoulder, she had a very large drink for me bought by a couple of guys around the corner, she pointed them out, I waved and took it. Ha! In your face I thought.

Jett said "Don't accept that!"

"Jeez you scared me. Why not? Jealous?" I received a couple more drinks and flowers, the waitress kept dropping stuff off. It did seem a little crazy. "Take one they're yummy."

"We're not here to drink, besides I didn't know you were a little lush." He said laughing. I punched him in the arm halfheartedly. He pulled me in close with one arm around my waist, I leaned back a bit put one arm around his neck the other still holding my drink. He slid his hand up the middle of my back slowly pulling me in closer, so close I could feel his breath on me. And then he kissed me passionately. Hearing an "Awwww" coming from the crowd. He pulled away and I turned my head to the right and there we were on the monitor. I hid my face in his shoulder.

He released me fast and grabbed my hand "Cale!" I slammed my drink down and Jett pulled me weaving us through the crowd to the back of the place and finally the back door. I tugged back on his hand "Get the car." He paused, "You stay here" and went out the back door. The bar was fun, but it had distracted us from Cale who was slipping away. He must have seen us on the video, because he wasn't supposed to leave so quickly according to my dream. I walked out into the alley, it was calm and quite, spine-chilling, I walked further out and didn't see Cale or his truck, I was startled by the sudden sound of Jett's car squealing around the corner into the one way alley the wrong way. I jumped in.

We passed one building then two, a truck turned on its headlights and was heading straight toward us. Jett slammed on the breaks and started backing up, we hit a pot hole and lost control of the car and backed into a dirt pile left from construction. The car was stalled but he had also blocked the alley way, his car started right back up. Cale slammed on his breaks, his passenger lunged forward not putting her hands out or anything.

"Huh" I let out a hard gasp "She's already dead!" Cale looked right at me and flashed his bright whites; I noticed how prominent his eye teeth were, he was glad I was there, he held my attention with a hard stare, pulled his cap down low, gave me a half evil grin out of the side of his mouth, and whipped his truck into reverse and headed out the alley way. It was definitely the truck we've been looking for.

Jett got the car started after the second try and took off after him. Cale stopped at the end of the alley opened the passenger door and dumped the body of out of his truck. He took off into the neighborhood. We got up to the girl and I jumped out, she was still alive but unconscious. Jett yelled at me to call 911, he took off after Cale. As I was running back to the bar a car passed me I glanced at the driver and she right back at me. I kept running and banged on the back door of the bar "I have to call 911! I yelled. I banged some more "someone's hurt!" A bouncer flung the door open; I made the call, hung up, slipped my piece of paper out of my pocket and called Grey.

I ran back into the alley where the girl was and Jett was sitting next to her, Jett pointed out puncture marks on her neck and told me not to touch her in case she had a neck or back injury. Declan, Rae and Nic pulled their car right by us, "What we're too late?" Declan said hopping out of his car.

"Just a little, we think Cale started early because he spotted us inside." I said.

By the time the ambulance and police arrived, I noticed the marks on her neck were faded, they looked like an old injury. I forgot to ask Jett if he noticed.

When his uncle showed up he was mad, just when he was about to start lecturing and yelling at us I let out an "Oh My God!" They were walking toward us. "I almost forgot in all the excitement. She knew it was happening too, but how? She said she had to touch someone to read them?" I told Jett and Detective Grey.

"Well..." she echoed, "I of course, touched you." It was Sheila and Cat.

"What are you doing here?" Grey asked. "I came to see Addie, I wanted to know if her dreams come true, I don't like being the only psychic in town. So you really did dream this?" I gave my head a one sided shake and a nervous smile, I mean what was I supposed to say.

Two days later and waiting in anticipation, we all met at the

Richfield Reading and Speech Center. Jett's uncle reported the injured girl, Callie, was shaken' up about the situation, but physically she was going to be fine. There were no leads on Cale and he was nowhere to be found, not the house or the apartment.

Sheila told us "As my uncle and have been reading all the journals and notes we have and are following the family lines, we have found that everyone who was experimented on directly never got sick but has died of good ole old age except for Cale and his cousin. Some of the offspring of the originals have special *'gifts'* and they usually appear after they hit puberty. We found some are very good athletes, runners, gymnasts, etcetera, possible psychics and none have ill effects when it comes to their health. Some are perfectly normal though, and one we know has several abilities, psychic and coercion abilities." Of course, she gave me a dead stare "...and from what Nic told me a very good athlete."

"... Is there anything else?" I asked.

"Yes." Sheila explained. "Cale and his cousin are obviously looking for a cure. So along with Addie and hunting for the celestial healer we think they are hoping one or both is supposed to make them whole."

"How do we find this healer?" Nic asked.

"Well we are not sure, she is supposed to, yes she, we found some mentions in our historical records about a clairvoyant savior that is born having a mark of an angel on her body, we are thinking a birth mark or tattoo of some kind. But we don't know who, we can't exactly strip search people to find the marking so we have no leads there so far." Sheila peered at me, I felt discombobulated.

"That would explain a lot." Jett stated.

"We have tracked Cale and his cousin in and out of hospitals getting blood transfusions for years on a regular basis, so unfortunately it's a huge probability they need blood to survive." Sheila explained. "And when we tracked all the blood lines of anyone connected Addie comes up as the best blood candidate as several of her grandparents had been experimented on. This is probably why you have Cale's attention."

"So you're saying I'm Wonder Woman to them? This seems so surreal...." Everyone agreed. I glanced at Jett he seemed excited about the news and he should be there may be a cure for him. I feel like I'm not even here, like I am in a dream state. This made sense, though, Cale said he was traveling every so often, but he

3:17 a.m. ...the waking hour

wasn't. I bet it coincides with when he gets sick and the reason why he's trying to get my blood from me, to try and cure himself.

"There is one little last thing I would like to mention" Sheila mumbled. "In one of the journals written by Dr. Rewtnic at the very beginning of a book was an unfinished entry '...*vehement acting as demons*. This with the celestial angel and a shaman should make them whole.' If we can find the book that precedes this book we may have a lot more information about Jett, Cale and his cousin's conditions."

I had nothing to say to that, if Cale or his cousin had the book we can't find them and if someone else has it who?

We met Declan and Rae at Papa G's Pizza, Declan raised his glass in a toast, "Here's to helping people in need and having fun in between." Jett replied "I'll toast to helping people, when we can."

Everyone clinked glasses. I hope they don't think I was going to be in charge of our crew coordinating rescue parties in pursuit of my dreams. We got lucky on where and when with this last one was but who knows what could happen next time.

I saw Declan lean over to Jett and started talking softly so I tuned in, "What's with your mom going crazy over a bunch of dead animals at your house about?" Jett stopped smiling as soon as he asked and replied "What?" delayed and said "Who knows, I think we have a coyote or something on our lot, probably had a baby or something." He was grouchy after that comment.

I wonder if my blood will heal Jett?

CHAPTER 27

Our parents took us camping this year for our family trip; we were rented a cabin that my parent's friends owned. The property was large enough for a couple of tents so our parents told us we could invite a couple friends, so of course I invited Jett and Nic. Jett decided to bring Storm as he thought that Nic and he should get together. I was hoping Nic would have found someone by now, and I'm actually shocked that she and Topher didn't start dating. I told Jett that Shelby may not like the idea and that's when Jett told me they had broken up over spring break. I hadn't even known. I hadn't really heard from Shelby as I thought it was because she was busy, I feel like a terrible friend but something I could fix.

The second morning of our trip Jett woke up and immediately went to grope my pockets, looking for a new note. I told him just once I wish he'd grope me because he wanted to, not because he wanted to know if I had another dream. He jokingly put both hands on my butt and then wouldn't leave me alone. After breakfast, I had retrieved my note from my bag and shoved it into my front pocket and Jett noticed it peeking out and got instantly mad; I had a dream and was hiding it from him. We were camping so I had no idea if I woke up at 3:17 or not so I didn't even know if this one was valid. I shoved it deeper into my pocket and asked Storm and Nic to go with me to check on my mom and dad fishing.

Jett got even madder. I gave the note to Nic and asked her to put it in my bag when she was done reading it.

When we got to their fishing spot it was the usual scene, my brother and dad fishing about 20 feet apart and my mom reading a book in her folding chair. My mom didn't like to fish and truth be told neither did I. We hung out a bit, Storm went over to help Kit re-bait his hook and Kit let Storm cast his rod and in no time flat he had a bite, he gave it a quick jerk and let Kit real it in. Nic went over to check it out and held the net for them while they tried unhooking the fish. It was a nice peaceful morning. It's funny how everyone acts in a different place, different environment.

When we went home on Monday evening I checked my bag for my note, and it wasn't there. I verified with Nic that she had put it in the front pocket of my bag; she said she did it when no one was around, but it was gone.

Jett's parents own a cabin by the lake in Michigan and I've never been there before, but I'd seen pictures. I'm not sure if I dreamt about his cabin because we were camping at the time or not. Nic and I had planned to go check it out. We had a back story for our parents and we would take a bus up to the cabin first thing Wednesday. I'm assuming Jett stole my note and read it but I don't plan on asking him about it because I'm not talking to him. I didn't want him to read it because I was still unsure of how valid my dreams really were and I wanted to check this one out first, do a little recon with Nic.

It turned out that Nic couldn't go; I almost didn't go by myself but then decided to at the last minute. When I got to the cabin and I was pretty sure I had the right one because of the tree in front and the brown siding and brick red shutters. I walked around back, sure enough Jett's car was parked in the carport, meaning he stole and read my note. Being all by myself this trip had made me nervous so maybe Jett's company would be better if I can get over being mad at him. I should have known he wouldn't be able to help himself from checking out my note. He goes on and on about me trusting him and he does this. Maybe I'm upset because there were some *'personal'* parts I didn't want him reading. I was here and I wasn't about to leave so I knocked on the door, wondering who else was with him. He answered the door and said "I made lunch for us, are you hungry?" He held the door open for me and slid my bag off my shoulder. I said nothing to him as I passed by him and into the kitchen, I could smell him, fresh air and soap, which made me feel at ease but still mad. He had no shirt on just a dark rope necklace and shorts, his skin was the color of a dark golden brown. I leaned up against the counter and crossed my arms maintaining my staying mad status.

He placed my bag in the next room which looked like a family room. "What were you going to do, break in our house?" Good point, I guess I would have been trespassing if he hadn't come. I looked at him and squinted my eyes "I brought a tent" I said coldly.

"Why did you even hide the note from me" he asked in a neutral voice. "That's my personal business and I wasn't about to share it with everyone at camp, besides who do you think you are going through my things and stealing it?"

"Fine, we both did something wrong – I want you to trust me and I want to help." He pulled the note out of his back pocket and handed it to me. I ripped it out of his hands and dashed outside. I was more embarrassed than anything that he undoubtedly read the whole thing. I walked behind the car port and started to pace. This is way crazy; I'm a nut job that has crazy dreams and Jett was going through some physical changes that who knows what they were about. He came up behind me, "I'm sorry and I did read the whole thing, it's nothing to be embarrassed about. I have dreams like that too – all guys do – I never assume girls don't."

He moved closer and put his hand on my waist and I started to cry a little, I wiped my tear. He moved himself in front of me and hugged me. "Shhh, at least it was about me, it was me, right? I mean at least the good parts." I shook my head and embraced him back. "I promise I'll never steal another note from you, I'll wait for you to share it with me. And I don't expect the part about me to come true at least not anytime soon." He told me in his deepest voice, true and blue.

"This is so messed up." I let go and took a deep breath. He gave me a peck on the cheek.

"There is a place in town, similar to what you described, plus the messed up part is I've caught a glimpse or two of Cale around here before, not much, but a couple of times in the past."

"So you think this dream could be valid? I don't want you to think just because I have a dream that it will come true, because I really have no idea if it will or won't."

"Agreed, some, not all? But you described the cabin to a "T." Let me show you around."

He grabbed my hand and pulled me through the family room, sure enough, it was just like in my dream. There was even a blue and brown plaid recliner with wooden arms. I pointed to the chair with my mouth open, and looked at Jett, he said "I know right!" He showed me the bedrooms even though I didn't describe them in this note, I felt like I was familiar with the rooms. One was all navy, I shuddered at the sight of it with an awful eerie feeling. The other room was all tones of green and the third was shades of rusty orange.

He grabbed me and gave me a hug. "I think we should go in town, check it out, see if we can spot anything else you recognize and look around for Cale. I brought a photo my Uncle gave me; we can ask people if they've seen him."

"Wow you came prepared."

We went back into the kitchen and we ate the lunch he made. They were only plain turkey sandwiches but I was glad for it, I was starving. He tossed everything in the refrigerator along with some sodas, and put his hand out to me "Are you ready?"

I took his hand "I'm feeling kind of guilty now, that I came up here without your permission, and I'm sorry about that. I would rather have been invited."

He pulled me out the door and locked it. "I'm feeling very guilty about reading your note too, and I wish I would have waited for you to give it to me." He gave me a peck on the lips and a tight squeeze. "Despite our guilt, let's just go hang out and have some fun. If we see Cale or find something really wrong we'll call my uncle and by the way consider yourself invited." I smiled.

We walked downtown, it wasn't far at all. They had some cute little restaurants and shops, and we went into all of them. "So you're a shopper then?"

"Oh yeah," he said. "My mom says she trained us well." His mom was right she did train him well I saw him perusing the clearance racks and he found me an orange tee for only four bucks.

We ended up shopping until dinner time; it went by fast and no leads. We went to a new Chinese joint it was decent, good food and the prices were economical. I was glad for it because I spent most of my money shopping. We filled up and packed up the leftovers.

Before going back to the cabin we checked out the hot spot in town, it was just like in my dream. The first floor had seating and no walls on three sides, the stairs were in the middle and it lead up to a huge bar that was under a roof, no walls on three sides again, room for a band and one was setting up, a dance floor and a nice size deck with plenty of seating out in the open. Everything was made of wood except the floor. The railing that encased the bar had big wood posts that held lights on every other post. Plus, they had white Christmas lights strung post to post even though it wasn't Christmas. It looked really nice and rustic. There were several people mingling around and seemed like the time to come because people started to stream in steadily.

"I hate Chinese food." I said to Jett as we found a table and clonked down.

"Why didn't you say something?"

"No, I hate it because I always eat too much and get sleepy but then in a couple hours I'll want more."

He laughed "Yeah, I know what you mean."

Dusk came quickly and the day was going fast. Jett asked me for a slow dance, "I thought you didn't dance."

"I can sway back and forth with the best of them, but if you don't want to..."

"Oh, I can sway too!" I replied.

After we sat back down I wondered how long we were going to wait around, I was getting very tired, my eyes were getting heavy. Jett thought we'd stay for another hour but as I was yawning I looked up past the bar and caught a glimpse of what I thought was Cale. I sat straight up and put my hand on Jett's hand urgently and looked toward Cale. We locked gazes no one moved not even Jett.

Jett got up slowly and walked to the opposite side of the bar. It was huge and when he got there Cale had put his arm around some girl's neck and started to leave. I followed Jett as he followed Cale. It wasn't easy maneuvering around all the people.

We got out to the beach and stopped. We had to look around as people were mingling everywhere. There were a few tables and chairs in the sand, I plopped all my stuff down on one of them; Jett went one way and I went the other.

As I was walking down the beach I saw Cale kissing the girl at the water's edge, it was brushing up against their feet. I started walking faster and stopped when he looked at me. Walking toward him again, slowly, he smiled at me with his dark eyes, pale skin and veiny face, I saw him bite the girl while still looking at me. She screamed. Jett grabbed onto me, "What's wrong." I realized it was me screaming. I pointed toward Cale who was continuing to suck the life out of the poor helpless girl. Jett turned to me, "Do you trust me?" I stammered out "of course" and before I could get another word out he said "Stay here" and took off after Cale kicking up sand in his wake.

As Jett approached rapidly, Cale let the girl drop to the ground and tossed Jett into the water. The girl stood up shakily, got her bearings and ran away. Jett went back at Cale on all fours, tearing through the water like it wasn't even there. When Jett reached him, Cale swiped his arm at him in a stabbing motion like you would a knife, but when he let go a syringe was stuck in Jett's shoulder. They wrestled around and when Cale got free he ran down the beach and through some residents yards. Jett followed but when he came back he was by himself, wet, sandy and walking with a limp.

He walked up to me, without slowing his stride, put his arm around me and out of breath said "he's gone, but I think he'll leave the girl alone." We collected our stuff and headed home. He was getting me wet and sandy and I was holding some of his weight, we were struggling. Halfway home he said "That son-of-a-bitch bit me" and started walking a little more on his own.

"He stabbed you with a syringe too." I responded, Jett reached around to feel his shoulder where he was jabbed, so he knew.

We were both exhausted when we got to the cabin. Jett unlocked the door grabbed some firewood before going in, tossed it into the fireplace, started it and headed for the bedroom. "I'll be right back." You could tell that was his usual routine.

I waited a few minutes before heating up the rest of the Chinese food. There was no TV, so I turned on the radio. Jett was on auto-pilot, he got more firewood and put it on the fire but held his back and moaned as he stood up. When he came into the kitchen with dry clothes he said "Awesome. Food, I forgot we had leftovers, I thought I'd have to make sandwiches."

He grabbed his plate off the counter and tucked two sodas into his arm, I grabbed my plate and followed him into the living room, we sat on the couch together.

When we were finished eating I took our plates to the kitchen and washed them. When I got back Jett hadn't moved. His head was leaning back on the couch. He looked lifeless.

I stepped up on the couch and pushed him forward sliding between him and the couch and started to rub his neck, rubbing deep and squeezing his muscles gently. I could feel all the tension in him. What he needed was a full massage. It was hard with his shirt on so I gave it a little tug and he leaned forward and I pulled it up and rested it on his shoulders. His skin was smooth and warm. His back was beautiful along with the rest of him. His shirt kept falling down, so I tapped his shoulder and said "Up" he lifted his arms up and I scooped his shirt off. I smelled it, it smelled of him, fresh air and soap.

"Lay on the carpet and I'll rub your lower back." He didn't move. "You hurt yourself right?"

"Yeah", he mumbled, he crawled forward to the carpet in front of the fire. I tossed him a pillow from the couch; he grabbed it and put it under his head and hands. His shoulders were much broader than his waist, his back long and tan. I was almost afraid to touch him. I sat on top of him and started to massage his neck, then shoulders all the way down to his lower back. "I must not be doing this right."

"Hmm" was all he said.

I put all my weight on my knees and leaned into it. "I must not be very good at this you're still very tense" I was talking softly, and without notice he turned over. "You're doing just fine."

He put his rough hands on my waist just under my shirt and pulled me forward, I put a hand on his chest for balance and just the touch of his skin sent a tingle through my body. He moved one hand to the back of my neck and then into my hair pulling me closer and kissing me softly, gently and then vigorously. I sat up a little and we held a gaze, I leaned down to kiss his muscular chest. He rolled us over and started kissing my neck. He held himself above me gently, not letting all his weight on me; I could feel the heat radiating from his body.

The phone rang, he stopped and didn't move. The phone rang again and we released each other and got up. I leaned on the counter across from him waiting to hear what was said.

"That was my uncle just giving us an update." I half smiled at him. The only light in the room was from the fire and it silhouetted his body perfectly. I slid myself to the other end of the counter where he met me. I laid my hands on his chest gently, and told him "I definitely need a shower."

He bent down and kissed me on the neck I felt his tongue glide up sending a shiver right down my spine all the way to my toes. He was kissing me again. I pushed on his chest a little and said again "I ah, need a shower."

He let his hands fall to my waist and said "me too." I opened my eyes wide, I was not prepared for this - no way! He looked at me and saw my expression. He let go of me patted me on the butt and said "Don't use up all the hot water."

"I thought you already took a shower."

"No I cleaned up a little and called my uncle, how do you think he knew to call us here."

"Oh yeah, I hadn't thought about that, my mind was elsewhere."

I tried to hurry, afraid that Jett might decide to join me. I went as fast as I could through the shower, but stayed under the hot water for a long minute before I came out and noticed a towel laying on the counter and my clothes gone. I can't believe I didn't hear him come in, plus, I know I had locked the door – I checked it again still locked. I towel dried my hair and dried myself quickly then wrapped the towel around myself tightly. When I was brushing my teeth I was reminded of Jett and his missing teeth at Nic's house.

I went to the door, opened it slowly and peeked out toward the family room, stuck my head out further and then turned the other way to dart toward my room. I screamed and put my hand to my chest, Jett was leaning up against the wall. With no shirt, no shoes no socks just sweat shorts and a towel on his shoulder.

He asked "Who you looking for."

My cheeks were flushed, and my hair still dripping. I stepped into the hallway. "You."

He stepped in front of me put his hands on my waist and pushed me back into the bathroom up against the sink. "I'm right here." He gave me a peck on the lips, and I waited, I didn't move or say anything. He went over to the shower and turned it on and said "Are you staying?" He put his hands on his shorts, ready to pull them off and gave me a half smile. I pushed off the counter and said "No way!' and darted toward the bedroom.

I got dressed quickly and picked out my hair, towel dried it some more and put some mascara on – Tori told me the least I should do is put mascara and color on my lips. It's not so bad, I found myself doing it more around Jett. I went back down the hall and the bathroom door was open. I peeked in and Jett was in a towel in front of the mirror brushing his teeth. I leaned against the wall across from the bathroom and watched him. He rinsed and turned around, leaned against the sink putting his arms on the counter on either side of him. They were flexed you could see all the ridges of muscle he had, I let my eyes glide over each one of them.

By the time I looked back up at his face he was smiling, he knew I was checking him out. I quickly looked at the floor and scuffed it with my foot. He made a sudden movement and was in front me with his shorts back on.

I kept looking at the floor, "You know as much as I ah, liked my dream," I stammered "I just don't think I am ready for *"it"* to come true." After my last word I looked up at him to see what his reaction was. He didn't seem to have one. He touched my forehead and caressed my face downward pushing my hair away from my face. "I understand." he said.

"You sound tired." I said.

"I am, I feel a little odd almost like I'm getting sick again. It's a tiredness I have a hard time fighting."

He led me over to the couch, he sat down and I sat in his lap, and put my head on his shoulder, he put his arms around me. We sat in silence for a while. It was nice, he was warm and I could hear his heartbeat. I closed my eyes, before I knew it I found myself kissing his chest - I stopped suddenly and moved to sit next to him.

He turned and kissed me on the lips pushing me back on the couch. My legs wrapped around his. My heart was beating so loud I could no longer hear his. I felt warmth run all over my body. He kissed my cheek and then my neck. "Stop" I whispered I couldn't move. He was kissing my breast bone and started moving toward my neck, where he bit me lightly and it sent chills all the way down my left side. "Please stop." I whispered again and pushed on him gently. Yet my head fell slightly back and he bit me again. This time I felt a searing pain in my neck, I released my legs from him trying to push him up "Stop" I yelled, trying to push him from underneath.

He pulled up his face, it was veiny and pale his eyes dark as night and he was panting, out of breath. He rolled off me quickly and ran into the bathroom. I just laid there holding my neck, frozen, not knowing what just happened. I was trying to put a logical thought together; he turns into whatever he turns into when he gets excited or mad...I looked at my hand there was blood, I felt a warm sensation roll to the back of my neck and put my hand back on it.

There I was in the middle of a cabin I didn't belong to, far away from home, holding my neck tightly, I felt an icy quake go through my entire body, a bitter sensation like no other. I could feel the warm blood spreading underneath my clammy trembling hand and it seeping through my fingers and spreading. I jumped up petrified with bare feet that were now rooted to the floor, not knowing if I should move, hide or even try to run. I just stood there in shock; the flames of the fire warmed one side of me and the other remained ice cold from fright.

I was so distracted, being in love not seeing all the signs of danger. But now I could see them all, I was finally having my moment of clarity, like I was seeing everything for the first time.

Cale is the monster who has been following me and trying to capture me, not sure why he wasn't successful, but I now know why he's after me; for a cure which had something to do with my blood, whether it be to change himself back to his human state or into a full monster I'm not sure, but I have a sneaky suspicion it is the latter.

Poor Jett, my first love, my protector, my soul mate got himself caught in the middle trying to protect me and now his life will be forever changed and not for the good either. I'm sure he blames me for what he is and what he is becoming, I know I would.

I tried moving again and my feet carried me shakily to the hall; the bathroom door wasn't completely shut. I walked over to it and pushed it open cautiously. He was sitting on the toilet, the lights were off and his head in his hands, "I'm sorry" he said in a very sympathetic and weakened state. "I'm not sure what I was thinking or what just happened" still not looking up. I could see all the veins in his arms protruding.

I leaned over the sink and slowly moved my hand away. My neck was stained red with a couple of small dark puncture marks. I turned on the sink to rinse it all away, when I was done I turned toward Jett, "If you left a permanent mark on my neck you are in so much trouble, my dad will have a fit!"

He let out a snicker "that's what you are worried about?" I went over to him and put my hand on his shoulder slid down and gave him a hug. He grabbed hold of me desperately and didn't let go. I think he may have been crying. I felt so bad for him. "We'll figure this out." I said hoping I sounded confident. I couldn't tell if he was the one trembling or me. I laughed a little and then pushed back from our embrace, "You made a mark" I said showing him my neck.

He caressed my neck with his index finger sliding it down my neck.

"Stop that!" I said excitedly and slapping his hand away. He stopped cold.

"I didn't mean to…." He remarked. "Aren't you afraid of me?" There was pause "Of what's happening to me or that I could hurt you?" He asked.

I got up and leaned against the bathroom sink and crossed my arms. "Na" I said. "You aren't scary yet, but just so you know I can drop your ass anytime I want, I got moves."

He really laughed at me "You are something else you know that Addie."

"I know. At least you're as big of a pain in the ass as I am now – creating so much drama I don't know if I can stand it."

He swung in for a kiss, I turned my cheek and we hugged.

He led me to 'my' bedroom and said good night. I went and crawled on top of the covers. He turned off my light on his way out leaving my door slightly ajar. I couldn't sleep I was restless, I couldn't stop thinking. I started counting….

I woke up screaming, or did I? I glanced around until they landed on the clock, I got that awful eerie feeling creeping thru me. It was 3:17a.m. My neck was wet. I ran to the window to see if it was locked. I checked Jett's room; he was asleep, I tried to wake him, nothing. I tiptoed into the family room and then the kitchen, the door was wide open. I creeped up to it, Cale was standing in the driveway. I walked outside cautiously. His arms were to his sides but restless, his eyes glowed like the wolf in my dream. He was wearing a pair of faded jeans that were distressed and ripped, a button down shirt with only a couple buttoned in the middle the rest were missing, it was splattered and stained of what I assumed to be blood. He was tanned from the sun but his veins still protruded all over his body, he had dark circles under his eyes that were crimson red and dark. No shoes. He shifted his weight. I moved back.

"We tried turning him you know. I'm sorry but some of them go bad. Bryce was trying to cure us. There's nothing you can do about that....Logan was a bad seed to start.... I wish to this day I would have jumped through that window and saved you sooner..." My breath caught and hitched in my throat. "But your brother, thank goodness for him right?" He was almost talking too calmly for me and in a low voice unlike him. "I'm sorry. I just wanted to tell you that..... and I haven't killed anyone, I don't know what's happening to the people around me, but I'm not hurting them. If I could have transfixed you, this would have been easier, but you're special Addie, I knew the moment I laid eyes on you."

I was frozen with fear, but I had a feeling he wasn't there to kill me because he would have already. I concentrated on watching and listening to him. A breeze came by blowing his hair and opened his shirt and revealed a nasty cut, it seemed to calm him, his fingers relaxed. The veins on him began to disappear. "What are you?" I asked hesitantly.

"Whatever we are Addie, there's no words for it, monsters. We crave blood, get violently ill and almost change at the full moon; almost a vampire, almost a werewolf but neither. Maybe ..." he stated as if in deep thought and then continued. "My father's journals state but don't elaborate that we are multifarious inbreeds with sanguinary tendencies and Bryce agrees..... Bryce and I have very different personalities, I am more, *good*" he hesitated, his brilliant eyes began to fade "and he's more..." He didn't finish that sentence took a deep breath and exhaled loudly. "We are stuck in limbo" he mumbled "an experiment my father didn't finish." I could tell he was starting to get tired. "He also thinks we could be hybrids, maybe a mix of both vampire and werewolf, but we aren't complete. That's what he's trying to figure out and he's close. We've been sick since we were kids and my father had tried curing us but gave us something else instead... more sickness. We ran out of the serum that kept us well and now we don't have all my father's journals to reproduce it. That's why we need you, to help us."

I cleared my throat "What did you do to Jett?"

"I didn't do anything to him" he said plain as day.

"I don't believe you Cale, when he changes he looks like you and why would anybody else hurt Jett, you're the only one that would….."

"That's not true, I really need you to believe me…" He backed up until he was in the shadows his eyes fired back up. I wanted to call out to him and ask him more questions but didn't after my consciousness kicked in. Last minute Cale added "You were right to break it off with me you know, I had ulterior motives… another thing I didn't expect from you, to really see me." He tapped his chest and contorted and yelped, fell to the ground on all fours. He looked up at me and growled, "it's working" he said under his breath. I heard bones crunching and things breaking and he said "you better run" in a growl. His eyes were ravage red and mirror like in the center. I ran back in the house locked the door and yelled for Jett, checked all the other windows and doors and locked them tight. Looked back outside for Cale, he was nowhere in sight. His shredded clothes lay on the ground.

Jett didn't come, I walked down the dark hall leading to his room cautiously wondering why Jett hadn't heard any of this. His door was ajar, I pushed it open all the way. He was laying there motionless, frozen in place I watched him intently not daring to blink and finally saw his chest rise and fall. I felt a rush of relief come over me. "Jett?" I said softly "Jett?" he didn't reply or move as if he was comatose. I tiptoed over, I didn't know what to do, I gave him a little shake but nothing. Exhausted I gave up and laid next to him and pulled his arm over me like a blanket.

CHAPTER 28

The next morning when I woke, Jett had his packed bag by the kitchen door, some turkey sandwiches and coffee made. He was reading the paper. I went back to get dressed and pack and I started to try and recall everything Cale told me. I should really find my pad of paper. It felt like it was all a dream. But it wasn't.

I had to leave my hair down to cover both sides of my neck, although the marks from Jett were barely visible. I threw my stuff in my bag and put it next to Jett's. Took a turkey sandwich and sat on the chair next to him and hugged my legs. "Good combination." I told him.

"Beggars can't be choosers" he responded turning the paper.

"True."

I blurted out "So what happened to your teeth? I thought you had to glue them in...didn't feel that way last night." He knew what I was talking about because he pushed the paper down and looked at me. He put the paper back up and mumbled something. I said "What?" He put the paper down and walked back to his room, and then I realized that he said *"they grew back."*

I followed him but he closed the door behind him. "What do you mean they grew back? You have new teeth?" I questioned him through the door. I knocked on the door and opened it haltingly as he was going through one of the drawers.

He turned to me "you get privacy but I don't?"

"I didn't get it so you don't either, besides you don't want privacy. Let me see your teeth."

"Ah, No."

"Why not?" He shrugged. So I pushed him onto the bed and sat next to him. "Open up!"

"No, it's none of your business."

"Sure it is, you already bit me no secrets there. Besides if you didn't want me to see you would have walked away by now. Are you embarrassed, you read my journal that was just as…"

"Good point." he said. "It's just weird."

"Open up."

He did and I looked really close, "Which ones are they? Your eye teeth?"

"Yeah, they feel weird in the back," he replied softly.

"Let's go in the bathroom, there's more light." I grabbed a pocket mirror out of my bag and headed toward the bathroom. I turned on the lights and sat on the counter – Jett came in slowly.

"Come here." He came closer.

"Open up…" I said as gently as I could. I knew he was feeling a little uncomfortable, yet he was still trying to act cool. He opened up slowly and I put the mirror under his teeth.

"Have you looked at them?" I asked and pulled the mirror out.

"Yeah, it looks like there are holes in the back of them."

"It sure does."

"I get food stuck in them sometimes too, it feels weird."

"Do they hurt?"

"When they came in they did."

"How come I didn't notice them coming in?"

"It only took a couple days and I was in so much pain I stayed home. I'm not sure if you noticed but I seem to disappear from everyone around me and get really anti-social when I'm sick, I do that because I have never been so – so – worried about anything before in my life. It's scaring the crap out of me."

I let out a sigh of relief. "Thank goodness, because I have never been more afraid of anything in my life either. I'm not afraid of you though, but what's happening to you and me." He put his head on my shoulder like he was relieved he could finally talk to someone. I thought I was going to cry and didn't want to, so I changed the subject. "Did you go to the dentist? Do your parents know? Is this why you haven't been smiling much lately?"

"No on the first two counts and yes, probably on the last one. You're the only one that knows."

"Do you know that this probably means you're a vampire?" I said with a smile and laughed. "Are you going to suck my blood some more?" I giggled a little more. He tried not to laugh but with such a weird situation you have to keep it light, otherwise, I think you could freak out easily.

"You really think so?" He asked with a half-smile.

"No." I replied. "If there was such a thing we would have known about it by now, besides look at you, your tan." He looked at his arms. "Do you crave blood?"

He looked at my neck, and then turned my head the other way. "What the hell happened to you?" He asked panicked. "Did I do that?"

I quickly responded to him, "No you didn't, you didn't do it!" I turned his face to look at me. "You didn't do it."

"Then how?"

"Ugh" came out of my mouth. "I'll tell you on the way back home." I walked into the kitchen.

"I want to know now."

"I am not quite ready. Can I please tell you in the car?" I changed the subject. "Thank goodness you came up – I have no money left."

"You wouldn't have spent all your money if I didn't come. Don't change the subject."

"Still, irresponsible on my part." I dug through my bag and grabbed my mom's gas card and held it up with a smile. "I can fill your tank though. That's if you're giving me a ride."

"Of course drama queen, I'll give you a ride..." he paused tilted his head to the side. "What happened to your neck?" I shook my head and said "I'll tell you in the car, I want to get going." What I really wanted to do was get away from Cale, away from here.

We got in the car after Jett checked all the windows and doors in the cabin and had cleaned out the fireplace. He pulled out and immediately put his hand out for me to put mine in his. I did and wrapped my fingers in his. I turned to him and said "I love you." He didn't say anything back he just gave my hand a squeeze. We didn't speak for a while.

"Did you dream last night?" Jett asked.

"Sort of" I replied and the word misvaad rang in my head and it gave me an unearthly feeling. I shook it off... I have got to write everything down before I forget. "After this trip I think I need to learn a little more about self-defense and fighting."

"You have me, you don't need to learn to fight....you defended yourself against Cale before....." Jett said.

"That's a joke – I have no clue what I'm doing. Plus, you slept like the dead last night. I couldn't wake you up. I need to learn self-defense, besides it won't hurt anything if I did. You could show me."

"You couldn't wake me? Oh my god tell me what happened to you neck!" I found a good radio station and turned it up. Jett turned it back down. "What happened to your neck, the side I supposedly didn't touch?"

I squeezed his hand tightly, I told him about Cale's visit. As soon as I said the name Cale he started to speed. I hadn't realized it but I had a death grip on his hand, my nails left marks in it. He pulled into a gas station to hear the rest of my story. "You should have woken me up last night! I can't believe you didn't tell me."

"I tried waking you and I even screamed twice but you were like a dead man!" He looked mortified that he wasn't able to help. "I mean I thought you were, it scared me." A tear escaped from me I wiped it away. "You know the syringe that Cale stuck in you, I was thinking that was what knocked you out." He added nonchalantly "Well not all of it got injected into me, I pulled it out before he could push the plunger. However, whenever I feed I always pass out cold." As soon as the words passed his lips he looked angry that he let that slip.

He got out of the car and walked away from me and over to the pay phone. I assumed he was calling his uncle with the news. I didn't mention how bad Cale's change was at the end last night, and Jett obviously didn't see Cale's clothing in the garbage either... I'll tell him when he calms down a bit. My big question is will Jett change fully now that he fed from me?

I dug out my pad of paper and pen and started writing everything I could remember from the night before including the words "multifarious inbreeds" and "sanguinary" because they sounded like technical terms. It took me a few minutes to remember his cousins name Bryce but glad I thought to write it down. I wrote down the terrible ending Cale had as well, this way when it came time to tell Jett I could just let him read my journal.

Next I started to recall my dream that not only could Cale turn into a Wolf but he turned into a panther in my dream as well and I just felt it in my bones that it was going to come true. Thinking all this through made in my mind made him a shape shifter that needs blood, bringing the term back to me, Misvaad. Cale and Jett are Misvaad's now I need to find out exactly what the means.

When Jett came back to the car, I was leaning on it waiting for him. He was calmer and wrapped his arms around me tightly "Are you sure you're okay? If anything would have happened to you...." He put his face in the crook of my neck.

"Mmhmm." I muffled into his shirt.

Jett shook his head and gave me another squeeze.

On the way home I kept thinking, does Cale need me to change, did my blood change him forever and will Jett change now. I inhaled sharply as I realized that Cale is trying to change people to be like him and experiment on them to cure them. Logan for one and Jett for another.

We stopped at Jett's house before getting me home. His parents weren't home. I stood in the kitchen, Jett pulled his shirt off as he walked into his room. I couldn't help but smile from the view. I knew he'd be awhile; he wanted to shower and to call his uncle again.

I flipped back through my notes and then called Nic, asked her if she remembered the technical term that Sheila told us the other day, *"vehements acting as demons"* she told me. I put those terms behind the others because they looked like they belonged at the end of sentence. It read *"multifarious inbreeds sanguinary vehement acting as demons, MISVAADS"*. Cale and Bryce were misvaads, 'mis' as in misfit and 'V' could stand for vampire, 'D' for demon or dancer and moon dancer is another term used for werewolves. Misvaad is very fitting. I turned around and Storm appeared. He stood right in front of me with his arms crossed, "What are you doing here?" he asked. "Jett needed to shower and call your uncle." I replied. "'What are you up to today?" I asked trying to make small talk.

"Can we talk?" he asked. I swallowed, I wondered if this was more bad news. He turned and walked into their formal living room, I sat in the wing back chair next to the couch. He planted himself on the coffee table across from me but then got up quickly,

I let my eyes follow him cautiously. "Is everything alright?" I asked. There was a long pause.

"No Addie, I don't think it actually is." Looking into his green eyes was like getting lost in a sea of water. They were solid and trusting, yet serious right now. "Addie, I think you have feelings for me." Gulp! My eyes got big, I didn't know what to say. He came and knelt in front of me and put his hand on my knee. "I love you Addie and I think you know that I do. And I know you feel what I do every time we're in the same room." He looked into my eyes; he was expecting me to say something.

I put my hand on his and after a moment I said softly "You're not wrong, but I love your brother and I'm with him." He got up and sat on the edge of the coffee table and ran his hands through his silky sand colored hair and rested his face in his hands.

"What if what we feel isn't real….. I break up with Jett and you find out you just wanted me because you couldn't have me?" He stood up, "No, it's not like that, I have never felt this way about anyone else before. Break up with him Addie, be with me, I love you." He held his hand out for me to take, but I was glued to my chair.

"I can't Storm. I'm sorry, but I can't. Your brother and I are together and I'll stay with him until he doesn't want me anymore."

"But Addie," he said and turned around, started pacing a bit, his arms were crossed over his chest again. "I don't think he loves you like I do."

I was trembling, I believed him, he turned his back to me. "So you don't think Jett loves me?" I asked. He turned his head just a bit "No he does, but..."

"Addie?" Jett called for me. Seeing the look of anguish on Storms face made me feel sick, he stormed out the front door.

"I'm in here!" My voice trembling, I cleared my throat.

"What are you doing in here? I thought I heard 'tow head'."

"Tow head?" I asked.

"Storm was born with very blonde hair, I mean it was white."

"Storm used to be blonde? He and I were just...talking about school starting next week." Jett's hair was wet and disheveled, I smiled at him.

"What did your uncle say?" "The Michigan police actually found Cale and followed him to the Indiana border. So they called the Indiana State police but they never found him."

We had a long awkward pause, I walked over to him and helped him pull his shirt on, he pulled me in for a hug. "What else?" I asked.

"He had a passenger in the car."

I fell asleep hard that night. When I woke startled at 3:17a.m. sitting straight up in my bed feeling a scream stuck in my throat, I had to look around and see where I was. My wolf had turned into a panther. "Shape shifters," I said aloud. I finally got it; Cale and Jett needed blood to replenish their bodies. Since they needed blood they thought they were vampires, but they fought themselves from changing into one because they didn't want to be monsters.

As soon as Cale gave up on the notion he was a vampire, which was after he stole my journals from Nic's room and read about my wolf he started to believe he was a werewolf. So somewhere between him convincing himself he was a werewolf and my blood he can now change. But they're not werewolves, they are part vampire and part shape shifters – Misvaads...

# # #

EPILOGUE

JETT

I sat there and pondered for a while, but then reached for my flashlight in the nightstand to read Jett's note which was under my pillow.... I know I have to read it even without his permission.

"I could feel every drop of water coming out of the spigot as though it were trying to pierce my skin, pelting me deliberately. Although the heat burrowed deep into me it felt great in the end. The bathroom filled with steam throughout and I couldn't even see myself in the mirror which was fine; to hide my monstrous face from me was perfectly fine. I'm not sure how much longer I could take these episodes filled with horrible excruciating pain."

"Every occurrence worsens leaving me battered and feeling defeated that there is no end. Knowing that every time, feeling like my body is burning from the inside out and every bone in my body starts to morph and crack. I don't think I can keep this up. I especially don't think I can take it if my body starts to change physically into a more monstrous form. If I were to ever scare away Addie or my family that would be it for me. I know then that I'd rather be dead than alive."

"This world is more mysterious than I ever imagined. When Addie tells me about her dreams, even the ones she calls "silly," I see them come true and I know there are things out there that can never be explained. I wonder if I'm the wolf that chases her thru the ravines. If I change into one will I change back, will I hurt Addie or my family? I've got to find out what parts of this folklore are true and not. I was scratched, not bitten and not killed, which tells me I'm NOT a vampire. I feel like I sound ridiculous thinking any of this could be true, but blood does revive me, it makes me feel like I have a new lease on life."

"I went into my room and peered out the window at the silvery almost full moon and had to look away; its brightness burned my eyes. I looked back when the clouds covered it and admired the golden glow that encircled them. The clouds whipped past and then I got mad. I felt the pull from it as though the moon could have something to do with the change. The sky looked so ominous, the way the clouds shifted over the moon effortlessly taking away its shimmer for moments at a time. Is it a full moon tonight? I felt a pang in my chest and fell to my knees, but then it was gone. I have one more night to go."

"Not that the moon is my only trigger. When I get upset it seems to initiate an onset and when I'm with Addie and I get... or we get involved... it seems to trigger my illness; anything that heightens my emotions. If I cannot be with Addie in every sense of the word, I'm not sure she'll want to be with me. I can't seem to bring myself to tell her all these things and I always engage with her despite knowing the possible consequences. But after this last incident I hope I have the courage to not let it get that far next time. I need to confess everything to her, but I can never bring myself to do it."

"Assuming Cale is still alive and he is looking for a cure, I will try and stay alive and find him to get the help I need. However, I cannot help but want to die every time the change starts. I wonder if he goes through the same thing I do. Does he sleep like the dead for a couple of hours after a transfusion or feeding? Does he have the insatiable hunger I feel and it worsens with each change? I have a lot of questions that need to be answered."

"I'm afraid to tell Addie too many details. If she finds out I have actually been feeding off animals when blood transfusions are not available to keep this torture of mine manageable, will she understand? I'm afraid she'd never want to see me again, ever. I'm tortured everyday about what I should do, who I should tell or confide in, and I'm tormented by the fact that I could possibly hurt someone eventually and …. It's exhausting. I have thought about ending my life but Addie seems to make me want to live and keeps me going, at least for now."

"If I am a vampire like Addie thinks, I was infected by being scratched, I wasn't killed or bitten or even fed vampires blood and I walk in the sun, eat food and garlic; maybe I'm not fully changed….or maybe those are all stories, myths…..maybe I really do have some kind of illness. All I know is that Cale holds the answers for me so I need to find him soon to stop this insanity… my insanity."

"Everyone wants to find Cale because of what he's done; I would like to find him to find out what's wrong with me and find a cure. I wish and pray that Addie could have a dream and find him for me, but she tells me she can't control what she dreams… or better yet maybe my Uncle Grey can track him down. I hope I can hold out that long."

"My fear is if Cale's in the same Hell I am and he likes having company and there is no cure. No way out, no light at the end of the tunnel just darkness. Just despair. Will Addie stay with me after the reality of me biting her sets in. After I fed from her it was the best I had felt in months. Everything was brighter felt more exhilarating felt more….. I'm afraid human blood will be…"

"I guess my next move is to try and find Cale and his partner along with Cale's father's notes from his experiments. Maybe that will tell us what he did and how to heal us. Sheila had read the whole list of people's names that were experimented on and supposedly they never got sick. Maybe they hid their illness like I have because no one knows what's wrong with me. I'll have to start a journal myself so I can see the progress being made, this will be my first. I wonder if there are any official records in books or news articles, I'll have to check the Akron library downtown. This is my new mission in life, to find Cale and find answers or I may not survive."

"I looked back at the silvery moon and a pain struck hard in my chest and quickly spread everywhere. I wanted to die. I squeezed my eyes shut and remembered how it felt when I bit Addie, the glorious rush of bliss I felt when her blood hit my veins, the sheer sensation of pure pleasure and ecstasy and that I could never do that again, ever. I would die first."

* # *

Thank you for reading my book. If you enjoyed it, won't you please take a moment to leave me a review at your favorite provider?

Thanks!

Shera Eitel-Casey

ABOUT THE AUTHOR

Photo © Shera Eitel-Casey 2014

Shera Eitel-Casey is a first time novelist living in the Chicagoland area. A web designer and analyst for the past 15 years. She started out writing down some ideas and eventually it lead to writing a novel. She is now working on her second novel "Time, The Addie Gellar Series" book 2 the sequel to "3:17a.m. ...the waking hour".

To learn more about the author or book updates go to CoeyFlyer.com/Shera/

Connect with Shera Eitel-Casey

Shera Eitel-Casey is the owner of Coey Technologies, Inc. She posted this book and did the artwork for it. Services for posting an ebook/book can be found at CoeyTech.com/services/ebooks.php

Made in the USA
Lexington, KY
07 March 2015